When the Jungle is Silent

When the Jungle is Silent

by

James Boschert

www.Penmorepress.com

ISBN: 978-1-942756-18-7 (Paperback)
ISBN: 978-1-942756-194 (Ebook)

BISAC Subject Headings:

FIC014000FICTION / Historical
FIC002000FICTION / Action & Adventure
FIC031000FICTION / Thrillers

Address all correspondence to:
M James
Penmore Press
920 N Javalina PL
AZ 85748. USA
Or visit our website at:
www.PenmorePress.com

1.

Dedication

This book is dedicated to the men and women who served in the Borneo Confrontation of 1963 to 1966.

To the British, Australian, New Zealand and Gurkha soldiers, sailors and airmen, some of whom died in the service of their countries, who went into the jungle to confront an enemy of far greater numbers and faced him down.

In particular this book is dedicated to the extraordinary men of the Special Air Service who give new meaning to the words **dedication**, **courage** and **determination**. Their skill at survival was legend in a jungle that, while itself neutral, harbored an enemy that was cruel and unmerciful to its victims. These few, intrepid men went into the jungle to become the British Army's eyes and ears in a war of cat and mouse that they dominated...even though they might have been the mice at times! In the process they befriended the indigenous people: the Dyaks and Ibans of Borneo, who shared their Long Houses with them.

It is sad to say that while the Iban and Dyak people have fared somewhat better under the rule of Malaysia than they would have under the Indonesians, they are still the victims of "civilization". Their habitat is being decimated by foresters and poachers and they are being forced to give up their perfectly balanced, happy lives in the Ulu.

Contents

Glossary:

Amok	To go mad Malay style
Armalite	American AR15 Rifle 5.56mm Caliber
Attap	An attap dwelling is traditional housing found in the kampongs of Borneo and Malaysia. Named after the Attap Palm
A Frame	A branch and leaf platform just off the jungle floor for sleeping on
Batu	Stone
Bukit	Hill
Bumped	To be ambushed or to make hostile contact with the enemy
Baluka	Dense secondary jungle very difficult to penetrate
Basha	Hut or makeshift shelter
Belt Kit	Belt that carries water bottles, bayonet, jungle knife, shell dressings, ammunition, grenades and some rations
Bergen	The large rucksack carried by the SAS
Bivvy	Bivouac. The Barracks or a place to bed down
CCO	Chinese Communist Organization

Claymore Mine	Plastic explosive in a curved shape containing many ball bearings; electrically detonated with a battery
The Clanger	Regimental jail
To drop a clanger	To screw up
Compo	The field rations of the British army; dried food was just beginning to be issued to the troops at the time of the Borneo war
"Confrontation"	The term used to describe the jungle war in Borneo with the Indonesians
'Color'	Color Sergeant in the Green Jackets: the equivalent to a Staff Sergeant
Dhobi	Clothes washing person who worked for the army. Usually Tamil people
Dyak	Native peoples of Sarawak Borneo
Durian	Jackfruit that grows out of the branches of the tree. Very pungent taste and smell. Found in the jungles of South East Asia
Gobbling Rods	Eating Irons: Knife, Fork, and Spoon issued to the soldiers
GPMG	General Purpose Machine gun. Belt fed 7.62 mm
Godown	Chinese warehouse
Gollock	British Army issue Jungle knife, about 14 inches long single blade
Gurkhas	Nepalese soldiers who have been employed by the British Army for several hundred years. Fearless warriors, excellent in the jungle. Have their own regiments and Brigades.
Fag	British slang for a cigarette

Field	Field Punishment, usually for a severe offence. 21 to 28 days in the tender care of the Regimental Police and confined to a cell when not doing work or on Officer's parade. Exhausting and very severe discipline.
Iban or Sea Dyak	Fierce warriors of the inland/coastal jungles of Sarawak; sometimes headhunters and pirates.
Indons	Indonesians
Jarit	Iban delicacy of raw pork and rice that is heavily salted and then buried in bamboo tubes for months.
Kukri	Traditional fighting knife of the Gurkhas with 12 inch long blade
Light Infantry	British Army Regiments of the Light Infantry such as the Green Jackets
Long House	The wide long houses high on stilts in the jungle that several families of Ibans or Dyaks lived in – sometimes a whole village
L-P	Landing Point
L1A1 SLR	Army code for the Self Loading Rifle
LMG	Light machine gun carried in a section. Looked like a sleeker version of the Bren Gun of the second world war
Manky	Filthy, dirty and sweaty
MG	Machine gun
On Stag	On guard duty, on patrol around a perimeter or sitting in a post on guard
OR	Other Rank. Non Officer
Padi	Rice field

Padang	Open area within a camp or village used as gathering place
Parang	Fighting blade of the Iban and Dyak: slender at the hilt, widening at the end of the blade
Panji or pungi	Concealed sharpened bamboo stakes that are used to injure or maim, often placed in rows around the perimeter of a camp
Primary Jungle	The more open jungle, with the trees rising sometimes to 150 Feet
Recce	Recce Platoon. The front end platoon that was used for scouting
RSM	Regimental Sergeant Major. The Senior Non Commissioned officer in a Battalion
RPKAD	Indonesian Para Commando
RP	Regimental Police
RPs week	Punishment at the hands of the Regimental Police, usually for a week
RV	Rendez Vous: location for pick up
SAS	Special Air Service
Sanger	Defensive dirt and wood dug out bunker
SARBE	Search and Rescue Radio Beacon
Sergeant Major	Senior NCO usually at Company level
SLR	British Army standard issue in the sixties and seventies *Self Loading Rifle* 7.62 mm. Replaced the Lee Enfield bolt action.
Skiving	Being lazy, hiding from work
SOP's	Standard Operating Procedures

Squaddie	Soldier in army vernacular
Tapai	Raw wine made from fermented rice or tapioca
To *rift* someone	To discipline; to sort someone out
To Tab it	Forced march into or out of trouble
Ulu	Malay for Jungle
Up Country	Into the fighting areas of Borneo, mainly near or on the border of Sarawak or Sabah
Winjing	Whining , complaining
82 mm	The 82 millimeter caliber mortar used extensively by the British
3inch	Three inch caliber mortar
2inch	Small portable mortar with two inch caliber barrel
One O Five	Field gun 105 mm caliber used extensively by the British & Australians in Borneo

Jahore Bahru
Malaysia 1964
Chapter 1

It was suffocating in the still, humid air and his shirt was soaked under the straps of his heavy pack which chafed his shoulders. His hips ached with the weight of more than twenty pounds of belt kit, ammunition, jungle knife, bayonet and two water bottles. The L1A1 self-loading 7.62 mm issue rifle was heavy and slippery in his sweating hands.

The jungle was full of the sound of insects in full cry and haunting bird calls which lent an unreal note that he found disconcerting, as though he were walking in a subterranean world.

The patrol of Green Jackets was following a narrow trail that wound its way through a mixture of dense *baluka* and primary jungle.

Well spaced out, about five to six yards between each man and very alert, the men moved with caution along the trail in the dim light of the afternoon. The few thin shafts of light that managed to get through the dense canopy above did little to illuminate either the path they were using or the surrounding bush more than to provide deeper shadows here or there. Even the saplings and leaves of the bushes were an indistinct dark gray or black in places.

Jason was at the rear of the patrol with Andy, another rifleman from the Pioneer section, some ten paces behind him. He was listening hard, trying to interpret the sounds of the jungle, the call of a bird or the bark of a monkey in the canopy high overhead. He was moving with care past the saplings, around outcropping tree roots and dense bushes. He was trying not to leave any sign of his passage, and in particular to make as little noise as possible while trying to keep the man in front in sight all at the same time. It demanded a lot of concentration.

When the Jungle is Silent

He paused as he watched the man in front come up to a large rotten log. The trail had narrowed even more, as there were now slopes on either side. He stopped, peered over the other side, then very slowly stepped over the log and moved on. Jason approached the same log and was about to step over it when the jungle erupted in gunfire.

Jason froze. The deafening rat-tat-tat of machine gun fire, the sharp crack of rifles, the even louder ear-numbing bangs as explosive devices went off nearby echoed and rebounded off the trees. Men shouted and the patrol began to return fire. Jason dived back onto the other side of the log and began to fire up into the jungle to the right of him. Behind him and to his front he heard his mates firing to the right and left. He wrestled himself free of his pack then continued to lay down heavy fire up the slope.

Jason heard a whistle, scrambled to his feet and charged, weaving up the slope towards the enemy, firing from the hip as he ran. He and his mates were yelling and screaming as they sprinted up the loamy bank, crashing past leafy saplings and through tangled undergrowth. Still shooting into the jungle ahead, Jason, Andy, and Jack, the corporal, drew together as they ran yelling but now panting up the hill. Jason saw a couple of shadowy figures ahead as men shot at them from only twenty yards away and began to make for them, frantically changing a magazine as he ran.

The next thing he knew he was flat on his face along side Andy and Jack. A tripwire had dumped them face down in the damp leafy floor of the jungle where they lay exhausted and stunned.

"Bang, bang, you dead, Johnny!" said a dark short man in green with crossed Kukri shoulder patches. Four of the squat men stood over the three Brits with their rifles pointing at them, grinning cheerily as they lay on the wet ground panting for breath.

"Bang fucking bang, you're dead if I can get my hands on you, Johnny Gurkha," swore Jack. He gave a tired grin, as did Jason and Andy, as they rolled over and stared up at the Gurkhas.

They all got up and stood towering over the four chattering Gurkhas. No one could understand a word that the others were saying but they grinned at one another amicably and waited for the whistle to blow again to mark the end of the exercise. Jason sighed. The umpires were sure to come and tell them how they had bolloxed the counter-ambush tactics, yet again!

The whistle blew and they all made their way down through the bushes and trees to collect their packs then to join the other men of the patrol and the Gurkhas at the open space along the track. The young lieutenant was getting a severe talking to by one of the instructors who belonged to the Jahore Bahru Jungle Warfare School for the British Army.

The men gathered in groups and took a drink of water or lit up while an intense conversation took place just out of earshot. It was clear to Jason that the instructor was not impressed with how the lieutenant had dealt with the situation and was telling him so. Both the lieutenant and the patrol sergeant were looking sheepish.

"Poor bastards," said Andy, wiping his heavily freckled face with his neck cloth, "Couldn't 'appen to a nicer pair of chumps, I say." He smirked at his own sarcasm.

"Fuck this for a game of squaddies!" Jason slapped irritably at a mosquito that was whining in his ear. "Give me the cushy life as a Pioneer. When are we ever going to need this shit?"

"Those Johnny Gurks can hide under a banana leaf, for Christ's sake. I didn't even see them before we were down," exclaimed Jack.

"Ah'm glad they're on our side, that's for sure," said Andy. "Just imagine seeing one of those little foockers coming at you with a blooody greet kukri waving about, yellin' blue murder. Ah'd die of fright before he ever got to me!"

The others snickered. Like all British soldiers, the Green Jackets loved and respected the mercenaries from Nepal. Renowned for their reckless bravery in battle and their cheerful dispositions, the Gurkhas were being deployed as the "enemy" for the seeming endless exercises being conducted in the dense jungle of Jahore on the south end of the Malay Peninsula.

The Green Jackets was being given an intense course in jungle fighting prior to being sent off to Borneo to fill the ranks of the Allied troops who were facing down the army of Sukarno, the Indonesian dictator.

To Jason and the other lads in the Pioneer section, who were also called Riflemen, although they rarely did front-end work, it was an endless waste of time. They would much rather be spending their time back at the main camp doing their particular trade work or finding ways to skive off altogether. But their bitching and skiving had drawn the ire of one of the color sergeants, who now made them do all the training the Riflemen were officially expected to do – and filthy, exhausting work it was, too.

He had slept out in the *ulu*, as the jungle was known universally by Brits, for many days now with the other members of the platoon; he was wet through, and filthy from the humid damp, his own sweat, and the repeated diving into the loamy soil when seeking cover during the training. Looking around at his mates' unshaven faces and filthy clothes, he thought they looked more like a band of heavily armed bandits than the usually smart and trim Light Infantry they were supposed to be.

Jason and his mate Andy were in this section while the others of the Pioneer section had been sent off to train with another platoon. In spite of himself, Jason did enjoy some of the aspects of the training. It was thorough and detailed so that he had learned quite a few things about this strange environment he now found himself living in.

"There's that fella again, the one wi' no insignia. Ah wonder wot mob they belong to," Andy ventured.

"I'll bet they're the SAS," Jason said, glancing over. He was wary of the quiet, intense men who wore no insignia. This man was talking in undertones to the lieutenant and the sergeant, who both looked chastened.

The story went that the officers had been taken off and given instructions on how to defend locations, direct fire and navigate within the dense and seemingly featureless jungle. They had to re-learn how to read a compass and keep track of distances covered. Many a cocky man had thought he could read a compass and find his way around in the Ulu, but the SAS had proved him to be wrong again and again.

Jason was tired to the bone from the short sleep breaks they had been given. That was another thing, the lack of sleep; the training didn't seem to have accounted for the fact that men needed sleep.

It was not easy but they struggled along gamely. Regimental pride drove tired men to do more than they would normally.

Jason, along with the other men of the regiment, was taught to move through the jungle very quietly, disturbing nothing and leaving little in the way of "trail" for skilled trackers to find. They almost never used their long issue jungle machetes, or Gollocks, as they were called. But again and again when they thought they had eluded their trackers, the boys from the Green Jackets had been caught up and ambushed as they played evasion tactics with their cunning teachers. It was very humiliating to find an instructor on the trail just ahead of the patrol with his grinning Iban tracker, who had not only followed the trail like it was a highway but had gone ahead to tell them so.

During his time with the platoon Jason had learned that to use soap, talcum powder or even toothpaste while on patrol was tantamount to suicide, as the air never moved and smells lingered for hours. They also learned not to speak out loud on any occasion, so that before long they called themselves with some pride the "Whisper Brigade".

Lieutenant LongAcre and Sergeant Baker came walking over to the men who were by now squatting on the trail, some of them smoking, which had been forbidden up to this point.

"All right, put your fags out and listen up!" said Sergeant Baker irritably.

Men grumbled as they stubbed out their cigarettes and put the dog ends back in their pockets. They stood up and waited for the lieutenant to speak. Jason looked at the lieutenant warily. Lieutenant LongAcre was very young; his smooth fresh face looked as though it had only just felt a razor. The men, although only a few years older, treated him with the scorn of old lags. He was clearly conscious of this and addressed them in a less than authoritative tone.

"Er...that last drill was a complete mess, men. We need to be a lot more aggressive when we get into a situation like that. Light MGs, you should lay down a very heavy fire both sides of the trail; that gives the rest a chance to move into a position for counter attack. The instructor told me that it sounded like a kindergarten party."

There were snickers from the men. "Silence in the ranks!" barked the Sergeant.

"We have to get very aggressive on these occasions. The front and rear sections have to move very quickly under cover of the protective fire from the MGs, find the enemy and start to roll him up," finished the lieutenant.

He had heard the same mantra for days now. The cheeky Gurkhas always seemed to be one step ahead of them no matter what they did. The young lieutenant droned on while some of the men fidgeted or, like Jason, switched off.

Finally the commentary was over. They were told to form up and prepare to leave the location and get back to base camp. The Gurkhas had vanished some time ago to wherever they went after an engagement like this. The instructor stood off to the side and watched as the group of men formed up in a line on the trail. At a low command, and with a collective sigh of relief, they set off at the fast pace of the Green Jackets, heading for the camp four miles away.

* * * * *

They arrived at dusk just as the cookhouse was opening for business. The men were lined up and rifles were checked for empty. They might have been using blanks during the exercise but the drill was still carried out religiously. Then they were dismissed to their primitive huts to clean up before dinner.

"Weapons inspection at o-seven-hundred-hours tomorrow! Dirty weapon means you're on a charge," Sergeant Baker hollered after them.

"Bloody 'ell," grumbled Andy. "I need a lie-in, not more of this bullshit!"

Jason nodded. He could not see much benefit for himself doing this kind of thing. "The Company Riflemen are the ones supposed to go out an' get manky and sweaty. They can play at being soldiers for fuck's sake! Our job is bein' Pioneers. That means to support and... well, encourage them's to be good soldiers!" Andy put it well, Jason thought.

"It's good for your 'ealth, Andy boyo," he said with a grin.

"That's enough out of you, yer Welsh git!" said Andy amiably. "We all know where you'd rather be, so don't give me that shit about this doing us'n any good."

He was referring to the girl friend Jason had met in Penang where the regiment had started its tour in Malaysia.

Andy stripped off his filthy, soaking clothes and, wrapping a towel around his waist, led the way towards the "showers." They weren't really showers, just Kerosene cans that tipped over and dumped cold water on a head after one had soaped. They were told to wear flip-flops to and from the showers because of the likelihood of hookworm getting into their feet. The day the MO mentioned this the troops who had been parading around with bare feet to show how tough they were went to the small NAAFI store and bought the place out.

Jason finished his shower and waited for Andy to emerge from his; then they set out for their hut.

6

"I wish they would teach us a bit more about explosives or something more exciting like that," Jason said as they tramped back along the dusty trail.

"I imagine it's because bloody idiots like you would blow yourself and the rest of us'n up wi' yer," said Andy while he combed his unruly red hair. "What 're yer going to do about that American chick? Did yer bang her in the end?"

Jason took a swipe at his friend's head, which Andy ducked. "None of your bloody business, Andy boyo!"

Andy grinned. "Shit, man, I'm jealous, she was a looker."

"*Is*, you mean." A pang of loss hit Jason. He really missed the girl, but they had been so busy here in the Jungle Warfare School at Jahore that he had not even had time to write. He resolved to get something off that night.

They went to the crowded, noisy cookhouse and had their mess tins filled with rice and curried spam, with tinned peas and some other green stuff that Jason didn't recognize which made up a mushy green mess. There was the usual tea, which legend had it was full of bromide to stop young soldiers wanking their brains out. He didn't believe it, but he was sure the awful taste was due to the water-cleaning tablets they dumped in it. The large tinned roof building resonated to the noisy chatter of more than a hundred other young men like themselves wearing only shorts and flip flops.

The ones in uniform were the unlucky soldiers on guard duty that night or the duty Regimental police. Even if they had just come in from patrol these men would have to stay up half the night on stag patrolling the perimeter of the camp alongside the Gurkhas. Jason thanked his stars that he had not been one of the chosen; he doubted if he could stay awake more than a couple of hours.

They joined up with others from the Pioneer section: Paddy, Jerry, Kevin and Geordie, who had arrived back from patrol later than they had. All of them complained bitterly about the six days spent in the fucking Ulu with no fags or booze.

"What kind of fookin' life is this?" bitched Geordie, his pockmarked face screwed up in anger. "Ah signed oop to fix things! Ah din't plan on goin' out and be'in a Warie! I'm fookin' knackered, that's what I am." He took a sip of his issue beer can. It was Tiger beer and warm, but no one cared as long as it was beer.

"You signed up to do or die, mate. And Color is going to make sure it's the die thing if he can!" said Jason. Geordie was always bitching, so Jason didn't mind ribbing him about it.

"Fock 'im. Ah din't see 'im ronnin' rond the Ulu like some fockin' ijot like we was," complained Paddy.

"That's because 'e's a Color Sergeant; they does the tellin' and we does the doin'," said Andy. After a couple of beers, he looked as though he was getting drunk; his watery blue eyes gave that impression, but it was an illusion. Jason had never met anyone who could drink like Andy.

"Them fockin' Gurks are good. Ah'll give 'em that," said Paddy. He was the oldest among the five of them at twenty-two, but even that small difference gave him some weight. His broad Belfast accent was difficult to understand sometimes, especially when he was upset.

"Did yer see that MG carrier? Wot's 'is name? 'E was really mad at one of 'em. I thought 'e was going to 'it 'im with it. Little bugger was just sitting under a banana leaf grinnin' at 'im, shoutin', 'Bang, bang, you dead, Johnny!'" said Jerry, laughing. He was a skinny youngster of eighteen who had joined the Pioneers only eight months ago. Jason liked his cheerful East London attitude to life.

"Yeah, I saw that," said Kevin. "Ah didn't think that would 'ave been the smartest thing to do, not with that bloody greet knife they've got."

The group fell to talking about their recent forays into the jungle with the real Riflemen. In spite of their grumblings they had enjoyed some of it.

Later, back in the *bashas,* as the huts were known, they began to clean their weapons by the light of the tiny oil lamps they had scrounged. No one wanted to wait till dawn and get late for parade and weapons inspection. Sergeant Baker meant what he said.

The three companies of Green Jackets had been in Jahore for six weeks now. The training they had undergone had supplemented the training they had gone through in the north of the peninsula when the regiment first came to the country. The Green Jackets had spent four months in Penang, arriving in January of 1964, acclimatizing and getting used to the jungle before coming south to the much more intense training now being meted out in the Jungle Warfare School.

Megan
Chapter 2

Jason sat in his *basha* in the late afternoon while his mates were off to the Jungle Warfare School NAAFI to get some beers, and wrote a letter to his girl friend. He missed her and he knew that his mates were beginning to notice that he was moping, always a bad sign. But it was hard for him to concentrate when his mind kept flying back to Penang Island up on the Northwest side of Malaysia where they had met. That was back in February, not too long after the Regiment had arrived in Malaysia.

*　*　*　*　*

The small group of tanned young men sat on the hot sand, swigging Tiger beer out of cans they had purchased from the Blue Café further along the wide beach. They were part of a sparse collection of European sunbathers and Malay boys who were enjoying the late afternoon on the sands of Batu Ferengi beach on the north coast of the island of Penang.

Jason was one of the young men finishing his beer while squinting out at the slightly muddy seawater that rippled along the beach. They had just stopped skipping stones out to sea, trying to hit the sea snakes that bobbed and wove about fifty yards away.

Sea snakes were supposed to be dangerous, but none of the men were sure. The three soldiers from the Green Jackets regiment were off duty and relaxing in the tropical heat of the afternoon.

They came here as often as they could, which was not that often, as a soldier's pay only went so far; but Jason always felt that he was in another world when the bus dropped them off after the forty-minute ride from Minden Barracks.

For Jason it was relaxing to sit with a book under one of the many coconut trees, listening to the muted splash and hiss of the sea as it moved in and out along the beach. The sea was ever in motion, but the waves were rarely ever more than a foot high. He enjoyed the fact that very few of the other soldiers seemed to come here. Further down the beach stood one small hotel office with a tin roof and some bungalows placed near by, while back in the coconut groves was the tidy Malay kampong. It was composed of pretty palm-thatched houses with steep roofs and wooden verandas. The houses were on stilts, under which chickens would scratch and children played. Fishing boats were drawn up on the sand, while others bobbed at anchor a hundred yards out to sea.

It was on one of these idyllic visits that he met Megan. She had been sitting at the Blue Café bar that belonged to the hotel, sipping an iced coke when Jason and the two other Pioneers came running up intent upon getting a cold beer after the bus ride out, jostling and acting the fool. They had all stopped the moment they saw her, and Andy and Kevin had immediately started grinning and nudging each other. Jason was embarrassed at his friends' behavior; he looked directly at her for a couple of seconds. Long enough for her to look up and catch his eye. She smiled at him; it was a friendly smile but not an invitation. He almost looked behind him he was so surprised. In fact Andy actually did, then realized she had smiled at Jason.

"Cor! Yer lucky boogger!" he whispered. "She fancies youse, mate."

Jason grunted and shook his head. He knew he was blushing and then collected himself and smiled back at the girl uncertainly, hating the fact that he was going red with embarrassment.

It seemed the others left him with a small space all to himself but he was unable to move or say anything. He dropped his eyes and concentrated on paying for a Tiger and then turned to leave. She had seemingly forgotten him, as she was looking out to sea through the shaggy eaves of the verandah.

His disappointment was strong, but he didn't know what to say in the presence of his mates, who were acting the fool just because there was a girl nearby. She ignored them completely. Giving a mental shrug, he walked out into the sun with the others and they headed for their favorite place a couple of hundred yards along the beach.

He had not been able to take his mind off the girl. He had noticed in the short time he had been able to observe her that she was slim, with long, dark copper-colored hair in a ponytail that fell down her back. She had been wearing a bikini top with a brightly patterned sarong around her waist. He had noticed a pair of very long legs and narrow ankles. Around one ankle was a small thin chain. His eyes had been rebellious and continually tried to look at her small but full breasts.

The young soldiers took off their shirts and got down to their trunks, ready for a long lazy afternoon in the calm of the warm beach and its picturesque surroundings. Their conversation was desultory, but of course centered on the good-looking girl at the bar.

"Wot's a good-looker like that doing 'ere, I wonder?" said Andy.

"She took a fancy to yoous, Jason, you 'ansom fart!" said Kevin. He fancied himself with the girls and was a little envious of Jason's obvious and rapid-seeming conquest.

"You're both full of shit," said Jason. "Ah bugger..." He looked around. "Anyone seen me book?"

"Na, I ain't seen it," said Kevin.

Jason realized that he might have left it on the bus or even at the bar.

"I'll be back," he said as he turned to jog off towards the bar. He left with their jeers in his ears.

He was not sure what he would say to her if he saw her, but he wanted to see her again. It was not often they saw a European woman, let alone one as attractive as this one, here in Penang. They stayed very much out of sight, and then mainly on the Butterworth side where the Australian Air Force was stationed. The soldiers mainly saw the Chinese, Indian or Malay women on the streets, who, unless they were prostitutes looking for business, ignored them completely as though they didn't exist.

He jogged up to the bar and his heart gave a jump. She was still there talking to the Chinese barman, who was wiping glasses with a not so clean rag. As Jason came in she glanced around and then there was that half smile again. He spotted his book on the bar next to her.

"I, er, came back for the book," he said lamely.

She looked down at it. "*The Moon and Sixpence*, by Somerset Maugham. Isn't this book about the South Seas?" Her voice was pleasant and sounded American.

"Yes, it is, 'bout the turn of the century," responded Jason. "Are you American then?"

She nodded. "From California, is it so obvious?"

He smiled. "I suppose so; we don't meet too many Yanks here in Penang."

"Well, technically I'm not a Yank, but I'll let that pass," she said.

She brushed a wisp of hair back from her eyes with a slim hand. He noticed there was no ring.

"What are you doing here?"

"Army," he said. "I'm stationed here with my regiment."

"Defending the Empire?" she said in an amused tone.

"Well ...we haven't done much of that lately," he said awkwardly. He was standing about four feet away from her and yet there was an indefinable, delicate scent of her that held him where he was.

"What are you doing here? Are you a tourist then?"

She shook her head. "Peace Corps."

"Peace Corps?"

"Here to teach children and their parents the American Way."

Jason wondered if she was serious, somehow he didn't think so. "So what does that mean? Are you really a teacher?"

She nodded. "Majored in English and history, then I grabbed the chance of getting out of the country, almost for free!"

Jason looked at her. He noticed that she had a fresh open face, a small nose and slightly wide mouth that when she smiled showed clean white teeth. There were freckles just below her hazel eyes. She looked frankly at him, as though sizing him up. He felt himself beginning to blush again. On impulse, he looked at the stool near her and asked, "May I join you? Would you like another drink?"

She smiled that wide smile again. "Yes and yes." Abruptly she held out her hand and said, "I'm Megan Hansen."

He took the slim fingers in his hand. "Megan, that's a Welsh name, isn't it?"

"My mother was Welsh, my father was Danish."

"Mine is Jason Griffith. I'm from Wales; my mother was English and liked the Greek heroes, so I got Jason, but Dad was as Welsh as you can get," he said. "I think we are both thoroughbred mongrels."

She laughed at that and he was captivated. Her laugh was light and infectious; he joined in with a chuckle of his own. He could hardly believe he was talking to an attractive girl like this. His experiences with girls had always been awkward and fumbling.

He asked the barman for a Tiger and then had her Coke replenished, paying for it with one of the few Malay dollars he still had. Payday was not until the end of the week so he had to be careful. He didn't want her to see how light he was in cash.

Megan toasted him with her cool glass; they touched with a clink. He liked the way that she looked directly at him. Most of the girls he had known in Wales never seemed to look at him, always off into the distance for some reason.

"You're the very first American girl I have ever met," said Jason after he had taken a swig.

"I've met a few Brits, but you seem nice enough," said Megan. "I met some men in Georgetown the other day at the E and O Hotel. I think they were officers of some kind."

Jason felt the familiar sense of inadequacy. So she had met the officers, which meant there was not much chance of his getting any closer.

He took another swig and said, "Orficers, you mean? Yeah they go there, us ORs aren't allowed in there."

She must have heard the slight bitterness because she said, "Well, I didn't say I lived there, nor did I say I liked them. They drank a lot and ogled me too much, so I left."

"Well anyway, I'm only a Rifleman, not even a corporal yet."

"What's a Rifleman? Is that a private?" she enquired.

"Yeah."

"But you read Somerset Maughan anyway. I have always liked to read."

Somehow she had turned the subject away from a sensitive area. Before he knew it, they were deep into books. She was very well versed in history and art and put his meager knowledge to shame, but not in a manner that made him feel stupid. He was grateful for this and let her into some of his favorite authors.

Her presence made him feel light-headed, and for the first time since he could remember he felt relaxed and comfortable with this girl from another planet.

He asked her about America and she told him of her life on a farm up in the hills overlooking the city of San Diego. Her father was a well-to-do farmer who had made his money off the land before retiring onto a smaller place that he could manage without needing help. She had gone to college, the second generation to do so, and then had heard of the "Peace Corps" and now she was in Malaya.

"Have you ever been to the Cameron highlands?" asked Jason.

She shook her head, her ponytail flying to and fro. "No. What's there, aren't they the central mountains?"

He nodded. "We went on an exercise up there about two months ago. It's cool and very beautiful. They grow tea and there are tigers in the Ulu. That's the jungle in Malay," he explained knowledgeably.

She nodded; she seemed to know the word.

"Do you know Malay?" he asked.

"Yes, some, I have to learn it to talk to the Bumi Putra when I am teaching, as not all of them know English."

He was impressed. He had made a halfhearted attempt at learning the language but there never seemed to be anyone to practice on in Penang, which was predominantly Chinese, so it had flagged.

"Do you spend a lot of time in the Ulu?" she asked.

"Yeah, I suppose so, it's what we are here for, and we are going to Borneo before too long. The Indons are making a fuss over there."

"Who is making a fuss? Does that mean they are fighting the Brits?"

"The Indonesians, Sukarno's men. Well yeah, I suppose so. They are trying to take part of it off the Malays and we've been told to go and look after them. They don't seem to be able to get it together over there."

He didn't want to think of Borneo now so he changed tack.

"So where do you live?" he asked.

"In a very small couple of rooms in the back alleys of Georgetown along a street called Armenian Street. It's old, mainly Chinese."

"I'm at Minden Barracks way over the other side of the town," he told her. "We get here by bus."

"Well, so do I, and it's a good way to get about."

He grinned at her. "On my pay it's about the only way I can get about!"

The sun was beginning to dip behind the tall trees to the west. The shadows were longer and creeping out across the sand, leaving only a few patches of sunlight. He realized that his time with her was running out.

"We've been talking for hours!" he said with some surprise.

"I know," she responded, looking back at him. "Do you have to go?"

"Yeah, I do, sorry, the lads will be here any minute. We have only a few buses that take us all the way back, and the next one is in about fifteen minutes." He was wondering how he could ever see her again.

"Um...how long are you staying here in Penang?" he asked.

"A few months and then I want to go and see some more of the mainland."

He coughed. "Megan?"

"Yes?" She was looking at him.

"Can I see you again? I mean can I...well, er..." he stammered to a halt. He dreaded the worst.

Cool fingers reached out and touched his hand. "I'd like that."

He was stunned. She smiled at his confusion and so he smiled back with relief. Then they heard the others coming towards the bar and the moment was gone.

"Can you give me your phone number?" he whispered quickly.

She nodded conspiratorially then fumbled in her woven handbag for a pencil and paper, wrote a number on a scrap of paper and handed it to him. He hurriedly pocketed it in his shorts just as the others came in.

"Wot did I tell yoous? 'E's chattin' up Gorgeous 'ere," said Kevin loudly, showing his large front teeth in a cheeky grin.

"'Ello, mate, been 'avin' a good time, 'ave we?" called Andy.

"My mates," sighed Jason. "Noisy but OK."

He introduced them to Megan who graciously greeted them smiling, and then began to collect her bag and a light cotton blouse that she put on. She joined the young men as they headed up the track to the bus stop next to the road to Georgetown.

"I'm going your way, at least to the town," she informed them.

Everyone was pleased and Jason was even able to find a place for Megan to sit in the crowded bus, while he and the other two stood with the Malays and Chinese, swaying with the motion of the smelly diesel bus as it negotiated the narrow road back to town. The strong smells of garlic and betel nut and unwashed bodies pervaded the interior of the bus, but Jason could only smell the light fragrance of the girl who sat near by.

At Penang Road Megan stood up, almost into his arms. He reached out and put an arm carefully around her waist to support her; with a quick movement she touched his wrist with her fingers. It was electric.

"Bye for now, Jason, call me," she said quietly.

He mumbled a reply and then watched her leave the bus and head up the street back from the stop. She looked back once but obviously could not see him, and in any case he was too shy to wave in front of the other two who were watching him.

"Cor, you're in there, mate!" Andy said enviously as the bus started up again for the last leg of their journey back to the barracks.

* * * * *

It had been four days of merciless ribbing and one guard duty before he could get to a telephone and make a call. There were only two telephones in the entire barracks that the ordinary ranks could use and these were, it seemed, forever occupied. Even then it had been harrowing as the exchange had to go through so many connections that he wondered if it would be simpler to call the UK.

Eventually the phone rang at the other end. It seemed to ring for ever before someone answered it, and then they did so in Chinese. It was a woman and she was very curt. He thought he had called the wrong number and promptly hung up. He peered at the number on the piece of paper and verified it again with the operator. Once again they went through the endless clicking and silences as the connection was made, and then the ringing commenced again.

Again the Chinese voice. He tried English. "I want to speak to Megan, American lady, please," he said loudly into the mouthpiece.

There was a pause then the voice said, "Amelican laydie?"

He nodded then said hurriedly. "Yes please...want to talk to American lady."

The voice said, "You wait."

He nodded again as though the voice at the other end could see him. There was a silence and then the voice shouted in the distance as though in a stairwell. He could not understand any of it but determined to wait it out.

Finally he heard the phone being picked up and then the unmistakable timbre of Megan's voice.

"This is Megan, who is this, please?"

"Megan, it's Jason...you know, we met at the beach? We met at the Blue Café?"

"Oh yes ...Hi there, Jason." She sounded cool, waiting. His mind registered the absence of too much warmth but he decided to plunge on.

"I wanted to call before but it is really hard to get to a phone and then I got guard duty. Sorry, I wanted to call before," he repeated lamely.

"That's all right, I was busy too."

"Can I meet you in town tomorrow evening?" It was Thursday and he would be paid by then.

"Where do you want to meet?"

"The café below the Loh Soo's bar. Do you know it? It's on the main street not far from the Ambassador Hotel."

"Yes, I go there sometimes. OK, what time?"

"How about five?"

"OK."

"Fine."

"Jason, are you coming alone?"

"Of course! You don't think I'd bring my pet monkeys with me, do you?"

There was the tinkle of laughter at the other end. It relieved the uneasy feeling he had been getting.

"Perhaps we could have dinner or something?" he said cautiously.

"That sounds nice. OK, I'll see you there at five. Bye."

He hung up feeling elated but confused as well. She had sounded very cool. He thought about it, deciding that he had probably left it too long and she had written him off. Small chance he had anyway if an officer showed up on her radar, he thought morosely. Officers drove about in the swift little Morgan cars, real "bird-catchers" by any standard. On his Rifleman's pay he could just about afford the taxi fare.

The next day he took a lot of time to prepare for the date. Andy and Kevin wanted to come along.

"Joost in case she don't show and you need some 'elp getting pissed," Kevin explained.

"'If you bastards show up with me she'll scarper for sure," replied Jason. "Keep the fuck away, or I'll pan the pair of you!" he threatened good-naturedly. His mates rolled about on their beds begging him not to hit them, pretending to be terrified. Grinning, he left, giving them the universal 'V' sign.

He arrived late because the corporal of the guard had checked IDs for the soldiers leaving the camp that evening and had sent him back for his. More ribbing from his mates.

Sweating in the warm evening heat radiating off the street, he had dived out of the taxi and headed for the door of the café. The usual group of trishaw drivers was parked along the side of the street next to the filthy monsoon drains, smoking their slim rank-smelling cigarettes.

"Hey, Jonny, you want good time, jigagig?" they shouted cheerfully at him. "Cheap woman, I take you. Blue movies, short time, long time ten dollar!" their automatic response to the arrival of a single British soldier. There was no hiding it, he thought ruefully; the haircut gave him away every time. He shook his head equally cheerfully.

"Not this time, mate," he called back.

He opened the door to the Milk Café and felt the cold of the air conditioning strike his damp body. He was impressed at how cold this place could be. Few of the other bars in the entire length of the main street had air conditioning, so this was a favorite haunt of the British teenagers from the garrison and the Australians from the air base in Butterworth. He could not see far into the gloom of the poorly lit place but could tell it was full. He stood looking around at the noisy crowd of young soldiers in jeans and civvies like himself and the kids who belonged to the families, searching for Megan.

He saw her wave from near the back and made his way over. The place was full of smoke and the music was loud, Jose Feliciano was sobbing out one of his songs on the battered jukebox in the corner.

He realized half way towards her that there were others at her table and his heart sank. She gave him a smile as he came up and then introduced him to her companions.

"Hi, Jason, these are a couple of friends of mine," she said cheerfully. Jason looked down on the two young people with her. They looked like hippies to him. The glow of the blue neon lights over the bar made everyone's face look as though it was made up for a cadaver show.

"Are you American too?" he asked.

The boy looked back at him. "Yeah, man. I'm Dale and this is Jan." He indicated the girl sitting against the wall smoking a cigarette. She smiled absently, waved her cigarette at him and then looked away.

Megan said, "You guys, this is Jason, the Brit soldier I was talking about. Come on, sit down and tell us what you've been doing."

Jason sat awkwardly next to her; he caught her scent again. It did not seem to matter where she was, the scent was the same. His skin tingled.

He looked across the table at the other two. "Are you in the Peace Corps too then?" he asked.

Dale looked at him with slightly vacant eyes. "No, man, we're just on the road, you know."

Jason turned and looked at Megan. She was dressed in a thin cotton printed blouse with a deep neckline and a linen print dress that covered her knees. His eyes threatened to stray again. He dragged them off her breasts and met her stare. She gazed back steadily, seeming a little amused at catching him out.

"How have you been?" he asked, feeling himself flush with embarrassment.

Her smile was secret, as though she could read his thoughts.

"Fine. You know, doing the teaching thing, it's fun. These two have been staying with me for a couple of days."

"Oh, where are you heading to?" Jason didn't know why but he wasn't sure he liked them.

Dale said, "We're doing the travel thing, man. Looking here and going there. We're going to Thailand for the good shit."

Jason was confused. "The good shit?"

"You know...the smoke, the best shit in the world!" Jason still felt confused. Megan leaned against him. "Marijuana," she whispered. He nodded as though he understood.

In truth he was still puzzled. But the fact that she had leaned against him was not at all bad. He filed the information away for future reference while he enjoyed her closeness. The other two were dressed in patchy faded clothes. Dale wore a denim shirt and jeans and had long hair with a thin multi-colored headband, while Jan wore a cheap cotton frock over which she had draped several necklaces of beads. She was not anything like Megan.

Jason was still impressed with their apparent poise in this place. They seemed to be part of it, whereas he felt awkward in his civvies and he was very conscious of his short haircut.

There was a short silence. Jason was not sure what to say to the others and they seemed disinclined to open the conversation. It was Megan who finally shifted in her seat and said. "OK, well, I'll see you two later?"

"Yeah, we'll hang out here for a while," said Dale. Jan had still not said anything.

Megan turned to Jason. "OK to go?"

He nodded hurriedly. "Yep, let's go," he said, not knowing where on earth he was going to go but ready to leave this place if she was. He got up and let her out.

"See you guys later," said Megan. Jason echoed her words while Dale waved a hand vaguely after them.

"Come on," said Megan. She took her woven bag and slung the strap over her shoulder.

They exited into the muggy evening street. The streetlights brought her features into sharp relief to his enquiring eyes.

She breathed the night air and said, "There doesn't seem to be anywhere in the tropics where a deep breath is very rewarding."

He had to smile and nodded; the stink of the street was suffocating after the air-conditioned bar. The monsoon ditches were always clogged with filth of some sort. The rotting fruit and other objects could put out a strong smell. But the rains always seemed to come along eventually to wash it all out to the sea.

"Where do you want to go?" he asked, standing next to her. She stood two inches less than his six feet.

"You promised me a dinner," she said, turning to face him with a smile.

"Come on then, let's go to the Ambassador, they do real steaks there," he offered rashly.

"OK, but I don't want a steak, I can get the best in the world at home," she said. "Let's just get a nice drink and talk for a little and then see if we are hungry."

He said, "OK, but I have an idea. I know of a restaurant near the sea, north of the esplanade, where we can get crabs or something like that. Would you like that instead?"

He felt suddenly a little freer. The atmosphere in the milk bar had not been much to his liking.

She nodded eagerly so he called over one of the trishaw men and they dickered over the fare, finally settling on a couple of Malay dollars for the half-mile trip to the restaurant located not far from the old fort. All along the beachfront were the houses of the rich Chinese, dotted here and there with restaurants that catered to the mainly Chinese population of the island and the occasional foreign visitor.

It was clear to Jason that Megan enjoyed the ride in the tattered trishaw, and she looked even more pleased when they came to the entrance of the ramshackle restaurant hard on the beachfront.

It was garishly lit with loud neon signs in Chinese on the front of the garden entrance. Inside, it was bustling, cheerful and very noisy as the sweating waiters shouted orders and customers talked loudly to each other and the waiters. Everyone seemed to be gesticulating, talking, and smoking at the same time.

They were shown to a table against the rails where they could look out on the straits and watch the lights of the shipping riding in the swells. The lapping of the small waves on the beach just below came clearly up to them in spite of the noise in the restaurant.

Jason ordered a Tiger beer for himself and a rum and Coke for Megan, then there was a short silence while they took stock of one another. Finally it was Megan who spoke.

"I think I like it here; I've never been here before. Is this where you bring all your girls?"

He grinned sheepishly. "Actually, I... er, I've only been here once and then I'm not sure how I got back to the barracks, I got so pissed."

She chuckled. "I don't meet many soldiers but the Brits and Australians all seem to like getting drunk a lot. Why's that?"

"Probably because there isn't much else to do most evenings," he answered.

"When do you go home?" she asked

"Back to the barracks?"

"No, silly, back to England."

"Oh, that. Well, we're here for four years – that's the standard posting."

She looked surprised. "Four years! Don't you go home in between times?"

"No, most of us can't afford to in any case. It's just Blighty anyway," he answered without thinking.

"Wow! Well, at least you get to live here in this lovely place. But you said that you'll be going to Borneo some time, wasn't that right? How long do you spend there?"

"About eight or nine months each time and then another five months here, then we do it all over again."

She looked a little stunned. "And you never go home? Don't you miss it at all?"

"Na, not really, it rains all the time there and the barracks are cold and miserable. Food's even worse than at the barracks here!" He grinned

The drinks arrived and they were silent while they sipped. The familiar taste of Tiger let him relax a little.

He could hear the restaurant all around but it seemed to be muted while he was with this girl. He decided that he really liked what he saw but a tiny warning told him to watch his manners and not to push it.

"Are you hungry, Megan?" he asked. She nodded.

"Let's eat that thing over there," she said, pointing to another table. "Do you know what it is?"

He nodded; it was called "Steam boat". He caught the eye of one of the hovering waiters and after much discussion they got him to understand that they wanted to have the same meal the Chinese were devouring on another table. Hot steaming soup that was kept at a boil by a Bunsen burner with dishes of meat and vegetables clustered about on the table. They decided to be adventurous and eat with chopsticks.

The meal was a success. Jason enjoyed picking the pieces up with the chopsticks, not always successfully, and placing them in the soup to cook and then fishing for them and squabbling good-naturedly with Megan over the cooked pieces as they floated in the soup. They chattered without a thought to the time. He was curious about her, asking about life in the United States, which she was willing enough to tell him. He quickly realized that although they came from very different worlds they were in some ways the same. He had grown up on a sheep farm near Brecon in Wales while she was from a cattle and fruit farm in California. They compared notes.

"Why did you leave the farm?" she asked

"Because I was sick and tired of heavin' the stupid, wet, smelly sheep about, and me dad was starting to make me feel unwelcome," he responded. He added that his dad had given him a hard time because he spent all his pocket money on books.

"I wanted the life of adventure...you know, visit strange places and so on, so the Army sounded like a good idea at the time."

"How old were you when you left?" she asked.

"Fifteen."

"What?" she gasped, her chopsticks halfway to her mouth. "No way! Now I know you're BS-ing me!"

"Na, really, I joined the Army at fifteen as a boy soldier and spent the next three years in a camp full of lads being trained by guardsmen. They were bastards!"

"You poor boy!" she exclaimed. "What was it like?"

He enjoyed her concern. "It was all right, I suppose. Lot of bullshit. Plenty of bullying went on, you had to learn how to look after yourself. Thousand boys, it's going to happen. When did you leave home?" he asked, trying to steer the subject away from an unpleasant memory.

"Oh, when I was eighteen and on my way to college. It was terrible leaving home for the first time. I took the train for Los Angeles and cried for days!"

"You look tougher than that," he said, admiring her features in the scattered light of the lanterns. "Did you have a lot of boy friends then?" he asked; immediately wanting to cut off his tongue.

She looked back at him thoughtfully. "A couple. There was Billy from the Rawlins farm when I was in High School. He never made it to college, claimed that was for eggheads and that farming was the way to live. I decided that I didn't think it was and we split."

She took a sip of her drink as though thinking about what to say next. "Then there was Ted at college, football player. A jock, nice enough in his way but after he had taken my virginity he left."

Jason stared at her. He had never met anyone outside his army mates who spoke so frankly about sex!

She gave a short laugh of self-depreciation and then turned her gaze back onto Jason.

He had been dreading this. "I've not had a lot to do with girls." He grinned sheepishly. "There weren't too many near the hill farm and none in the Apprentice school."

In fact, while at the Army boy's school, he had gone to the town and then through all the usual sweaty groping that went on in the cinema with this or that girl picked up at a pub. Only a couple of times had he actually gone "the whole way", as his mates would have put it.

Megan studied him. "You aren't bad looking, you know." She smiled at his discomfort, and then reached out and placed her hand on his. He blushed but there was a glow in his chest that made him return the smile.

"I should say the same for you! It's not that easy to get with a pretty girl who can talk about all sorts of things when you're a squaddie."

"Have you ever been with one of the... you know, the women here in Penang?"

"No!" He even sounded shocked to himself. "The MO keeps telling us that there are all sorts of horrible things you can catch," he explained. "Lots of the lads do anyway and don't seem to get into trouble, but to be honest it just don't appeal to me. Besides, what would I do if it dropped off from some dreadful lurgy I'd picked up in town?"

She giggled helplessly. "You come out with some of the silliest things! I thought that you soldiers had a girl in every port!" she spluttered.

"That's the sailors; we squaddies spend most of our time in dark, wet, and 'orrible places avoiding nasties. Doesn't make for too much romance," he said ruefully, grinning at her amusement.

"Well, Jason, Rifleman, I think I like you. Are you on your best behavior tonight?" she asked him archly.

He decided that he liked her too; she kept him just a little off balance, which was turning into fun.

"I'm on my best behavior but wait till midnight, that's when I change, and then you need to watch out, lassie," he growled.

A band made up of young Chinese musicians started up with a local pop singer shouting out his song in Hockien to an appreciative crowd.

The noise was deafening. Jason wanted to stay and talk but that proved to be impossible now, so he waved the waiter over and paid. It cost him a lot but there was money left for the weekend if he needed it.

Megan got up and waved over to the beach. "Why don't we go for a walk? What time do you have to be back at the camp?"

"I have a late pass but if I'm late for parade in the morning I'm for it," he explained. "Come on then, let's go for a walk on the beach, it goes for miles, but there are some rocks over there" – he pointed to the east – "where they fish and we could sit in the quiet."

She nodded and they set off. She quickly took her sandals off and moved her feet sensuously into the still-warm dry sand. It was almost white along this stretch of beach.

"Come on; take your shoes off. It's wonderful."

He complied, trying to balance as he took off first one shoe and the sock and then the other. He rolled up his pant legs and agreed with her it was a nice feeling.

Their walk quickly took them away from the crashing music pulsating from the garishly lit restaurant. The warm dark of the night closed in around them. Jason held his hand out and she took it, her cool slim fingers gave him a sense of well being he hoped would not stop.

"I love this island, much better than wet old Wales," he said. "The sea is all around but I have almost never seen it very choppy or rough. It always sounds like it is now."

She just squeezed his hand, saying nothing. He decided to enjoy the night in silence with her.

They soon came to the line of rocks that jutted out into the water. There were small lights from lanterns at its extremity where the fishermen were still trying for one last catch.

Above them the night sky was almost clear, the black shadows of the clouds partially obscuring the half moon that tried to shine through. It provided enough light to glimmer off the black sea, lifting and dancing on the small crests of the wavelets and reflected off the white beach.

He found a large rock, flat, that allowed them to sit facing the sea in relative comfort.

She sat next to him still in silence. They watched the ships' lights at anchor in the straits and further south along the coast towards the harbor.

In the distance they could see the brightly lit Penang-Butterworth ferry plowing across the narrow strait. Nearer at hand the chug, chug of a junk making its way home from some fishing trip, or even a trading journey, carried clearly across the water.

The smell of the seaweed and the water nearby was strong with the taste of salt and iodine while the light breeze brought the smell of the dank vegetation from the trees behind.

It was cooler now and she shivered in her thin cotton blouse and snuggled closer to him. He put his arm around her shoulders. He would have gallantly shared his jacket if he'd had one but he wore only his short-sleeved shirt.

He could feel the straps of her bra beneath his hand and for some reason it made him become very aware of her physically. He had suppressed this firmly after he had brought her to the restaurant, as he knew he would blunder and lose her if he said or did anything stupid. But now he felt the urge to touch her, so he gently stroked her back with his left hand. Her response was to tip her head back, enjoying his hand as he moved it over her shoulders and then her neck.

He turned towards her and looked at her face barely illuminated in the half-light of the moon. She lifted her chin so that she presented her mouth to him. He leaned over and kissed her, gently at first and then with some more pressure as she responded. She turned into him and put her arms around his neck and opened her mouth. Jason drank deeply of her proffered lips; his tongue touched hers and slid onto her teeth.

Megan made a tiny noise and forced her mouth more firmly onto his. With great care Jason moved his hand so that it settled onto her right breast and rested it there. He could feel her nipple grow tight under the light material of the bra and her blouse.

His blood was racing and he got a jolt in his groin. There was nothing he could do, he just grew. He wanted to adjust himself but that would mean losing the moment so he clung to Megan for a few seconds longer. They parted breathlessly.

"Mmm, that was nice!" she murmured, leaning back in his arms. Jason decided that he had gone far enough for the moment. He tried to relax and enjoy the darkness and the girl in his arms.

Jason was beginning to wonder where things would go next when she asked him the time. It was almost midnight. Megan sat up.

"Darn it, I have to get up in the morning. Can you walk me back to a taxi?"

He hid his disappointment as well as he could and helped her up. She stood facing him and brushed the sand off her backside with her hands and then reached up and put both hands on his shoulders.

"You are a nice man, Jason Rifleman. I have really enjoyed the evening. Will you call me?"

His heart leapt. "Why don't we meet tomorrow night?" he asked tentatively.

She looked at him, it was difficult to see her expression in the dark, but her kiss told him what he needed to know. "Hmm, I'd like that, Mister Rifleman Jason."

Jason put his hands around her slim waist and gave her a squeeze. They went back towards the restaurant hand in hand.

The Date
Chapter 3

Despite the fact that he had said he would meet her the next day after their first night out, it had been a full week before he got out of the camp again. He had been nailed for guard duty on Friday, which had thoroughly pissed him off. Desperately he had tried to sell the duty to his mates, but they were engaged on some activity and couldn't or wouldn't help him. Finally he had had to make the dreaded call. It had been difficult and he had worried that she would be fed up and just ditch him. Megan had seemed to understand, however.

"I'm going off to a Peace Corps thing this weekend, Jason," she said, "so what about next week, Thursday?"

He wondered if he could last that long. "That's fine, Megan; have a good time, I'm sorry about this bloody guard thing, nothing I can do about it."

"That's all right."

"Miss you."

"Miss you too, it was fun last night."

"I'll say! Er, yes, it was, wasn't it?" he corrected himself.

He heard the tinkle of her laugh and knew it was all right.

"Take care then, love. I'll see you at the same place?"

"Yeah, see you, Jason." The line clicked off.

The week had dragged by; he had occupied himself with reading and writing letters and finally on Tuesday evening he succumbed to going to the camp movie with Kevin, who told him that *The Last Patrol* was showing. They watched the French Foreign Legion patrol go out on its tragic last patrol where, after fighting off hordes of Arabs, only the one man came back. The music was haunting as it was the last post, per the Legion, and was played as background music throughout. He went out into the dark humid night, whistling the tune to himself.

"Blooody glad Ah never got the urge to join that lot," said Kevin. "Them'ns didn't stand a chance from day one!"

"Nor me!" said Jason. "Never could understand fellahs who's sign up for that kind of shit."

"Yeah, well, soometams it was the guillotine or the Legion. Ah know which one Ah'd take any time." Kevin gave a theatrical swipe across his throat. "Booger the Legion for a game of Squaddies."

Thursday came and Jason went through the ritual of getting ready and was subjected to the usual ribbing by his mates. Andy and Kevin, who had met Megan, told the others about her and what a looker she was for the hundredth time. He felt good because of the obvious envy from the others. No doubt after payday some of them at least would be in the brothels this coming weekend.

He had an idea where he wanted to take her but first he had to get to town and meet her. The café was full, but this time neither Dale nor Jan was there with her. She looked cool as always, dressed a light blue blouse and cotton print skirt with a pair of sunglasses perched on her head, her hair in a ponytail. He wanted to look at her legs but they were safely under the table. She got up when he came and they kissed. Then they sat down. It felt good suddenly; his worries melted away. Here he was in wonderland with this girl from California, feeling good.

"How have you been?" she asked, giving him her direct look.

"On guard duty; bored most of the time, and missing you," he added, looking back into her eyes. "How was the Peace Corps thing?"

She smiled. "OK, you know. I wanted to get a chance to look around the Cameron Highlands, same place where you went, but there wasn't time. I'd love to go to one of those... I don't know what they call them, hotels?"

"Rest Houses?" he offered. He knew about those as once he had been sent to Singapore with a staff sergeant to do some work on weapons, and they had stayed at the Rest Houses dotted down the length of the country.

"Yes, that's it, Rest Houses, up in the highlands... they say it's very beautiful with mists and tigers and things. We just stayed at a cheap hotel and it wasn't so nice." She seemed excited at the thought of going back to stay at a more romantic place.

"Then when I got back Dale and Jen had almost trashed my apartment!" she finished, sounding upset.

"Are they bothering you then?" he asked, an edge to his voice.

She looked at him sharply. "No, not enough for me to want to throw them out just yet, so don't feel you have to defend me." She grinned at him mischievously.

"Well, where do you want to go to tonight?" he asked, grinning back.

"You seem to know this town a lot better than I do. Why don't you take me to another of your haunts?" she said with a smile.

"All my haunts are near the sea, I love to eat and listen to the sea," he said tentatively. He didn't add that one of them was the bar upstairs where he had often stayed late and had even taken part in a brawl with his mates against some men from the Royal Marines who had come to town. It had been a good scrap and they had all made up later in another bar. They had wrecked this one.

"Sounds fine to me. Let's go!" she said, standing up. He was careful where his eyes strayed.

They took a trishaw again and enjoyed the in-and-out maneuvers the driver had to make along the noisy streets. They passed temples and old Chinese shops that looked as though they had been there for a hundred years, old wood-painted dragons twisting and turning among their eaves. Their conversation was light; there was a comfortable feeling between them, so in the short silent moments when there was only the swish of the tires on the road Jason was not concerned. He was beginning to learn that Megan spoke when she wanted to and not all the time. He rather admired her composure.

This time they came to a bar that sat just off the beach nearer to the fortress where Jason had spent many an evening with his mates, sitting outside listening to his favorite music: Joan Baez, Ray Charles and Jose Feliciano. When they were especially maudlin, Ray Charles would be put on as loud as the drunken soldiers could turn it up.

They went into the dark interior and Jason was relieved to find there were very few men from the battalion this evening. They nodded recognition but said nothing other than to stare enviously at Megan. He nodded to the bartender and then ushered Megan out onto the patio that overlooked the beach.

It was quiet outside with only a few couples, mixed Chinese and Australian, sitting at tables with small Chinese lanterns hanging from trees and posts swaying gently in the cool breeze.

They sat down at a quiet corner. Megan looked around approvingly. "This is nice. Hello again, Mister Rifleman," she said, moving her hand across the table.

"Hey. It's good to see you," he said and took her hand in his.

The music was muted out here, allowing them to talk. The waiter came and wiped the blue and white plastic table cover then asked them what they wanted to drink.

For Jason it was Tiger and Megan settled for a San Miguel.

"I don't know how you can drink that stuff," she said with a small grimace.

He grinned. "I told you, it was made 'specially for the Brit squaddies, it tastes horrible but doesn't cost much, and we have neither taste nor money to spend."

She laughed at him, her white teeth gleaming. They toasted and drank. It was a humid evening, but it had rained earlier that afternoon and it was unlikely it was unlikely to rain again. A light wind cooled them and the waves were noisily lapping at the sand of the beach below. In the dim light of the Chinese lanterns he could see her face and liked what he saw.

He pointed up at a huge full moon, which was only partially obscured by the fast moving clouds.

They ordered shrimp and crab from the menu. Wine was offered but they stuck to beer.

Jason wanted to hear more about the fabled California and she told him about the type of country it was there. Her father had been the first in the family to go to college to study for a degree in Agriculture. Her Grandfather had come from Oklahoma. They spent some time drawing the USA in beer on the table and she showed him where the relevant states were situated with respect to one another. Jason learned about the Great Depression for the first time and Megan told him to read *The Grapes of Wrath*.

He liked the sound of the dry country and the deserts beyond to the east. She told him that they had often gone into a desert known as the Anza Borrego to camp and walk.

He told her about his life on the hill farm, how he had grown up near Brecon, deep in Wales. He told her of his love of the Brecon Beacons, which he could always see from the Eppynt, a range of hills to the east and north that ran between Brecon and Sennybridge.

"I used to ride our cob out onto the Eppynt and look over at the Beacons; they were always different. Every time something had changed: the heather or the color of the peaks. They were moody mountains," he told her.

"Did you like the life on the farm?" she asked him

"I loved the open air and the weather; it rains most of the time but I didn't mind that much," he said. "I just got fed up with the sheep!"

"Isn't it cold over there in Wales?" asked Megan, pretending to shiver.

"Compared to here it is. Probably compared to California too, I'd guess."

The food arrived and they ate, enjoying the hot sauce that came with the shrimp and crab.

As the evening progressed, they found themselves almost alone on the verandah, but Jason's antennae were out. He knew there were squaddies in the bar: it had become noisy. Soon some drunken Riflemen from the barracks with too much booze in them started a fight. The shouting grew in volume but someone turned up the music as though to drown out the noise. There was a crash of something getting broken. Jason wondered who might be there but certainly didn't want to get involved. He looked apprehensively towards the bar.

He glanced at Megan and got the impression that she wasn't paying much attention to the noise. Still he decided it was time to leave. He had just called for the bill when there was a loud crash as the doors from the bar onto the verandah slammed open and a tangled mass of fighting bodies tumbled out. Jason and Megan were nowhere near the exit door of the bar, but suddenly the whole patio seemed to be full of fighting men.

He sighed. The Kiwis were in town. They always had to fight everyone in every bar. It was hard for the Green Jackets to turn them down. After all, they were Kiwis and everyone loved them, but most Brits wished they would stick to fighting the Aussies, who were their favorite scrapping partners.

Jason stood up quickly and threw some money onto the table.

"Come on, love, it's time to leave," he said. He looked behind him to see if there was an exit but there was none. It meant they had to get past the six or seven men brawling it out on the patio. They had already demolished some furniture and the barman was screaming abuse at them in Chinese and waving his arms angrily.

A rangy New Zealand sailor was in the classic boxing position facing a short stocky Rifleman who was dancing about on the balls of his feet. The Kiwi lashed out with his fist and nearly connected with the man's face. Jason recognized the Rifleman; he was one of the men from the Recce platoon from B Company. A very tough man from Cornwall who really knew how to fight, Faulkner was his name. Faulkner merely dipped his head as the huge fist came at him.

"Thaat the best ye can do, yer silly booger?" he jibed and dipped his head, skillfully dodging the punch. Then his foot came out from behind him and slammed into the man's midriff. The man gasped but he was a lot harder than Faulkner had imagined.

"Fuck you, Pommy, try this!" he roared. They set to furiously with fists and boots.

Jason guided Megan along the edge of the battle, past men cursing and shouting insults at each other. It was definitely not a good place for someone like Megan as far as Jason was concerned. One man came stumbling backwards into Jason's unwelcoming arms. Jason turned him round roughly and gave him a good shove back towards the bloody-faced Rifleman who had sent him in that direction in the first place. The Kiwi got another very hard punch from another Rifleman. The man flew back, toppled over a table and fell with a crash behind them. Megan gave a startled giggle.

But Jason wasn't going to get away with it; another man stepped into his path and swung a punch at his head. Jason ducked and punched the man in the ribs. The man, not one of the Kiwis or a Rifleman, grunted as the air was knocked out of him and then leaned forward to swing again. This time Jason was nearly caught off balance, as he had been watching for trouble from another quarter. The fist grazed his ear and made it sting. He pushed Megan forward through a gap in the fighting men and punched the man in the mouth. It hurt his fist but the man disappeared and he was able to skip past the rest who ignored him.

Running and dodging now, the two of them ducked onto the small pier that ran out to sea, and then Jason jumped down onto the sand. The pier was only three feet high at this point but he held out his arms and Megan leaned down and dropped into his arms. He enjoyed holding her and she seemed in no hurry to be released.

"That fight could go any way right now and I don't want to be here when the MPs come," he told her.

There were curses and more crashes, then they heard the squeal of tires on the main road outside and the thump of running boots on the sidewalk followed by whistles being blown as the MPs arrived.

"Come on, Megan, we need to get some distance from here," said Jason urgently.

They ran off down the beach into the shadows. Megan was giggling.

They came to some rocks and sat down.

"You seem to be able to handle yourself, Mr. Rifleman, Jason. Are you all like that?" she asked him, sounding puzzled.

"Not always, love. But sometimes the Aussies or the Kiwis come to town and we have a rumble. And before you ask, no, I don't look for fights. I did learn to fight in the Boys' School though. You had to there."

"You Brits are nuts, you are all nuts!" she exclaimed, laughing.

He grinned and rubbed his ear. Then he took her hand and they moved out onto a more comfortable slab of rock and sat down. Jason was nursing his fist; the man's teeth had left marks on his knuckles. Megan leaned over and took his hand.

"Does it hurt?" she asked solicitously, peering at it in the dark.

"Na, not really; hope he didn't have rabies though!" They giggled together. He glanced back down the beach towards the restaurant. He was sure that he could see some MPs on the pier looking up towards them. He hoped they wouldn't come along the beach. If they did, he had Megan as an alibi anyway.

"Looks like the MPs are checking to see if we are within reach," he said.

Megan looked back the way they had come. "I'll tell them you dragged me kicking and screaming out here to have your wicked way with me," she said.

"You wouldn't!" he exclaimed, pretending to sound panicked.

He wanted to kiss her but waited. They sat in silence catching their breath and listening to the lapping of the wavelets among the rocks. They were sitting on a black slab, leaning back against a rock, looking out over the sea that was lit by the moon.

Megan said dreamily, "There is so much texture to this place, you know what I mean?"

"No, but it's beautiful, that what you mean?"

"I suppose so, silly. Kiss me," she said.

Putting his weight on his elbow and oblivious of the discomfort Jason leaned over her and kissed her. It was a long, lingering kiss.

His hand traced a pattern on her stomach and then inched up towards her breasts. She reached up and pulled him down onto her.

"Careful," he mumbled, "you must be feeling the rock."

She giggled; her hand went down to his pants.

"I guess I am," she laughed.

He laughed too, embarrassed, suddenly very aware of his condition.

They kissed again and he became bolder. His hands were gently kneading her breasts. He tried to undo her buttons, which she let him do just enough to expose the silky material of the bra. He pressed his lips against the material, enjoying the sensation and the tantalizing feel of her breast and the nipple beneath.

His hand started to wander down towards her hips even as they kissed. She pushed it away firmly but not violently and then eased him off her. They were both a little breathless by now.

"OK, soldier, don't overdo the standing to attention thing." She laughed a little shakily.

Jason was so aroused that he was unable to come back with a response. The blood was rushing into his head and nether regions with such fury that speech was impossible. He sat back and let his breathing ease. Megan began to button her blouse and tidy her hair distractedly.

"I'm sorry, Megan, I didn't mean to..."

"Let's go to my place," she said softly.

Jason nodded mutely. He could hardly believe he had heard correctly!

"OK, we need to go past the restaurant and get a taxi." He offered her his hand and pulled her up. She stood on her toes and kissed him. They scrambled off the rocks and arm in arm went back the way they had come.

The brawlers had been rounded up and taken off to the military police station. The very angry owner of the restaurant and his Chinese staff were shouting and waving their arms about as they cleaned up the mess. Jason and Megan slipped along the pier to the main road without attracting attention.

The taxi dropped them off in a seedy area along Armenian Street. Jason was wary. They warned the troops at the camp that a lone soldier in the back streets of the town was liable to be robbed and possibly worse as the Chinese Communists were still deemed to be active in the Chinese areas of Malaysia such as Penang, but he had never heard of any incidents. He was, however, willing to believe it of these incredibly shabby rows of tiled houses. The people never seemed to sleep. Even at this hour it was busy, with the street vendors open for business. The aroma of cooking fish, pork and boiled cabbage pervaded the air in the street. Lanterns swayed in the light breeze, moving shadows about like living things.

Megan seemed quite comfortable here though, so he decided to take her lead but keep alert. They crossed the street and entered an arched gateway. The paint was of an indeterminate color, flaking away all over the square pillars and the archways. There were the usual old wood shutters with peeling paint on the windows overlooking the street with a glimmer of light showing behind them. The street lights shed a dull light on the walls of the shabby buildings. But there were dark shadows cast by the overhanging roofs and in the deep doorways.

They went into a small rundown courtyard. Some Chinese women were sitting playing Mahjong noisily on a metal table, the tiles clicking as they dropped them into place while smoking their acrid cigarettes in one corner. They looked up at the arrival of the pair and fell to watching and talking about them.

Megan led the way across the courtyard towards the stairs on the other side. There was a light on the first floor and the shutters were half open. She nodded upwards.

"That's my apartment," she said in low tones.

They started up the stairs; the place smelt of incense, camphor and boiled food. The slightly rancid odor of ghee, the local cooking oil, clung to the walls of the stairwell. Jason found it a little cloying but his attention was focused on the legs of the girl climbing the stairs ahead of him. Megan led the way along a narrow landing and then opened the door at the end.

They were half way into the room when she stopped abruptly right in his path. Jason almost fell over her.

He quickly saw the reason. Dale and Jan were making love on the futon laid out on the floor near the window. They had not heard the entry, they were so preoccupied with their own activities, both quite naked in the missionary position, thrusting away at one another, Jan squealing happily for Dale to "Do it, do it, oh yeah, oh!" Dale seemed happy to oblige but just at the point where he was peaking Jan glanced up and saw the two standing there staring at them.

She nudged Dale sharply but he was in the throes of his orgasm and paid no attention to her. "Yeah!" he exclaimed, his hips pumping. "Oh yeah, baby! Oh yeah!"

Then he became aware of the fact that something was wrong. Jan was banging him on his forehead with both fists.

"Stop it, Dale, stop it, dammit!"

"What the fuck's the matter!"

He stared down at her for a second and he realized that she was looking over his shoulder. He spun his head around, his ponytail whipping across her face and making her wince. Hurriedly he pulled a light quilt over them and rolled off Jan.

"Shit, Megan, you might have knocked!" he complained.

"I shouldn't have to knock," said Megan sharply. "This is where I live! You could have at least done it on your bed!" she whirled away saying, "Get off my bed and stay off it, you bastards!" then led the way back along the landing and almost ran down the stairs.

Jason followed. He knew the evening was gone and hated Dale for having made it so.

"Christ!" he thought. "I could kill that bastard!"

When they got to the courtyard the women were still there. Megan looked around almost desperately for a secluded place to sit, away from their prying eyes. They found a low wall near the one papaya tree in the yard. Jason sat silently next to her. For a couple of seconds they said nothing. Megan was breathing carefully, her teeth clenched.

Then Jason said, "It's all right, love. It wouldn't have done to stay."

Megan looked at him in the darkness. "I'm sorry, Jason. Dale is a pig. I wish I had never let him stay at my place."

"Did you know him from before?"

"No, not really, but we Peace Corps stick together, and these guys have been shifting from one site to another. I can see why they don't stay long anywhere. They piss everyone off."

"Well, they certainly pissed you off, and come to think of it, they did me, too!" he said with annoyance in his voice that he couldn't hide.

She laughed and the tension was broken. Her hand came out and she laid it on his arm.

"Was my soldier all pumped up?" She giggled.

"Yeah, he was actually! Rigid! At attention and ready for anything, except this!"

She was laughing silently now, and he had to join in. They sat giggling for a long moment. She was leaning against him, her forehead pressed to his.

She was serious for a moment. "Do you think I'm a loose woman, Jason?"

He was shocked. "No, love, I don't. It seemed like it was the right moment; you know, it was right," he repeated. He took her hands in his. "I've had a wonderful evening, love. One of the best I can remember, fight and all."

"Me too, fight and all," she said smiling, tilting her face up at him.

"Do you mean that? I mean I'm only a squaddie, you know."

"Shut up, you idiot. I liked you from the first time we met. Anyway, you don't act much like a soldier. I like that."

He kissed her then and felt the now familiar heat rising as he pulled her close to him.

"Can I see you again, then?" he asked when they came up for air.

She pretended to think about it for a couple of seconds, her head angled up and away from him. Then she grinned impishly at him.

"OK... I guess so. Let's meet in town and we can walk. What about the Esplanade by the old fort? This Saturday? I love sitting there. Can you come alone?"

He nodded happily, able to breathe again. "You bet I can, what time?"

"Can you make it in the morning? What about eleven? I have to close the class at ten thirty," she said.

"Sounds good." He looked at his watch. "Heck, I'd better go. Can I get a taxi near here?"

"Just down the street. Take care, Jason. I'll see you Saturday." She reached up and kissed him goodbye.

"See you, love." He walked briskly out into the street, looking back once to see her still standing there. She waved her hand at waist level. He grinned and waved back then went to look for a taxi.

Major Johnson
Chapter 4

The single rider broke free of the melee of other players in the middle of the wide green field and rode his pony hard towards the club house. Major Johnson flicked the ball forward with his mallet on its second bounce, lifting it into the air; then at full gallop he swung his mallet in a swift strike that connected with the ball just before it landed. The white ball seemed to float lazily over the two red wicker goal posts situated thirty yards in front of the club house. The Syce standing well back from the goal posts raised a red flag and waved it high to signify a score. The crowd on the verandah of the club house and seated on the wicker chairs lined up facing the field clapped appreciatively.

The Major acknowledged the applause with a lift of his mallet and turned his pony to canter back to the middle of the field, where his team members were already gathered for the throw in. He was a big man who made his pony seem small, but he was a good if not an elegant rider, so it was barely noticeable to the critical observer. He lifted his light cork helmet and rubbed his forehead, then pushed his matted light brown hair back before replacing his helmet.

There were enthusiastic congratulations from his team and nods of approval from the opposition when he joined them. The ball was tossed in by the umpire and the players jostled each other, snapping their sticks against one another's as they tried to tap the ball out of the melee.

Johnson, who was playing number three, caught the ball coming out from a mass of ponies' legs and tapped it out of the crowd forward towards his number two who had broken away, waiting for just this moment. He managed to hit the ball once with a good long hit down field but was ridden off hard by one of the Chinese players from the other side.

The major was carefully watching the line out as players marked one another. He rode his pony comfortably and controlled the eager animal easily with his left hand, waiting for an opportunity to push his opposing player aside and take the ball.

But the number three of the other side was a good player; he rode off his opposite number and hammered the ball back towards the major's goal in a high arc with a very skillful back hand.

Everyone including Johnson hauled their ponies round and raced them back up the field to get to the ball before the others. His number four, Captain Romney-Smith got to the ball easily, but just as he tried to back the ball himself he was ridden out by the man who marked him.

This left the major and the man who was marking him now at a flat out gallop towards the major's goal. They rode into one another in a furious back and forth play, hammering into each other as each tried to line his pony up with the swiftly moving ball and ride the other out of the way. It was the major who just managed to get to the ball, but instead of striking it with a back hand he tipped the ball forward off to his right with a flick of his powerful wrist.

Almost standing in the stirrups, guiding his horse with his legs and a light touch on the reins, he rode it in a half circle, tapping the ball along as he went. By now he had slowed his excited pony to a canter and tapped the ball in a tight arc that denied his opponents an easy chance to ride him off. It also gave his team a chance to get forward and position themselves for the long pass that they knew was coming.

Sure enough, he now had the ball lined up facing the opposition's goal and he was just short of the half way line when he gave the ball a terrific hit that lofted it high into the air. The others raced after it, watching it soar right down the middle of the field to land bouncing high on the short grass within forty yards of the opposing side's goal. He heard the distant bell ringing for two minutes before end of the game and prayed that they would score before the whistle blew for the game to end.

His number one, Lieutenant Graham, reached it with his opposite number racing to catch him. Graham only had to tap the ball but his stick was hooked and he lost it. Johnson's number two, riding right behind the others, managed by dint of some wild leaning out to just hook the ball enough to get it started towards the goal and then he too was ridden into. The shock of the two ponies coming together nearly unseated Lieutenant Stevens but he hung onto his horse's neck and recovered long enough to lean out again and tap the ball over the line.

There were roars of approval from the crowd at that end. Many of the watchers were men from the Green Jackets who had come to watch the playoff for the final match the next day. Major Johnson nodded his approval and cantered back to the center with the others. But the whistle blew for the end of the game just as the players began to line up again. After the handshaking and back slapping, the Green Jackets team, led by Major Johnson, walked their tired and sweating horses back to the pony lines. He leaned over and patted his pony on its wet neck and gave it all the reins so that it hung its head and plodded home.

"That was a nice goal, Roger."

The young officer blushed with pleasure.

"Thank you Sir. He nearly unseated me! That Ken Seong can pack a wallop when he rides one off!"

The others laughed. The Chinese and Europeans on the other team were good players and would be going on to the finals the next day, but the officers from the Green Jackets all felt that as a scratch team they had done well.

Major Johnson was pleased with the team. They had only just started playing at the Penang Polo Club. They had lost this game by only one goal and that was no disgrace against the more experienced team they had been playing.

The Chinese and Europeans played better in the heat and certainly were much more experienced. The only one on his team with a handicap was himself with a one goal, and Captain Harley-Smith had a zero rating. However, his team of starters was showing the others what the visitors could do.

There was much in the way of congratulations for the winners and the losers as they gathered upstairs at the bar of the club. It was crowded and full of smoke in the bar room, everyone talking loudly to one another. The sweating Chinese barman was kept busy with orders for gins, beers and whiskey sours demanded by the thirsty crowd.

The other teams who had played that day or were to play next in the three day tournament were all there, drinks in hand, faces flushed and talking animatedly with one another. He almost sneezed; the Chinese members were heavy smokers.

Major Johnson searched for his wife in the crowd. He saw her among a group of wives and waved. She smiled and waved back. holding their young son by the hand. He pushed his way carefully towards them, receiving complements and commiserations from the many new acquaintances.

When he arrived he leaned over and kissed his wife and ruffled his smiling son's hair. "Hello Darling! Hello Tony. How are you two? Did you see anything of the game?" They had arrived late because Anthony his son had still been at school.

"Hello Darling," responded his wife Barbara, a slim woman in her thirties with light brown hair and dark blue eyes he always enjoyed looking into.

"Yes we did, Daddy!" piped up his six year old son eagerly. "That was a terrific goal you scored. Cor! I wish you could have won!"

The major smiled. His son was very partisan when it came to his father's polo matches.

"I suspect we could have if I had been on Prince, Anthony," said the Major with a smile down at his boy.

"Well, it was an exciting game, and everyone was very complementary about our boys. Especially you, dear," said Barbara comfortably. "How long do you think we will be staying?" she asked.

The Major knew his wife was not one to socialize very much, so he nodded and said, "I probably need to say hello to the colonel. I spotted him with some of our hosts so...probably half an hour to an hour, darling. OK?"

They had moved onto the landing just outside the bar.

"We'll go and have a look at the horses then. Would you like that, Tony?" she asked their son.

"Oh, yes, Mum. I'd like that. See you in a while, Daddy!" Anthony said excitedly.

He kissed Barbara on the cheek, ruffled his son's hair again and went back into the crowded room to do his duty. He spotted the Colonel who was standing with his wife at the window, talking to one of the Europeans who lived in Penang. Obtaining a gin and tonic, he walked over to them, gave a polite short bow, and smiled at the colonel's wife.

"Hello Janet; hello, Sir." He greeted them. Colonel Barkar-Hollingworth greeted him by raising his glass. "Well done, Nigel"

With them were a couple of the Chinese business men who formed the larger portion of the club membership, still in their boots and breeches. The Chinese were very capable players, owned good horses, and were also very generous and willing to share them with the officers of the Green Jackets until they could buy some of their own. They were happy to have some new blood in the club, if only for a short while.

"That was a tight game there, Nigel; we will have to keep an eye on you Army types!" said John Lehman, one of the opposition players, a European who had lived in Penang for over twenty years.

He grinned. "A lot of missed opportunities, John. But it was also a lot of fun, gentlemen, thank you for your generosity," he said, raising his glass.

The others smiled back and raised theirs in response. "You are a welcome addition to the club in this remote part of the world," remarked the Chinese man standing next to the colonel.

"John and Ah Sew here were discussing the recent events going on in Singapore, Nigel. That man Lee Kwan Yew is proving to be an interesting person to watch," said the colonel.

"Why is that, Sir?" asked Nigel who was unsure of the name.

"Because he is going to finesse Singapore out from under the noses of the Malays! Just like you British did with the Dutch, I think," said Lim Sew with a laugh.

Nigel knew Lim Sew was a lawyer, most of the rich professionals in Penang were either doctors or lawyers, and it was fashionable for them to either have race horses or polo ponies as part of their image. He wasn't sure if he liked Lim Sew but he was polite to him nonetheless. The Brits were here on invitation, not as the overlords any more. Besides, these men had their fingers on the pulse of the country and were worth knowing.

"Really? Why would he want to do that, Sew?" he asked carefully.

"Because the Chinese are sick of the high-handed way the Malays treat them when, after all, they represent the economic backbone of the country," interjected John Lehman.

Nigel almost looked around, he was so surprised at the words. He was not sure if there were any Malay people who were members of the club. He fervently hoped no one had heard that last sally.

"There might be something in that from what I hear. Tunku Abdul Rahman, the Malay premier, is at least listening to what the Chinese are asking for," said Lim Sew with a sharp glance at John.

"What if they don't listen?" asked the major.

"I think that it is an unsaid thing, but there is genuine fear in Kuala Lumpur that there could be a return to the jungle by some of the hotheads."

This was said by another tall Chinese man who the major knew as an influential man in local politics. Doctor Ah Seng.

The major looked sharply at him. Having been in the Malay Emergency as a young subaltern, Johnson was keenly interested in what was going on in the now independent country with its mixture of native Malay people, Chinese, and Indian minorities, as well as Europeans. He remembered the tension of the time then and wondered if it had eased at all in the last six years.

"What does he intend to do? Make Singapore a Chinese independent nation?" he asked, with a glance at the colonel.

"That's about it, but he has not only the Malays to convince but the British too. There are some communists in the mix as well, it seems. It could get interesting," said Ah Seng.

"Well, we are more interested in the shenanigans of that fellow Sukarno right now," said the major." Any news in the papers from that quarter?"

"He is sending thousands of troops across Borneo to try his luck with Brunei from what I have heard; that is mostly what the papers are saying, and they are desperately looking for news," said John.

"Do you think he will really try for Brunei?" asked Nigel carefully.

"He is mad enough to try anything, that man; don't forget that Brunei is swimming in oil." said Lim Sew. "One might hope that it will take his mind of the Chinese that live in Indonesia for the moment. I am sure you British will deal with it if it comes to a fight; at least you are good at that," he said tartly.

Major Johnson wondered where he had heard the name Lim Sew before. Not for the first time, he wondered if the man had been involved with the communists; the name seemed somehow familiar.

"Well, I suppose that is why we're here after all," he responded coolly.

"I think Sukarno wants the whole of Borneo to add to his collection of islands," said John Lehman with a smirk.

"In that case, your Commonwealth forces have got their work cut out for them. Borneo is a large place, mostly jungle, ridgeback hills, and swamps in the south, while over in Sabah it isn't much better." Ah Seng said.

"Have you been there?" asked the major politely.

"Oh yes," Ah Seng said. "We have some interests in the logging business on the Kalabakan River near its delta, not far from Tawau. Miserable place! Horrid place to fight a war from what I can tell." He grinned at the assembly showing a gold tooth.

Ever the diplomat, the colonel tried to get the conversation away from politics. He turned the talk back to the game and what the Club's chances of winning the Malay cup might be on the morrow. As the talk went back and forth over the relative merits of the visiting teams he excused himself from the group and took the major's arm.

"Need to talk to you and the other company commanders, Nigel. Come and see me in the morning after you have dealt with your company business, would you?" he murmured quietly.

"Of course, Sir. I'll see you at 0900 hrs?"

"That would be fine, Nigel. See you then. Well played. We might not be the cavalry but we can still show 'em, I suppose. Go and see your family. I will try to get this lot onto other things." He smiled and left Nigel to go back to the group.

Nigel spent some time with the others of the team and a couple of the other senior

officers at the bar, then went to see his wife and son at the pony lines.

*　*　*　*　*

Major Johnson arrived punctually at the colonel's office in the main administration area at 0900 Hrs. He found the other company commanders waiting there. They greeted one another quietly and then waited for the Adjutant, Captain Patterson, to come and collect them. The fan above them only just managed to move the air around in the room, so they were all soon sweating in

47

the humid air. Johnson felt the moisture patch growing down his back. The jungle green jackets of light cotton material were heavily starched but rarely lasted longer than a couple of hours in this hothouse humidity before looking rumpled.

The major guessed that they were to have a briefing on when they were to go to Borneo. He was very keen to get going. He, like everyone else in the regiment, considered the island of Penang to be an enviable posting, but he was after all a soldier, and Borneo sounded like a promising place to have the occasional scrap and perhaps some recognition, which did no harm in a so-called peace time army.

Finally they were all admitted to the large, cool office of the colonel by the Adjutant, who then left the room and shut the door. The colonel greeted the five company commanders by name and then went straight to the point of the meeting.

"I have been informed by GHQ that they want to beef up the south of Sarawak earlier than anticipated," he said. "The Paratroop regiment faced down the Indonesian trouble makers in Brunei, and now GHQ wants to reinforce the border with more troops. Kuching is to have the Green Jackets and the Gurkhas as a barrier to the Indonesians if they should try for it. The Hampshires have been there for longer than they were originally intended and need to be send back home for some R&R."

The officers seated opposite the colonel began to stir and shift.

"Sukarno has already made a bid for Brunei where his men got bumped by the Paras and kicked out. This means the Green Jackets have to get down to Jahore Bahru sooner than expected and get some serious training under way. He might try for Kuching next, and that is what we have to stop happening."

Now there was an excited murmur from the officers. At last they were to do something about the situation over there, and sooner rather than later. Johnson was pleased because there had been a niggling feeling that they might miss all the action.

The colonel gave a wry smile.

"We all like Penang, I am sure; it is probably one of the most idyllic places in the world to be garrisoned, but it isn't what the Light Infantry is about. So start preparations to leave immediately. Remember this show is called a 'Confrontation' and that officially we are not involved, so the less our people talk to the civilians about it the better."

"Quartermaster," he addressed the major in charge of all the camp stores. "Please ensure that the weaponry and supplies are up to standard; get as much as you can out of Singapore. Transport to Jahore by train, and then I am told the regiment will be shipped to Kuching where we will jump off for the various places each company will be staying."

He then addressed the other officers. "You may think that we have done some good training up to now, but I am told by the Brigadier it will be nothing compared to what the SAS and the Gurkha training battalion have in mind for us in Jahore. Make sure the junior officers have their map reading up to par and hone their navigation skills, we are going to need them, I hear."

After he had dismissed them the major walked back to his own lines and informed the officers of what was coming. He was excited by the news and the challenges to come. This was what he wanted, but he knew Barbara would not be happy, although she would accept it as being the life of a soldier's wife. He would tell her that night over dinner.

The Train South
Chapter 5

Almost the entire regiment crossed the straits of Penang on a special ferry and then took the train south to Kuala Lumpur from Butterworth, the town opposite Penang Island. Despite the misery of the parting with Megan, Jason had enjoyed the leisurely ride south. The carriages resembled those he had seen in westerns.

There was a small railed platform at each end of the carriage he shared with his mates where the men could stand in small groups to smoke and watch the jungle go by on either side. The train had traveled almost all day before clanking and hissing slowly into the capital of the country, Kuala Lumpur. The troops had leaned out of the windows and stood on the platforms of the carriages, staring back at the curious crowds on the sides.

As the troops were forbidden to disembark, they stayed aboard and sweltered in the stuffy carriages. There was not much talking by now as everyone tried to find a place to sleep. The lights of the train station and the city had been exciting to watch at first, but as nothing new happened they grew bored and turned in. Jason and his mates stood smoking and talking on the connecting platforms of the carriages.

They were rewarded with the sight of small groups of pretty women walking alongside the train.

"Ah'll bet them's prosis," said Kevin as they watched a small group come towards them. Others had realized this too and the bargaining began as sex-starved soldiers vied with one another to get the services of the women. Dressed in elegant sarongs, with tight bodices that showed off their small breasts, they were all appetizingly petite. Andy and Jerry, who was still a virgin, excitedly called to one of the women to haggle with her over the price.

"Fooking Aida, them's aboot as tasty as any Ahv seen in Pinang!" exclaimed Kevin.

"'Ow much for a quickie, Jiga Jig?" asked Andy of one of these svelte-looking creatures.

"Ten dollar. Short time, Jonny," she said, smiling gold teeth at them.

Ten dollars appeared and was handed over.

Then Jerry said, "Oi want two's up! 'Ere's another ten!"

"Yer'll get a dose 'o the clap, yer silly fokers!" Paddy commented.

"Betchyouse it drops off before we get to Borneo," said Kevin, nudging Jason. "Wot, not interested, Jason? 'ad enough in Penang, did we, Taffy?"

Jason didn't answer. He was numb with the parting from Megan. He realized that he had come as close as it was possible to actually deserting. He shook his head and moved out of the way. They stood aside when the girl was helped onto the carriage platform and the two lusty boys took her off to their compartment.

"Give us 'alf an hour, mates, and no lookin'," called back Andy.

"Betcha yoos'll be done in a second. Be cheaper to 'ave a wank!" Paddy jibed.

"Hey, Jerry! D'ya ken where to put it? Want me to show youse?" called Kevin, grinning.

Jerry gave him a v-sign and trailed after Andy, looking nervous. The others speculated about their chances of getting the clap while they waited on the carriage platforms.

It was not long before more were on the train and compartments became steamed up as the prostitutes dispensed their services.

There was a whistle and the train began to move. Some of the women became agitated and wanted to leave, but the men wanted to have more and prevented them from getting off, telling them that they could disembark at one of the stations further on. However, somewhere in the middle of the train a discovery was made.

Not all the pretty women were women. The men who found out, being Riflemen, were none too gentle with these.

One burly rifleman put it this way, "Oi din't expect a pair of 'airy balls when I went up 'er skirt! Got me really bovvered that did!"

As the train gathered speed, these unfortunates were tossed off into the passing jungle. Their shrieks of distress were fuel to the loud, and by now excited and destructive squaddies, who started to look for more who might be hiding. Fortunately for those who were the genuine article, their partners, like Andy and his mates, defended them against the rowdy men looking for victims. Fights were quelled by the corporals, the only men with authority at this time and place.

One of the problems with a train full of British troops, especially Green Jackets on their way to the never-never land of Borneo, was that the officers were at one end and the senior NCOs at the other. Thus the middle carriages were a kind of no-man's land that the sensible officers and NCOs didn't visit while the train was on the move. The corporals and senior Riflemen who were not drunk used their fists and boots to restore order.

They steamed into Jahore Bahru in the early hours of the next day. Bleary-eyed troops disembarked and were quickly herded by color sergeants and other NCOs with their clipboards onto the three-ton Bedford trucks, the mainstay of transport in the British Army. The trucks whisked the Green Jackets men past the rows of small shops owned by industrious Chinese and Indian tailors, restaurant owners and hardware traders. They drove along tarmac roads and then along dirt tracks, the jungle on either side. The trucks ground their way along potholed and very bumpy tracks that wound among coconut palms and banana plantations. They drove past rubber plantations with their attendant villages and their distinctive cloying stink of smoked latex that made the men groan and hold their noses.

Finally they headed into the wilderness to arrive at a camp on the edge of the jungle proper. The main jungle warfare school was some way off from the area where the regiment was placed. That was a well-tended camp with tennis courts and a nice officers' mess. The Green Jackets, however, were not here for a holiday.

They were met by more of the advance guard from the regiment who had come down by plane to prepare for the arrival of the troops. The condition of the accommodations had elicited a groan from the tired men but they had accepted them without much complaint.

Jason and the others of the Pioneers had mixed feelings about the eight to nine months they were to spend in Sarawak. They had heard that was to be their destination. First Division was located near and around Kuching, the capital of Sarawak. The officers spent a lot of time looking at maps with members of the spooky group of men who were the instructors. Rumor had it that most of Borneo was unexplored and men speculated endlessly on the added rumor that the huge island was full of people called Dyaks, who were headhunters. Other strange people were seen occasionally, known as Iban trackers, who stayed close to the instructors and spoke to each other in a language that resembled Malay.

Training began and Jason and the other riflemen resorted to their usual defense; they just hated them and got better at what they were being trained to do. They even beat the Gurkhas once or twice, which gave them a ridiculous sense of achievement. The Green Jackets, which included the unwilling Jason and his mates in the Pioneer section, took to the jungle very well, and soon they all had the pasty-white look of men who have not seen the sun for weeks on end. There was no time for sunbathing in this place, and the men were worked so hard that there were few disciplinary problems.

They became very good at setting ambushes and moving fast but quietly from one place to another. Their officers and sergeants became proficient with the compass and the method of estimating distances. They could not better the SAS, but those people had gone native and were hence considered Choggies, which was what the Riflemen called the Malay soldiers.

Sir Galahad
Chapter 6

The day finally arrived when the command came down from General Headquarters in Singapore for the regiment to embark for Borneo. They were to leave by troopship from the naval port on the island of Singapore, located on the other side of the causeway across the Straits. The base was one of the last naval ports the British had access to in this part of the world. Jason and his mates packed up their kit and made ready. There was an air of expectancy among the troops. This was the jump of point for the sharp end. The senior officers and the advance guard were to be flown to Kuching while the men were to take a troop ship called *Sir Galahad*.

The Bedford trucks came and picked up the Green Jackets from the jungle warfare school and took them in a long convoy across the causeway, and then they went east towards the naval base.

Jason could hardly believe his eyes when he saw their vessel: a very old cargo ship that had been converted to accommodate troops. It elicited a collective groan from the men – this rust-bucket was to be their home for four days and it looked barely seaworthy. The general feeling was that they were being sent to the ends of the earth to fight the Indons in unknown, unmapped country in a vessel that was bound to sink before they even got there.

They trooped aboard and were herded in their sections into the cramped cabins, six to a room,where they found two sets of three-tiered canvas bunks and not much space to put their gear. The Pioneers found themselves in one of these steel closets with only one porthole to let smells out and the hot air in. Of course, there was no air conditioning, not even a fan, so they stripped down to their drawers and flip-flops. Rifles and other weaponry were stacked in corners and men got into the bunks and resigned themselves to a long, hot journey.

Andy commented, "Fookin' Aida! Good job they didn't give us any live ammo yet. There's more than one squaddie Ah know would use it on the fookin' ship's captain. What a tub!"

The ship didn't leave port until late that night, by which time the men were tired of watching the sea and the dockside. Most had gone to their cabins before the ship cast off and slowly headed out into the eastern seas. They took a southerly course for the remote town of Kuching in Sarawak. Jason woke during the night and felt the ship rising and dipping to the swell of the high seas. He turning over in his bunk, stared at the steel wall in the dark and felt lost.

The first day was spent doing all the usual drills that the Army feels is mandatory when it goes to sea. The senior NCOs explained the drills to the men grouped on the main deck, Jason among them.

One NCO who Jason didn't know said loudly, "It's not that we don't trust the Royal Navy, it's just that ships have a bad habit of sinking when you least expect them to, so pay attention!"

This drew some derisive laughter from the sweating men but most of them just glowered and put up with it.

The men sweated through the safety drills and lifeboat drills and the fire drills and all the other drills that military functionaries, who themselves have probably never even been to the beach, consider important for soldiers to perform at sea.

By the second day, the men were used to the routine and spent most of their free time on deck. They could be found lying around sunbathing almost everywhere except the bridge, which was strictly out of bounds to all ranks except the officer in charge.

They lay around on the bow deck and the afterdeck, along the main decks and on the wide canvas covered hatches, sunbathing wherever they could find a place to sit or lie. The mixed crew of Malays and other indeterminate sailors learned not to disturb the men of the Green Jackets because these men wanted all the sun they could get. They were quite sure that they were going to live like troglodytes when they got to Borneo and didn't want to be disturbed.

Jason and his mates did the same. He had a couple of books that he got into and on occasion found someone to play chess with. There was a hot competition going on for an unofficial champion at chess and he fancied his chances. But there were a couple of good players among the company, so he wasn't complacent.

On the second night, in a desperate attempt to keep the troops from going completely nuts, the sergeant majors and their NCOs started a Bingo session. Jason and his pals Andy, Paddy, Jerry and Kevin went to play. Geordie had been selected to go on the advance party and had been flown with others directly to Kuching.

They took their places and counted their money, which didn't come to much, about twenty-five dollars Malay. Payday wasn't until they got to Kuching. This would pay for a couple of beers each and two sessions of Bingo. The game was played between decks after the soggy dinner had been served. The mess was cleared and chairs were placed to face a small platform where one of the color sergeants was calling out the numbers.

Jason and his mates passed on the first few games and enjoyed the cold beers they had bought. The ship had a cooler of some size and for the first time in weeks they could revel in the taste of cold Tiger beers. The evening progressed with the usual shouts as one person or the other got a run or a sheet. The rewards were modest amounts of money or extra beers. It wasn't long before there were some tipsy squaddies making fools of themselves. Jason finally bought a ticket for the last round of the evening and settled down to listen for the numbers. He wasn't paying much attention to the calls, he was mooning about Megan as usual, but evidently Kevin was.

He suddenly gave a shout. "Bingo! Bingo! Fookin' 'ell, Jason, can't yer see? Bingo! Bingo!" There was a collective groan as the others in the packed mess hall peered at their own tickets hoping it was a mistake.

Jason was taken by surprise but he allowed Kevin and Andy to take the ticket up for scrutiny by the skeptical sergeant; he sat where he was and waited, sure Kevin had gotten it wrong.

But Kevin let out a whoop and turned back to him shouting, "Youse looky boogger, Jason, youse won the last 'ouse and the fookin' snowball all in one! Ah don't believe it!"

Nor did the sergeant who double-checked the ticket, but he then turned to the color sergeant and told him that it was correct. The other men in the mess hall cursed the Pioneers and began to leave. Soon the only people in the room were the Pioneers and the two NCOs.

"Well, how do you want it?" asked the color sergeant.

"Can I have it in beer, Color?"

The two NCOs looked at them. "You can have it in beer or money, I don't care. Just don't fall overboard or I'll put you on a charge."

Andy and Kevin snickered and Jason grinned. "I'll take it in beer, please, Color."

The group of Pioneers took the five crates of cold Tiger beer up on deck. Andy suggested that they go to the very front of the ship where they could enjoy the beer without being interrupted.

"We don't have to get on parade in the morning and it's cooler at the front than in the 'ole we have to sleep in," he pointed out.

The gleeful group of Pioneers took the crates onto the small deck at the prow of the ship. The cool breeze was delightful to the young men as they swigged the first of the many cold beers. Soon a party was going on. Some of the men who got on well with the Pioneers came to take advantage of the bounty and some stayed. The stories and lies got under way and it wasn't long before people were well and truly tipsy. Later, however, the five Pioneers were left with the remaining two crates of beer that they were very determined to finish off before dawn.

The moon came out and the throb of the ship's engines seemed to become more pronounced as some of their mates went to sleep and the companions sat quietly drinking, enjoying the bright moonlit night. Jason was restless and stood up. He wobbled to his feet and stared forward towards the horizon. He peered blearily ahead for some minutes and then called over to Andy.

"Hey, Andy, come and 'ave a look at this."

Andy scrambled slowly to his feet and, like Jason, swayed while he too peered forward.

"Somethin's wrong, Andy," slurred Jason.

"Wot yer mean?"

"Does that look like land to you over there? See the long black line ahead?"

Andy, who had now found his feet, wiped his eyes and peered harder at the horizon. "Fuck me. We're heading straight for the land!" he exclaimed. "That's land, right? Hey, Kevin, get up 'ere and have a look," he called.

Kevin, who was about to go to sleep along with Paddy and Jerry, climbed shakily to his feet.

"Wassamater with you booggers?" he slurred.

"Tell me that that's not land dead ahead, mate," demanded Jason.

In the bright moonlight and the almost cloudless night, they could all see the horizon and what appeared to be a long dark strip of land dead ahead that went right across the entire horizon.

"Yarright, it's land ahoy!" shouted Kevin.

"Shurrup, you noisy bugger," said Jason. He squinted thoughtfully at the black line ahead. "What bothers me is that this ship is not slowing down. At this rate we'll crash into it and that will be that," he said reasonably.

"Fockin' captain's dronk! That's wot he is," said Kevin truculently.

"Someone 'as to go and tell 'em," said Andy firmly. "We're all going to fookin' drown because that boogger's drunk!"

"Tellem what?" asked Jason stupidly.

Paddy stirred. "Shurrup! Noisy wankers!" he murmured.

Jerry stirred and snored.

"Tellem to change course or stop engines, that's wot," said Andy.

"We're noo allowed onte' bridge," said Kevin.

"It's a ma'er of life or death!" said Andy insistently. "You're noo allowed to go rammin' oother people's coontries wi' a ship. Noo even the Royal fockin' Navy!"

"I carrnt swim anyway. Not in this big, wide fuckin' ocean. It's full of sharks," mumbled Jason apprehensively. "Whose going to tell 'em?"

"We draw lots," said Andy solemnly. The others nodded agreement.

He fished out a couple of matches and broke one.

"The one gets the short end goes and tells the captain to change course."

They drew lots and Andy got the short one. The other two were relieved and sat back down and began to drink again. Andy was going to sort it all out. They were safe now. He disappeared.

They watched the bridge to see if there was any activity. The bridge was a dark silhouette against the moonlit sky so when Andy did arrive on its port wing they saw everything as though it was some kind of shadow theatre.

He appeared on the wing and then disappeared into the bridge proper. The next thing they saw he was going backwards and what is more he was leaning backwards while the silhouette of the officer of the watch, who was leaning forward, was walking after him and shouting. Andy waved his hands in the air then the officer disappeared back into the black bridge proper and Andy disappeared somewhere.

"I hope he 'asn't fallen down the gangway," Jason mumbled. He was having trouble staying awake.

After what seemed like hours Andy got back to his mates. He found Kevin half awake and Jason asleep.

"Hey, wake up, Jason," he slurred. "The captain's an asshole and waz very rude ter me. We are going to ram the country ahead so let's have another drink."

Jason woke up in time to hear the last part and agreed with the sentiment. "Let's have another," he said drunkenly and fell asleep against the warm side of the ship.

He woke up the next morning with a bad headache and the sun shining brightly on his face. By the feel of it the ship was still moving. He quickly stood up and stared forward. The sea was empty of all traces of land. He shook his aching head in bewilderment and headed shakily down to the cabin to sleep off his hangover.

Sarawak Borneo
Kuching
Chapter 7

The old troop ship HMS *Galahad* was nudged gently alongside the wooden quay by the tiny, puffing tugboats. They had nursed her along ever since she came into the muddy waters of the Sarawak river estuary. There was virtual silence from the green-clad troops lining the starboard side of the ship as they contemplated their new home.

Most of the town of Kuching was out of sight from the harbor, hidden by a dense wall of green, allowing only a glimpse of the whitewashed government buildings perched on the sides of the low hills beyond the harbor itself. Coconut palms lined the back of the single quayside, interspersed with banana trees. Along the length of the dilapidated quay were buildings constructed of rusty corrugated iron that housed the customs and police offices. It was hot and muggy here on the river, with the added threat of rain as huge cumulous clouds gathered over the hills to the south.

The crowded ship came to an all stop, then the rumble of her engines resumed, changing direction. The brown water boiled beneath her stern for a few minutes, then the engines were brought to a final stop as the ship came to a gentle bump against the roped walls of the wood pilings that shook its steel frame.

There was suddenly a lot of activity on the quayside. Official-looking men who had been watching the arrival of the old troop ship shouted at some native dock workers who rolled the ramps forward. The gangplanks were lowered and the bustle of disembarkation began.

When the Jungle is Silent

A long row of three-ton Bedford trucks waited at the end of the quay near the main road, ready to take the first batch of men from the Green Jackets to their new base outside Kuching, a barracks that they would learn was called Semengang.

The color sergeants, crisp in their newly dhobied and starched greens and black insignia of the Green Jackets, with black stripes on their sleeves, began to shout out for company groups to disembark and then to form up on the quay. Men carrying their kit bags, packs and rifles moved down the ramps looking rumpled and untidy. They were relieved to be on land again after three days at sea. In spite of the steaming humidity and the heat of the afternoon sun, they were thankful to be leaving the cramped quarters of the "old rust bucket", as they uncharitably called the aged troop ship.

The men, all five hundred of them, fell into platoons and were marched rapidly, at the Light Infantry pace, towards the distant trucks, where they loaded up and were whisked off to the camp.

One of the first things Jason and his companions in the Pioneer section became aware of was the stink of the river as the trucks drove along the bumpy road that followed the banks of the Sarawak River before turning inland towards the jungle. The tide was out and the black mud gave off a stench that could not have been only mud. It seemed to the troops holding their noses that the town of Kuching drained its sewer into the river. Here it blended with the muddy waters and the other offal thrown by the local residents living alongside the banks in bamboo and Attap huts. These were mostly the coolies and the very poor.

The road to Semengang camp wound round the outside of the town of Kuching so the troops saw almost nothing of the town itself and knew that they would not get much chance to in the future. The men were silent as the three-ton trucks ground their way along the narrow roads, watching the surrounding country. For the most part, it was light jungle interspersed with coconut plantations and the occasional house on stilts, its walls and steep roof constructed of palm and Attap thatch. All the houses and huts had open entrances to which a short ramp led from the beaten earth yards. Knee-high, sharp lallang grass patches were interspersed with groves of banana trees and the more dense patches of high trees covered in vines.

After half an hour the trucks pulled up at the chain-link gates of a camp set back off the road. It was a large wired compound within which was the camp itself. It was full of long barrack huts, and just like almost all the non-government houses in the area, the buildings were composed of wood and thatch. Most of the buildings had large window openings without glass and doorways without doors. Set a couple of feet off the ground on short stilts, they all had spacious verandahs, along which soldiers of the advance guard lolled as they watched their mates from the main party come into the camp. The trucks stopped on the main parade ground and the men dismounted. There were shouted greetings, then they were shown their billets by members of the advance party.

Jason and his companions from the Pioneer section were taken over by one of their own, Geordie, who had been there a week and behaved towards his mates with the condescension of one who knows all. They gazed about at the stark surroundings they were to make their home in for nine months.

"Reckon it's goin' to take some scrounging to make us comfortable," remarked Paddy.

"Nothin' a few parachutes won't fix; coupla extra mozzie nets and we'll be set," said Jerry.

Jason said nothing. He was beginning to really miss the clean airy Minden Barracks they had left behind a good six weeks ago in Penang. Megan was very much in his mind as he contemplated his new home.

Like soldiers who had been around for years in an unsympathetic army, they had all given a mental shrug at the sight of their quarters. They instinctively resolved to transform it into something more than what it was, and to push the permissible limits of comfort over time.

"Where's the cookhouse, Geordie? I'm ready for a decent nosh," asked Jason eventually when they had all dumped their kit on their respective beds, dragged out cigarettes and lit up. The smoke hung in the still humid air, drifting slowly out of the open windows.

It was getting late, so the first thing any of them wanted to do was to eat. The bedding and the unpacking of kit could take care of itself later. Mess tins were dragged out of packs. Knives and forks, "gobbling rods" as they were otherwise known, were searched for, and then armed with the appropriate tools they all headed for the cookhouse. A lot of others had the same idea, so it became a rush to get into a queue which was getting longer by the minute.

Jerry wrinkled his nose. "I can smell the shit from here!" he exclaimed. "I bet it's rotten old meat and tatties. Don't those fucking cooks know 'ow to cook anythin' else?"

"Look out, there's an RP! 'e's checkin' to see who's left his rifle be'ind," murmured Kevin, nudging Paddy.

Fortunately none of the Pioneers had left his SLR in the barracks; they were all slung over their shoulders. Jason and the others watched as the Regimental Policeman found a couple of luckless Riflemen without their weapons. He promptly pulled them out of the queue and told them to go and get their rifles. There were sympathetic looks but not much comment. They had all been warned about this by their platoon sergeants. This was active duty and the rifle stayed with a man even when he sat on the toilet.

This RP was called Robbie, one of the more decent ones. He could have placed the men on a charge but didn't. All they lost was their place in the queue, which might mean nothing for them to eat by the time they got back.

The small group of Pioneers shuffled up to the long tables where the sweating cooks were doling out rice or potatoes and curry or beef slices with the green sheen of old meat. There were even vegetables that had been boiled to the point where the carrots were a red sludge and the cabbage was a fibrous mess in the bottom of the steel pots. The curry and rice looked marginally better to Jason so he took a chance and loaded up on the green mess, hoping that it was chicken.

"Any old man wivout teeth could gum 'is way through this load of shit!" murmured Kevin as they stared unhappily at the mess in front of them.

Jason took his full mess tin and a cup of muddy tea with him to an empty table and then warded off others who might have wanted to share it, keeping it for his mates. They soon came along and sat down to their first meal in Sarawak.

"Oive naver seen a chicken bone this fockin' big!" said Paddy.

"Well, maybe it's not, then," said Jason, poking at his meat.

"What the fock d'youse tink it is then?" exclaimed Paddy, looking at the bones sticking out of his mess tin.

"Ain't yer noticed 'ow few dogs there are int' camp?" enquired Geordie conspiratorially, grinning at their discomfort.

"You'd be'er be kidding, yoo Geordie twit," said Kevin, looking peeved.

"That's it, I'm going on full-time compo from now on," said Andy. "When do they give out the beer?"

Later they were lounging in the barracks hut that was to be their home, sitting in the dark, as no lamps were issued at this time. There was a mosquito coil burning to give the illusion that it would keep the ever-present whining insects away. The electric cables had not yet been run to this end of the camp. Despite the large number of men in the camp, the noise from the insects as they started up their evening chorus all but drowned out the conversation. Listening to the sounds coming in from the square around which the huts were placed, Jason and his mates smoked and discussed their new home.

"It's a fockin' dump, that's what it is!" remarked Paddy.

"Could be worse. The camps up coontry are just 'oles in the ground," said Geordie.

"How d'you know that, Geordie?" asked Jerry.

"Well, remember what it was liek at the Joongle warfar' school?"

They all nodded in the gloom.

"The camps are just clearin's with everything undergroond. Foock living like a mole. Ah'll stay here even if the RSM's here an' all."

There were chuckles. No one liked to be near the Regimental Sergeant Major. RSM Waldon was the bane of everyone's life; even the junior officers avoided him.

"So what do you hear that Indon is up to?" asked Jason.

"Dunno. Ah heard that 'e tried to get into Brunei and the Paras gave him a bloody nose, but from whot Oi 'ear down 'ere, it's not the Indons so much, it's them Chink Commies."

There was a collective "Ye' wot?"

"Yeah, well, what I 'eard was they tried to blow somethin' oop in Kuching and then the cheeky boogers got awa' with it. The Tankies in their Saladins chased 'em and ran into some oil the clever boogers had poured across the road. Sent the cars into the monsoon ditch. Way-aye, boot that must ha' bin good te see!"

There were unsympathetic chuckles at the humiliation of the Tank Regiment. Infantry rarely had a kind word for the boys in armored vehicles, and the feeling was reciprocated.

There was silence. None of the boys here was a fighting company rifleman. They

were the Pioneer section. The thought that sneaky Chinese Communists could get into Kuching and then out again without being stopped was not reassuring.

Paddy flicked his cigarette out over the balcony.

"Wouldn't do that, Paddy, the color sarg'nt will 'ave youse cleaning the square with a toothbrush in the morning if he finds it," said Geordie.

Paddy groaned and went to get the dog end and put it out in an improvised ashtray made from an old 105 Howitzer casing.

"Fock me," he muttered. "The baastards niver let up, do they?" There were grins from his mates.

"Well, one thing's for sure: the food isn't any better 'ere than it was in Penang. Is there a chai wallah 'ere, Geordie? I could do with an egg banjo," grumbled Jason.

"Yeah, 'is name is – wait for it – Ali! He makes soom really good egg banjos and 'am sarnies. Milo's not bad neither. But he's not around tonight. Them's likely stopped 'im at the gates because yous were comin' in."

Geordie was referring to the native vendor who would come round with tea and milo and serve, for a few cents, a cooked egg sandwich, called a banjo.

The whine of mosquitoes started to make itself heard over the general noise of a regiment settling in for the night.

"We're going to have to get some more coils," said Jason. He got up to make ready for bed.

The men turned to in the dark, ensuring that the nets were adequately placed. Their smoking had kept the insects away but now the mosquitoes were swarming and becoming a nuisance. They were soon asleep.

*　*　*　*　*

Jason was woken by the bugler playing Reveille. He hummed the tune to himself. "Dah Dee Dah Dee Diddle Dee Dum!

"Ah, fock off, will yer?" came from Paddy's bed.

There was a certain comfort in that ageless sound of the morning awakening by the bugle. Jason had listened to it for three years now and expected it to be there each time he woke up in the barracks.

The men of Support Company who had come in the night before formed up on parade at 0800 hrs. Having found that there was to be no hot water for the duration, it was a fairly disgruntled company that fell in.

The company commander was there with the company sergeant major, who bellowed, "Officer on parade! Stand to your front! Compana-ayy!"

There was a muted thump as sixty jungle boots stamped into the ground. Their rifles were jerked up to the inside of the right arm. Right hand on the pistol grip, the left palm slapped against the stock for a count of two and then snapped to the side. Every man stared straight ahead. The sergeant major saluted Major Denniston and informed him that all were present and ready for inspection.

"Thank you, Sergeant Major," said the major.

Sergeant Major Welch spun around on his heel and shouted, "Stand at ease!"

Rifles were grounded, the men stamped their feet apart, and their left hands snapped behind them. The morning sun burned down. Men sweated.

"Right, men! This being the support company, we will be split up into support roles at the various locations this regiment is responsible for. The mortar platoon is to go to Bukit Satu with B Company." There was an apprehensive ripple among the men.

"Where the fook is Bukit Satu?" came a sotto voice.

"Silence in the ranks!" shouted Welch. "Next man talks I'll 'av 'is name!"

The major continued. "The Pioneer section stays here in Semengang and the Clerks and Paymasters section remain. The cooks will be distributed among the companies, HQ A, B and C both here and up country. Radios will be mobile.

"I should remind you of a couple of things while I am here. Paladrin is to be taken every day; this country is infested with malaria. Do not drink un-boiled water; there is an unpleasant thing called Leptus Pyrosis in the streams and rivers. It's something to do with the large brown rats that infest the place. You will get very sick indeed if you don't purify water while on patrol, and some of you will mark my words.

"You are to report any suspicious behavior inside the camp. We have a lot of native labor here, from dhobi washing to gardeners and cooks. Not everyone is happy that we are here, even if it is for the benefit of the Malaysian government." He paused. "The Chinese Communists Party is active in the area of Kuching and there is nothing they would like better than to embarrass the British Army. All time off in Kuching is therefore cancelled until further notice. No one has permission to leave the camp unless cleared with myself or the sergeant major. You will be sent off to your various stations over the next week. Make sure you are kitted out properly at the Quartermasters before you leave. There will be very little to be had when you get to your destinations. That's all."

The sergeant major shouted them to attention and saluted the major, who tipped his peaked hat briefly with his swagger stick and walked off.

The men remained at attention. "Stand at ease, men," said Welch gruffly. Now that the major was off the square and the RSM was nowhere to be seen, he visibly relaxed and spoke to his men more informally. Jason relaxed as did the rest of the men. He liked the sergeant major who rarely shouted at his men.

"You all need to remember that not to take Paladrin is a chargeable offence, and if you get malaria you will be on a court martial," he told them. "That's if you live to be marched into one! Also, two Scots Guardsmen were killed in Kuching the other day while off duty, and we think it was the CCO. That's why you are confined to camp unless on duty elsewhere. If you are sent up country you will be attached to the company there."

There was a collective murmur at this. Although everyone on the parade was a volunteer, very few had actually been in action. Most men on the square were somewhere between eighteen and twenty-two years of age.

Sergeant Major Welch continued. "The medical officer has told the NCOs that there is a very high incidence of gonorrhea and syphilis in Kuching. If any one of you wankers gets a dose you will be on cookhouse duty for a hundred years."

There were guffaws and nudges. Some men had already picked up a dose in Penang; they still smarted from the humiliation of being examined by the medics and then being subjected to the ribbing of their mates as they recovered.

"Quiet in the ranks! So if any of you wants to go AWOL and prove you are a hard case... Phillips." He glared at a luckless rifleman who grinned sheepishly while his mates chuckled around him. "You will do time in the clanger and wish that you had been sent out to fight the Indons all on your own!

"Weapons to be carried at all times, nothing up the spout. One mag on, safety on, even when you are taking a shit on the bog. If there is an accidental discharge of a weapon, that man goes to the clanger and can look forward to twenty-eight days field punishment. Am I clear?" he bellowed at his men.

There was a collective "Yes, sir!" from sixty mouths.

"Compana-ayy, dismissed!" he roared. There was a loud thump as the men came to attention. Rifles were flicked up with the front sight into the right armpit, the men turned to their right, stamped their left feet down next to their right, paused for the count of two and then they walked off.

The small group of relieved Pioneers ambled back to their barrack room and set about cleaning up.

"Well that takes care of that then. We stay here. Poor Mortars! The buggers are off; it's the up-country life for them," said Jason cheerfully.

"Wot's 'e mean, 'if we go on patrol'? A'hm focked if A'hm goin' on any patrols!" said Paddy.

Jason and the others nodded. Not for them the business of wandering about in the Ulu, they decided. They were the Pioneers; the Riflemen could do that.

"I 'aven't got a clean piece of kit; everythin's manky after that trip on the old tub," complained Jerry.

"What matters 'ere is 'ow clean the rifle is and 'ow sharp the old gollock is. Ain't it, mates?" Geordie indicated the long jungle knife that they had all been issued prior to embarking on the boat.

"I could shave with mine," he said proudly of the eighteen-inch single-edged blade on his belt.

They were interrupted by a shouted command out on the main square. They all stopped what they were doing to watch as two riflemen double marched past their barracks hut. The men were in full pack kit and gasping and sweating copiously in the sun.

There was another distant shout. "Ma...ark time!"

The two soldiers began to double march on the spot. They continued to do this until a smartly dressed regimental policeman strode up to them and barked another command.

"Get those knees up, Fisher, or you'll get five more days," he yelled. "By the front, at the double, for...ward march!"

The two red-faced, sweating men began to double forward again. The RP repeated the commands at regular intervals to allow himself to catch up

"Poor fockin' bastards," said Paddy. "Ain't that Billy Fisher? Wot did he do this time? 'e's always in trouble."

"'e got twenty-eight days' field for an accidental discharge. Them both did," said Geordie. "Serves 'em right, could 'ave killed some one."

"Wot's your problem, Geordie? You're always bein' holier than thou," said Paddy irritably. He didn't much like Geordie and even less when he pulled his old soldier ways.

Geordie turned his pockmarked face to Paddy and glowered.

"Fook off, Paddy, they deserved it," he said truculently.

"Joost ye wait till yoose 'ave to do twenty-eight days and we'll see 'ow you like it. In this heat, it's got to be brutal," said Andy.

"Ah'm noo goin' te do any field time," said Geordie confidently. "It's goin' to be one of yoo's idiots."

"I dunno who's calling the kettle black 'ere, Geordie," said Paddy. "After a', we didna hang the monkey, did we now?"

He was referring to the legend that went back to the time of the armada from Spain that had come to invade England. Storms had driven many of the ships up the east coast and wrecked some of them. In one case the only survivor had been a ship's monkey. The local people off the coast of Northumberland had thought it was a Spaniard and had hung it as a spy.

Geordie knew Paddy was looking for a scrap so he let it go. He got up off his bunk, took his rifle and left. The others snickered at his huffy behavior.

"You should ease up on him, Paddy," said Jason. "He doesn't mean any harm."

"Ah, doan't mind him, Jason, 'cept when he's wishing bad on oothers. Ye know 'ow rough field punishment is. We've all done some. Ah used to be so knackered at the end of the day! Then when yer hanging off yer chinstrap they'd make ye clean all yer kit and stand on officer's inspection at 10 p.m. Ah could barely stand oop by the time 'e came by. Geordie enjoys seein' others suffer,"

Paddy had a keen sense of fair play and hated people who enjoyed pain at the expense of others.

"Yeah, I know Geordie can be a right wanker at times. I got two extra days when I was nailed because the bloody guard sergeant found some creases in me bed pack," said Andy. "Ah was so knackered Ah was 'angin' off me own chinstrap most o' the time, Ah was!"

There was a collective chuckle from the old lags, who knew what it meant to do field.

Jason had so far evaded field punishment and fully intended to continue to do so. Still he was impressed with his mates, as it seemed a bit like some kind of initiation to have been given field punishment. It looked really harsh but that was what it was about, he realized.

"They want us so scared of the fucking sergeant majors that we'll go and fight any fucker in the world rather than do field, I suppose," he said to the group at large.

"Recon youse is right there, Taffy," said Kevin. "Me when I got out of it, Ah was so fit Ah could ha' run the fuckin' marathon twice over a' then beaten the shit out a' gross of marines!" He chuckled. "The bastard sergeant used to come lookin' for fags in the cell. Oi could hide them well no matter what he'd do ter me."

'Bet youse din't piss 'im off once youse were out though, did yer?" said Paddy with a laugh.

"Na, but if Ah iver do meet 'im on a dark night, 'eel niver know wot 'it 'im, Ah'll stab 'im to death slow like, wi' a spoon!" said Kevin comfortably.

"Well, I don't see anyone looking so sharp over here," remarked Jason laughing, continuing the earlier conversation. "It's not like the dhobi is going to make everything as starched as cardboard like it was in Penang, is it?"

"Geordie told me there's a dhobi but no starch here." said Andy. "Ah've noo idea wot's go'in ter hold me up right on t' parade ground wi'out starch in me fookin shirt!"

"It'll be the rest of us likely, yer wanker," said Paddy with a grin.

"Hey, have yer seen them Ibans 'anging around the place?" asked Kevin, changing the subject.

"The Wots?" asked Jason and Paddy together.

"The Ibans ...you know, the little wallies from the Ulu. Din't you see them at the cookhouse this morning? Trackers, I think they are. 'Alf naked, and covered with tattoos. Them's the real thing. They're 'eadhunters, I bet," said Jerry with satisfaction.

"Yeah, I did, matter of fact," Kevin said. "Wot do all them tattoos mean anyway?"

"One of those boys in 'A' company who was going up to Padawan told me that if you see a tattoo of what looks like a bloke on the front of his throat, 'e's killed a man," Jerry said with hushed tones. "Have you seen their knives? They're a fuckin' yard long!" He was referring to the long slim knives that were a feature of the Iban trackers. "Ah also 'erd that they make 'em from car springs," he said knowledgably.

Despite itself, the group was interested. Jason leaned forward

"Are they really 'ead hunters then?" he asked.

"Dunno, but yoose could lop an 'ead off easily with one of them bloody greet knives they've got. No problem!" stated Paddy, who had also spotted the Iban trackers in the cookhouse. "Hey, Jason, wot 're those weapons they've got? They don't look like issue."

Jason thought for a moment. "I think they're Brownings and they aren't loaded with birdshot, that's for sure."

The shotguns he was alluding to were almost as long as the Iban trackers were tall. But none of the soldiers would have thought to laugh at these tough little men who came from the jungle.

"Why are they here in Kuching? Aren't they supposed to be up country?" asked Jerry.

"I think the SAS is here for a visit with the Colonel. Putting him right on the lay of the land, I suppose. I guess they came with 'em," said Kevin.

Their conversation was interrupted by a shout from outside. They scrambled to turn out of the room as Corporal Bates shouted at them.

"Where the fuck have you all been? Don't yer know where yer supposed to be workin? Get your manky arses into gear or I'll rift you lot for skiving! Hey, Jason and Paddy, get your arses up to the armory. The Staff is waiting for you. The rest of you lazy buggers, coom wi' me!"

Amid the suppressed groans and insults to Bates's heritage, the group broke up and headed off to their places of work.

Jason and Paddy walked off to the small room called the armory where they would spend their days working on the rifles, machine guns and mortars that came in for servicing. Jason and Paddy were the product of the British Army Boys School system and were quite at home in the rough company of the riflemen they lived with. They had joined the army at fifteen.

The SAS Officer
Chapter 8

In the Regimental HQ, Major Nigel Johnson sat with Colonel Barkar-Hollingworth and the other company commanders in conference. The only other men in the room were a well turned out captain going slightly bald who was standing next to a thin hard-looking man with no insignia other than the cloth crown looped onto his shoulder tabs. It wasn't really much of a room by the standards of Penang, Johnson thought, glancing around. The walls were made of Attap and the windows were huge openings in those walls. God alone knew what lived in the thatched roof and walls.

He sat up in his chair; Colonel Barker Hollingsworth was introducing the newcomers.

"Gentlemen I would like you to meet Captain Hendricks who is with the Army Intelligence unit based on the airport and Major Stanford who is the officer in command of the Special Air Service squadron here in Kuching. They have a lot of important things to tell you so please pay attention."

Captain Hendricks seemed to have just come from the parade ground. His uniform was starched and clean, in sharp contrast to the uniform of the SAS man. He stood up and approached the large scale map of Sarawak that had been pinned to a black board then indicated the area that would be First Division's responsibility and in particular the zone that would be that of the Light Infantry. He peered at the map through thick glasses then pointed with a cane at various names on the map and ran off their significance to each company commander. He informed the officers as to what they were to expect at the various locations they were to be shipped up to.

Some would go by road and others by helicopter but in each case they would relieve the troops in those positions seamlessly with their own, and as quietly and as unobtrusively as possible. In each case the advance guard had already gone ahead to prepare the way.

He talked for a good half hour about how the British should have been supporting the Malays but due to complications with logistics and some politics they were on their own along with the Australians, mostly artillery and some New Zealand special forces. "You will find small contingents of Malay soldiers in most of the villages but not along the border itself. You need to maintain a good relationship with them but they are not allowed to make decisions on their own, having to refer back to a Malay Brigadier here in Kuching who in turn does not make too many decisions without first getting in touch with Kuala Lumpur," he finished with a sardonic smile.

Listening to the officer talking Johnson decided that if he ran into difficulties with the Malays in his area he would just make his own decisions and move on. He found that his area comprised one large village that actually had a road leading to it although as Hendricks pointed out it was merely a dirt track that could just take a three tonner on a dry day. The other place that came under his command was an obscure dot on the map almost on the border that Hendricks called Sapit.

After Hendricks had finished his summary he went on to describe some of the known Indonesian units that were placed on the other side of the border. Finally he said.

"You will want to hear what Major Stanford has to say on the subject because at this time the SAS are our eyes and ears along the border. I should really turn this over to you now Sir." He said differentially and stood back.

Major Stanford stood up and walked to the board. He was dressed in the jungle greens and boots as were the other people in the room, except that his uniform, in sharp contrast to the well-pressed greens of the Light Infantry officers, was stained from much wear and very rumpled.

The SAS major had spent the last six months in Sarawak with his men and trackers following the activities of the Indonesian army as it probed the defenses of the British, Australian and Malay forces in the region. He looked gaunt and tired. Johnson wondered when he had last seen a decent meal and taken any leave.

The major addressed the map of Sarawak which itself was interesting. There were huge areas on it that were completely unmarked. He pointed to the map.

"There are large tracts of Borneo at this time that are relatively unexplored and unknown by white men and the only maps that are available are derived from the old Second World War charts that the Dutch and British colonial offices could provide."

"We have recently completed an exhaustive and thorough exploration of the former British areas of Borneo, right up to and sometimes beyond the border. That includes Sarawak and Sabbah, both now part of greater Malaysia." He remarked almost casually

Major Johnson was impressed. He remembered the jungle he had been in on the peninsular of Malaya as a young man and the work they had done in Jahore Bahru. These men had performed a notable feat in his eyes. He began to pay keen attention to what Stanford was saying.

In fact the men and officers of the SAS had logged distances and marked mountains and rivers where none have been marked before, bringing topography to a region mostly unknown and only inhabited by inland Dyak tribes and Ibans. This little group of men had patrolled almost twelve hundred miles of border on their own over that time, a vast area by any standards.

"We have been careful to make friends with as many of the "people of the long houses", as they are known, because a whole village can live in one long house. We used the same technique known as "hearts and minds" that the British used in Malaya during the Emergency. Giving them medicine and treating festering sores, eye problems, that kind of thing. For the most part it works but one has to be careful as some villagers play one side off against the other."

Pointing at Kuching in the bottom left corner of Sarawak, he then moved his finger south and east towards a spot called Padawan.

"The Hampshire Regiment have been here for a while and had few contacts up to now, however it is a juicy target because it has access to the road to Kuching. The Hampshires have built some defenses here but it could do with some more work. There is every reason to expect that it will be bumped one of these days if the activity increases." He paused.

"There is an Aussi artillery group there with two 105 L5 Pack Howitzers. They are very good so if you are out and get bumped in an ambush they can reach all the way to the border and beyond. Just make sure you know where you are when you call them in."

There was an uneasy chuckle from the officers as they stared at the contours of the map. The major Johnson remembered the map reading work and navigation they had all painfully gone over again and again in Jahore Bahru and hoped that it had stuck in the minds of his junior officers.

"You will notice that the border is very hilly," said the Major. "It will be a lot harder here than it was in the Jungle Warfare School in Jahore. You climb one side and slide down the other side they are so steep. We know there is increased activity in this region as we have discovered camps the Indon has made on both sides of the border.

"They don't seem to have artillery that can do much damage at present, however they do have mortars. These camps," his finger pointed to three locations on the map all very close to the border, "have all been mortared in the past by three inch pipes. Even if they are wildly inaccurate they will still keep you awake.

"We have seen a lot of activity here." He pointed at a place near to one of the mountain ranges not far from a small base call Sapit. Johnson sat up even straighter and listened intently

"My people have been watching them on and off for months. There are a couple of villages in these areas with friendly Ibans in them." He pointed to several locations along the region of the border that now belonged to the Light Infantry.

"The Indon has made himself generally unpopular with the villages along the entire border. They treat everyone they come into contact with badly, bullying the villagers and taking food without payment.

However, be careful when you patrol near them as one can't be all that sure. There have been cases of informers passing stuff to the Indon, although that is rare, most of the time they are giving us info. In any case they will see you long before you see them!" he added. There were rueful smiles.

He continued. "We have spent months visiting the Iban and Dyak villages in the regions along the border, providing medicine and help where we could. The policy of " Hearts and minds" that was begun in Malaya during the Emergency is important and we should all bear it in mind when coming into contact with these people. They are beginning to appreciate us and have given us crucial information as to what is happening on the other side of the border from time to time. Unfortunately we usually have to go to them as they are not inclined to come out of the Ulu and tell us. They don't like nor trust the Malays ...or the Chinese very much." There were raised eyebrows from some of the men at that. It had not occurred to them that there might be issues with the interaction between races to contend with as well.

Major Johnson was not so surprised as he remembered his time in the jungles of Malaysia during the communist insurgency known euphemistically as "The Emergency" and then too there had been friction.

Major Stanford continued. "This means that we have individuals out there along with a couple of trackers each, either from Intelligence or our boys, who visit Long houses from time to time and glean what they can to pass back. They will visit your locations and pass along information as they do, please make them welcome. They will often as not need a new uniform so please alert your QM's."

He turned to the colonel. "I understand that there is to be no cross border patrolling at this time, sir?"

The colonel nodded. "We have express orders not to do so as yet Major. However, we have orders to patrol very aggressively this side and not to shrink from contact whenever we get the chance." There was a ripple of excitement from the officers.

The major continued, "My people are in these areas on and off. We don't have much in the way of radios when we are out there but you should check with HQ as to any concerted activity, just in case we run into one another. We will be showing up in your camps from time to time to pass along intel' as we get it."

The briefing continued with the company commanders, all men who had served for some time although not all had battle experience. Some of the older men like Johnson had served in Africa and Malaya before. They instinctively respected the major. Their questions were respectful but probing. They would be living here for eight or nine months before they rotated out of their positions. It was vital that they gleaned as much information from him as he was willing to provide.

"Are you expecting any concentrated activity that we need to prepare for, Major?' asked the colonel.

The major stared at the map for a moment. "We have been playing cat and mouse with the Indon for months now, sir. They are not sure of our strength, which is just as well as they outnumber the combined Brits and Aussie forces almost five to one. But they are not very good in the jungle as whole units. They leave a lot of trail for us to follow. However we have not as yet found enough sign that indicates they are building up in one area in preparation for some kind of push. There is the possibility that one of the hill forts could be a target but we don't know which one. These are Bukit Satu, Bukit Scrunch and Sapit." He indicated the places on the map. All were right on the border perched on high ridges.

"Who is my backup in case I need reinforcements?" asked Major Johnson. He glanced at the colonel who nodded.

"You have the Fifth Gurkhas, who can be moved very quickly into an area to either entrap or reinforce," stated Hendricks. "I imagine the brigadier will confirm that, sir."

The colonel gave a comfortable nod, as did the others. Who better to have in support than the men from the Gurkha regiment? "That's Colonel Marshall, isn't it?' enquired the colonel of the captain.

"Indeed, Sir, it is,"

The colonel nodded again, "Captain Hendricks, we will need to discuss some details further, please join us for lunch." He turned to Stanford. "Will you have lunch with us at the mess, Major? We can't provide a terrific meal as yet, but we are working on it."

The major smiled. "Thank you, sir, I have to get back. There is a patrol due in today and I have to debrief them. Very kind of you, sir."

"Very well, Major, thank you for the insight you provided. I expect we will be meeting again. I shall inform the brigadier of the meeting this evening when I visit him. If there is anything we can help you with, please do not hesitate to call upon us."

The major nodded. "Thank you, sir, very much appreciated." With a brief salute he hefted his Armalite AR 15 rifle and left the room. Two dark, heavily tattooed, wiry men, clad only in sarongs and carrying long shotguns, who had been squatting on the verandah, stood up as he came out. They greeted one another in the local dialect and then they were in the Land Rover and driving out of the main gate.

The colonel had watched the departure from the entrance to his office. Turning to his officers he said, "Thank you, gentlemen, I hope it has been instructive. I'll see you in the mess." The colonel dismissed his men with a casual salute.

"Strange men, those. They go completely native; somehow they manage to disappear into the woodwork and only come out when they really have to." He said to his adjutant.

His adjutant nodded in agreement. "I'm glad to have them around, sir, but they certainly keep their distance. How many of them are there here in Kuching?"

"Only about fifty at present, as far as I know, Peter. They spend most of their time up country wandering around in the jungle, but they are based here in the town. There is a rumor that they are living in a haunted house that doubles as a whorehouse," he chuckled. "I imagine that gave HQ some raised eyebrows, eh?"

Major Johnson strode off towards his company lines, deep in thought. There was a lot to do, as he had to make sure that his men were packed off to Padawan in good shape that very day, and there was still the formal meeting to be held with the brigadier. After that, it would be an evening with the Governor, who was going to host a welcoming party for the senior officers of the Green Jackets.

A Letter
Chapter 9

"You've got a letter from your soldier boy, Megan!" called Matt, the senior Peace Corps representative on the Island as she came up the steps to his bungalow, which doubled as an office and home.

Megan smiled at him and his girl friend Krista as she climbed the stone steps to the verandah where they were sitting drinking lemonade and enjoying the early afternoon.

"Have a drink with us, Meg," said Krista, smiling. "Its hot out there and we have some ice!"

"Hi, you two, I'd love to." She smiled at Krista. "It *is* hot, but it's going to rain. Have you seen those thunder clouds over Butterworth?"

She sat down with them on one of the large unpainted wicker chairs and gratefully accepted a cold glass of lemonade. Her friends were colleagues in the Peace Corps, but both were somewhat older, and Mat had been all over Malaya. They were dressed in colorful sarongs and loose short sleeved cotton shirts. Both wore flip flops and looked comfortable compared to how she felt in her working clothes.

"How did the day go with the students, Megan?" asked Matt. He was about twenty four, with a sparse blond beard and long hair tied back in a pigtail in the style of the hippies in San Francisco. Krista was a blonde girl with an open face, freckles, and bright blue eyes; she was beginning to gain some weight but had a very friendly attitude to the world at large.

"Oh, OK, I suppose; the Chinese kids are very different from the Malays but they all seem to enjoy learning English. Why the Brits don't bother to teach them I don't understand." Megan said as she took a sip. The drink was very sweet but cool, which was nice. She had learned to like tea the way the Chinese drank it, but this was fine.

"The Aussies do over in Butterworth," said Matt. "The only Brits on this island are the Army and some of the old Colonial boys who never left and still think of it as a colony. They have other things on their minds, I guess."

"How is Soldier Boy doing over in darkest Borneo?" Krista asked with a smile. They teased her gently about that because everyone now knew of her relationship with the British soldier and how she felt about conflict and wars.

"In his last letter he was just settling in to his new barracks in Kuching. I looked the place up on the map we have. There isn't much there at all! I think he's OK, but the way he talks about the food makes me feel ill. How can they eat the stuff they are given? Yeuch!" she grimaced and they all laughed.

"There is something funny too. The radio from Butterworth talks a lot about the war going on in Vietnam these days, but I have never, ever heard it talk about what's going on in Borneo. I wonder why? Is it secret or something?"

No one could answer that one.

"Why don't you stay and have dinner with us, Megan." Krista wheedled her. "We have some really nice left over curry and there's plenty to go round."

Matt even tried to bribe her.

"I have some San Miguel, nice and cold, Megan. Don't be moping now, stay with us this evening."

"She's smitten by the Soldier Boy! Let her be, Matt," said Krista with a grin at Megan, who poked her tongue out at her, feeling a blush start.

"Ok, OK! I'll stay, but leave me in peace while I read this letter, will you?"

'C'mon, Matt," said Krista, "Let's go and get supper, and leave our girl with her boy friend. Bring her a beer while you're at it, Lover."

Matt grinned and touched Megan on the shoulder as he went by.

"Beer coming up!"

She relaxed back in the wicker chair and took out the letter. She recognized Jason's careful, forward leaning writing easily now whenever she collected her mail. The letters were often stained and crumpled so that she wondered where Jason could be that the paper was in such a state. Nonetheless, each time she received one of his infrequent letters she felt a little light headed.

She shook her head. The whole of the region was going to war, and she had fallen in love with a Brit soldier who was in the middle of one of them. The irony was not lost on her, given her views on the subject. She slit the thin air mail paper and began to read.

My Lovely Megan,

Miss you, miss you a lot. Thanks for the last letter. I liked that bit about your Dad and the horses. I would like to have a chance to ride again, that Polo thing seemed fun, didn't it? Do you miss home? Do ya miss me? Huh Huh? I miss you really badly.

She smiled at his silliness; at least he seemed in good spirits, she thought to herself

She continued to read:

We have been in Seramban for a couple of months now and not much has changed since I last wrote. I have pulled a lot of guard duties lately, which has ticked me off, but there are a lot of worse things to have to do. I could be up country at the sharp end, which is not so good I am told. A lot of Ulu and it's crawly with Indons.

It is hot and sweaty today, I think it is going to rain and that means I am dripping onto the paper again! Wish we had a bigger fan in this hut.

The others are off to the canteen for a beer so I decided to write, it's been a while.

I got guard duty <u>again</u> last night. We sit around in a large tent by the main gate during the time off from Stagg (that's when we have to go out and patrol the camp and the perimeter) and play chess or cards till it's time to go

out and have a look around for a couple of hours. We are supposed to be watching for invaders or Indons or something like that, but most of the time we're catching the prostitutes coming in or going out. I don't know how they do it but they get in no matter how much we watch for them. I reckon it's the randy bastards in the HQ company that smuggles them in. Most of the ones I have seen are pretty awful.

It's all right on the early Staggs but the late ones, the ones in the early morning, are killers. I can hardly stay awake sometimes. But the penalty for sleeping on duty is 28 days field and I don't want to do that. I've seen the poor buggers running around with a full pack on all day and then they have to do full bullshit parade in the 10pm Officer on Guard parade! Talk about hanging off your chinstrap!

I am nearly at the top of the chess league now. There is one guy in the Paymasters unit who was a County player back in Blighty who is my next victim. Ha Ha. He will probably give me a good kicking in the backside, but I am having a good time with the chess, although there is not much else to brag about.

I went into Kuching the other day to service some weapons for another unit. There were some Aussies there who use a weird sub machine gun, can't remember what its name is now, I think is called an Owen gun. Sounds Welsh so I told them so, but they don't know who Prince Owen was so they just laughed. I stayed with them the night as there was a full curfew, so I got a lot more beer than I can at our camp. Those Whallies really like to drink! I could not go back as the Chinese Commies are back in business and making a pest of themselves.

I saw one of the biggest moths I have ever seen while there. It was most likely eight inches across and a really nice gray color with white marking that looked a bit like eyes in the middle. They are common here but that was the first time I ever saw one. You would like the butterflies and the birds, Megan, never seen so many different colors, also there are so many!

There are stick insects about six inches long that live in our roof and Christ knows what else. I get into bed at night and that mosquito net is tight all around. I once found a huge spider sitting on my pillow and nearly died of fright! I bet someone put it there, so when I find out who it was...! The boys are always playing tricks like that on each other. I guess they will never grow up.

We've made the rooms a lot better than they were with parachute material and stuff like that. We now call it the Ritz and it is the envy of the whole barracks. It's become quite the home now! We use heaps of those Mozzy coils. The Mosquitoes here are as big as sparrows, I swear. They come in the evening in clouds! More like squadrons and dive bomb us! The malaria is really bad in this neck of the woods so we all take our Paladrin each day .If you don't it is a chargeable offence and more Field!! We are all slowly turning Yallah!!

There are spiders here that would carry off a new born baby, they are so bloody big. There are also lizards that make the geckos look like match box toys, that the natives eat. Considering how horrible the food is in the canteen I wonder if that could be any worse. Don't even want to talk about the snakes, they are everywhere but most of them are grass or tree snakes.

There was a cobra found in the Sergeant's mess the other day and everyone thinks it was put there by one of the lads with a grudge against the RSM (that's Regimental Sergeant Major) who is a right bastard. Would have served him right if he had been bitten. But then he would have died and we would have had to get into our best kit and go on a bullshit parade so it was probably for the best that he wasn't.

Most of the time I eat the breakfast food, as it is cereal and some grand fruit, and not even the cooks can mess that up. But the lunch time food is manky and I can only eat a bit of that. The meat is often green, and I never know what the veggies are they are such a mess. So I go and have a sandwich from Ali the Chai wallah who comes round at night. At least his sandwiches are edible. We are all losing weight.

Andy got five days RPs. That's five days of company hard labor for talking back

to one of the corporals. Wasn't Andy's fault, but some of those new NCOs are full of shit and this fellah was all over Andy for no good reason. I suppose it could have been worse; he could have had twenty-one days of field punishment. In which case we would not be seeing him again for a while except when he came running by in full kit with an RP screaming at him to get his knees up and mark time again. That's brutal!

Geordie went up country to do some work and we have not heard from him for a while. I might be going up country soon too, as I lost the toss on who should go. Paddy stays and I go. Should be able to write from there I think. They live underground up country which does not sound like too much fun to me.

The Indon is pretty busy up there too, so I hope that I don't get into a place that is bumped by them. Here it is nice and peaceful, which is just as I like it, and it's only the Chinese who are a bother and that is in Kuching which is about five miles away. They leave us alone.

Miss you badly, Megan, can't get you out of my mind, especially our last time together. That was wild, wasn't it? Mmmm.

I love your letters. Please keep writing.

Take good care, Love. Miss you and love you.

Lots of kisses.

Jason

Megan finished the letter to find a beer sitting on the table near her right hand. She had not heard Matt come out and deliver it! Within a few sips Krista called her into the house to eat supper.

Over the meal, the two of them bombarded her with questions about how Jason was and what he was up to. They had briefly met him once and both had decided that they liked him.

"He seems to be OK, but he is going "Up country" whatever that means, and he

says the camp is crawling with snakes and other creepy crawlies."

"If the camp is like that I wonder what the real jungle is like," said Matt with a grimace.

"I got as close as I ever want to the real thing in the Cameron Highlands," said Krista through a mouthful of rice.

"That's in the highlands too, where it's cooler. Borneo isn't very high anywhere, is it?" enquired Megan.

"Well, there are some fairly high ranges, I think, along the back bone you might say, and there is this one big mountain in the north. A lot of it is basically uncharted," said Matt.

"They are always on the edge of getting punished in the British army," said Megan.

"What do you mean?" asked Matt.

"He keeps talking about 'Field Punishment' and things like that. I think the discipline must be brutal."

"Probably has to be, to keep those boys in line and willing to fight. By the way, anyone know why they are there? Is it something to do with that Sukarno guy?" asked Krista.

"Jason told me that the Brits, the Aussies, and the New Zealanders were there to help the Malays fight the Indonesians in the jungle because the Malays weren't very good at it," Megan said.

"The Brits must have come a long way since the war then," Matt responded. He knew something about the recent history of Malaysia.

"What do you mean, Matt?" asked Krista.

"They got their butts kicked by the Japs in Malaya during the war. But I guess they must have learned a lot since then. Did you know they chased the Chinese Commies all over the Malay jungle for the last twenty years?"

Neither of the girls did, and the conversation moved on to their own interests in Penang and how they were doing with the Malay schools. Matt pressed another beer on Megan and then she felt it was time to leave. It was nearly nine pm and she had to get up in the morning. Also, for some reason, she wanted to be alone.

"Love you both, and thanks, but I have to get back to the pad. I'll see you tomorrow."

She kissed them both goodbye and left.

Megan took the letter back to the apartment where she read it again. There was some comfort in being in her own nest, as it were, when she opened one of the thin letters that came via the British army mail system to Matt's office. This time she had not had the heart to refuse her friends' invitation, and besides, she was restless and had needed some company. She read through the letter and then folded it up and put it on the kitchen table. Everything seemed to be so normal here. Even if it was still Malaya and not home in the US. The familiar smells of cooked cabbage, garlic and cigarette smoke wafted up from the ground floor where the Chinese family lived. One of the Chinese women was shouting at someone while the baby was crying again.

Out in the street there was the honking of horns as the occasional car drove carefully along the narrow street, trying to get past the uncooperative trishaw drivers and street vendors who hogged the middle of the road. She listened with half an ear to the 'cling' 'cling' of the trishaw's bells as the drivers looked for business. It all seemed perfectly normal, for Penang anyway. It had been such a change from her life in California when she first came. Her friends had been very kind and helpful, and the training provided by the Peace Corps, brief though it was, had helped prepare her somewhat.

Now she felt a lot more at home. The Chinese were still cool and distant, but they would now smile and speak to her, although that was often a conversation between two people who understood not a word of each other's language.

The windows were wide open to take advantage of the light sea breeze drifting over the town from the straits. To take her mind off things she made herself a cup of tea, something she had learned to enjoy in this tropical country. Tea was supposed to be cooling. The radio was still on from when she had left in the morning. The news from the local Australian station was all about the American forces being sent to Vietnam. President Johnson was sending reinforcements to boost the flagging South Vietnamese forces and conscription was being debated in congress. Nothing at all about what was going on in Borneo.

Jason seemed to have gone off to a wild, weird place where people lived in holes in the ground or in Attap huts, like the Malay fishermen did on the coast the other side of the island. She wanted to show him that part of the island when he got back, for he had never been there. In his last letter he had mentioned that the Dyaks and Iban tribesmen who lived in the jungle were head hunters. She shuddered at the thought of what men did to one another.

Her mind went back to their last time together, which had been intense. Jason's words had brought a lot of memories flooding back.After he had told her of their impending departure, they had gone for a walk and later to a restaurant, the one they both liked most on the waterfront where he had first taken her. It had been a quiet meal, subdued for them, but very pleasant despite the noise of the restaurant all around. Somehow they had made a bubble for themselves, and Megan had desperately not wanted it to end. Later, after a walk on the beach, they had sat on the rocks talking for a long time, listening to the water and the boats out in the straits as they chugged by. Megan had been acutely conscious of Jason nearby. Finally they had kissed; he had been very gentle and she had loved him for that. But then things warmed up and she had almost let him make love to her then and there on the rocks in the darkness, her need had been so urgent, his too, by his behavior. She smiled at the memory.

Instead they had rushed home to the apartment, and almost before they had made it into the door she had turned on him, and the two of them had kissed fiercely in a tight embrace. Kicking the door shut they had fallen onto the bed behind her and his hand had gone down to her thigh, lifted her dress and slid up to cup her buttocks, then he began pulling urgently at the fabric, which, as they fell onto the bed he had almost torn from her.

"Wait, Jason! Not like this, wait!" she had insisted, laughing and pushing back onto his chest.

"What is it, Love?" he had asked impatiently, leaning over her on hands and knees, peering down at her with his hair disheveled and his face flushed. The he saw her laughing and grinned sheepishly.

"I want to be naked, and I want you to be as well!" she whispered urgently.

He nodded and fumbled with his shirt, but in the end she had almost dragged it off him while he fumbled with her dress and then her bra. They tore off the rest of their clothes and fell upon one another, giggling and kissing hard.

They had made almost desperate love that made her cry out and which left them both panting and sweating in each other's arms. The slow turn of the fan did little to cool them. He had lifted his head and tenderly kissed her on her damp breast in a manner that

even now made her feel weak at the memory.

Megan woke up from her reverie and shook herself; the memories were very clear and her body was tingling. She decided to write a letter to him and to make him feel wanted. She smiled again, at herself this time. This was not the Megan who had arrived from the States with a rather prim outlook on life. Jason had done something about that. but the climate had also helped, she told herself firmly. She wondered what he might be doing now, this minute just as she was thinking about him.

Padawan
Chapter 10

The Bedford three-ton truck ground its way up the last slope of the dusty red track that passed for a road followed by the Saracen armored car it had as an escort. The scout car was in the lead. Jason shielded his eyes as he stared forward towards the opening in the jungle that indicated they were almost there. He and several riflemen from A Company were perched on the supplies being taken to Padawan. It had been a long, bumpy and dusty trip along a track bulldozed out of the jungle only a matter of months ago. The constant swaying and jerking of the large truck had tired them all out. Several of his companions were napping as only young soldiers know how to, lolling against the sacks slackly, dozing, not quite asleep, while several kept watch. The other Riflemen slept whenever and wherever the opportunity offered itself. Jason had only just woken up, bleary-eyed, to see what his new temporary home would look like.

Padawan was not a remarkable place. The road ended at a shallow river that almost encircled the village. On the other side of the steep riverbanks were the usual collection of sandbagged Sangers, mortar positions and machine gun emplacements. Men who would help to unload the truck were crossing a rope bridge slung across the river.

They were mostly Ibans who lived in the village itself, along with several Riflemen led by the Quartermaster for the company, Color Sergeant Wilson. He was along to see that the goods destined for his stores were not going to get lost – or "relocated", as he was fond of saying. All the men from the regiment wore jungle-green trousers and boots but were without shirts, their rifles slung over their bare shoulders.

Without ceremony the men in the trucks jumped down, collected their gear and then, while Jason reported to the Color, made their way across the bridge that traversed the river.

"Griffith, Color. I'm here to do small arms inspection," Jason said.

"You are, eh? OK, well, you might as well get to the other side with your gear, and when I'm finished here I'll find you a billet." The Color Sergeant looked him over briefly, then he moved on to shout pidgin Malay at the Iban laborers.

Jason walked gingerly across the rope bridge, looking down at the muddy brown river flowing sluggishly eight feet below him. He noticed the banks of the river on both sides were festooned with dense rows of nasty looking bamboo spikes stuck in the ground; he knew them as 'pangies'. In the Jungle Warfare school they been had shown them and how nasty they could be if planted densely.

He was greeted by some of the men from the company doing duty in the emplacements. Most knew him, for he fixed their weapons when they needed him to. He squatted in the shade of a banana tree with his kit and waited for the Color, who came back in half an hour followed by a train of laden men carrying all the equipment from the now empty trucks. He watched enviously as the drivers turned the trucks and drove off in a cloud of dust back to Kuching and a cushy billet.

Color Sergeant Wilson motioned Jason to join him and then led the way into the area where A Company had made their home. There was a large beaten earth open space known as a *padang* in the middle of the village area where some men were playing football. Jason saw that they were Malay soldiers,, and then he noticed that on the far side there were a lot of long low huts made of bamboo and thatch. They had long, wide verandahs, open doorways, and windows. There were sandbagged defensive walls all round them. The men from A Company were living here, and it didn't look too bad; he had been led to believe that the forward men lived in holes. He noticed a pair of large, two-storied wooden buildings located at either end of the *padang*. These were the only proper wood buildings in the entire place. Color Wilson led him towards the far building, which he told Jason was the Quartermaster's stores, and then indicated the other building, telling him this was the cook area and mess hall.

"I need to get the stores up there, and then we'll find a billet for you."

"Right, Color, I'll wait here," said Jason diffidently.

It was very hot and stuffy. He peered about at the surroundings. To the east of the area he noticed several attap huts, some on stilts, and assumed that the Ibans lived in these. Around the *padang* were the huts where the men from A Company lived. It looked basic even after Semengang and he wondered, not for the first time, why he had come here, but he had not volunteered. The call had come in that weapons were not doing well in the jungle and that an armourer was wanted. Paddy and he had flipped a coin and he had lost.

To the south of the camp there was a small hill that was covered with barbed wire and rows and rows of pangies, placed such that they pointed out of the ground at various angles, all guaranteed to cut a leg to ribbons if anyone was mad enough to venture in among them. There were thousands of them, and most of them looked as though they had only just been put in the ground: they gleamed in the sunlight. In fact, wherever he looked he saw barbed wire strung in coils along the river bank, and in among the wire more pangies. He noticed the guard emplacements at the entrances to the village and the packed sandbags everywhere.

There were two businesslike 105 Pack Howitzers squatting at the base of the hill on the edge of the *padang*, with an Australian gunner cleaning something nearby. It was always easy to recognize the Aussies: they insisted on wearing their distinctive hats no mater where they went. The Brits envied them their large-brimmed issue felt headgear; it gave a rakish air to a soldier. All the Brits were issued was a floppy, shapeless green hat.

Jason's inspection was interrupted by the Color, who came down the stairs of the ramshackle wooden building and gave a call to one of the riflemen lounging at the guard hut near by.

"Hey, Dobbs, show Griffith to the Sanger where Williams, the radio fellah, is. You can bed down there, Jason. I don't expect you will be here that long."

Dobbs took him down to a tiny bamboo hut, known as a sanger, its walls surrounded by sandbags, which he was to share with the radio repairman. It was one of the smaller huts on the south side where most of the men were billeted, and Jason was told to stay away from the Iban village. They found Williams asleep under a mosquito net. He woke up quickly when they came into the little hut.

"Hey there, Jason! What brings you to Padawan?" he croaked.

"Hey, Allan. They're telling me that their rifles are fucked up. I lost the toss."

Dobbs left without a word and the two young men sat down and began to gossip. Allan was from the Royal Electrical & Mechanical Engineers. He was shunned by most because he was considered too brainy to associate with, and this made life a bit lonely for him. He was obviously pleased to see Jason, and told him what the dos and don'ts were, in the time-honored tradition of ordinary rankers who don't want their mates to fall foul of authority. He also warned Jason that there was something going down but no one had said much as yet.

"I reckon the Indons have crossed the border in a couple of places and we're waiting to go after them. I think I heard that the Gurkhas bumped some out at Tebidu only a couple of days ago," he said confidently.

"Bet they regretted that!" said Jason. They both laughed. They actually felt sympathy for anyone who was attacked by the Gurkhas.

This coincided with the air of expectancy that Jason had sensed but could not place. The men of A Company were braced for something, he could tell, but it was not clear what. He set his kit down and then made his way to the mess area with Allan, where they hoped to be able to get a mug of tea. He was greeted by many of the A Company men as he went by, and more than one complained about his weapon jamming. They were not complimentary about the SLR Rifle. Almost as if it was all his fault!

He told them he was going to set up at the mess hall and they could bring their rifles with them for him to look at.

It was not long before there was a sizeable queue chatting and smoking outside the mess hall, waiting to have their SLRs looked at. The British L1A1, or SLR as it was known, was a good rifle when used in the right conditions, but the jungles of Borneo and Malaysia had tested it badly. Jason went through the usual routine of checking for unload on each rifle.

"Take your fucking mags off and clear the weapon or I won't look at it," he called out to the assembled men.

He would never forget the time when he had taken a shotgun off one of the Iban trackers back in Seramban and failed to check it. During the inspection he had accidentally pulled the trigger and blown a huge hole in the side of the hut he had been working in. What had impressed him most was the hole in the six-inch-square beam overhead: massive! It told him what one of these weapons could do to a man. That would take the man out as well as the banana tree he was hiding behind, he had thought.

There had been the usual hell to pay for it and he had been lucky not to find himself on a charge. The Regimental Sergeant Major had not been amused and had blamed him for the incident; he came very close to getting twenty-eight days' field punishment.

If there was an "accidental", they were the ones who were going to do twenty-eight days, not him. Most of the complaints were about the bad re-cocking action of the rifle. It might or might not re-cock, they told him and that was fucking bad when a patrol really needed firepower. He reset the gas regulators to max, told them it would kick but at least it would reload.

The work was interrupted by a thunderstorm that moved overhead late in the afternoon. They all took shelter in the cookhouse and drank the stale tea, watching the rain as it sheeted down onto the *padang*. The area was under a couple of inches of water within a few minutes, the thunder and lightning barking and flashing close enough for men to sit looking at one another apprehensively. The temperature dropped abruptly to Jason's surprise and he shivered. Water was pouring off the roof of the building in torrents and some spray blew into the open area where they were sheltering.

However, within twenty minutes the storm moved on and the sun poked its head through the clouds scudding by. Steam rose in tendrils from the *padang* and the tin roof of the nearby huts and sheds.

Jason got to work again as Riflemen reassembled in a line, waiting for him.

The rest of the day passed in a blur of work as he went methodically through the First Platoon's weapons. The sun was low on the jungle horizon by the time he packed up his gear and joined the lines for dinner. Mess tins were out and men jostled each other for a place near the smelly cooking area. Mosquitoes began their relentless attacks, so now the men wore their shirts with the sleeves down, slapping and cursing the invisible whining attackers as they shuffled forward to the glutinous mess called stew made by the sweating cooks.

Jason found a place among some men from First Platoon at the cookhouse and settled in for a long-awaited meal of beef stew, hard tack biscuits and tea. He was told by his mates that he could draw on the two beers he was due, after stand-to. He relaxed as the noise of loud conversation and clatter of a company of young men dining on the culinary best that the British Army could muster swirled around him. Hot compo! Not even the cooks could fuck this up! It was food and he was hungry!

Just as he was beginning to relax with another mug of tea, he was startled by a scream.

"Take post!"

He whirled and stared at the area where the guns were situated. The yell had come from there. The gunners came boiling out of their huts and rushed over to the two howitzers. Within seconds they had the covers off, the breech blocks jerked open and a round rammed up the breech with a fist. A clang of metal and the breech was slammed shut.

There was a shout. "Reada...ay!" followed by a brief pause, then the guns fired together. The noise was deafening. The air around Jason seemed to shove hard against him and he slammed his hands over his ears.

One of the Riflemen next to him said, "Boogers do this every night, just before stand-to."

There was a whistle and the whole camp became quiet. Then men began to run silently to their battle positions, diving into trenches, or going to specific places to take cover and face out of the camp. Jason joined the cooks and waited it out.

For fifteen minutes life in Padawan camp stopped and men waited. During this time the gunners fired three rounds from each gun and then made them secure. After this the whistle sounded again and the men from A Company stood down.

That night he made the acquaintance of the monkey called SAS. Someone had brought the small pigtailed macaque into the cookhouse. Jason only noticed it when he saw the furry little thing with its wizened, old-looking face sitting several tables down from him facing one of the Riflemen. The beer ration had been issued to every man and soldiers were comfortably taking a swig of their lukewarm brew and no doubt dreaming of an ice-cold Tiger. All they got, courtesy of the British Army Quartermaster's stores, was two cans of warm. People lit up cigarettes and the general chatter of a cookhouse full of well-fed soldiers began. Men swapped stories and told filthy jokes, played cards or chess or simply read, as this was the only place with enough light to read by in the evenings. Suddenly there was a burst of laughter and Jason looked up. The monkey was just putting down an almost empty can of beer, having taken a drink of the dregs.

The laughter seemed to provoke it into activity, for it leapt onto the shoulder of one of the men and then bounced from him to the attap walls, where it scrambled up onto one of the beams of the roof.

At this time of night there were many large moths flying about in the room, rebounding off the Tilley lamps, while up in among the rafters, huge cicadas that lurked in the beams would from time to time rasp noisily, as though competing with the general noise of the soldiers. The monkey was nothing if not a performer, for it went up to one of these insects and seized it in its paw. The monkey's little hand could barely encompass the body of the struggling creature that promptly started to sing noisily in protest.

Waiting until every eye below was focused upon him, the monkey then bit the head off the insect and chewed on it while dumping the still-struggling body on the disgusted but cheering Riflemen below.

There were shouts of laughter as the men cheered it on, so it ran along another beam and repeated the exercise for the benefit of those below.

Before long it became bored with this, returned to its friend for the evening and began to drink more of the beer dregs in the cans. It was clear to Jason that the monkey was tipsy, but it was not a cheerful drunk and fell about making a nuisance of itself. The man who had brought it in took it away to the jeers of his mates.

The next morning Jason was walking near to one of the barrack huts when he saw the monkey again. It was now chained and was sitting on a pole. He nearly burst out laughing. The poor animal had a hangover. It crouched on the platform on the pole clutching its head in a manner Jason had seen all too often performed by his own mates. He stopped near by to commiserate with it but was greeted with a snarl, then the damned thing attempted to run up to him and bite him. Jason backed off, wishing it a blinder, and left.

When the Jungle is Silent

The next few days passed uneventfully as he worked his way through the weapons of the company. He finished with the mounted machine guns, or GPMGs, and finally his favorite: the platoon weapon, the L4 A4, a magazine-fitted fast-rate machine gun, a descendent of the old Bren.

No one knew much about the thin, unshaven man who came into the camp from the trail that led off to the south. He was dressed in jungle greens but wore no insignia; he carried a Browning 9mm pistol on his belt and, instead of the standard jungle knife known as a gollock, he wore a Kukri, one of those large curved fighting knives the Gurkhas were issued. He carried one of the very new AR15 weapons that the Americans were now touting as the best thing since sliced bread. Jason knew about it, having serviced a few in Seramban.

The mechanic from the SAS lines in Kuching used to come in with a couple from time to time, but Jason had never met the men to whom they belonged. The thin man was accompanied by two tough-looking Iban tribesmen, who were heavily tattooed and who wore nothing more than a sarong around their waists. The riflemen told Jason that every time the man came in he would go immediately to the bunker where Major Johnson kept his HQ and spend an hour there, while his two trackers would squat outside smoking their thin smelly cigarettes. After this, the man, who everyone was sure was SAS, would go to the cookhouse and get a meal, no matter what the time, and then disappear into a hut in the region of the Iban village.

The soldier came up to Jason one late afternoon when there was not much he had to do and asked him in a low voice if he could check out his Browning pistol, as it was jamming. Jason diffidently took it from him, made sure it was unloaded, and then worked with the mechanism. He quickly stripped it and found what was wrong. Replacing the small spring in the trigger mechanism, he reassembled the weapon and returned it to the watching man. He felt uncomfortable under the direct gaze. Just as he handed the weapon back, he saw something that made his eyes pop. A face poked itself out from the opening in the man's brown issue shirt – a tiny monkey.

Jason almost dropped the tool he was carrying he was so surprised. The man noticed the direction of his look and smiled.

"My trackers killed his mother. We ate her and he is now living with me," he stated calmly. "My trackers would like to have their weapons checked too if you don't mind." Jason knew it was not a request but an order, even if it had been put politely.

"Sure," he said.

Each man gave him his weapon. Out of long practice, Jason unloaded each of the shotguns and checked them out. The Ibans, unlike the man they were with, did not seem to look after their weapons very well at all. In one case Jason found water inside the breech. He spent an hour cleaning them and checking for loose or rusted parts while they stood watching him. He then handed the weapons back with the admonishment that they should be oiled more. The uniformed man spoke to them and pointed to Jason. They nodded their heads and grinned at him, then they were gone.

Jason took guard duty the next night. He had become almost used to the routine of the camp, avoiding the sergeant major, the Color, and the officers as much as possible, for attracting their attention was a sure way to collect extra duties. He confined his activities to the weaponry, and as often as not sat with friends under the attap-covered roof that housed a tea shop. Most men liked a drink called Milo, a sweet chocolate kind of drink that reminded men of Bovril back home. They would sit there and tell silly jokes or play chess if they had the energy.

Guard duty meant sitting in a sanger for two hours in every four. He pulled duty at the east side of the camp where the trail led up to the camp from down by the river, which flowed by sluggishly.

This was also where he would test fire the rifles if he had made a modification that warranted it. He had gained something of a reputation for good shooting after he kept a beer can in the air for four shots at a time. He had always been a good shot ever since his time as a boy hunting crows with a .22 in Wales.

The route to the sanger was between many huts and past the notorious dugout where the officers had the radios. He wanted at all costs to avoid upsetting the officers. Then the path wound past the showers, little more than stalls with a five-gallon kerosene can on a stick that rotated when pulled, and dumped water on a person's head. One then had to move along a wood walkway that followed a sharp bank with a cesspit on one side and a nasty row of pangies on the other. It was all done in the dark, and Jason had a dreadful fear of falling into the stinking cesspit. The pangies were more desirable, as the cesspit would invoke vast amounts of amusement later on if he fell, whereas if he got wounded by the pangies he might at least get some sympathy.

When the Jungle is Silent

The first night was uneventful and he spent the time in whispered conversation with his companion, heads down in the sanger, peering out over the sandbags from time to time to make sure there weren't hordes of Indons charging up the path at them. In any case, the trip flares and booby traps would have provided the two young soldiers with plenty of warning, whereupon, Jason reasoned, they would be the first killed in any case. Another reason not to be a dumb Rifleman, he decided, yet here he was, doing the unthinkable, being just like them.

The next day there was tension in the air. News had come that the Indons were moving into Sarawak in force and one group was possibly on its way to Padawan. A real prize, if they could take it. Men were told to put their shirts on and wear battle gear, which meant all belt gear: water, wound dressings, bayonet, gollock, grenades and ammo. They carried loaded rifles.

The mortar group were sent up the hill and bunkered down in a deep trench while all the positions full of nervous Riflemen were regularly inspected by equally nervous sergeants and corporals who made threats to lippy squaddies and took names.

Jason was trying to get his head down that evening when there was a massive explosion near by. He jerked up and fell out of the bamboo bunk, scrabbling for his rifle, cursing. There was another monstrous bang, and another; the concussion seemed to bend the air. He dived out of the hut to see the Aussies just about to load the two 105 howitzers for another round. He put his fingers to his ears and watched. The two explosions came very rapidly. There were brief gouts of flame, the guns jumped, dust swirled around the sweating crews as they slammed open the breaches. Smoking shell cases leaped out, another round was rammed up with a fist that pulled back quickly, and the breach snapped shut.

The now familiar "Readaaay!" was screamed by the loaders, and the gunner snatched the lanyard back that triggered the round. Again there was a terrific double explosion, and again the tightly rehearsed procedure. Finally, they stopped, and life resumed. Jason was impressed. The Aussies were good. He wondered what they might be firing at. One of his mates told him that they sometimes fired at the border to support a patrol that might have run into trouble. He decided that he never wanted to be on the receiving end of one of these guns.

The thought of anyone being out there in the dark and the jungle struck Jason as being insane. The jungle was ominous enough during the day, harboring all sorts of unpleasant things, including a lot of hostile Indonesians. But at night it became doubly so: dark, menacing and dangerous.

Jason was put on guard duty for the second night in a row, which pissed him off, as he was tired from the first night and had not had much sleep during the day. His position, if the company was bumped by hostiles, was his not most favorite place: the very sanger that he distrusted so much. He would have to run there flat out and carry two metal boxes of ammo to supplement that of the men there already.

He was just going to sleep, as he was off duty, when he was roughly shaken awake. "Stand to!" the corporal of the guard said in a hoarse whisper. "Take your posts!"

Jason scrambled to his feet, groped for his rifle and the two boxes near by, and charged out of the guard hut at a sprint. He ran hard towards the east side, noticing that a flare had gone up. The night was lit with an unearthly orange and reddish glow that threw enormous shadows, which flickered about as the flare came down, swaying gently on the end of its small parachute. The quiet was unnerving. He came tearing round a corner and then started sprinting up the slope to the ridge where the sanger was situated. Others were running silently in all directions as they too hurried to their posts.

Jason ran straight into a low-hung field telephone wire, which took him just under the chin. His legs continued running for a split second so that he was pivoted and swung almost horizontal, before gravity took over and he was dumped flat on his back, rifle going one way, the boxes going the other. He lay there stunned and choking for breath. His throat felt like someone had cut it. As he lay in the mud, he heard the rat-tat-tat of a machine gun opening up on the other side of the camp.

"Oh fuck, oh fuck, oh fuck!" he gargled, clutching his throat that felt as though it had been torn open, rolling about, looking for his rifle in the dark. He found it, then scrabbled about for the boxes. The firing continued for a couple of seconds and then stopped. There was absolute silence, no insects, no shouts, nothing at all. Complete silence! The jungle was eerily silent, it seemed to be listening.

He got to his feet and wobbled shakily off towards his destination, his heart pumping furiously. His greatest fear was that the boys in the sanger would hear him and shoot him as he came up. Everyone was going to be trigger-happy this night.

He galloped along the narrow path, hoarsely calling his name to them. He fell into the welcoming dark of the sanger and lay there for a minute getting his breath. The two Riflemen inside said nothing, their full attention was on the darkness of the jungle ahead.

Slowly the jungle came to life again and the interminable rasp and buzz of the insects became a solid background noise, punctuated by the deep boom of a bull frog in the cess pit behind them.

Later, the three young men whispered to one another as they peered into the darkness, waiting for figures to come charging out of the night. Jason didn't like the idea of having his head above the sandbags so he lay at the entrance where he could look out and down the trail without being a target if they were illuminated from behind. They began to speculate on the firing at the other side of the camp.

"Some silly bugger got trigger happy, I'll bet," said one. Jason thought his name was Jeff.

"Who has the GPMG over there? Mickey, isn't it? 'E's in the shit then. Sergeant Major is going to slap him on a charge, bet you, boyo," said his companion. Jason said nothing; he just didn't want to be there.

But there was no more shooting that night; within an hour they were relieved by others and he was allowed to go back to his hut and sleep. He had a huge welt under his chin and it was hard to swallow.

The next day the company stood down from the alert, but then paraded. Major Johnson came out on the parade ground and had a few words to say about the night's exercise.

"The stand-to last night was a drill. For the most part you did well, but I will have the balls off anyone who shoots off his weapon without serious cause next time. There will be more of these, as I want this unit to move into gear like clockwork and twice as quietly. You could have been heard in Jakarta with all the racket you made. Sar'Major, I will take defaulters in my sanger at eleven hundred. Dismissed."

Jason was called over by the Color and told to report to the officers' sanger. "Wear a shirt, Jason," he was told.

He put on his shirt apprehensively. Defaulters was at eleven and that was when he was to report. He wondered what he might have done to incur the wrath of the officers.

As he came down to the company commander's sanger he saw the defaulters lined up waiting to be marched in for punishment to be administered for various sins,

The sergeant major was standing facing the three luckless unfortunates about to be sent in.

Then he heard a bellow from within the depths of the sanger, "Right, Sar'Major, let's get on with it! March the guilty bastards in!"

The shout had come from 'Scrappy' Johnson, the Major in charge of the base. Jason realized with a thankful sigh that he was not one of the poor bastards going in to get field punishment.

The sergeant major bellowed a command. "Atten...shun!" The three men in jungle greens thumped to attention rigidly, staring straight ahead. "Right Turn, by the front, double march!" bellowed the sergeant major. "Lef Ri, Lef Ri, Lef Right! Get your knees up, Simpson, or I'll 'ave you back 'ere tomorrow for more!"

Jason realized that Mickey Simpson was one of the defaulters; he was the one who had fired off the machine gun without calling in first. That meant at least 21 days of field punishment. He didn't envy Mickey Simpson at all.

The sweating men disappeared into the sanger and Jason thankfully stood at ease, well out of range of the doorway.

Soon after, Captain Romney-Smith came out and greeted him.

"Ah, there you are, Rifleman Griffith, isn't it?" the officer asked in a slightly plumy accent after Jason had snapped a salute which he casually returned.

"Yessir."

"A chopper is coming in today that is going to Sapit. You are needed there to help with their GPMG, Griffith. It has been jamming. Be ready within an hour."

"Yessir." Jason saluted and jogged off.

Sapit! Wasn't that somewhere up in the really sharp end? He wanted to go in exactly the opposite direction, back to Kuching. But the orders were clear. Nervously he packed his kit and another small bag with items that he thought might be necessary for the repair job. Allan wished him a good trip.

"I have heard of that place. It's just a bunch of holes in the ground, which the fellas share with the insects, lizards and snakes. You're bound to like it there, Jason, me old Mate," he said with a grin.

With a nervous grin back, Jason told him to fuck off.

An hour later he was standing with two other Riflemen and their kit, waiting for a chopper to take them to the hill fort Sapit.

The scout helicopter could be heard long before they saw it. It was one of the new type of low-slung, tight-looking aircraft, with large front windows and sliding side doors, called a Scout. The chopper flew in low over the treetops then swept in an arc into the camp. It landed in the middle of the *padang*, its rotors blowing dust in all directions. A couple of men in green stepped out with their weapons and packs, there was no insignia. They looked businesslike to Jason, but he didn't have time to wonder about them. The Color was shouting at him and the two Riflemen to grab their kit and get aboard. They ran, crouched low, towards the noisy aircraft and clambered aboard behind the pilot's seat. There were doors, but they were kept open by another man with a helmet who sat facing the soldiers as they settled in. Next to him was a GPMG machine gun on a mounting pointing out of the door. There was not much room. It seemed to Jason as he looked around that it could only take about five men and their kit.

Within a couple of seconds of getting on board, the chopper's engine changed its note to a higher, more intense scream, and the rotors picked up speed. With a light jerk, the snub-nosed craft lifted off and rose above the huts of the camp. Jason watched as the whole camp of Padawan became laid out below. He could make out the defenses very clearly from up here, and the way the brown river wound around the camp, confining it within a peninsular curve of flat, cleared land. All around the camp was dense primary jungle.

The chopper sped directly south-west, staying low over the trees that seemed to be so close he could reach down and touch their foliage.

They hurtled in a straight line for perhaps twenty minutes, and then the beat of the engine changed. Jason could see nothing below him other than that they were rising, because ahead was a large range of hills. The ridge ran from the north-east to south-west. Its sides seemed to be steep and sharp, even though it was clad in the usual dense jungle. The chopper rose above the ridge and then made for a small clearing ahead. Jason only saw the clearing as they started their decent.

He could hardly believe his eyes. They were going to land in that! Sure enough, the chopper came cautiously down into the clearing. There were a couple of men with rifles standing off to the side, but from Jason's vantage point there were no huts or accommodation to be seen. His heart sank. Were they going to have to march off into the jungle somewhere?

The crew man, who had not spoken to them the entire trip, shouted at them and waved his hands, pointing out towards the clearing. It was clear that they were to exit, and quickly. This they did and ran, again at a crouch, lugging their weapons and packs towards the two men.

The chopper began to rise almost immediately and was soon gone back the way it had come, leaving the jungle to resume its deafening chorus of insect sounds.

Jason came up to the two Riflemen. One was a corporal he knew by sight, who grinned at him and the other two; then the corporal wordlessly led the way off the top of the hill. They wound their way among dense rows of pangies and barbed wire towards what appeared to Jason to be a jumble of half-buried sangers. The entire place seemed to be mostly underground. After negotiating some coils of barbed wire and a couple of barriers, they descended into a trench. The two men split up, and the corporal continued to lead the way towards what Jason assumed was the command sanger, as it had the only large antenna in the camp atop its roof. At the entrance they were told to stop; the corporal went into the hole and there followed the murmur of voices. A sergeant came out, greeted them, and sent the two Riflemen to their stations. Once they had shuffled off, he turned to Jason.

"I'll take you to your bivvy, but along the way I'll show you where the GPMG is located so that you can get to it quickly, Griffith," he said in a friendly manner.

"OK, Sarge. When do I get out of here after it's fixed?" Jason asked cautiously.

"Could be a couple of days," returned the sergeant.

"Shit!" Jason thought. "This place is probably swarming with creepy-crawlies!"

The jungle seemed oppressively close and made this manmade place seem insignificant. He was sweating heavily in the suffocating heat; his shirt was wet through with perspiration. Wiping his forehead with his neck cloth, he contemplated his surroundings with severe misgivings.

What a dump!

As though the gods had heard him, there was an ominous rumble of thunder right overhead. He glanced up and saw the clouds were on top of them, black and dense with water. He hurried after the sergeant as they descended into the earth and moved along the narrow trench towards the black hole where he guessed he was going to be living for a couple of days.

Jason gave a start as a huge lizard scuttled along the bank at eye level. It stared back at him with one disapproving eye then disappeared into the thick ground cover that was already growing in between the barbed wire. He shuddered. "Christ, I hope there aren't any bloody snakes in these sangers!" he grunted to his guide.

"Na, just some fucking great spiders from time to time and the usual scorpies; so be careful what you do with your boots."

The first drops of rain began to fall just as they made the entrance of the sanger. It wasn't the one he was going to sleep in but the one with the machine gun he had come to repair. With a loud clap of thunder , the cloudburst opened and rain began sheeting down; and as if to punctuate it, there was a blinding flash of lightning and another huge clap of thunder right overhead. Jason ducked.

The GPMG poked its businesslike snout out of the long horizontal slit that had been shaped out of the earth with reinforcement provided by sand bags. The whole sanger looked well protected and provided a good field of fire. There were a couple of Riflemen Jason only knew by sight leaning against the outer wall, looking out at the sheeting rain. Another was preparing a meal using hexamine blocks and mess tins. The now familiar smell of the burning hexamine filled the fetid air of the shelter. A tiny breeze came into the hole in the ground but it did little to alleviate the dense thickness of the air within. The dank air of the sanger stank unwashed bodies and old curry, mixed with the acrid smell of hexamine tablets that were used for cooking. He greeted the men and got a low-toned acknowledgement from them. They looked fed up; they had been in this post for more than a month already.

The sergeant left in the rain, sloshing back the way he had come along the water-logged trench. The light in the sanger was poor, only improving with the intermittent flashes of lightning. Jason still managed to strip the machine gun under the inquisitive eyes of the three riflemen. He noticed that the feed pawls were damaged and thanked his lucky stars that he had thought to bring some new ones. With some difficulty, he replaced them and then re-assembled the weapon.

One of the men, Lewis, gave him a metal mug full of tea. He tasted the hot brew; it was not bad considering how it had been made. Jason knew the rumor that Compo tea was believed to have been recovered tea leaves dug up in Portuguese rubbish dumps that were dried and sold to the Quartermaster's for use in the British Army. Something to do with when they had been allies fighting the French. Couple that with the water full of chlorine and the pervasive additional taste of hexamine and it was 'Hot 'n wet'. A man put up with it as long as it was 'hot and wet'.

By the time he finished, the rain had moved on and the thunder was miles away. The soaked earth gave off a wetter smell than usual and the insects, temporarily silenced by the ferocity of the rain, began their deafening chorus again. Frogs croaked and competed with cicadas while mosquitoes whined and stung.

"We should test it sometime," Jason said to no one in particular.

"Need to get Sarge's permission then," said Lewis. "Hey, Robbie. Go an' ask the Sarge if we can send a few tracers into the *Ulu*."

Robbie grabbed his rifle and left, sloshing ankle deep through the new layer of mud in the open trench outside. The others continued to eat their food. Jason wondered if he would get fed and asked where the cook was. He was given directions as to which sanger the cook lived in and where he prepared the food for the soldiers.

"You need to watch what the bastard gives yer, mate."

"Why's that?"

"Well, one day the chopper brought some semolina and rice. Jesus, I am sooo fuckin' sick o' rice. Anyway, he gives everyone a dollop of this goop and along with that we get some canned peaches. Imagine that, peaches!"

The other Rifleman snickered. "Man, oi scarfed it down like there weren't no tomorrer. Tasted great!"

"Trouble fucking was," continued Lewis, "it weren't semolina!" He paused dramatically. "It was fucking target glue! Can you believe it – they sent target glue, don't ask me why, mate. Why would the stupid bastards from Quartermaster's send that shit here at all?"

Jason laughed. "What happened then, did you all get sick?"

"Nah, most of us couldn't shit for a week. We all wanted to kill the stupid cookie. He's so dense that he only found out when it was too late. Never trust a cook, that's my lesson," said Lewis.

"I blame the bastard QMs," said the other Rifleman. "Them's the stupid bastards sent it in the first place. Them div'nt give a shit for us'ns oop at the sharp end." His Lancashire accent was so thick Jason could hardly understand him.

Robbie came back with the sergeant in tow. "Griffith, I'm told you want to test it?" asked the sergeant.

"Yeah, Sarge, should really, make sure there's nothing else goin' on."

"OK. Well, in a few minutes the Aussies are going to shell the border a few hundred yards ahead. When the shells come over you can fire the thing. No more than half a belt now," he admonished.

"OK, Sarge."

They set about loading the GPMG. Lewis cocked the weapon and they waited. Not long after, as dusk was setting, they heard the unmistakable rocketing sound of missiles hurtling through the thick air overhead. Seconds after the sound had gone by, there was an explosion in the jungle about five hundred yards ahead of the fort down in the valley below. Lewis looked at his watch. "Like a Swiss watch, they are, those

Aussies!" he said, "OK to fire, Sarge?"

"OK to fire."

Lewis, who was now the gunner, sent a burst into the jungle at the base of the hill. In the confined space the bark of the machine gun was very loud. Jason could see the tracer, one round in every five, curling lazily down in a shallow arc to ricochet off the trees. Lewis fired short bursts that spread neatly into a line as he moved the GPMG on its mounting. The shell cases clinked onto the floor and there was a strong smell of cordite in the thick air. As they fired the machine gun, the Aussies sent six more shells overhead.

"That's enough, its working fine now," called the sergeant over the noise. "Stop firing!"

They all grinned at Jason. "Thanks, mate," said Lewis.

"Where do I bed down, Sarge?" asked Jason.

"Robbie will show you where. Robbie, take him to the sanger off to the east of here. Stand-to in five minutes."

Robbie sloshed along the muddy trench with Jason towards the place where he was going to sleep. "There'll be a bed o' sorts inside on the shelf. I'll do Stand-to here with you, mate."

There was the muted sound of shuffling feet and the metallic click and snap of weapons being checked as the entire unit roused itself, even those who had just completed their stint on guard. Every man went quietly to his battle position and stood staring out at the darkening jungle below. They stood there in silence for fifteen minutes and then stood down on the word being quietly passed along the trenches.

In the dark Jason climbed onto the bamboo platform inside the sanger and lay on the camp bed. He loosened the laces of his boots but left them on. Pulling his mosquito net around him, he lay back on the crude pillow of his poncho with his hands behind his head, listening to the jungle sounds outside, not ready to sleep. His mind drifted back to Penang and Megan and the first time they had been together.

Batu Ferengi
Chapter 11

The week following the incident with Dale and his girlfriend had crawled by for Jason. Life in Minden barracks continued with its inspections and parades. Added to the fact that his pals Andy and Kevin were openly envious of what they considered his conquest and ribbed him mercilessly, the first morning after the brawl at the café he was tired. He had made it back to camp by midnight but reveille was at 0600. The familiar tune woke him. The bloody bugler was standing out on the road right opposite their barrack room! There were irate yells from the other Riflemen for him to bugger off and wake the officers instead.

They weren't really living in rooms so much as divisions made up of eight bed areas, separated by solid wood screens laid out on the huge floor space of the colonial-style buildings. It was like this on both the ground floor and the second floor. Six beds to each area. This is what made up the many barrack rooms of Minden Barracks.

The buildings were airy and spotless from the spit and polish lavished on the floors and walls by the riflemen each week in preparation for the inspections that were a routine part of their lives.

He walked down to the cookhouse with the others, dressed only in his blue PT shorts, a vest and PT shoes, to gulp down breakfast then get ready for the 0800 hours parade.

Later, during the parade, Jason was standing at the "Ready at Ease" position, sweating lightly from the humidity in the early morning sun, along with the rest of the platoon. They were dressed identically in starched green cotton shirts and shorts, facing front, waiting for the sergeant to finish the inspection. Jason's thoughts drifted to the night before.

He still couldn't really believe his luck. True, there were women to be had from the hospital over in Butterworth, but the Aussi Air Force boys usually got the nurses long before the luckless Riflemen on the island even had a chance. A lot of the boys went to the brothels in town, despite the dire warnings from the medical officer. Many got a dose of the clap and had to report to the Indian doctor and have the humiliation of having their penises examined by this finicky man. He would admonish them in his singsong voice not to repeat the stupidity, knowing full well that the majority would be right back in the same loathsome dives the moment they were pronounced well.

Some of the regimental lads were known cradle-snatchers, dating the more promiscuous daughters of the married ordinary ranks families. That was tricky, as sergeants had once been privates and they knew all the angles. If the rifleman got into trouble with the girl, the father would nail the lad. Jason let his thoughts drift to the time on the rock. He was so far away that the command "dismiss" came as a surprise and he was caught still standing at Ready Ease while the others all snapped to attention, turned left sharply and moved off.

"Coom on, dream-boy," said Kevin, punching him on the arm. "Hey, Andy, lover-boy's lost it!"

"Did you fuck her yet, Boyo?" asked Andy slyly.

"Shut up, you prick!" said Jason. "I'll pan you if you keep on about it."

The others grinned at each another. They walked down towards the quartermaster's area where they all worked.

Minden Barracks was well laid out. Incredibly, someone had taken the numerous hills that the extensive camp covered and designed the officers' mess, sergeants' mess and barracks in such a manner that the two messes were situated on separate hills from each other and had very good views of the straits, while the barracks for the ordinary ranks were placed so that the noise of numerous young men horsing about and generally being vulgar would not disturb the tranquility of either of the messes. The school for children was well away from all of the troop locations, as was the hospital.

Numerous mature trees lent shade to tennis courts and the one swimming pool down near the guardhouse. Jason wondered sometimes if there had been an accident and that the place had been mistakenly designed for something else: it was such a pleasant barracks compared to the wooden huts most soldiers were familiar with in the UK.

He woke early on Saturday morning. No guard to do and a weekend pass from the platoon lieutenant.

"What disgusting things are you going to do, Jason?" Lt Graham had asked good-naturedly. Jason had mumbled that he knew some Aussies staying at the other end of the island who had invited him along and he didn't want to have to get back to the camp by midnight.

He wasted no time, showering and changing into his slacks and sandals with a cotton print shirt. He took his trunks, as he was pretty sure he wanted to go swimming. He also made sure he knew where the other two were planning to spend their weekend. He need not have worried. They had blown their wages during the week and couldn't afford to go out even if they'd wanted to. They would get drunk in the NAAFI on tab this weekend.

The sun was climbing high into the sky as he made his way down the hill road towards the guardroom where his pass was checked. After passing that gauntlet, there was the walk down the road to the gates at the far end of the playing fields on the perimeter fence. Beyond the fence was the road that led back to the town, and across the road a short strip of land and then the sea. The shoreline was hazy in the gathering heat as the humidity picked up. He glanced at the sky. It almost always rained at some time of the day. His practiced eye told him that the distant white puffs would gather and become towering black pillars of water-filled cloud by mid-afternoon and then it would rain, so he had at least three or four hours yet.

The rattletrap taxi was driven by a cheerful Chinese in tan shorts, a dirty singlet and the usual flip-flops. The few remaining teeth in his mouth were all gold. Their way took them along the Jalang Jelutong road, through the suburbs and slums on the outskirts of Georgetown. The stink of the open monsoon ditches and poorly maintained sewers hung rank in the humid air. The taxi drove at breakneck speed along the narrow road, windows open to all the smells. These changed with each quarter mile or so, from diesel fumes to rotting fruit, the gagging stink of durian, and even a ditch full of offal. Jason was used to the smells and hardly paid any attention, only wrinkling his nose when it got too rank. They changed roads and drove fast along Jalan Perak Road heading for Macalister Street.

The poor houses gave way to the larger buildings of the schools and depots, which in turn led onto the more conventional houses of the middle-class Indian, Malay, and Chinese people who worked in the town center. The streets grew wider, and were better maintained. There were tree-lined avenues with private dwellings set back from the road along the way.

Then they came to the center of Georgetown, and the taxi driver turned right up Macalister towards Penang Road. He drove along the main streets, honking loudly, avoiding trishaws, scooters, motor bikes and bicycles alike as they went. Jason watched the small shops go by with their garish Chinese signs as they made their way down the streets seething with activity. The noise of people shouting, cars honking and the scooters revving their engines as they flew in and out of the traffic was deafening.

Finally they came to the calm of the old town nearer to the harbor, driving past the law courts, the merchant banks, past the Hong Kong and Shanghai Bank building and the large merchant *godowns*. Here were wider streets; Jason admired the well-maintained monsoon drains and clusters of the old government buildings built in the traditional colonial manner, dazzling white in the sun from their many coats of lime wash. The buildings were constructed with huge arches protecting wide-open corridors along their length. Most had imposing frontages with impressive signs in English and Chinese. Mature trees dotted the lawns in between the buildings.

The taxi dropped him at the entrance of the fort. He paid the five Ringit – Malay dollars – then strolled over to the main gate of the old Cornwallis fortress. He stopped by the Seri Rembal cannon, which pointed out to sea. On a plaque next to it, he read that it had been gifted by the Dutch to the Sultan of Jahore. The Achenese had stolen it and took it away. Then the British captured it from the Achenese and brought it to Penang. Jason wondered about the past of this island as he walked up onto the earthen battlements where he could get a good view out to sea.

He was somewhat disappointed to find that the place was deserted but for a few Chinese couples walking around, aimlessly enjoying the lawns and relative cool of the seaside. Of Megan there was no sign, although he told himself it was only just after eleven. The humidity was growing and there were now thunderheads off to the east, but they were far enough away for him to be unconcerned. He sat down near another of the huge cannons that were dotted along the fortress walls. Someone had once told him that the Seri Rembal cannon was good for women, that if they touched it they could conceive. The Chinese were a superstitious lot, he decided.

He gazed out at the straits of Penang, watching the cargo ships moving with steady deliberation along the center of the narrow straits. He could barely see Butterworth because of the haze coming off the sea. It was always a busy sea lane. Among the larger steel ships were the junks and smaller sampans plying their trade, some of the smaller boats seemingly loaded to the point where their gunnels were almost level with the water, but whenever a big ship drove by, they seemed to bob over the wake without trouble.

He noted that the sea was greener today, which meant that for sure there was rain to come. It was also choppy, the waves not high yet, but more agitated as they slapped against the black, slick rocks below the fortress walls. As he gazed down at the rocks he could see the small crabs running about in the ponds created by the tide and the constant movement of the sea.

Jason was contemplating the rocks and the sea, lost in his thoughts, when he felt a touch on his arm. He whirled about, rising at the same time. Megan stepped back, a look of alarm on her face.

"Hi! I didn't mean to startle you!"

"Sorry, love, habit, never get used to it. Hello, yourself." He leaned over to kiss her.

She closed with him and returned the kiss.

Despite the muggy tropical air, Megan looked fresh and trim; a light tan enhanced her slim figure. She was dressed in a cotton skirt of white linen that came down to just above her knees, while her blouse was of orange-colored cotton with a pattern of tropical flowers. He noted that it was close in all the right places. It helped to accentuate her small but full breasts nicely. He stood back and stared frankly at her, liking what he saw very much.

She looked at him, smiling. "Do you like?" she asked, doing a little pirouette on her leather sandals. He admired her slim ankles and feet. Her legs were perfect. She carried a large woven straw bag with a towel showing at the top.

"I'm not sure I'm going to behave myself today," he growled, pretending to look fierce. She laughed, showing even teeth, except where one of the front ones was a little turned in, a tiny defect that he liked.

"How long have you been here?"

"Only a few minutes," he lied. "I can see why you like it here, though. I haven't been to the fort for a long time."

"Let's walk a little," she suggested. He was very willing to agree.

Before he knew it, she was telling him about the fort and challenging him about the history.

"Do you know who made this fort?" she asked him.

"Us Brits, weren't it?"

"No, not quite, although they did what they always do, they took it for themselves after a fight."

"Yeah, that's how you get an Empire for yourself," he said.

"Well, you don't own this anymore, do you?"

"No, wish we did. It's beautiful, isn't it?"

"Silly. It's their country and always was; you guys just came along and stole everything from them."

Jason felt defensive. "No we didn't! We gave them trade and laws and things."

"They were probably very happy with what they had before you Brits came along and made them work for you!"

They were into a friendly argument that went on until they came to the end of the walls and were walking onto the strip of land to the north of the fort.

"Boy, you are anti-empire!' he exclaimed.

"Anti-imperial, you mean," she corrected him. "No, I'm not a communist or anything as rabid. But I believe that it's the right of people to run their own affairs."

"What about this Sukarno thing then? We're the same people you've been condemning, doing a favor for the Malays."

"I know; that's a puzzle. The Brits never did anything for nothing. Then there's that other thing happening up in Vietnam as well. We Americans are meddling in that, saying it's to protect the people in the south. I'm not so sure. Our government isn't any better than yours in the long run."

He shrugged, feeling a bit out of his depth but enjoying the conversation because it was very different for him.

"We're told to stay away from politics and religion in the Army. But I like the way you make me think. Come on, let's get into the shade, all this talking has made me thirsty."

They were near a seating area on the beach side of the road and moved to sit in the shade. He noticed a light sheen of sweat on her upper lip. He longed to kiss her but restrained himself, simply enjoying her company. She noticed him looking at her and her mouth dimpled.

They ordered sodas, which a young Chinese girl brought in glasses filled with ice.

"Do you know how all these Chinese got here?" she asked him as she sipped her drink.

He looked at her. "You're going to tell me anyway. No, I don't know."

"The Brits brought them here to make ships for them."

"Why did we want the ships made?" he asked a little stupidly.

"To fight the French and the Dutch, silly! You guys can't get along with anyone for long!"

He laughed. "We can too. Look at me – I'm putting up with all this anti-imperialist crap from you, an American, and not giving you a hard time back."

"That's only because you want to make love to me."

He sat back. She could take the wind out of his sails so fast. He grinned at her.

"Right you are, love. When do I get my reward then?"

"Boys! Down, Jason, we've only just met!" She grinned back at him, taking the sting out.

"How are things with your friends?" he asked.

"Oh, them! I asked them to leave tomorrow."

"Did they agree?"

"Yes, because I threatened to turn Dale in for smoking drugs. That's a very serious offence here."

"I've heard that they can hang someone for taking drugs in Malaysia. We keep getting lectures on it at the camp."

"I think that's true, and that's why I told Dale I wanted him to leave. I know that the Chinese smoke Opium near where we are, but that doesn't make it any safer if the cops decide to come," she told him."I'm sure they would be very selective as to whom they arrest."

They sipped their drinks in companionable silence for a while, watching the traffic and people walking by.

"Have you noticed that even when it's hot the Chinese seem to be in a hurry all the time?" She asked him.

"Yeah, I know, half the time when it's this hot all I want to do is to find some shade and take a siesta." He laughed. "Come on then, why don't we go to Batu Ferengi for a dip? Did you bring your bathing things?"

In answer, she lifted the edge of her blouse so that he could see the top of her bikini. Jason felt his blood pressure go up a notch or two. She smiled as though she knew.

They paid the girl at the stall, then hailed a passing taxi and for the next few minutes haggled over the price. When they had settled on about twelve Ringit Malay, they climbed into the hot vehicle and shot off north along Lebuh Light Road. The taxi turned onto Lebuh Farquhar, past the E & O Hotel that Jason glanced at resentfully, wondering if he would see any officers.

Then they were on Ahmad Shah road and going by the Penang Club, making for the coastal Jalan Sultan Road. It was a pleasant drive, as this part of the coast side was known as the Chinese millionaires' row. The houses were all colonial style, with tiled roofs and wide balconies. Their fronts gave nothing away as to the people living there, but without doubt Jason felt they were rich people. He could see Mercedes parked at most of them. It seemed to be the favorite car of the wealthy Chinese.

They drove along the pleasant coast road of Pesiaran Guerney that was right along the coast, and then past the restaurant where they had previously eaten dinner. They enjoyed the view of the beach below. The taxi then drove out of the main part of Georgetown.

It was sticky with the increased humidity and the thunderheads were piling up on the mainland. Jason didn't care if it rained. The showers were always over within the hour and brought a cool in the aftermath of a storm. They both opened the windows in the back of the taxi to obtain some relief from the sweltering heat. The taxi had no air conditioning and was, like most of its kind, a battered old Mercedes that had no right to be on the road.

The taxi driver didn't want to talk, which suited Jason fine; the man probably sensed that they were content to be left alone. They themselves didn't say much except to exchange looks and a smile from time to time. Jason never tired of the coastal road out to Batu Ferengi. It turned and twisted in and out of the jungle-clad hills, giving tantalizing glimpses of the sea from time to time. They would swirl past a small cove where Chinese boats bobbed in the choppy wavelets, and then it was back into a green tunnel as the road briefly turned inland. The sawing of cicadas and other insects would return in full force, clearly heard over the rush of air through the windows and the sound of the car's old motor.

They emerged through a cleft in the hills to see the coconut plantations below them with the road cutting a straight line through the trees. Off to the right was the sea again and the longed-for golden sands of the beach. They could see that a squall was approaching from across the strait, so they made haste to pay and then, holding hands, ran into the bar that belonged to the hotel on the edge of the beach just as the first drops landed. Jason grinned at Megan. "That was close!"

She laughed and he felt his heart constrict.

They stood near the door watching as the rainstorm roared in from the sea. The trees nearby began to sway furiously in the increasing wind. It tore at the palm fronds as though trying to shake every one of them off the trees. The sea disappeared from view as the center of the squall roared onto the beach. They ducked as the rain hurled itself at the hut, which creaked with the strain. Penetrating gusts of wind blew items off shelves and onto the floor to be recovered by the cursing Chinese barman.

There were few guests other than themselves. An older European in tropical whites was trying to read a paper, and a couple of Chinese businessmen were sitting in a corner, drinking brandy, chattering animatedly, and chain-smoking. Within minutes the squall had swept over the bar hut and moved on with a last flash of lightning and a rumble of thunder.

"Let's have a drink," suggested Jason. Megan nodded in agreement. They settled down to stare out at the now brown and choppy sea. The sun came out and the day instantly brightened.

"I think we might still be able to get a swim and some sun," said Jason hopefully. He was really looking forward to seeing Megan in her bathing suit.

"I'm not sure about the swim, but I'd like to laze in the sun for a while," she answered.

Their beers came and they strolled out onto the balcony to get a better view of the beach. It was now almost deserted. Some

Malay boys were playing in the distance with some driftwood, but other than that they had the beach to themselves. They sat down on the rattan chairs, ignoring the wet surface, Jason giving a contented sigh.

"Ah, but this is the life!" he said, taking a swig of his beer. He was used to the taste, but not so Megan, who pulled a face. "Is this Tiger stuff really beer?" she asked incredulously.

Jason laughed. "Tiger beer is the worst beer ever created. I think there is more varnish in it than anything else! It was designed for us flint-poor bloody Brit soldiers, I'm sure of that. Take another swig, it grows on you."

Megan grinned. "Don't they pay you Brits very well?"

"Ah, we do all right, but compared to, say, an American squaddie, we are paid like Coolies!"

"That bad, huh?"

"Yeah, not to worry though, over here everything's cheap. Tell me more about you," he said, to get them off a sticky subject.

They both began to talk at once, and then, realizing he was being rude, Jason said, "Sorry, Megan, you talk, I'll listen."

She sipped her beer again. "I never thought I would ever come to a place like this, for one thing. It's like paradise. I love the coast line of California, but somehow this place gives the feeling of a real paradise."

"Yes, I love it. After Wales it is quite a difference."

"Don't you miss home?"

"No. Who would if they lived here most of the time?"

"I thought you told me you were going to Borneo."

"Yeah, that's the rub. We get to stay here and do some jungle training in Jahore, and then we are into the real stuff in Sarawak."

"Do you want to go there, Jason?" she asked him directly.

"Not really, but... well, you know... it's what we came for, I suppose."

"I hate war!" she said with some passion.

Jason looked at her with a twinge of alarm. "Do you hate squaddies too, Megan?"

"Not really, most of them like you don't have much choice where they send you," she said thoughtfully. "You seem different, not like your 'mates'. They look tough, like soldiers. That's not to say that you aren't tough – it's just that you... well, you like reading, for instance."

"I've always liked to read. I read under the bedclothes at home when I was a boy. I had no problem with my 'O' levels in English and Maths and Geography, but I didn't have enough to become an officer."

He looked out over the beach. The sand was drying out invitingly.

"Come on, we're losing the afternoon sitting here talking, when we could do the same on the beach."

They picked up their beers and walked onto the sand. Megan took his hand. Jason didn't know when he had been happier.

They found a sandy bank with a coconut tree growing out of it at an angle. Jason looked at Megan and then started taking off his shirt. She seemed to slide out of her skirt effortlessly and then her blouse came off. He was half way towards getting his trousers off standing on one leg when he got a good look at her in only her brief tropical patterned bikini. He promptly fell over with one leg still in his trousers.

"You shouldn't stare at a lady, it's rude," she said, laughing down at him. He was looking up at her standing in the way she did, her body weight one leg with the other casually placed, the toes pointing out to the side.

"You look like you were a dancer or something," he said to cover the sensation that was beginning to take place in his groin.

"I used to do ballet dancing. Strictly amateur, but it kept me fit."

"I'll say!" he said, getting to his feet. He looked at her frankly, admiring her form. The bikini hugged her curves, both the top and the bottom. He had to look away as the sensation had started up again and he didn't need that embarrassment just now. But it was as though she knew what he was thinking.

She stared back at him. He was clad in brief trunks himself. Her eyes traveled from his legs up to his waist where they lingered and then moved up to his chest. Jason was well built without being over-muscled and was not ashamed of his body, but this scrutiny was almost too much. There was suddenly an electricity in the air.

Then she laughed, breaking the tension. "You're not too bad yourself!" she said.

"I'm sorry, Megan. It's hard not to stare at you. You are lovely," Jason said apologetically.

"It's OK, I'm used to it, but it's sometimes fun to do it back," she said, grinning.

He smiled back, shamefaced. "Well, now we have that settled, would you like to go for a swim? The water won't be that cold."

They ran into the brown shallows and spent the rest of the afternoon swimming or sunning themselves. Jason resisted the impulse to behave like Tarzan, knowing instinctively that Megan would not appreciate the macho approach.

Later they watched the sea from the bank they were sitting on as the sun went behind the jungle to the west. The long shadows thrown out by the palm trees and jungle began to work their way along the grassy bank and down onto the beach itself.

"We should get a room and then something to eat," said Megan. "I'm starving, Jason."

He looked at her. Somehow he had not quite planned that far ahead but had simply hoped it might come to this. Now she was casually stating that they needed a room. He felt a tiny glow begin in his stomach.

They were by now reasonably dry so they put their clothes back on and walked back to the low-roofed hotel on the other side of the bar.

There was no trouble getting a room, although Jason half expected the Chinese to ask if they were married; the man was not very friendly. Nonetheless, they were given a key, after Jason had paid the twenty Ringit.

They found one of the bungalows some way from the main building. Megan was pleased with it even though it was a cheap bungalow with a thatched palm roof. There were shrubs and flowers along the path to the bungalow and potted plants by the door. He plucked a hibiscus flower in passing and gave it to her; she put it in her hair. For Jason it was becoming a heady experience.

The room was plain and unadorned but clean, and there were large windows with a cool breeze coming in from the sea. There was a large bed with a huge mosquito net hanging off the ceiling above it. The fan was on, turning slowly and generating a little air movement.

There was even a bathroom off from the bedroom, something Jason had never had before. In all his time in Wales the toilet and bathrooms were always a long way from the warmth of the bed, down a long droughty corridor. At his grandparents' it had been at the end of the garden. Here, luxury of luxuries, they had a shower and toilet right off the room.

"I'm going for a shower, want to come too?" she said quite naturally.

He nodded dumbly and watched fascinated as she took off her blouse and then her skirt. He fumbled with his shirt, but his concentration was on the apparition in front of him, who was now beginning to take off her bikini top. Somehow Megan managed to make it seductive and erotic without even trying and there was that half smile again.

The bra slipped off and then all she had on was the bikini bottom. Jason was still getting his shirt off; he nearly tore some buttons off as he dragged it over his head. Megan came up to him and put her arms around him. She wanted to be kissed. He held her in the crook of his arms and then sat down on the bed. They kissed for a long moment, savoring the sensation of being physically close. He tasted the salt on her lips.

She lay back with her lower legs off the bed and he stood up to look down upon her. Once again he had trouble with his trousers, almost falling over. It was hard to concentrate while he looked at her. She watched him as he came toward her, an amused look in her eyes.

His eyes were now roaming greedily over her slim body as she lay on the bed. They took in the thick pile of her dark copper hair framing her oval face, her full lips, then followed the line of her jaw down to the curve of her neck, the slim shoulders and the smooth roundness of her small, full breasts. Then his eyes moved down her rib-cage and her taut stomach to the bikini, held tight and low across her hips, They moved down to the smooth rise of her pubis under the fabric. That set his blood on fire, and his pulse became loud in his head.

He reached out with both hands to touch her thighs with his fingertips. Gently stroking and kneading her thighs, he moved his hands higher until his fingers touched the edge of her bikini. He glanced up at her face as he did so; her eyes were half shut and her lips parted as though waiting. Gently he moved the tips of his fingers onto the rise of her and stroked the fabric, pressing gently, enjoying the slick feel of the material but sensing the softness of her underneath.

Megan shivered and sighed. She said, "Oh my, that's nice. You are so gentle, where did you learn that? It wasn't from the sheep in Wales, was it?"

Jason choked and sputtered with indignant laughter. "Megan! That's not fair!"

She gave a giggle and said, "Undress me, let's have a shower."

He complied willingly, easing off her bikini and admiring the view of her entirely naked body as he did so.

Jason followed her into the bathroom. They soaped one another under the shower, exploring each other. He was in awe of her ease around him in her stark naked state, but she managed to put him at ease too. He had been reacting to her in an unmistakable manner for some time now; she teased him with her fingers, cupping him and stroking him while he tried to kiss her slippery body.

They soon reached a point where neither could wait any longer. They did a kind of two-step out of the shower and fell onto the bed, still wet. The mosquito net tore as they struggled, with fits of suppressed laughter, to get under its folds and then they were lying together entangled on the bed.

The kissing began again, but soon Megan said urgently, "Jason I just can't wait, I want you now!" she guided him and then clutched at him, giving a low moan of pleasure as they came together. Leaning over her he could only wonder at the situation in which he found himself: they were finally in bed together after a couple of false starts.

But then the moment caught up with him and the urgency of her movement beneath him concentrated him on her. They moved as though they had done this many times, rocking gently together. Jason was terrified that he would be too quick and disappoint her, but he need not have worried. Megan was rushing to her climax and came gasping and clutching at him, her hips driving into his. Jason wondered if it had been the fact that she was staring straight into his eyes, her mouth slightly open saying his name that brought him to his own shattering climax, whereupon Megan promptly had another orgasm. It left them both inert for a few minutes afterwards, lying in a tangle of sheets and limbs trying to catch their breath.

"Wow!"

"Wow yourself," he said.

"Make love to me again," she growled softly as she kissed him. "Kiss me all over."

That night Jason felt he had died and gone to heaven. Megan taught him a few things about women that he had not previously known, showing him where to kiss and how. They never made supper, finally falling asleep in each other's arms under the mosquito net, exhausted.

They did not hear the noisy people at the distant bar, nor the chorus of the night cicadas and tree frogs, or the geckos chirruping as they ran about the ceiling upside down, chasing flying insects.

Sapit

Chapter 12

Jason was jerked out of his sleep by the explosion that came from above and behind his Sanger. He groped for his rifle in the dark, desperately searching about for his belt kit and trying to get his feet deeper into his boots. He hurriedly laced them up, his eyes searching the darkness for clues as to what was going on.

There was another explosion, this time to the front of his position, on the wire perimeter. Clods of earth struck the front of the Sanger and something large howled just past the opening. There were shouts coming from the trench that led into the small dugout he had been told to sleep in. He felt a deep fear in his stomach and wanted to crap and pee both at the same time. This was no exercise!

A machine gun opened up off to his left. The savage bark of the weapon made his blood run cold. It was coming from the trench where he had been earlier that night checking the mechanism. He had replaced some feed pawls in the loading mechanism. It appeared that it was working well enough right now. He glanced out of the Sanger in the direction of the chattering gun and saw a tracer arcing towards the perimeter and the jungle below.

His mind registered this as he tried desperately to understand what was going on. A gnawing fear gripped him. Were they under attack? It couldn't be possible, not here, not now! Not while he was here! He hurriedly laced up his boots – he had slept in them– clipped on his belt kit and searched for his rifle in the dark. The he went back to the slit where he could look out with his weapon placed in front of him on the ledge of the opening. His eyes searched the darkness desperately.

He looked out over the slope down into the jungle about forty yards away. Between his Sanger and the edge of the jungle was a net of stretched barbed wire, two densely coiled rows, then hundreds of pangies in thick rows in between the wire, their sharp new bamboo blades white and menacing in the flickering light.

They stuck one or two feet up out of the ground. They looked formidable enough in daylight, now they looked like the bared teeth of some hellish dragon with its mouth wide open. Nonetheless, he was in a fever of worry: he was alone and quite unsure what he should do other than remain where he was and presumably fire into any shape that came out of the jungle. He cocked his SLR, pulling hard on the cocking handle and releasing it quickly to make sure it took a round into the chamber, then laid it back on the parapet, waiting nervously.

When the explosions started to occur at regular intervals he realized that this was a mortar attack; the noise was deafening. The earthen roof of his sanger dumped small clods of earth on his jungle hat and shoulders each time another round struck behind his position. There would be a flash that illuminated the surroundings and then the explosion that shook the ground. He hunched his shoulders and squinted into the darkness, trying to see what was happening outside.

There were shouts near by as the men of forward platoon raced into their defensive positions. A black figure came shuffling out of the tight corridor that made up the deep connecting trench and his dugout. Jason whirled with his gollock clenched in his hand. There was no room for the rifle – it would have blocked his way. The figure shouted at him to stay were he was.

"Do you have enough ammo?"

"Yes, Sarge," he said back hoarsely, recognizing the platoon sergeant. The figure lurched out of sight and shouted at some others grouped behind him, a couple of whom came rushing into the sanger. There was a huge flash and a deafening explosion just outside and the sergeant vanished in a choking cloud of mud and spray. One of the figures that had come into the sanger lurched against the earth wall and then slid down onto his hands and knees, choking.

Jason had been well into the sanger, but even so the blast had thrown him into the back wall. He picked himself up and staggered over to the others. The remaining man, who he now recognized as Peters, was bending over the other on the ground.

He felt a rush of adrenaline that threatened to paralyze him for a moment.

Then Peters shouted. "'E's hit, mate, I'll try to get at the wound. You watch the front. Those Indons are serious this time."

Jason nodded in the darkness and peered over the rim of the trench wall out of the slit. The night was illuminated by a ghostly flare that someone inside the perimeter had fired. Probably the lieutenant, he thought, as he peered out at the night. An eerie reddish glow illuminated the night as the flare glided earthwards on its small parachute. Mortars exploded, flashing white briefly, followed by a terrific *bang* if they exploded on the surface, or by the whine of metal fragments, or a deeper *crump* if they went into a trench or hole, tossing earth high in the air.

His training told him that these were at least 81mm mortars. Those packed a wallop.

"How the fuck did they manage to get these heavy things all the way here?" he asked himself.

Jason heard the rattle of a machine gun again and watched the red tracer arcing into the jungle, ricocheting off trees as it hit. This was off to the side where the GPMG was being manned and he could hear a lot of shooting out of sight of his position, to the right. The loud chatter of the other defensive GPMG came from somewhere behind to the south.

He heard a whimper as Peters pulled his companion over to try and find out where the wound might be. In the dark it was almost impossible to see anything. He was muttering encouragement to his mate.

"Hey, Toby, tell me where the fuck it is, will you?" But Toby convulsed in the dark, his heels drumming in the mud for a few seconds, then lay still.

"Fuck me, 'e's gone! 'E's dead!" exclaimed Peters. "Those bastards killed him and the sarge! Can you see if any of 'em is comin' this way?" he asked Jason loudly.

Jason shook his head in the dark. "Bloody hell, nah! Something's going on over to the south of the fort, though. I think the Indons are trying to get in."

"You believe it, mate, this time it's serious," said Peters as he came up and peered cautiously over the lip of the slit. The bang and crump of the mortars never seemed to let up. Both of them were shouting at one another, the noise of firing and explosions was so continuous. Smoke drifted over the slope below, white in the glow of the flares. There was an acrid smell in the air from the burnt glycol explosive.

Peters suddenly grabbed Jason by the arm. "There're some of the bastards down there!" he said, pointing excitedly. Just as he did, the flare went out. Another was quickly sent into the night sky from the top of the hill behind them.

"There!" shouted Peters. "Shoot the fuckers, shoot 'em! There's fuckin' 'undreds!" He began to fire his rifle down the slope towards the edge of the jungle where a small group of figures had emerged, running in a zigzag fashion, roughly towards their position.

Jason jerked his rifle into his shoulder and sighted down the long SLR barrel. He could see almost nothing through the sights, so he estimated the distance and started shooting. The crack of the rifle, the jerk into his shoulder served to steady him. He settled down to fire more carefully at the group of men trying to get across the wire. The effect of their shooting was quickly apparent. Jason saw at least two he had hit throw up their arms and fall like bundles to the ground. Peters was firing steadily and hitting regularly.

There were faint screams from down the slope, but Jason didn't care; he was now caught up in the excitement of the shooting. The rank smell of cordite filled the closed space of the sanger. The spent cartridges from Peter's rifle were bouncing off his hat and one or two onto his bare forearm, where they stung from their heat. Jason found he was stepping on spent cartridge cases, treading them into the mud on the floor.

The two men were well protected by the dug-in position and the overhang of the sanger roof. Even so, Jason was surprised to hear bullets suddenly thudding into the earth above and around the opening. He flinched briefly as dust and splinters of wood flew past his face, but Peters continued to shoot carefully and without seeming to notice the return fire, so he carried on shooting too. He wished that they had more people with them. He felt that then they would be able to deal with the figures who did not seem to be discouraged much by the well-aimed shots the two soldiers were putting down.

The flare went out and this time stayed out for a longer period than before. Both soldiers peered anxiously into the dark below. Now they could see nothing of any activity down the slope. There was a lull in the shooting and the mortar fire slowed too. Then Jason realized that the machine gun was silent. He nudged Peters nervously.

"What's happening out there?" he whispered.

"Dunno, but it don't sound too good to me." The whites of Peters' eyes showed in the dark.

Then there was a whistling sound and another explosion, followed by more, and the fighting resumed. A flare went up but there was no GPMG firing into the jungle and the shooting on the other side of the hill intensified. Now there were screams and the smaller bang of grenades going off. A phosphorous grenade was tossed out of one of the defending sangers to the left of Jason's position. It fell in among the pangies and wire. It exploded with a loud pop and the white spray flew in an arc, curling lazily, high over some figures now trying to get out of its way as they realized the horror about to descend upon them. The night was lit by the phosphorous and flares now, in some nightmarish flickering glow where men ran one way or another while the riflemen tried to kill them.

Then there was a long whistle that seemed to dominate all other sounds followed by an enormous explosion just outside the perimeter. The ground shook! There was a long pause as though everyone was trying to understand what new event had occurred when this was followed by another explosion and then another.

"Those are the One O Fives!" exclaimed Peters. "They're shelling our perimeter!"

The two men looked at one another in alarm in the shadows, both realizing that there had been a break-in. The enemy was within the perimeter! Jason and Peters peered out of the slit down the hill. There were a lot of bodies, lying either inside the wire limp or twitching, some impaled on the pangies, and another corpse hanging off the wire with his arms wide open as though blessing the men inside.

"I don't think that crowd will bother at this side any more, we had better see if the lieutenant needs help," Peters muttered nervously. "Come on."

He seized a bandana of bullets from the firing stand, reached down to grab several grenades from his dead companion's belt, and motioned Jason to follow him. Jason, who already had his belt full with magazines, water and jungle knife, took one of the proffered grenades. He tried to remember the drill he had learned. Take the grenade in the right hand and pull the pin hard with the left fingers through the ring.

He glanced at the cotter pin and moved the wings closer together to ensure he could pull when he needed to. He resolved that he would count the prescribed three seconds. Then they were out of the sanger, stepping gingerly over the dead body of the sergeant and another man, both lying in an untidy heap half buried in the mud of the trench. They ran crouching, peering forward and listening to the fighting going on above them.

Bullets smacked into the mud off to their right but not close enough to worry them just yet. Rifles at the ready, they headed for the north of the hill, upon which the fortress was perched. Jason was sweating and very frightened. Peters seemed to be calm enough though and led the way, moving quickly and purposefully along the trenches, looking for the connecting trench that would take them to higher ground.

Some way along the trench Peters paused and seemed to be listening. Jason could just see past him in the flickering light of a fire. A mortar had landed in a position they came to. The three men inside were dead, half hidden under fallen beams and dirt. Suddenly Peters jerked his rifle up. A figure loomed over them, standing on the top of the trench. He shouted some words that were not English down at them. Before he could do anything else Peters fired three shots into the man, who fell down into the trench in front of them with barely a cry.

Jason was so surprised that he nearly pulled his own trigger. He was glad that he had not, as he would have shot Peters in the back.

Peters turned and looked at him grinning wildly, a mad expression on his face as he turned away and jumped over the dead man then scuttled along the trench. Jason scurried after him, certain that the enemy was all around. The shooting was falling off ahead of them. Someone screamed a terrible, long-drawn-out scream that penetrated into Jason's skull and almost paralyzed him with its intensity. He was sweating; he felt the mud of the trench sucking at his jungle boots as he sloshed along, trying to keep up with Peters.

The mortars had stopped, replaced by a lot of yelling, shooting and more screams. A flare went off again, lighting the whole hill. Jason realized that the hill was swarming with people and they were not Green Jackets. His instinct was to turn and run and hide. But Peters was looking for a fight it seemed, and all he could do was to follow and hope that they were not killed.

He did not get the opportunity to find out. There was a shout, followed by some shots that thudded into the wall of the trench. Peters turned half way towards him and then fell against him loosely, his rifle dropping with a splash in the mud. Jason barely had time to try and catch him when there was a huge explosion and his whole world went black.

* * * * *

"Sir! Wake up!" The night duty signalman in the large bunker that housed the radios shouted for the major without any ceremony.

Major Johnson came out of a deep sleep instantly and rolled quickly off his camp bed.

"What is it, Witley?" he demanded, rubbing the sleep out of his eyes. There was a lot less ceremony in the forward positions than back in Kuching.

"Sapit is under attack, sir, and it's very heavy. They are being mortared and there is at least a company of the Indons trying to get in," Lance Corporal Witley said urgently. "'Ere, sir, it's Lieutenant Harper on the line and 'e's in clear."

The major blinked. That in itself was unusual. To call in on the radio in clear was very serious. He seized the mike and Witley fiddled with the dials to make sure the signal was not lost.

"Alpha Charlie Oscar here, over."

"Harper here, sir. Sorry to get you out of bed, sir, but I am under attack and they seem pretty determined about it, over."

"Do you have any numbers, Robert? Over."

"Estimate a company and we are taking a lot of mortar fire. They are trying to breach the perimeter, over."

"I have your co-ords, Robert. I will ask the Aussies to lay down a perimeter barrage."

"That should help, sir. I'm taking losses. I think Sergeant Williams is dead and at least ten others. They got really close and then opened up with what seem like eighty-one's or three inch pipes, not sure. Over."

"Wait, out," the major told him. He turned to Corporal Witley.

"Witley, get all the officers in here *now*, and that includes the gunnery officer from the Aussies. Hurry, man!"

The adrenaline was flowing, but he also had a deep sinking feeling of helplessness. Harper was a good young officer who had a platoon of men with him of good riflemen, but against a company of Indons and ten men gone already his fort might not be able to hold out, and then there would be hell to pay.

He fingered the mike again with a hand gone slippery with sweat.

"Robert, this is Charlie Oscar. Do you read me? Over."

"Reading you, sir ...this is Corporal Goff, sir. Lieutenant Harper is directing fire, over."

"OK, Corporal. We are going to drop fire onto your perimeter from the One-Oh-Fives here in Padawan. It will take a little while. Are you able to hold? Over."

There was a pause that seemed to last minutes and then the radio crackled again. "Harper here, sir. We need the artillery just as soon as you can get it down, over."

"Roger that, Robert. Keep your heads down. I can't get help to you until daylight – can you hold out? Over"

"We'll do our best, sir, over."

"Wait, out." Johnson turned, as men in jungle green came stumbling into the dimly lit bunker. His captain and the three young platoon officers followed the sergeant major. Their shadows thrown up by the light of the 'Tilley' gas lamp played large in the recesses of the earth and bamboo walls of the bunker. The sergeant major spoke first. "Company is on stand-to, sir." He did not salute. Major Johnson was not a man for that kind of thing, especially at a time like this.

"What's going on, sir?" This came from Captain Richard Romney-Smith, a normally debonair officer who now looked very much the jungle soldier. They all wore their jungle hats casually on their heads at various angles, the blue crosses in front.

"Sapit is under an intense attack. Harper thinks it's at least a company, and they have three inch mortars, or perhaps the Chinese eighty twos with them, and are pounding him. He is taking casualties," returned Johnson curtly. He looked at the men.

"Troy," he said to the Australian gunnery officer. "I want you to set to and drop rounds all round the position. Do you have the co-ords?"

"Yes Sir, I do, we have taken post."

"Good man. Off you go! They need all you can give them. Send a runner to this bunker. I'll use the field line, but I might need to change the co-ords as this goes along."

"Right away, Sir." Lieutenant Troy got out of there fast.

The other officers kept quiet until he had gone, then Johnson addressed them. "We have to kit up and be ready to go in tomorrow, by chopper if we can get some out of the RAF, or on foot. Harper is in serious trouble."

There were glances between the five men. It fell to Captain Romney-Smith to ask the one thing they were all thinking.

"Is he going to be able to hold out, sir?"

"We'll see; he seemed calm enough when we talked a few minutes ago," snapped the major, but his insides were churning. He glanced at his watch; there were too many hours before they could get help to the unlucky people in Sapit. He felt helpless and frustrated.

As he finished, a huge boom resounded that shook the roof, and a flash lit up the open doorway as one of the 105 mm howitzers fired its first round. The tight knit team of Australian gunners worked feverishly to reload.

The other one went off almost immediately with another loud, mind-numbing bang that seemed to split the air, shaking the dust loose from the roof of the bunker.

Johnson picked up the mike. "Johnson here. Do you read me, Harper? Over."

There was a long pause and then Harper's voice crackled through.

"Harper here, read you clearly, sir."

"Artillery is now firing, Harper. Observe for effect and correct, over."

"Roger that, sir... Here it comes."

Again a pause, then the radio crackled. "First was down fifty. Bring it up fifty and that should put it right on the outside of the perimeter. Move left, sixty."

The voice sounded tired but firm.

"Roger, up fifty and left sixty. Wait, over."

Johnson lifted the field telephone and called in the numbers, but then shouted for the runner to ensure that the commands got through. He gave the private the instructions and sent him running headlong into the thunderous night.

He turned to the young officers standing around.

"Get to your men and see that they are fully kitted out for seven days' rations and ammo. Stand them down after you have inspected them," he commanded. "Richard, stay here and keep on the air with Harper. Sarn't Major, get me Regimental HQ in Kuching on the other radio. I need to tell the colonel what's going on."

Captain Romney-Smith nodded and took the mike from him.

"Harper, come in. Do you read me?"

The line crackled but nothing came back. Richard looked anxiously at the lance corporal, who stared back at him. "We are A-OK here, sir," he offered, indicating the radio.

"Harper, do you read me? Come in, Harper, this is Richard. Over," called the Captain.

The line crackled and then very faintly a voice answered.

"Harper here, sir, they are inside the perimeter. Your rounds are landing on the outside. We cannot hold them – they will overrun us very soon. Change co-ords to this location. Repeat – change co-ords to this location, we all know what they do to prisoners!" The voice stopped.

"Harper! Do you read me? Please confirm situation, over." Richard was almost shouting. He turned to the major.

"He said they were being overrun and to drop the rounds on his position, sir."

The major could see his face had gone white, even in the poor light of the gas lamp.

Major Johnson looked at him hard. "He what?"

"He told us to drop the rounds onto his position, sir," repeated Captain Harley-

Smith tightly. He swallowed. "Then he was cut off, sir."

There were beads of sweat on the captain's forehead. "Do you confirm, Corporal Witley?" he asked the ashen-faced corporal, who nodded mutely.

"Yes, Sir, I...I heard 'im."

Major Johnson wiped a hand over his unshaven face; sweat was pouring off it and down the back of his neck, forming a dark uncomfortable band around his shoulders.

It was stifling hot in the bunker. They were all tense and sweating as the men stared at their CO, who had to make an awful decision.

There was no way he could simply let the Indons take the place without giving them a pounding. The only thing he could do, he reasoned, was to make the place untenable for them.

He nodded to himself, and then, his face grim, he called the runner who was hovering in the doorway. This time it had to be in writing.

"Tell Lieutenant Troy to follow my orders. Do you understand?" The private nodded wordlessly. Johnson wrote the co-ordinates of the Sapit position quickly on a piece of notepaper, *'You will fire on this position at once with twenty rounds.'* He signed it then handed it to the private. The man ran off.

Major Johnson turned away from the men watching him. It had all happened so fast that he was still stunned at the end result. Now it was highly likely that the men of 4 Platoon were either dead or wounded – or worse, prisoners. He could only hope that the guns would maul the Indon company badly enough to make them head for home after this. He clasped his hands behind his head and stared at the bamboo roof.

"Those poor bastards."

Then he thought. "This is also the end of my career."

The guns paused outside and then resumed their firing. There were two howitzers and the men of A Company boasted that they could put five in the air when the Aussies were in top form. They were slower tonight, but when the guns got going the area around them seemed to be a mad patch of hell that had just surfaced.

The major shook his head and turned to the sergeant major. "Have you raised the colonel yet, Sarn't Major?"

"I got the signals people, sir. They're looking for the colonel. They think he might be at the governor's."

"I don't care where the fuck he is!" snarled the major who almost never swore. "Tell them to get him on the fucking line! I want to talk to him."

The sergeant major hunched his shoulders and spoke loudly into the microphone. Corporal Witley moved the dials with his knowledgeable fingers and fine-tuned the frequency for the regiment at Kuching.

When the Jungle is Silent

Richard Romney-Smith, Captain, who didn't smoke, took one from the pack on the map table and lit up.

Escape
Chapter 13

Jason woke to a monstrous noise that would not stop. He was choking and there was a great weight on his back. He found that he was lying at the bottom of the trench with someone on top of him and his face was being pressed into the mud. He could hardly move and had a terrible headache. He slowly tried his arms and legs and found that they were still attached. Twisting his head and moving his hands under him, he heaved and pushed upwards. The body slid off and lay on its side next to him. It was Peters, dead, soaked in blood. Jason gasped and pulled himself into a crouch.

He remembered what had happened, and suddenly all his fears came back. The Indons, they had overrun the place and were probably just waiting to kill him. For a couple of seconds he crouched there in a state of abject terror while the world went mad all around him. At any moment he expected a gun barrel to be poked into his back.

There were deafening explosions all around; each was preceded by a wailing howl then the impact that shook the ground. This was followed by a white flash, an enormous explosion, and then stones and mud would descend all around him like rain. In his abject state he realized that the position was being shelled. Somehow, even in his terror, he managed to think of his own survival. He began to realize there were no Indons about; they were all cowering in holes just like him. Dimly he thought of escape.

It took an enormous effort of will to lift his head and peer first down the narrow trench and then over the rim to try and get his bearings. He glimpsed the wire about fifty yards away, the ground in between was churned up like a deeply ploughed field.

He tried not to think beyond that wire. Having retrieved his rifle he noted that it was covered in mud, and then he saw a bandolier lying near by. He checked his own water bottle then reflexively went through the gruesome task of shifting that of his former companion out of the way so that he could check for more ammunition.

Peters was not co-operative, but as he rolled him over Jason noticed that Peters had been armed to the teeth before he died. There was blood all over his front and a darker patch in his chest region. His face was partly obscured by mud and one eye was watching him balefully. Jason swallowed nervously but took the two HE and the two phosphorous grenades off him, then let the body roll back into the mud.

Finally he started out on the long journey towards the shattered wire of the perimeter. First he had to get over the lip of the trench. That done, he began to crawl on his belly through the loose earth, holding his rifle in front of him, praying no one would pay any attention to him in the madness of the night. He had no idea whether or not his rifle would work if he did run into trouble. As the howl of an incoming shell announced itself, he would cringe into the mud, hoping it would find some other target.

Without realizing it, he had followed a path that took him onto the roof of one of the still intact Sangers. He wanted more than anything to avoid any contact with the Indons, but his way went down from the Sanger. He realized that if anyone at all should look out of the slit while he was still crawling down to the wire he would be a sitting duck that they could not resist and he would be killed immediately.

His heart was beating so loudly he was sure anyone nearby could hear him. He crawled over the roof and listened. Sure enough, he heard murmurs from inside. It wasn't English, he was certain of that. Wondering how many were crammed into the small space beneath him, he drew out the phosphorous grenade. He knew from his training that these could inflict horrendous damage in a confined space. His heart was beating furiously, but his only thought now was survival; so he drew the pin, unsure how long the fuse would burn. Seven seconds? Five? He decided to count to four and then lob it in through the slit at the front.

One thousand, two thousand, three thousand, four... He leaned far over the ledge and tossed the grenade firmly into the darkness below. Then he pulled back quickly. He heard a terrified shout, the grenade made a loud popping sound and the phosphorous exploded. There was a thump under his belly, then streamers of phosphorous arced out of the slit as the explosion incinerated those within.

The screams of the dying men could be clearly heard over the explosions of the shells. Moving quickly now, and shutting his ears to the awful sounds coming from below him, Jason threw himself over the ledge and, stumbling and crawling, headed blindly for the gap in the wire where he remembered it to have been. He miraculously missed most of the pangies still embedded in the ground, slashing his calf on only one as he slithered by. He barely felt the cut as the razor-sharp bamboo tore at his trouser leg and sliced into his calf.

Then he fell into a hole in a tangle of wire and mud. He popped his head up just as another shell landed on the other side of the hill. It illuminated the whole hillside; the former fort was unrecognizable: mangled beyond recognition by the continuous salvos coming in. He didn't care to think why the fort was being shelled by his own side.

He knew he had to get deep into the jungle or he was finished. Panting now, his mouth dry, he steeled himself for the last few yards between his position and the doubtful safety of the jungle on the slope below.

He checked his rifle and his water bottles, then jumped up and made a wild dash for the comfort of the trees. He had just about made it to the darkness of the looming jungle when he heard two shots slam past him and crackle through the *baluka* ahead. With a shout of fright, he threw himself forward. As he neared the jungle he dodged and weaved – someone was still alert enough to have spotted him and was trying to nail him even as the shells came down.

Panting and crying with the effort, he dashed into the cover of the trees and slid behind the roots of a large Tualang tree. Its huge roots fanning out provided good cover, at least for the moment. There were no more shots.

But he could not see anything now it was so dark. The flash and deafening bangs of the shelling suddenly stopped behind him, so there was an eerie silence. The jungle was absolutely silent. No sound from above and behind him on the ruins of the fort, or ahead of him in the darkness.

When the Jungle is Silent

He was sweating profusely in the close damp air and longed for a drink but knew that he had to keep moving, there was no time left. He had to lose himself as deeply in the protection of the jungle as he could. If anyone survived the onslaught of the barrage and remembered having seen him, they would come looking for him. He was convinced of that.

Carefully he started out; he remembered that the instructors in the Jahore jungle warfare school had told them that even on the darkest night a person could see once their night vision kicked in. That is, they could begin to distinguish one tree from another. He shut his eyes for a few seconds and then opened them again. The night above the canopy was clear so there was no cloud cover yet, which meant that some stray light could filter down to the jungle floor.

It was a steep slope; Sapit had been perched on the top of a narrow ridge. Sarawak seemed, in this area at least, to consist of a series of very steep ridges joined into ranges. Without a compass he was not sure which direction he would be going in. North would be where he wanted to go. South was where the Indons had come from. However, just now he wanted to put a lot of distance between himself and the remains of Sapit.

He slid and slipped down the steep hillside for about an hour. As he put more distance between himself and the summit he became aware that the former silence of the jungle had been replaced with the sound of insects. Their noise began to intrude upon his consciousness and he wondered what sort of creatures were coming out for the night while he was blundering about in it. His normal fear of creepy crawlies began to come back as the fear of Indons and Sapit receded.

Jason was careful where he put his feet and equally careful what he hung onto. But his fear of being taken prisoner drove him on, overcoming his fear of stepping on a snake or some loathsome insect. It was difficult not to make any noise. Try as he might he could hear himself sloshing through the mud and breaking damp twigs as he went. He wondered how good the Indons were at tracking. However, apart from the endless chirping of frogs and the rasping of the multitude of insects, he could detect no sound of pursuit in the night.

Gasping for breath by the time he came to the bottom of the slope, he paused and listened. There was a trickle of water from a stream somewhere nearby but no other sound that might spell danger. The cleft led even further downwards so he pressed on.

His vision was now good enough to make out the dense black of a tree or a rock, but other than that he blundered through vines and small bushes constantly in his blind effort to put distance between himself and pursuit.

His legs ached and he was wet through from both sweat and the damp foliage. It had rained recently, and the floor of the jungle was still sodden with wet leaves from bushes that slashed at this face as he staggered by. His sopping jungle greens stuck to his skin, chafing, and his canvas jungle boots were saturated.

Several hours later, he collapsed near the roots of a large strangling fig root tree and simply sat there, his chest heaving. He wiped the perspiration from his face with the net rag he still had round his neck. Ignoring the whine of mosquitoes, he took the first drink of water since he had left Sapit. Even in his exhaustion he was proud of himself; he had not succumbed to the temptation of drinking. He knew he could not drink the water on the slopes without tablets or he would get very sick, the instructors had mentioned that too, so he decided to be miserly with what he had.

Very slowly and carefully in the darkness, he checked the state of the rifle. It was covered in a slime of mud that was in danger of getting into the working parts, but as he could not see well, he decided to leave it until there was enough light to clean it by.

His legs were too tired to take him further so he decided to burrow deeper into the tangle of the huge flat roots and get some sleep.

That proved to be difficult. The insects were everywhere, and every mosquito in Borneo seemed to be homing in on him. He put his net scarf over his face and rolled his sleeves down to the cuffs, pulling his hands into the sleeves as far as they could go. With the rifle between his knees, he crouched against the tree and fell asleep, exhaustion finally overtaking him. He was not aware that he twitched and moaned in his sleep, and neither the eerie call of the howler monkeys high in the canopy nor the rustle of small animals on the jungle floor woke him until the early hours.

*　*　*　*　*

Jason awoke with a jerk as the false dawn filtered some light into the jungle. He was stiff and sore. There was a sharp burning pain in his right calf, which he tried to examine in the gloom. His trouser leg was torn and bloody, and something was hanging off

145

the wound. He knew without examining it more closely that leeches were on his leg.

Jason wondered what exactly had caused him to wake. He looked around apprehensively to see what was happening in his immediate vicinity. He could make out more of the trees, but there were still great patches of darkness wherever he looked along the slope he had come during the night. He wondered how far he had come, then his stomach rumbled. His mouth was dry, so he took a sip of the precious water.

His mind refused to focus. There was much that he didn't want to remember but it came back. Like a nightmare it came back in a wave as he recalled the horror of the night before. As his predicament became more apparent to him, he crouched deeper into the dark of the tree roots.

Self-pity overtook him and tears began to course down his sweating face. He wanted to howl and cry out, but a sense of self-preservation was still there. He buried his head in his arms and sobbed quietly. Where was he? No compass and no food. The Indons would surely find him and kill him – or perhaps worse, take him prisoner. The barracks rumor of what they did to prisoners was foremost in his mind.

With a huge effort he took hold of himself and lifted his head. Staring ahead, he ground his teeth and told himself to stop being a coward and to start thinking of what he could do.

He reasoned that if he could stay out of sight in the area it would not be too long before British forces came to find out what had happened. How long would they take, he wondered. Sapit had been a disaster; it would not be too long. All he had to do was to stay out of the way of the Indons and keep his water from running out.

Jason wiped his eyes on his damp sleeve and realized that he could see far better now. The gloom of the jungle would never be replaced by bright daylight, but enough light was beginning to filter down from the canopy to allow him to see more than a few yards. He was still in primary jungle, and although the taller trees were well spaced there were endless varieties of small saplings and large-leaved shrubs trying to compete for what little space was left.

He sat very still and peered around. The slope of the hillside was all there was to tell him from which direction he might have come the night before. Even though he knew he had walked along the side of the hill he could not tell for sure which way was north.

He pondered his next move. His location was not that reassuring. If there were Indons searching for him they would quickly see him moving about in this kind of jungle. He remembered one of the instructors at the Jungle Warfare School saying that the best place to hide was in the densest thickets known as *baluka*.

He also knew that he was on the wrong side of this range of hills and had to somehow get back over the ridge and down the other side where he might stand a chance of meeting up with a British patrol.

Sitting here wasn't doing any good either. He shifted his cramped limbs carefully and tried to remember his training. The Pioneers had not really been involved in much of the ambush training and deep jungle work that the rest of the companies had undergone, so it was sketchy at best. He knew that he could not and should not move quickly, as that was a sure way to being seen.

Belatedly he took stock. He had in his possession one rifle and about a hundred rounds of ammo in magazines and another hundred in the bandolier. The rifle was covered in mud, and he thought it remarkable that he still had it. He also had three grenades and two water bottles. He patted the pocket on his left leg and was delighted to find two chocolate bars, but other than that he had no food at all. He also found in his pockets a piece of string. He had on his belt his large gollock, and nothing much else.

Jason looked at the rifle critically and decided that he had to clean it. Checking to see that there was no danger nearby, he quietly removed the magazine and tried to move the slide back with the cocking lever. The slide refused to move back. Trying not to panic he very carefully snapped the locking latch and opened the SLR in the middle. It was caked with mud inside. Carefully he drew off the cover, removed the carrier and block, and peered into the breach. It was not too bad, but the parts needed to be cleaned urgently. He laid the parts on his hat and again using his neck cloth he cleaned the components very carefully. He still had some oil in the metal tube in the butt of the rifle, and he used it sparingly. Lifting the opened breech he peered along the inside of the barrel. He could see that although it was dirty from the firing it was not blocked. When satisfied, he replaced the parts.

Taking great care not to make too much noise, he pushed the magazine back on with a click and tried to cock the weapon. The block and carrier slid back and then forward easily and he had a round in the breech. Somehow this automatic operation restored his morale by a few notches and he felt a lot better. Having heard other riflemen from the line companies complaining about the SLR not re-cocking after firing, he set the gas regulator at nine. This would give a kick but at least it would reload. Now he had a weapon.

Next he had to look at his leg, no matter how bad it might be. He peered down at it and choked. There were four large leeches attached to the skin around a long, deep slash in his calf. The white of his skin threw them into sharp relief. He knew enough about leeches to know that if he tried to pull them off they would leave their teeth in his skin and this would lead to bad ulcers. However, he could not light a cigarette in order to burn them off either.

He decided to scrape them off with his gollock. Sliding it free from its canvas sheath, he got to work, gritting his teeth as he did so. None of them came off easily, but finally and almost blind with sweat he had forced the writhing creatures off his skin onto the ground, where he proceeded to squash them. He was pretty sure that they had left something behind, for there was a raised, reddish ring where each had been.

He now had to bind the leg and stop more of them from getting to the wound. His neck cloth was all he had, so he cut a strip from that and tried to tie the rip in the trousers with it to prevent more of them getting in. Where had he heard that leeches were good for some things? The whole effort tired him, so he rested for a few more minutes. Then it was time to get going. The slope was not that steep at this point but he trod carefully. There was no trail and he intended to stay off them in any case. He was not even sure that there were trails around but assumed there were some – how else had the Indonesians made it with mortars? That had taken some doing.

Trying to imagine how skilled soldiers like the SAS would have moved through the jungle, he lifted his feet with exaggerated care and placed them with equal care. It was hard going. Keeping an eye on the surrounding jungle and still moving forward taxed his concentration considerably.

As he moved up the slope, he stopped to listen. He heard voices and looking over to the right he thought he heard people moving, although he saw nothing. It had to be the Indons, he was sure of that. No British soldiers would make a sound, let alone talk while on patrol. He had heard his mates in the Green Jackets bragging that they were the "Whisper Brigade."

Sweating with the closeness of the humid air and the thought of the Indons still moving about near by, he crept up the slope. He was almost on hands and knees as the slope was very steep. He pressed on, peering forward and back, moving as quickly as he dared, trying to put distance between himself and the voices.

But then he heard a sound above him, and looking up he thought he heard the stealthy movement of men moving over the slope. He now lay in the undergrowth with only his head above the tangle of vines and loam, watching and listening. He began to realize that the area he was in was full of people, and it was more than likely that they were Indons looking for him and others who might have escaped.

His leg throbbed but he dared not attend to it, he was deathly afraid of moving now lest he make any noise. He wished that he had taken the other way farther down the slope; he might have been better off.

Very slowly, he slid back down the way he had come, clinging to the ground, gritting his teeth as he wondered when he would get too close to a snake or some bloody great spider. But his danger was too present – he had to get out of the area. He soon found himself back at the base of the very tree where he had spent the night. When he looked at it carefully, he realized that it was an enormous tangle of roots that climbed high into the canopy. Huge vines climbed its trunk, while another tree seemed to be resting against it half way up. The effect of this, and the dense cluster of small leafy saplings at its base, gave him the idea that it might be a good place to stay. He rested there for a long half hour, wondering what to do, figuring that he should probably stay where he was. Any movement was going to attract attention sooner or later.

With that thought he decided that he was too conspicuous where he was. Carefully he dug into the loam near the roots of the tree. He pushed the loam outwards to make himself a shallow hole, turning out grubs and other insects in the wet, soft soil. He recoiled when he turned out a huge centipede that wriggled away past his cringing legs.

Then he looked at the dense cluster of young saplings near by and decided to take a chance and cut some so that he had some cover. He was glad that he had sharpened the gollock so well. It had been a point of pride to demonstrate how sharp he could make a blade, and now he used it to good effect, a quick slash and hardly any noise. One large-leaved sapling fell. He listened carefully, nothing. Again he cut, then again. When he had finished he had about six or seven of them around him. He pulled them towards his shallow hole and then stuck them into the soft ground all around. Their large leaves were almost at ground level. If he crouched in the hole he could see out and up the slope without being seen unless he moved. He had the wit to cake the bright slash marks on the stumps with mud so that they disappeared.

Jason wiped some mud onto his face to disguise it from keen eyes, then settled into the hole and waited. He was ravenously hungry now, so he carefully pulled out one of the bars of chocolate and broke off two squares. He told himself that he had to somehow make do, so he savored the squares as he chewed and then took a sip of water. It did not do much for his hunger. All he wanted to do was to eat the whole bar.

His thoughts drifted even as he chewed. He would have given anything to have had a breakfast of sausage and eggs, sitting on a slab of bread and chips. Even those greasy chips from the cookhouse at Seramban would taste like heaven just now. He wondered what his mates were doing. Probably goofing off as usual, he thought sourly. He wondered if they knew about Sapit yet.

What was the army doing about it anyway? He wondered if he would ever see Megan again but recoiled from that thought and tried to concentrate on what was going on in front of him. All these questions went through his head as he smeared his face with mud, pulled his hat low on his brows and peered out of the hide he had made.

Something moved up the slope. He peered into the gloom tensely. Where had he seen that motion? Could it have been an Indon patrol? They could easily have seen him, he thought, his heart pounding wildly, and were just getting into position to shoot at him. His eyes strained to detect any movement, and then he caught another shift in the foliage. The muzzle of a rifle barrel appeared first, very slowly followed by a brown hand gripping the stock, and then a man in the green-striped uniform of an Indonesian soldier edged into view. The man was watching the slope away from Jason, but he was only ten yards away. Jason inched his rifle round slowly to point in the general direction of the stealthily moving man. Then a good six feet behind the first man came a second. Both were very quiet and very intent on the forest ahead of them.

Neither thought to look at his tree, then a third appeared well behind the second man, who had almost disappeared from Jason's view. This man was looking around carefully and his eyes even rested on the leafy blind for a few moments before he moved on. Jason felt that he had looked directly into the black eyes of the soldier. His finger had curled around the trigger ready to shoot first. He wanted to pee so badly his groin cramped.

But the soldier moved on, quietly following his companions as they scanned the hillside ahead. No one followed the men but Jason stayed frozen. He was holding his breath. Very slowly and quietly he let his breath out. He lay rigid in his cover, waiting for them to come back. He could not believe that they had not seen him; he was sure they would come back any time, and then it would be all up. With surprise he realized that he could smell very faintly the rank odor of sweat and curry the men had left behind. He wondered how badly he smelled and how they could have missed him for that alone.

His bladder clamored for attention; he wanted to pee badly but was afraid to move from his hide. He remembered what someone had mentioned about ants.

"They are all over the place and they will find you. If you leave anything at all out they will find it, and then a tracker will find you!"

"If you have to crap then do it well off the trail, and don't piss on the trail either."

Well, he had to pee and he had to go now! He dug himself a hole in the corner of the roots and then, kneeling, he relieved himself as quietly as he could. The relief was enormous but his fears quickly returned. He buried the damp spot with fresh earth, then moved carefully back into position to observe his front. His clothes stuck clammily to his skin and he was itching from dozens of small sores that threatened to become ulcers if he didn't stop scratching them.

There was no further movement that he could detect anywhere near him, but far off he heard a rifle shot. There was only one, and it seemed to be a flat, dead sound in the distance, the sound dampened by the dense trees and the thick tepid air. The jungle itself seemed to be holding its breath and listening.

He wondered wildly what it could mean, but as no clues presented themselves he stayed right where he was, hoping that the Indons had moved away. The jungle slowly came alive, the insects that seemed to sense when all was not well on the jungle floor resumed their scraping and buzzing. The cicadas in a small clearing began their interminable singing. He then heard the woof of one of the numerous monkeys that lived in the canopy as it warned others away from its favorite tree. He started when he heard a loud "wa-waauw" from down the slope from his tree; he guessed it must be another monkey of some sort. A frog began its monotonous bellowing song nearby.

He spent the rest of the day in his hole, hoping that this would give the Indonesians time to leave the area. That evening, as the jungle darkened, the sawing and scraping of the cicadas and other insects rose to a deafening crescendo.

Jason settled into his hole, shivering with the cool of the evening. Then it began to rain; he could hear it on the canopy high above him long before the first drops splattered the leaves on the saplings all around. But then the water ran down the trunk of the tree he was hiding near and soaked the ground all around him. He was soaking wet and wretched it was a cold and uncomfortable night. Darkness descended and he shivered again, and wished he was back in Penang.

Encounter
Chapter 14

Jason woke wet and chilled. It had rained intermittently throughout the night and he was soaked to the bone. The mosquitoes had attacked remorselessly in between the squalls until the chill of the early hours stilled their persistent whine. His face and the soft areas around his eyes were puffy from their bites and his hands swollen. He itched everywhere, and the cut on his leg had acquired a couple more leeches. Jason removed them and retied the wound. He could hardly control his shivering as he pulled out one of the bars of chocolate and ate another two squares. The impulse to eat the whole thing was almost overpowering.

Huddled in his little dugout, he wondered if he would ever be back in Penang. He longed to be out of this hell hole and be with Megan, enjoying the hot sands of Batu Ferengi. Shaking his head, he promised to keep that in the forefront of his mind and get out of this stinking place. She had been really distressed to see him go, which gave him hope that she might still be there if he managed to get back.

It was time to move out from his hiding place and try to make his way back to the British lines. He reasoned groggily that he had to climb the hill in order to set a course towards Padawan, whereas to continue on down the hill and up the other side would put him firmly in Indonesian Borneo.

Quickly taking stock of his surroundings, and listening for some minutes for any noises that might sound like men on the move, he vacated his hole by the tree and once again set off up the hill.

He would walk a few yards then crouch, listening. His nerves were drawn tight from the effort of keeping quiet and trying to hear anything out of the ordinary. Nothing seemed to be threatening his safety; the jungle woke up with its usual noise. A light mist hung below the canopy, making the trees ghostly, their trunks seeming to disappear into the sky; but this gradually evaporated, and he could see much better. Working his way up the slippery hillside was very hard, made even more severe as he was concerned about leaving a trail. On more than one occasion he stepped on some small twig that broke with a snap. He would freeze instantly and wait, listening, his heart pounding.

Eventually he realized he was nearing the summit of the steep hill, so he slowed down even more. Dropping into a crouch, he moved up the last few yards until he was level with the top. There were fewer trees along the sharp ridge, but the saplings were denser. He looked around him and then listened for any sound coming up from the slope below.

He was concentrating so much on what was behind him that he failed to pay enough attention to his front. A voice said very quietly.

"What are *you* doing wandering about in the *ulu*?"

Jason nearly fell over backwards he was so surprised, but reflexively he jerked his rifle up and pointed it in the direction of the voice. He peered about but could see nothing but jungle.

The voice spoke again. "Easy with that, laddie, we're on your side."

Then Jason could see him. A man in jungle greens was sitting on the ground, almost hidden by the overhang of a branch full of thick leaves. His hat obscured his features. The man stayed where he was and motioned Jason to move towards him. As he did so, he could make out the figure more clearly.

It was the same man who had come to him in Padawan to have his and his trackers' weapons examined. He wore no insignia at all and now wore a few days' growth of beard. The man's jungle hat looked as though he had torn the sides off and turned it into a cap. Resting on his knees easily, held in his right hand, was the new rifle Jason had inspected, the AR 15. Suddenly Jason realized that the man was not alone. Nearby were the two dark trackers he had been with in Padawan. They were almost naked and carried the fearsome Browning shotguns, and huge knives about three feet long resting on their knees. They grinned at him, showing gold teeth. His surprise seemed to be very amusing to all three of them.

"Where did you pop up from, then?" The question was friendly but insistent, and delivered in a whisper.

Jason swallowed. The man motioned him to sit down or squat. He did so. He cleared his throat. "I got away from Sapit, the Indons overran the place," he whispered back.

The man stared hard at him. "You alone?"

Jason nodded. The man looked thoughtful. "Did they take the place then? We heard the racket a couple of nights ago and wondered what was going on."

Again Jason nodded. He could hardly believe what was happening. Could he be out of trouble? Was this man a scout? He was sure he had met up with one of the fabled SAS that they all talked about back at camp.

"We were coming to have a look. Anyone else get out?"

Jason shook his head. "Don't know, don't think so. Heard a shot yesterday but nothing else." Reaction was beginning to take hold. He found himself trembling.

"You OK? You hurt or something?"

Jason shook his head. "No," he whispered. "Bit tired."

The man turned to his companions and whispered something to them. Jason thought it might be Malay. They nodded as though in agreement, looking at Jason.

"Did you hear anything of the Indons since you got away?"

"Yes. They're on the slopes of this hill, but I don't know how far away they are, I just heard some voices and then a patrol went past yesterday."

"Did you see their shoulder flashes by any chance?"

"Looked like a Tiger Head. I'm not sure."

"That's the RPKAD, the Indon Paras." The soldier nodded to himself, then shook his head as though in disgust. He whispered to the Ibans again. They grinned at one of his comments and grunted replies.

They all stood up slowly. "Come with us," the man commanded. "Stay in the middle and don't make any noise."

The party of four moved cautiously along the ridge. One of the trackers took the lead while the other took up the rear. Jason realized that he should not be too close but needed to keep them just in view.

The soldier went about six yards ahead of Jason and seemed to be well tuned to their environment, his head slowly but constantly swiveled as he watched the sides of the trail they were moving along.

They paused at one point when the tracker lifted his hand. Jason was motioned down to squat by a sapling, and suddenly one of the men disappeared for a couple of minutes. He reappeared with a well-loaded Bergen type rucksack, which he handed to the soldier.

The man was thin but appeared to be very fit, making light work of the heavy-looking pack. More than ever Jason decided that he had had the good fortune to run into one of the SAS.

The soldier came close to Jason. "We have to get out of this area; it seems to be crawling with Indons. You need to keep up but try not to make any noise...it carries." Jason nodded that he understood.

The man took out what looked like a compact folded piece of cloth from his trouser pocket. When he opened it up Jason realized with surprise that it was a map. He peered at the intricately marked cloth map while the man checked something against his compass. Jason had never seen a map made of cloth before. He guessed that these people were among the few who were issued such things. The man seemed satisfied with his calculations and folded the map up into a small package the size of a cigarette pack and put it away. The compass he continued to hold onto.

"Keep your distance, about ten yards between us, and watch for my hand signals," he whispered. He then followed behind the lead tracker, who had started off.

They were well spaced out by now, and Jason had forgotten his tiredness as he concentrated on the figure ahead who moved through the undergrowth without a sound. They began to head down the other side of the hill. The man and his Ibans seemed to move through the jungle effortlessly. They never cracked a twig, nor broke a leaf in passing. Try as he might Jason found himself making more noise than he meant to and cursing his clumsiness.

Once he slipped on the steep incline and barely stopped himself from sliding into the soldier. The man looked back as though annoyed but otherwise displayed little emotion. His concentration seemed to be on where they were going as he read his compass often, making small changes in direction. He signaled his companions in silence and they seemed tuned to him so closely that no one needed to even whisper.

They made the bottom of the long slope after what seemed to Jason to have been several hours. He was tired but determined not to slow them down if he could help it. His stomach rumbled and he needed a drink; but although they would pause frequently to listen, they never stopped for a drink or food.

At the bottom of the hill they stopped briefly, and he was able to take a long drink of water. The soldier huddled with his trackers and they seemed to be trying to decide which would be the best route to follow. There was much hand pointing in various directions. Eventually the soldier sidled back to the waiting Jason.

"My boys have heard noises to our front and are worried that the Indons have made it this far forward. They might be waiting to ambush our own people when they come to see what happened. We are going to have to move more in an westerly direction to try to warn any patrols we can."

He paused, looking at Jason thoughtfully. "If there is trouble, head further west and then go north again. OK?"

Jason nodded, his mouth dry. He wanted to ask how the hell he was to know which was which when he had no idea where he was to begin with, but decided that it would not do to be smart.

They went back into the order they had been in and set off. Once again there were many pauses. They would all squat on a hand signal and listen, then it was up and off again. The day was became well advanced and Jason wondered if they would ever stop for a bite to eat. But the three men were tireless and continued to move, first west, and then the patrol turned north by his reckoning once again. There was urgency to the way the soldier checked his compass repeatedly and spurred the others on.

The jungle was dense in places as the *baluka* swarmed into open spaces in the high canopy, but Jason never saw the sky, not even once. Noiselessly they moved over the dense but soft ground cover, drifting between tall saplings, sliding carefully past leafy shrubs in their path. They were not following a trail that Jason could tell. He had no idea how they could keep track of where they were, let alone where they were going.

Then the tracker up front motioned them all down and squatted. He stayed there for longer than usual. The soldier moved forward carefully until they were next to one another. The tracker pointed forward; he seemed to be worried. They continued whispering for a little longer, the tracker pointed to the front once or twice, and then they began to move forward again.

Now, however, the two men in the lead were very tense, and Jason sensed the tracker behind was, as well. They hadn't told him anything, but he felt the tension and concentrated even more, fingering his trigger, keeping the weapon pointed forward but not towards the man in front. The jungle seemed to be unnaturally quiet. Jason knew enough to realize that if the jungle was silent there was trouble somewhere ahead. The two men ahead were looking around them very carefully as they placed one foot ahead of the other.

The crash of rifle shots stunned him. The air reverberated with terrifying ferocity as firing appeared to come from all around. He stood frozen for a couple of seconds in total incomprehension. His disbelieving eyes saw the distant lead tracker swept sideways in a storm of fire, and the soldier had disappeared. Several bullets smacked past Jason. That was enough; his survival instincts took over and he threw himself down. His training activated automatically and he fired his rifle repeatedly in the direction of the incoming fire. He had been told during his training that the only way out of a well-placed ambush was to fire back with all you had, and seek cover. Within seconds he had used up twenty rounds. He quickly changed his magazine and continued firing, spreading his rounds and firing at knee height in the vain hope that he might be lucky and hit someone.

He heard firing ahead of him and assumed that the soldier was firing back at their ambushers. Behind him he heard the boom of the shotgun being fired and the eight gauge shot howled over his head. Another boom, and again the hum of the lead balls hurling overhead. He ducked and, seeking more cover, rolled to his left towards a dense thicket that refused to let him in – he was tangled in a 'wait-a-while bush'! There was brief, horrible panic, then he was free. He wriggled deeper into the thicket. Bullets were flying at about the three-foot level and made a noisy cracking sound as they passed through saplings and bamboo. The noise was deafening, but he now began to hear where the main fire came from; it was not all around as he had formerly thought, it was off to the right and well forward of his position. He desperately wanted to run and hide somewhere but forced himself to crawl forward and see if he could find the soldier. Without him he knew he was in deep trouble. His mouth was dry and he desperately wished he were somewhere else, but he set off. The firing subsided as the Indonesians failed to find targets.

In the silence that followed Jason became aware of his thudding heart. The quiet seemed magnified after the noise of shooting, but now the jungle was silent too, as though listening with him. His eyes flicked everywhere, searching the dense undergrowth for movement.

Slowly he began to slide forward, flat on his belly, the rifle cradled in his arms. He did not have to go very far; the soldier was crawling back towards him. Incredibly he was dragging the Bergen behind him. They briefly pointed their weapons at one another until recognition came and then they were lying together, facing the direction the fire had come from.

Jason glanced at his companion and gasped. There was blood all over the man's left thigh. The soldier's face was gray under his beard. He noticed Jason's look and whispered, "I have to stop the bleeding. Can you keep them off while I fix it?"

There were beads of sweat on his forehead and he had lost his cap. It was clear to Jason that he was in a lot of pain. Jason nodded and peered forward, while the soldier moved back behind him a couple of yards and, grunting with pain, started to deal with his wound.

Jason peered intently into the dense thickets ahead. Through the slim trunks of saplings to his front about twenty yards away, he noticed movement in a space created by a large fallen log. He waited tensely as the vague forms of at least two men appeared and moved at a crouch towards him. He removed the HE grenade from his belt and pulled the pin. Then he let the lever fly off, counted two and tossed the grenade as hard as he could in their direction. He fired his rifle rapid fire at the men.

The instant he fired they seemed to freeze; one went down abruptly with a scream and the other disappeared. The grenade went off with a terrific bang and shards of shrapnel hummed through the leafy saplings overhead. But it had done its damage. There were screams at which Jason continued to fire as fast as he could. He changed another magazine and fired to the left and the right of the area to discourage anyone from working around. There was no return fire. He stopped and listened, fearful that they might be working around him, half expecting to receive fire from behind. But the jungle was still and silent again. A thin tendril of smoke drifted up from the end of the barrel, leaving the bitter smell of cordite in the damp air about him.

Jason licked his dry lips with a tongue that felt like a piece of cardboard. He was trembling with the reaction of the firefight. He glanced back at his companion and saw that he was facing slightly away with his rifle at the ready, listening too. He had placed a large medical pad on the wound, but it was already soaked with blood.

Jason knew the man would not be walking out of this predicament and almost panicked. That left him on his own again. The two lay there listening until it was almost too dark to see clearly. The enemy had either settled in to wait them out or had left due to the unpleasant reception they had received. Jason had no idea how many of them there had been or if they were still there. He slid back to the soldier and nudged him. "What do we do?" he whispered.

"We wait, all night, if we have to. Have you seen or heard from the trackers?"

Jason shook his head in the gloom and whispered. "I saw your lead man go down. I think he was hit. The man behind me fired twice and that was all."

His companion nudged him and pointed. Behind them was a dense thicket of saplings with a tangle of vines and some bamboo. "We should get into that and then we have some real cover," he whispered.

Jason agreed. Although they were quite well protected to their front, they could be seen at any time from the flanks. They shuffled backwards on their stomachs into the thicket. The soldier groaned softly, only once, but Jason was acutely aware of how serious the wound had to be. There was a lot of blood, and flies were already landing on the padding. It would not be long, he reasoned, before the ants came.

They found that they could watch their approaches quite well, even in the gathering gloom. Finally, when he seemed to feel more secure, the soldier whispered, "We got off lucky there. I hope Nighan made it."

"What the fuck do you mean we were lucky?" exclaimed Jason incredulously in a hoarse whisper.

"They were trigger happy. They didn't wait until we were all inside the killing zone. Someone was too eager," the soldier replied calmly.

Jason could not believe it. There they were with at least one man dead on their side while the soldier, his only hope of getting out of the jungle, was wounded and probably unable to walk, and the crazy man was quite calmly evaluating their situation and telling him they were lucky!

"You are fuckin' mad. Do I call you sir?"

"No. Sergeant White will do." He winced and looked down at his leg.

"I'm Rifleman Jason Griffith, Sarge."

"Pleased to meet you, Jason. You did OK there. You kept your cool. You could have scarpered; I'm glad you didn't."

"Thanks. I'm really scared fuckin' silly, sarge."

Sergeant White grinned, his teeth gleaming in the gathering dark.

"We have to stay here until we are sure they have moved off. I'm hoping that they think we've done a bunk, which we would have done if I hadn't been clobbered. You put down enough fire to convince them that we had a sting."

"How's the wound doing?" Jason asked.

"Have a good look and tell me if the artery is cut. It pumped a lot when it happened."

Gingerly Jason unwrapped the thick shell dressing and lifted the wad off the wound. He flinched when he saw the black entry hole. Under all the congealing blood, some still welling out, it looked red and swollen already, but he was relieved to report that there was no arterial blood pumping out.

"Did the bullet go all the way through, Sarge? No bones broken?" he asked.

"No, missed the bone, but I can feel it right near the skin on the other side."

Sergeant White took the shell pad off his belt and gave it to Jason, who applied it to the leg and tied it tight.

"Do you think you'll be able to walk?" he asked the sergeant nervously.

"Not sure, maybe. We can try to tab it out or wait till a Brit patrol comes along," was the laconic reply.

Jason felt his heart sink. Then his belly started complaining again. "Sarge, do you have any rations? My belly thinks me throat's been cut."

"Have a rummage. I could do with a drink of water. How are we doing in that department?"

"I have one bottle left and you've probably got some still."

They did a quick inventory of rations and the more important water supply. The pack revealed that they had enough food for three more days at most if they ate sparingly; his mouth started watering at the sight of the three tins of sardines he saw among the food packs. But the water supply was low. Two bottles only.

"I've got some tablets that we can use if we get to some water," whispered Sergeant White, then he gripped Jason's arm and indicated silence. Evening was descending upon the jungle and the insects were into their mad chorus, but White was listening hard and so did Jason when he saw his intent expression.

Then Sergeant White pointed. Moving out of the shadows were three Indonesian soldiers. Walking warily towards the two men lying in the thicket, they were making the classic error of staying bunched together.

Sergeant White moved his weapon forward to point at them, but his head was swiveling to the right and left looking for others. Jason slipped his safety off and eased his rifle up to his shoulder. He prayed that the men would go away, but they continued to come towards them, looking so hard at the thicket that it was as though they could see them hiding there.

"Be ready," whispered White. "These buggers aren't going away."

Jason sighted on the one at the rear, assuming that White had the other two in his sights.

"Now!" Sergeant White said and fired. The sharp rat-tat-tat of his weapon on automatic was deafening, but Jason immediately pulled the trigger, felt the recoil and saw his man go down. The 7.62 mm round knocked the man over backwards. Sergeant White was not so lucky. One of his victims went down immediately but the other one, although apparently wounded, staggered off with a scream.

"Get him, Jason!" commanded White.

Jason stared at him. "Get him, hurry, while you can!" urged the sergeant

Jason scrambled to his feet; his heart was in his mouth. He charged after the wounded man, ran over the other two lying where they had fallen and saw the man staggering off into the gloom. He fired two rounds quickly at the retreating figure and then followed at the run. He nearly fell over the body where it lay face down among the bushes. There was a large patch of blood on the man's back.

Reaching out, he turned the slight figure over and immediately felt sick. The bullets had torn large holes in the chest as they exited; he could even see the shredded bone and bloody flesh, and blood still welled. The dead man's face was young, the wisps of a moustache on the smooth brown features. His eyes stared sightlessly past Jason's shoulder. The Indonesian soldier was not much more than a boy.

Jason felt sick, but his fear of there being others made him quickly crouch down and look around fearfully. It was terrifyingly quiet. Once again the jungle was silent, listening; but he sensed no further danger, so he moved back slowly towards the hideout, peering into the gathering gloom.

When he got back to the thicket he found White lying back with a slightly dazed expression on his face. Are you OK, Sarge?" he whispered.

"Yeah, I just took some morphine, that's all. We need to get some sleep. We can't move about in the dark like we are. First light we move out and go west again, all I can hope for is that a Brit patrol heard this; we can't be that far off the trail to Padawan."

He slumped back and seemed to settle himself more comfortably. Jason noted that he never let go of his weapon and resolved to imitate the man. He sucked on the package of cold curry and rice that he had been about to eat before the action, took a small swig of water and tried to settle himself to sleep.

They spent a miserable night. The insects from the jungle floor found them and so did the mosquitoes. Already soaked with sweat and two days of rain, Jason hovered between exhausted sleep and half waking. At one point in the night he gave a start as he heard some snuffling off to the area where the dead men were. He lay awake, listening to the regular breathing of the sergeant and the noises coming from that direction, wondering if whatever it was would come and investigate them. The smell of blood would have attracted animals to the scene.

Before dawn, he heard a rain squall pass overhead. The only indication that it had rained was the drip, drip of water on the leaves and falling off the high branches into the undergrowth afterwards. He heard the sergeant mumble something in his morphine-induced sleep but nothing else. The jungle was quiet at this time, a light mist forming among the trees; he dozed off.

They woke to the call of the Bornean gibbon, its loud high-pitched call seemingly right above their heads. Jason opened his swollen, gummed-up eyes and immediately checked his surroundings. Sergeant White was awake, listening to the jungle as though ticking off the various sounds, ensuring that none of them was threatening.

He looked over at Jason.

"Much as I'd like to stay here in this comfy bed and wait for a Brit patrol, I think it's more likely it'll be an Indon one coming to see what happened. We have to get out of here as soon as possible. There are some villages just to the west of here where we might be OK." He took out the cloth map and squinted at it in the half light. Jason peered over his shoulder as his finger traced a path and stopped at a point somewhere between the point marked Padawan and the mountains to the south that they had left the day before.

"We are about here," he said, "We have to keep moving west; there is a small village in that direction."

"Can you trust the Dyaks around here, Sarge?"

"Ibans. Not always, but if we stay on this side of the high ridges we should be OK. They don't have any love for the Indons. If we could just get to some high ground and make an L-P for a chopper I might be able to get the SARBE signal to work. These old maps are not such large scale that I can tell easily where there might be a good hill."

"What's a SARBE?"

"It's our method of telling our people we are in the shit and need to be got out."

"How far are we from Padawan?"

"About fifteen thousand yards."

"That's all? Can't we try to make it there?"

"Fifteen thousand yards in the *ulu* can take up to three days or more when you're fit, and there is no trail especially as the place is swarming with Indons. If I'd not been clobbered I would take the chance, because I'll bet your boys are tabbing it this way to see what happened at Sapit."

They crawled out of their hiding place. Jason hefted the heavy pack and then helped the sergeant onto his feet. At one point it looked as though he was going to fall over, but he held on grimly and stood swaying on one leg, the other hanging loose while he leaned on Jason. Then he gingerly put some weight on it, gasped with the pain but persisted, and then hobbled forward, holding onto Jason with a vice-like grip on his arm.

"We will have to make a crutch for me, or I won't last very long." He muttered.

In this manner they took a compass bearing and headed west at a shuffle. Jason knew White had to be in a lot of pain, but the sergeant kept pressing him to move on and get some distance between them and the site of the engagement.

"We have no idea how many of the Indons there are," he said. "We have to take our chances outside this area, even though our own boys could be near by as well."

Jason saw the logic of it, although he was afraid that with all the noise they were making they were sitting targets.

They headed towards what Sergeant White said he thought might be a ridge where they could make a small helicopter pad out of the jungle and call in assistance with the SARBE rescue beacon.

Enquiry
Chapter 15

Major Johnson surveyed his men as they stood sweating in the early morning sun on the *padang* of the camp. Padawan was a tense place today. The major was red-eyed from lack of sleep and felt ten years older than he had the previous morning.

Everyone in the company knew of the awful decision that had been taken the night before and that was uppermost in all their minds. Surprisingly, no one seemed to blame the major for his decision. At least not overtly; all the officers had come to him at one time or another and expressed their support and approval. No one was happy that the Indons had overrun a position that belonged to the Green Jackets, but they were now eager to get to grips with the enemy and take it back.

At first light the Recce platoon under Lieutenant Thomas Hammond had left, heading due south, accompanied by a group of men from the SAS with Iban trackers in tow. These eight SAS men had arrived by a large Wessex chopper from Kuching as dawn was breaking. Two of them had had an intense discussion with Major Johnson in the privacy of his sanger, asking penetrating questions as to the conditions and what he knew of the situation at the time of the battle, then they had joined the patrol and left.

Now the remaining platoons were assembled with full kit, ammo and weapons, waiting for his orders to leave. Captain Romney-Smith would lead the two platoons, 3rd and 5th, with Lieutenant Michael Powell as his second. Padawan camp was going to be left with Lieutenant Robin McGregor and Sergeant

Major Goff. He, Major Johnson, was to be flown back to Kuching to explain his actions to his colonel and the brigadier.

Hiding his concerns, the major waited until the sergeant major called the men to attention then marched up to him and stamped to attention, with a salute.

"Company ready, sir."

"Thank you, Sergeant Major. Stand them at ease."

"Companaayy, stand ...at ease!" bellowed the sergeant major.

Major Johnson walked forward to where he could see everyone and be seen.

"You all know what happened last night, men. The Indon overran Sapit. It is too early to try and put men in with choppers as there are no other clearings near by. You have to hoof it. You need to move along the trails like only the Green Jackets can. If the buggers have an ambush along the trail you'll be through it too fast for them to react

anyway."

There was a collective chuckle from the ranks.

He continued. "The last we heard of Lieutenant Harper he was being overrun and there is little likelihood that there were many survivors. We can all be sure of one thing. Fourth Platoon went out fighting as only this regiment knows how."

Again, there was a murmur from the men, an angry, low growl that told him what he needed to hear.

"You are going to avenge Fourth Platoon and there is no time to waste. I wish I was coming with you." He paused; it was difficult to speak for a minute. The men stared at their CO. They all knew what he must be suffering. Major Johnson was a well-liked and respected CO.

He cleared his throat. "Captain Romney-Smith will lead. Good luck, men. Get on with the job and show them that they can't get away with this kind of thing. That's all, Sergeant Major. Dismissed."

He was about to turn away when a lone voice from the ranks called, "Three cheers for the major!"

Before the Sergeant Major could shout for silence, the fifty men were cheering. Their CO stood still, straight as a ramrod in front of them.

"Silence! Silence in the ranks!" bellowed the sergeant major, but those nearest him would have been able to see that he had a grin on his normally stern face. Eventually the noise stopped and there was an awkward silence. Major Johnson saluted his men and turned away to pack his kit.

Within half an hour the men had disappeared into the surrounding jungle, hastening towards the ridges and Sapit some eleven miles overland, looking for a fight but also desperately hoping to find some survivors.

The only people left in the camp were the Iban villagers, some Malay soldiers who were not consulted about the expedition, and the HQ platoon, severely depleted.

Rain came down in buckets that day and the next, and Johnson was informed that there were no choppers available because of flooding in Kuching. This ensured that the major had to endure a wait that nearly drove him mad. He resigned himself to listening on the radio for his men.

There was no contact as they hurried towards Sapit and were firmly under radio silent mode. The trouble was that eleven miles in this country could take three days: there were few trails, and despite his flippant remarks they could not afford to run into an ambush. The waiting was terrible. He spent a sleepless night tossing and turning on his camp bed, waiting to be called by the radio man. Nothing came in, no contact with the enemy that would have resulted in a signal being sent; nothing.

The scout helicopter came the third day and took Major Johnson off towards Kuching. As they were flying over the jungle, the major grimly contemplated his future. He had no doubt that he was flying towards his court martial and that his career was over. But he was not going to submit weakly, he was determined about that. They didn't call him "Scrappy" for nothing. If the brigadier didn't like his explanation then they could all go to hell in a bucket as far as he was concerned. He wondered what on earth he would do when it was all over and he was ousted as a civilian.

The jungle canopy below sped by and after forty minutes the River Sarawak appeared, winding sluggishly through the dense jungle, then civilization in small clearings. Kampongs began to show up, half hidden by the towering trees, followed by villages with tin roofs, which were inhabited by Chinese. He wondered if the SAS was having any luck finding the elusive CCO. According to Intelligence, the Chinese Communists were strong on the ground in Sarawak, and were involved in an unholy alliance with Sukarno.

All too soon they came to the RAF base on the outskirts of Kuching and landed in a cloud of dirt and sprayed mud from the recent rains. Collecting his rifle and kit, Major Johnson nodded to the crewman and, crouching low, ran towards two men standing next to a Landrover parked on the gravel road near by. He noticed a lot of activity as he jogged over. A couple of Wessex helicopters and a Belvedere troop carrier with its distinctive twin rotors were winding up, and a long row of men were preparing to embark. They were Gurkhas and looked businesslike.

He recognized the adjutant, Captain Patterson. "Hello, Peter. How are you?" he asked as he came up.

Patterson, dressed in jungle greens and wearing the green beret of the regiment with its distinctive cap badge, saluted him. "Good to see you, sir. Sorry about Sapit."

Major Johnson said nothing; he tipped his scruffy jungle hat. The driver was a Rifleman and it would not do to discuss the situation in front of him. They climbed into the Landrover and headed for Kuching. Major Johnson realized that they were not going to Semengang; instead, they seemed to be heading for Brigade HQ.

So be it then, let's get this over with, he said to himself.

The Landrover pulled up at the entrance to a large fenced compound with neatly trimmed hedges behind it, obscuring the view to anyone wishing to look inside. On either side of the gateway were two low sandbagged emplacements with watchful soldiers from the Gurkha Regiment peering out. One walked over to inspect the Landrover, and the adjutant told him they were expected by the brigadier. He nodded and saluted smartly,

then stepped aside.

The barrier was raised and the thick gravel of the drive crunched under the tires as they drove the short distance to the large, double-storied, colonial-style building. Johnson barely noticed the beautifully groomed gardens, the frangipani trees, the carefully trimmed tree ferns and immaculate lawns; his thoughts were elsewhere.

Sentries were standing either side of the steps that led up to the first floor of the whitewashed building that was Brigadier Whiley-Carrick's HQ. Major Johnson knew a bit about the man. He was one of the old school soldiers, who had spent most of his

military career in India. He had fought his way down into Burma as a young lieutenant with General Wavell during the war, spoke several languages, and had served in the Gurkhas with the legendary Brigadier General John Masters. Johnson knew he would be better off just telling it as it had been. Besides, he was disinclined to do otherwise. He felt that he had made the right decision at the time.

They climbed out of the Landrover and walked up the steps. The major still had his rifle in his hands and now he didn't know what to do with it. This didn't seem quite the right place to carry one about. Peter saved the situation by offering to take the rifle and leave it in the vehicle with the driver. He came trotting back and they went into the cool interior of the large colonial building.

Dressed in the heavily starched issue shorts and tropical greens, their kukris at their sides, the immaculate Gurkha soldiers standing at the entrance slammed to attention and presented arms as the two officers went by. They stayed frozen in position until they were saluted, then they slammed back at ease.

The polished floors and cool atmosphere within were a far cry from the muck and basic life of Padawan. There was the bustle of a busy HQ. No one wore a hat; officers and NCOs strode about with wads of files in their hands as they went from one office to another. The two newcomers stood at the entrance, getting used to the dim interior after the bright sunlight outside, uncertain as to where to go.

A well-starched captain came towards them, giving a nervous smile of welcome.

"The brigadier and Colonel Hollingsworth are in his office and will see you now, sir," he said diffidently He eyed Johnson's rumpled and stained jungle uniform, the muddy boots and belt kit disapprovingly, but wisely said nothing.

"This way, sir." He went ahead, knocked, opened the door and announced to someone in the room beyond, "Major Johnson has arrived, sir."

"Ah, thank you, Stewart, please show him in," the voice of the brigadier boomed back.

Captain Patterson indicated that he would wait outside while Major Johnson went past his guide, Stewart, into the spacious room. The door shut quietly behind him, leaving him alone with the men in the office.

The colonel and the brigadier were standing by the brigadier's desk. Both looked serious. However, when Johnson snapped as good a salute as he knew how and stood rigidly to attention, the brigadier came marching over.

"Hello, Nigel old chap, how have you been?" He held out his hand.

"Very well, sir." Johnson took the firm, dry grip in his own not so dry hand, and they shook briefly.

The brigadier smiled a tight smile. He was much shorter than Johnson, stocky, and although he was tending to fullness around the waist he still looked quite fit. His hair was sparse on top, but he made up for it with a good moustache. A pair of bright gray eyes looked the major up and down appraisingly. The brigadier indicated the rattan chairs off to the side of the office with a view out onto the verandah.

"Let's have some tea and you can tell us all about it. Hmm?"

Colonel Barker-Hollingsworth came over and shook his hand as well. He was tall, with that deceptive thinness that seemed to indicate frailness. Most people were deceived only once.

"Hello, Nigel. Rum do, this. We wanted to hear all about it from you directly, that's why we called you back."

Major Johnson was not sure how to respond, so he followed the two men in silence and settled himself onto the edge of the large rattan chair he was shown to.

The brigadier eyed his belt equipment, the magazine pouches, water bottle, jungle knife and pistol. "Would you like to get rid of that for a while, Nigel?" he asked solicitously.

The major nodded and took off the belt, placing it carefully on the gleaming floor near by. He felt badly dressed in front of these two very senior men who wore starched jungle green uniforms with creases that could cut, with their polished shoes and Sam Brown belts. He wished fervently that he could have stayed in Padawan.

Tea was ordered and served by an impeccably dressed servant, and they all took sips out of delicate cups. The colonel and the brigadier indulged in small talk as they drank, but finally the Brigadier put his teacup down and said, "Now, Nigel, tell me in your own words what happened the other night at Sapit."

Major Johnson began his story. He continued until it was lunchtime. In all that time the brigadier watched him silently, as did the colonel. Neither asked any questions, they simply let him tell it chronologically. When he had finished there was a long pause.

Major Johnson could hear the voices of men and women in the distance through the open windows. The creaking of the fan overhead sounded clear in the silence and he was surprised by the high-pitched call of a peacock in the lush green gardens outside.

Then the questions came, and he girded himself for a battle. The two senior men asked question after question as though they had rehearsed the act. He stuck to the story, answering clearly, trying not to contradict himself. He felt that he had given them what they wanted, but by the time the questions stopped, he was sweating in spite of the cool air from the fan overhead.

There was once again a long pause while the two senior men seemed to be digesting all that he had said. The brigadier glanced over at the colonel and then said to Major Johnson, "Nigel, thank you for being so frank and straightforward. I need to talk to Richard for a few moments and then we will call you back in. Is that all right?"

Major Johnson picked up his belt and stood up. "Thank you, sir. I'll wait outside."

He walked slowly to the door and let himself out.

* * * * *

Inside the room the two older men looked at one another.

"Bad show this one, Richard, but I believe Nigel is telling the truth, don't you?"

"Oh, absolutely, sir. Nigel is not one to embellish things. What do you feel you have to do now? Court martial?"

The Brigadier smacked his knee with the flat of his hand.

"I think we bloody well have to, Richard. He fired on his own, you might say. Although I am not at all sure I wouldn't have done the same thing under the circumstances. Trouble is, he knew the co-ordinates of the place. If he could only claim he had not, we might have been able to wriggle out of this corner."

"We could say that he was firing on a position the enemy had already taken, sir."

"Yes indeed, that was done in the war, prisoners or not, as I recall." The brigadier glowered, looking fierce. The colonel could read the signs; the brigadier was getting angry at a situation he could not control.

"I'll tell you what I'll do. He's a cracking good officer and I would hate to lose him at this juncture. There will have to be a court of enquiry at the very least, and if they decide it has to go to a court martial then so be it. I don't have to convene it until this mess is over, though. Send him back to his company, Richard. He would die here in this spit-and-polish environment; that's clear enough."

The colonel smiled for the first time. "Thank you, sir. His men love him and probably need him back there if I'm not mistaken. Shall I go and tell him?"

The brigadier smiled thinly under his moustache. "Lucky bastard, he's going back to all the fun. You and I are too old to be traipsing about the jungle, Richard, but I do miss the action sometimes. Give him the talk. Do you want to go out there?"

"I have no objection to going, but I fear that if I do it will send all the wrong messages, sir."

"I agree; it's his show, but tell him that it's not over and there must be a court of enquiry; however, that can wait."

The colonel got to his feet. "Thank you again, sir. Right away!" He saluted and left quickly.

He found Major Johnson sitting uncomfortably on one of the cane chairs within easy call of the office. The major stood up quickly when he saw his colonel come out of the brigadier's office. He felt nervous and defeated.

"Nigel, the brig says you are to go back to your company and get on with things. When this rumpus is all over there most certainly will be a court of inquiry, but it is going to be put off for a while. Can you handle the wait?"

He must have seen the relief in the eyes of his officer.

"Thank you, sir. Yes, I can deal with it. I'll leave right away."

"Not quite so fast, Nigel. I want to look at the maps with you, and there is Major Phillip Stanford, SAS, who, you might remember, gave us all a briefing when we arrived. He's going to be visiting your location and you should get to know him. Let's have lunch at the mess where we can meet Stanford, then we can get you back to Padawan before nightfall; if not, you can leave in the morning. I'll tell Radios to call them in Padawan and let them know.

"Right, sir. That's fine." Major Johnson allowed himself to take a deep breath for the first time in hours.

They went out and found the adjutant standing, waiting for them near the Landrover. "I've got some things to deal with, so I'll take mine and see you two at the mess," said the colonel.

The mess was a luxury after the basics of Padawan. Major Johnson could not help but be envious of the HQ staff of the regiment as he walked into the cool interior of the building. The fans were running hard to keep a cool breeze going, which was pleasant to stand under after the sweltering heat outside.

The other officers greeted him with undisguised pleasure, and while they waited for the colonel to show up he caught up on events in Kuching. They, on the other hand, wanted to know as much as he could tell them of the action at the sharp end, although they were diffident about asking exactly how the Sapit incident had occurred.

It was a relaxed group of officers who sat down for a late lunch when the colonel came in. He brought with him the thin officer Major Stanford, who greeted the others with a slow smile. The colonel introduced him and asked him to sit near him with Major Johnson close by. It was clear to both that the colonel wanted them to meet and hopefully get along.

It was not hard to do. Both men were keen professionals who loved what they did. Before long they were planning how they could not only take back Sapit but prevent it falling again and kicking the Indons back over the border.

"Are we allowed to go over the border and take it to them after this, sir?" asked Johnson.

Stanford looked approving at that and looked to the colonel for confirmation.

"I believe the brig is about to allow us to go over and do some damage of our own. Sapit probably pushed him to it a little earlier than he had intended," said the colonel cautiously.

Both men were pleased. The colonel then asked Major Stanford mischievously, "Haven't your boys been over the line in any case, Phillip?"

There was a brief silence as Major Stanford looked down at the table. "Well, sir, actually we might have strayed once in a while."

"Hmm, given your men's map reading skills that is an interesting word," the colonel said drily.

There was laughter from everyone in the room, even the colonel was smiling. "It's all right, Phillip, I won't tell. We might need your help before long to guide us over, though. In spite of the work you and your men have done, our maps are atrociously short of information."

The meal was finished in a good mood by the officers of the Green Jackets. They were eager to have the wrong put right and were very pleased to see that one of their own, Major Johnson, was not going to be locked up for doing something all of them agreed he had had few choices about.

Later the three men, with the adjutant in tow, went into the colonel's office and pored over the sparse maps that represented the region near the border where the camp of Sapit had formerly existed.

Major Stanford was able to add a considerable amount of information to the map, much to the colonel's relief. He and his men had spent three months in the region mapping and doing the "Hearts and minds" program with the local population. He was able to point out where the villages were, which ones were trustworthy, which was nearly all of them, and the rivers that were still unmarked. He knew where the unmarked trails were too, and mentioned several good ambush positions between Padawan and the border that could be used one day.

By the time they had finished it was time for dinner, and the officers reassembled in the mess. It was a subdued meal, but there was also as sense of optimism; these men were clear in their minds that the regiment would be avenged and that Major Johnson would be allowed to lead.

Early next day Major Johnson reported to his colonel, and once they had discussed the situation as the colonel knew it to be, they shook hands and parted.

"I want you to be sensible, Nigel. Don't go charging off after the men just because you want a fight. Make sure you do a good job of running the show. D'you hear?" the colonel admonished him, looking as stern as he could.

Major Johnson saluted and grinned somewhat sheepishly. "Yes, sir, I'll be sensible."

Peter dropped him off at the RAF base with the cheeky comment, mimicking the colonel. "Now behave yourself, sir. Be sensible and make a good job of it!"

"Fuck off, Peter," he said, grinning.

"Good luck sir. We are all behind you on this." Peter said more seriously.

They shook hands smiling, then he grabbed his rifle and pack and walked over to a dispatcher who was waiting near a scout chopper with its rotors turning.

"You for Padawan, sir?" the man said, without saluting.

The major nodded, and clambered aboard. Within minutes they were airborne again and he could relax for the first time in three days.

Major Johnson arrived back to find the camp in a state of high excitement, which became jubilant when he appeared. No one had expected him back for the duration. He noticed a Bell helicopter parked on the *Padang* and wondered who had brought it in.

The sergeant major snapped him a cheery salute and said, "Welcome back, sir. Welcome back. The men are on stand-to, sir."

Johnson grinned and tipped his hat. "Good to be back, Sergeant Major. Keep the men on stand-to for the time being. Whose is that chopper? What's happening at the sharp end?"

"The chopper belongs to the Aussies, sir. One of their officers is here to chat with the battery. I'll ask him to come over when you are settled?"

"Thanks, that would be good. Let's go and see what's going on."

Leaving his kit to be picked up by someone else, they hurried off to the radio Sanger. Johnson wrinkled his nose at the stink of the closed air inside the gloomy Sanger. The mosquito ring burning on a table lent its noxious fumes to air foul with unwashed sweaty bodies and stale curry smells, but this was home for the time being and he felt good to be back.

Lieutenant McGregor was concentrating on the map as they came into the dark of the interior. He stood up sharply.

"Oh, hello, sir! Didn't expect you to be...well, er, back so soon," he stammered, remembering to salute at the last minute. "Glad to have you back though, sir. Things have hotted up a bit since you left."

"What's going on, Robin?"

"Witley got a short call early this afternoon. The Recce platoon has arrived to within about two miles of the ridges; they came across what looked like an ambush site, day or so old. They found several Indons dead and one Iban. The SAS boys said he was one of theirs."

That explained why the SAS was so interested in the situation. Why not? They were the ones who had done all the hard work up to now, Major Johnson reasoned to himself.

"Are we in touch with them right now?" he asked. He was thinking hard. If someone, perhaps the SAS sergeant who worked the area, had been ambushed, then it was good odds that the Indon was probably further forward than everyone had originally anticipated. He wanted Recce to wait for the main body to catch up before they pushed on.

"I think we can raise them – they're sitting still waiting for the others to catch up, sir," said Robin nervously. "I took it upon myself to advise them to wait."

"Well done, Robin, I was going to say exactly that." Johnson clapped his lieutenant on his damp shoulder. The room was stuffy to the point of stifling, but none of them cared. The excitement in the room was tangible.

Lieutenant McGregor put the microphone to his mouth. "Alpha Romeo, this is Alpha Charlie Oscar calling. Do you read, over?"

They all listened. There was a long pause, then the radio crackled, a voice whispered, "This is Alpha Romeo, did you say Charlie Oscar is there? Over."

The major took the microphone. "Yes, Tom, this is Nigel; can you give me a situation report? Over." he said in clear. No one was using codes very much at this time.

The radio crackled, again the whisper. "We came across an old ambush, dead Indons and one of ours, Iban tracker. The chaps we have with us think he is one of theirs. They pretty sure he's one of the trackers that came with the man who lives with us, you know? It looks like he's now either a prisoner or wounded somewhere in the area. They seem to think there has been quite a fight that moved around all over the place.

There are several dead Indons and they found a lot of blood in one location where it looked as though someone, who might be wounded, had stayed and fought them off. Shell cases all over the place, over."

"Are the guests still with you? Over."

"Four of them left with one of the Ibans to follow the trail they picked up of two men going west – two, not one, and the other man is not the other tracker! That's a bit of a puzzle. The other four with two Ibans are staying with me; they're well up front of my position, over."

"Good. Wait there until your backup arrives, then call in, over," he ordered.

"Willco, out."

There was silence in the earthen cave as men thought about what had taken place at the ambush site. Major Johnson had some sense of the loneliness of the single man, or was it two now, who had been fighting for their lives in the depths of the jungle. Who was this other man? he wondered.

Here at least they shared the danger with others around them. It was hard to grasp how isolated those two must be feeling now.

This gave the major time to digest events. The radio-man Witley swiped a cockroach off the map onto the floor. He had gotten into trouble the last time because he slapped it onto the map, which now had a dirty brown stain on it that could have denoted an unexplored range of mountains. When he had done it the last time the major had caustically remarked, "The SAS and others went to a lot of trouble to get the salient features in this area right, corporal. We don't need you to provide features on the map that do not exist!"

The sergeant major came in with some tea from the cookhouse for the two officers. "I thought you might want some refreshment, sir," he said.

"Thank you, Sergeant Major. How's morale?"

"Couldn't be better, sir. Now you are back," he added with a grin.

Major Johnson nodded and sipped his metal mug of sweet tea flavored with condensed milk, reflecting on the life in Kuching compared to his here. He gave a mental shrug. This is where he wanted to be and where he would stay until it was over, and then he would go back and take his medicine. He wondered how many hours it would take for the remaining platoons, the 3rd and 5th, to catch up with Recce platoon– not too long, he thought.

"Witley, put me in touch with the colonel, would you, please?"

Major Johnson gave the colonel a full update on the situation as he saw it and also reported the news of the strange ambush that had been reported. He wanted the information passed along to Major Stanford. The colonel thanked him for his report and agreed to pass the information along, then they broke the connection.

Major Johnson was dozing on his bed when the radio crackled again. It was now six in the afternoon and the heat of the day outside was beginning to lessen. All the same, he was soaked in sweat from simply lying on the canvas frame.

Witley answered. "We have you one-by-three, Alpha Romeo, say again?"

"Main party has arrived, over."

"Got that," said Major Johnson. "Put Alpha Three-Four on, over."

Captain Romney-Smith came on. "All together now, Charlie Oscar, glad to have you back." His whisper over the air sounded faint. Witley turned up the volume control.

"Listen up and acknowledge, Alpha Three-Four. Bivvy down for the night but tomorrow you are to proceed with all due caution towards the target. It's a fair chance that they've planted ambushes along the way, over."

"Roger that, Charlie Oscar, over."

"If you're bumped, get good grids and get back to me ASAP. We have fire power, over."

"Roger that. Our guests have a good idea of the grids, over."

"Good luck, out."

Major Johnson sat back and wondered what else he could be doing. If there was some way to get men into the area by parachute he would have asked Major Stanford to consider it, but the trees were well over a hundred feet high, some nearly two hundred. How could a man parachute into that without getting into a real mess? He suspected that the SAS could, but no one else he knew.

He called HQ and asked where the Gurkhas were at that time and was told that a lot of them were to the east of his position in Tebedu, too far to do much good. Not only that, they were finding traces of incursions in their areas and were out trying to flush the Indon from the bushes themselves. It seemed as though the border had come alive with Indonesians. He asked if some could be sent to Padawan as backup behind the Green Jackets.

The colonel came back an hour later and told him that he could have the reserve company, consisting of a mixed bag of new Light Infantry recruits   – about forty in all – and a few seasoned Riflemen and the NCOs who were training them. These men were getting ready and would accompany thirty Gurkhas. They would arrive the next day at dawn. Johnson decided that he would have to make do with that. He was confident that his men could take the fort back if the Indons were not too deeply entrenched, and he did have the Aussies after all, who could pound it back into the mud again if they had to, even at that range.

Then he had an idea. "Sergeant Major, please go and find the Australian officers and bring them here. I want to talk to them."

Within minutes, two tall Australian men dressed in the usual greens, but with the Australian felt bush hats and insignia, came into the cramped sanger. Johnson knew Lieutenant Troy well, and the other man, he discovered, was Captain Leslie Scott of the Royal Australian Artillery.

He motioned them to sit down and told Lieutenant McGregor to join them, then he told Witley to get the whiskey out, and when they all had a glass in their hands he toasted them. Each man gulped the fiery liquid.

"Captain," Johnson said, "I want to borrow your chopper for a couple of hours."

Captain Scott looked surprised and a little alarmed. "Where are you going, sir?"

"I want to go where my men are, Leslie. It's important."

"I see, sir." He sounded uncertain.

"It's a very normal request, Leslie. I have men in the field, about to go into action, and I should be there with them. I intend to leave you in charge, as the senior officer." He didn't look at Robin, who he was sure was disappointed. "Robin will act as your liaison officer with the Regiment, both at the front with me and back at Kuching. The Sergeant Major here is the man to muster the troops. There is a very good chance that I will need your guns as backup. Will you do this for me?"

"OK, sir. If it's today, we don't have a lot of light left." Leslie was looking excited at the prospect of being in command.

"Not today, I need to set it up with my people."

"OK, sir."

Major Johnson called Kuching and spent half an hour persuading his reluctant colonel to allow him to move forward with his men.

"They are my men out there, sir, and they were my men who went under at Sapit. While I have a lot of faith in Richard, I truly feel that is where I should be, sir."

"I shouldn't even be talking to you, Nigel, but I suppose I can't stop you. For goodness' sake, be careful and make sure that this goes well. Your future depends upon the success of this."

"I know, sir." He didn't want to dwell upon the unspoken situation regarding his future. "Thank you very much, sir."

"Good luck."

He walked out of the bunker, calling the sergeant major to come with him, and went off to find the Australians.

"We need to talk disposition of reinforcements as well, Leslie."

That got the captain's attention. "Reinforcements, sir?"

"Two groups of men are coming in at first light, a large platoon of Gurkhas and a platoon of Green Jackets. The Gurkhas are to stay with their choppers and fly to the same co-ordinates that I will be using. They will be met by men from the Green Jackets I will leave there at the helipad and to guide them in to my position.

"The Green Jackets who come in are to be dispersed around the perimeter of Padawan at your orders, but the sergeant major will know what to do with them. That right, Sergeant Major?" he asked his man.

"Yessir, no problem, I'll work with the captain to deal with their arrival, sir," barked the sergeant major happily.

"Join me for a tour to familiarize you with our layout," Johnson ordered the two Australians. They walked as a tight group around the entire perimeter on an impromptu inspection of the defenses while on the way back to the command sanger. The men in their trenches and bunkers made it clear that they were delighted to see him back.

"Get me Captain Romney-Smith, will you please, Witley?" he said when they got back to the radio shack.

"Yessir."

Captain Romney-Smith came on with a whispered enquiry.

"This is Nigel, Richard. How long will it take you to clear a patch for me and reinforcements to land in tomorrow, about a thousand yards behind your position? Over."

There was a long silence, and then, "About four hours. Are you coming in? Reinforcements did you say? Over."

"Yes. Make it large enough for a Wessex. I will head for this co-ordinate. I will come in first after you have sent confirmation that the hole is cut. See if it fits and then get going in the morning, over." He provided Richard with the new co ordinates.

"Roger that, we will make a hole. Over."

"Thanks, Richard, out."

It was time to eat a meal and settle in for the night. The whole camp stayed on stand-to and meals were given to the men in relays to ensure that no position was left unattended. Major Johnson dined on compo spam and rice curry with his and the Australian officers and the sergeant major in the Sanger, listening to the radio.

At one time, eerily, the radio came to life and they all sat up to listen for a call-in. It was late in the evening. But what came over the air was a conversation between two American pilots in Vietnam who were about to attack a bridge. The men in the sanger listened fascinated as this freak radio conversation, thousands of miles away, came over the air for a couple of minutes. Then it went quiet and they heard no more. In the silence that followed, the men looked at one another.

"I wonder how they'll do with that war," said the Major reflectively.

*　*　*　*　*

The next morning after stand-to, the major had another whispered conversation with his captain.

"We sent men back to the RV at first light, sir. They should be done in about four hours."

Barely able to contain his impatience, the major acknowledged the information. He looked at his watch. It was six a.m. so they would not be in the air until ten, and then not on the ground until about eleven. He wanted a full day to go for the ridge so he had to consolidate his position and make sure he knew where the enemy was before he began. They waited.

183

Then they heard the sound of helicopters in the distance. Major Johnson went out to greet the men, leaving Lieutenant McGregor at the radio.

He met Captain James Robinson as he disembarked with his Gurkhas. Very quickly Major Johnson outlined the plan and told the captain to settle his men for a couple of hours before they remounted for the last leg out. The Gurkhas formed into a group over on the side of the Milo stand and squatted down to await events.

The sergeant major quickly took charge of the Green Jackets newcomers, dispersing them among the older soldiers around the perimeter.

The camp of Padawan settled in to wait for the men in the jungle to prepare an RV.

Finally they received the message from Captain Romney-Smith that there was a hole in the jungle and they could come in.

There was a brief pandemonium as the sergeant major and Corporal Smith rushed about getting the major's kit, weapon and some rations together. Then he was herded out of the sanger, still issuing instructions, towards the Bell helicopter with its bubble front that was revving up on the Padang.

He had a hurried conversation with Captain Scott and the two lieutenants, telling them to stay on the radio at all times and be ready to accept co-ordinates for fire if needed, then he was on the chopper and lifting off.

The men on the ground turned away from the downdraft, their backs hunched, holding on to their floppy hats as the dust from the chopper's ascent blasted them. The men from the Gurkha platoon were making ready to embark even as he took off.

It was only when he was up in the air that Major Johnson wondered if he had done the right thing. However, the die was cast now and there was no going back. He wanted to be with his men when they went into action and that was that. He was glad that he had the colonel's blessing. What would the brig do, court martial him?

They flew fast and low in a straight line, the pilot constantly checking his bearings and occasionally making a call to the men on the ground. Within what seemed to be a very short time the pilot pointed, and they could see the high ridge where Sapit was located and the border beyond. The pilot slowed the aircraft and went forward cautiously. Both the pilot and the major were looking for the hole in the jungle that denoted a helipad cut for their arrival. The major tapped the pilot on the arm and pointed off to the right. A flare had gone up from out of a small opening in the canopy below.

They banked low over the trees and carefully approached the opening in the jungle. It was easily big enough for the small Bell helicopter to settle into, and the pilot went down confidently. There were armed men off to the sides and one who guided the chopper down with hand signals. As soon as he saw that he could jump, Johnson took his rifle and pack and stepped out onto the sled-like runners and then nodded to the crewman. He jumped the last few feet, landed well balanced, and scuttled off out of the way. The chopper immediately lifted off, cleared the trees, then headed back the way it had come. The jungle seemed very quiet after the roar of the chopper motors had died away in the distance.

Major Johnson listened while crouching near some bushes, as did everyone else in or near to the clearing for a couple of minutes, and then Sergeant Frostell from the Recce platoon came to meet him. His jungle greens looked very lived-in by now, and Johnson registered the blue cross in the middle of his hat. This had been mandated by Gen HQ some time ago as the Allied forces consisted of men from the Gurkha regiment, Green Jackets and others. Distinguishing one another in the gloom of the jungle could prove difficult when a life hinged upon a nervous trigger finger and a quick decision. Now all British and Commonwealth troops wore a small light blue cross on their jungle hats.

"Welcome back, sir, good to see you," said the sergeant.

"Glad to be back, Sergeant, are we all set? Then let's go."

Without more discussion the major joined some of the men from Recce section as they moved out tactically at a fast pace back towards the main unit. The Gurkhas would be coming in very soon after; the remainder of the section would guide them in.

They could hear the sound of the choppers that would bring the Gurkhas in within minutes as they moved off.

Several hours later, deep in the jungle at the site of the ambush where it looked as though the SAS man had fought off the Indons, the three platoons of British soldiers waited quietly in hiding. Their officers and members of the SAS conferred.

With the major were the senior SAS man, Sergeant Mike Denning, who was squatting with Captain Romney-Smith,

Lieutenant Tom Hammond, and Lieutenant Michael Powell, with their platoon sergeants in a shallow depression looking at a crude map of the region by torchlight.

The other SAS men of the four-man patrol with their two trackers were well forward of the Green Jackets positions, watching the jungle ahead. They had sent word back that there were a lot of signs that the Indons had been around, so everyone was on high alert.

The Green Jackets were in a defensive perimeter at all points, while in the center were radios, the major with his officers, and senior NCOs. The British soldiers were settling in quietly as they could; there would be no bashas this night. The jungle insects began to bring their calls to a deafening crescendo.

Later, a soft challenge went out at the rear of the British lines and was answered by a cheery-faced Gurkha soldier. They had covered the distance very quickly indeed. There was a hurried conference between the major and Captain James Robinson. The Gurkhas were to stay close behind the Recce platoon and move up to join them if a contact was made, to add beef to the center. The Gurkhas settled down for the night with the Brits.

Sergeant Denning pointed to a spot on the map near to the ridge base they were headed for. "We are here, with about two thousand yards to go to reach the base of the ridge, sir," he whispered.

"What's the terrain like from here on, Sergeant?"

"It's thick with *baluka* patches, some primary, and then a steep climb to get up the hill. It might be wise to spread the platoons out and have my people guide them towards the target from several angles, sir. If they're waiting for us, it will be at the base of the ridge and then at the top, where they can retreat to."

The major agreed. He didn't want to end up with all his men bogged down in some narrow enclave while the Indons potted at them from some higher elevation.

"We move out at dawn," he said.

There was no point in trying to move around in the dark, either now or in the early hours. No one would be able to see and the noise would certainly alert any Indons. He was confident that his men could move stealthily into a counter-ambush position if they could detect the presence of Indons early enough.

He was relying on the SAS and their trackers to do this for him. The whispered conference continued for another half hour, then the group of men broke up and headed for their respective places in the nearby jungle. The large body of men spent a restless night waiting for the dawn.

The major waited until he was alone with Captain Romney-Smith. "You do know why I came out, don't you, Richard? It was nothing to do with your competence. That isn't in question; I simply had to be here."

He could make out the flash of teeth as Captain Romney-Smith grinned in the dark. "I won't say I'm not a little disappointed, sir. But in your place I would have done the same. Your place is here."

The major nodded in the dark. "Thanks, Richard, that means a lot."

In the trees some distance away, some long-armed baboons hooted, defining their territory to one another. Down on the ground the British troops tried to find a comfortable way to rest throughout the long night.

Rendezvous
Chapter 16

Jason stared into the dense thickets all around them. They had been walking – more like hobbling. The sergeant now had a crutch that Jason had cut from some thick sapling so he could make better progress, but it was still very slow – along in a westerly direction for about four thousand yards if Sergeant White's map and estimates were to be believed, and it had taken many hours. Jason was unfamiliar with the fine measurement of distance in yards, but it made sense somehow. Sergeant White thought that they should be coming to some slopes before too long that would take them up into higher elevations.

They were resting. Jason had dumped the Bergen but held onto his rifle, as did Sergeant White, who was lying propped against the pack facing back the way they had come. He had mentioned to Jason that he was a bit surprised that they had not been followed and worried about it. Jason was equally nervously looking ahead of them into the seemingly endless depths of the jungle, wondering when they would be ambushed again. He was soaked in sweat, his filthy clothes chaffing him under the arms and his crotch. He itched all over from the bites of the mosquitoes and other insects.

Once again they had a look at the sergeant's leg. It was swollen and obviously painful but aside from the occasional grunt if they knocked it against a tree in passing, or if he had to lift it higher than usual, he endured it without comment. Jason might not have been medically trained, but his common sense told him that they would have to do something fairly soon or it would go septic, and then the man would be in deep trouble.

"Once the land starts to move upwards you'll have to leave me and go on and look for a good place where we can bring in a chopper," the sergeant said.

"Are you sure, Sarge?" Jason asked.

"Yes, I can get into some kind of hide and stay with the Bergen. You can move faster without it. Just take your belt kit and a bottle. All you have to find is a fairly level place on the top of a small hill where a chopper can get in. Then you can come back for me."

Jason didn't say anything. His biggest fear was that he would get lost and not be able to retrace his steps once he had found a place.

As though reading his mind, White said, "Do you know how to read a compass?"

"Yeah, I did map reading in boys' school."

"Good, then follow a bearing and count your steps. Use a piece of string with knots to count off every hundred steps. Pay attention to your surroundings and keep looking back along your trail, don't weave about."

He gave the compass to Jason with the threat that if he lost it he would be in such deep shit that he would never resurface. They agreed on the bearing using the silk map that Sergeant White dragged out of his map pocket. He estimated that they were somewhere in the region of the mountain called Bukit Knuckle, still very close to the border. He also thought that there might be a village a few thousand yards off to the west, but that was not an option for the moment.

Jason was awed by how sure the man was of his position. As far as he knew they were somewhere in Sarawak and most probably on the wrong side of the border. But he had learned to trust the quiet-speaking sergeant; it helped keep under control the panic that constantly lurked just below the surface.

They munched on the meager rations that Sergeant White dug out of the Bergen. Jason estimated that they were almost out of food, but as they had not eaten that morning it was imperative that they ate something. The sludge of the curry and rice mixed with a tin of sardines tasted like nectar, and Jason sucked every drop out of his plastic bag. They then put every single piece of rubbish back into the pack.

His various and numerous sores were itching, particularly the bites from mosquitoes and other denizens of the jungle. He scratched without thinking. But Dave noticed and admonished him, "Try not to scratch because you will open them, even a little, and then they will become septic ulcers. Very painful, and then you really get sick."

"Jesus, is everything in this stinking hot-house bad for you? My crotch and underarms are sore as hell!"

"No, but that is one thing we find ourselves treating even the Dyaks for. Starts as a little bite for one of the kids, which then gets infected because they scratch it; not long after, it is as bad as a raging boil. You've probably got Tinia, that's why it's sore."

Jason sighed and with an effort restrained himself from scratching.

Later on, he left Sergeant White lying deep inside a thicket that still gave him a decent view of their back trail. It was also far enough off the trail to allow people to miss him if they were concentrating on the main track. He pointed out signs of their passage to Jason and made sure he tidied them up: a deep footprint in the loam, a broken leaf here or there. Jason knew enough by now not to leave unnecessary signs. In spite of the labor of helping the sergeant to hobble along, they had been very careful, the sergeant insisting that he pay attention to what they were walking into and how they moved through the jungle. They had not cut their way through anything, much to Jason's surprise, either going round dense areas or over rotten logs and being very careful to make sure that there was nothing lying about on the other side.

In fact, once there had been. As they peered over one large log, to Jason's horror the thing behind it had risen up and they were face to face with an enormous snake. Both men stood stock still, their rifles pointing directly at its huge head. There was a double 'snick' as two safeties came off. For long seconds the three had stared at one another in total silence, and then the huge snake had gone down and slithered off into the depths of a thicket. Jason had felt sick with fear.

All Sergeant White had said was, "Couldn't have been very hungry."

Jason had glared at him.

"What the fuck was that? A python?"

"No! A king cobra. Nasty fellas, those!"

Jason felt a little queasy.

Their progress had been painfully slow.

He felt a lightness and some release as he made off. Overhead he sensed that the weather was about to get worse and prayed that it would not rain until he made it back to their base. He moved with exaggerated care, using the compass more than he needed to, but it was all new and he was terrified of losing his way. In this manner he still made good progress and had counted about four hundred paces when he heard what he thought was the sound of water rushing in the distance.

Not knowing what to expect, he slowed down even more and made his way cautiously towards the sound. As he approached, the sound of rushing water became the dominant noise and the normal sounds of the jungle became muted by comparison.

Very carefully he moved towards some high trees and peered round the large roots of one when he came to it. Below him, down a steep bank, was a fast-moving stream. It tumbled down large rocks and spewed over some barriers of rotten logs and storm detritus, making for a series of short waterfalls. His eyes searched the other bank carefully, but he saw only the dense jungle with high trees. Going down on hands and knees, he crawled forward to lie in the shrubs on the bank overlooking the tumbling water. It would be a difficult job to get the sergeant across this, he thought glumly. On the other hand, they could refill their water bottles and take care of that problem.

He peered up stream but could see no sign of danger, then did the same for the down stream side. Again he saw nothing. He crossed the stream by jumping from one wet rock to another and made the cover of the other side, thankfully without any sound of alarm. Rechecking his bearings and his back path, he continued forward. Now the land began to rise sharply and he was soon struggling up another of the steep hills that are so common in Sarawak.

Fortunately it was not one of the high ridges that he had encountered near Sapit. After half an hour of cautious climbing, he came towards the summit to find to his delight that the jungle seemed a lot thinner. Glancing about, he saw that for the first time since he had left Sapit he could get a good view of the sky. He turned and gazed back across the jungle. The view was intimidating. As far as he could see there were hills similar to the one he stood on, all of them clad in dense jungle. He barely acknowledged the beauty he was looking at; his concerns were too pressing.

He turned back to stare at the green-clad summit of his particular hill. To his surprise, he noted that around the summit in a large round space most of the tall trees were absent; some lay where they had been felled in a tangle of limbs and trunks. It was clear that the hand of man had been present. Warily he moved forward to get a better look, and could see that some point the area had been cleared, burnt, and crudely cultivated, then allowed to return to the jungle. He supposed that the local Dyaks might have been the farmers at one time. Nonetheless it looked useful. He realized that he would have to clear a little more of the jungle but not that much to allow a helicopter to drop into the space. He felt elated, but then thought of the effort it would take to get the sergeant across the stream and up the hill.

He stared up at the sky. Thunderheads had formed and it looked like rain again. He gave a mental shrug. He was soaked through all the time now and felt that some more wet was not going to make a lot of difference. For the first time in a day he began to feel the slash on his leg. He glanced down at his calf, but it was tied tight with the rags of his face net. The cut had become painful, however. He sat down to have a better look, taking the crude bandage off. He didn't like what he saw. The long slash was inflamed and there was puss along the ridges. It felt sore. He retied the bandage, resolving to try and wash it in the stream when the opportunity presented itself.

Jason found the sergeant with difficulty, although he congratulated himself that he did at all. The rain commenced as he made his way back down the hill so that by the time he reached the stream it was torrential. As it was he almost walked past the hideout, and the sergeant had to whisper loudly to him to catch his attention.

They huddled together in the hide and waited for the rain to pass. Sergeant White wanted to move off as soon as they could so that they would be on the hill before nightfall. Jason was not sure that they would make it but agreed they should at least get to the stream. They were out of water.

Two hours later – late afternoon by Jason's reckoning – they approached the stream. Jason reconnoitered the area again and then filled the bottles. He was glad the sergeant had tablets, as he had nothing.

Sergeant White was looking very pale in the evening light that filtered through the leafy roof. The stream opened a space for them to see fairly clearly so Jason took a chance.

"Sarge, we should bivvy here for the night and then take the hill in the morning. It's a heck of a climb, and you are not in good shape right now."

White nodded reluctantly. "You're right, Jason; we have to do something about the wound as well. I have to get the bullet out."

Jason started to sweat. "Oh shit!" he thought.

"We'll have to take a chance with the water, it's probably full of muck and other horrible bugs, but we have to clean the wound with what we have after you've taken out the bullet."

"Me, Sarge?"

"Yes, you, Jason, wake the fuck up! I have to get it out and you have to help me," White whispered fiercely.

Jason nodded dumbly.

"I'll take you through it but you have to do it. OK?"

"OK, Sarge, whatever you say."

White told him to get the Bergen and set things out. There was a sharp Swiss knife in one of the pockets, and plenty of dressings, as well as a basic first aid kit with antibiotic creams and plasters. Jason even found a suture kit, which the sergeant put aside.

"I'm going to take another morphine dose when we start but I'll still be awake. Help me get my pants down."

He struggled to get his blood-stained pants off with Jason's help and exposed the white, bloody thigh. The whole area looked badly bruised, with yellow and black patches in the region of the wound. Jason gingerly took the dressing off and exposed the lesion. It was swollen and black at the entrance. Lifting his leg painfully, White showed Jason where the bulge was that the bullet made in the back of his thigh. It was black and blue in the vicinity of the bullet and when he touched the area the sergeant flinched. Jason put his fingers on it and felt something hard underneath.

"OK, Sarge, I can feel it," he said, trying not to let his stomach betray him.

"Right, I'll take the morphine and then you get to work. Cut it out and clean the wound as best you can. Make sure you get any cloth or other shit out before you bandage it up."

Sergeant White took another of the small vials he carried around his neck with his dog tags and drank it. It didn't take long. He lay back with a sigh and then turned onto his front.

"OK, Jason, get on with it," he ordered.

Jason took up the Swiss knife and checked the blade: it was very sharp. He applied its tip to the area, hoping to make a cut. The blade barely grazed the skin. Feeling queasy, he dug harder and felt the sergeant jerk. But blood flowed, and he realized that he had to swab it away or he would not see what he was doing. Taking one of the dressings, he patted the wound he had made. It was not very deep. Groaning inwardly he dug deeper and this time the blade went in about a half inch. It felt more like he was tearing at the wound, the flesh resisted his efforts as he cut a slit in the area of the bullet. He was rewarded with the feel of the blade scraping on something metallic. There was a lot of blood and the pad was already soaked. He gritted his teeth and made a cut about an inch long. He then probed for the piece of metal. The blade grated on something and he tried to lever it out. The piece moved away from the blade and he realized that he was pushing it in deeper. Sweating now, he paused.

The only way he could get the piece out was to find some kind of pliers, but they had nothing. He looked about. Quickly rummaging in the Bergen, he dug out the knife, fork and spoon kit belonging to Sergeant White.

"I have to use your gobbling rods to help get it out, Sarg." he said. White merely nodded. Jason went back to the prone body of the sergeant, tapped him on the shoulder and said, "I've found it, but I need these to pull it out. How are you doing?" The bearded face turned towards him. It was gray with pain but White croaked reassuringly, "Just get it out, mate. I'll be all right then."

Jason nodded and then concentrated on the operation. Using the Swiss knife and the handle of the spoon, he managed to trap the jagged piece of metal and began easing it out of the flesh.

He was trembling with the effort when he finally managed to pull the bullet out; it seemed to resist his efforts all the way. There was a welling of dark blood behind the object as he extracted it. Exultantly he picked it up in his bloody fingers and passed it over the hunched shoulders.

Sergeant White took it and turned it over. "Doesn't seem to have broken up into pieces. Now you have to wash everything a lot. Be thorough, Jason."

Jason washed the wound liberally with water from the stream, even going back to replenish the bottles. Later on White rolled over slowly and painfully then sat up.

"Help me put the sulphalidimide into the wound then bandage both holes," he said groggily.

Jason complied, liberally dosing the powder over both holes and bandaging the leg firmly; then he sat back to examine his handiwork. The leg was well bandaged and somehow looked a lot better than previously.

They struggled to get White back into his pants and then rested. The sergeant looked over at Jason. "You did well there, lad. We'll make a soldier out of you yet!" He grinned weakly.

Jason shrugged, embarrassed. "I wouldn't have known where to start without your help, Sarge," he said awkwardly.

"Call me Dave. This should keep until we get back to Kuching."

Jason said nothing. He admired the matter-of-fact way the sergeant saw things and hoped that he was right about them getting out the next day. He contemplated the filthy and ragged man seated in front of him in the twilight. He took in the soaked, torn uniform and the man's thin frame. His beard was now well grown but did little to hide the gaunt, sunken cheeks. Jason noted the feverish eyes but marveled at the determination still there in them and the set of his mouth. The man was just not capable of giving up, it seemed. Jason's flagging spirits lifted somewhat as he thought about this. The wound must have been enormously painful, but the sergeant barely seemed to acknowledge it, forcing Jason to keep paying attention and moving forward.

They decided that they needed to rest the night by the stream, although it presented problems for them if anyone came along. They would never hear anything because of the noise of the gushing water.

Sergeant White, ever cautious, insisted that they move back into the jungle a few dozen yards to a better hide. The light was almost all gone by the time they were in place. The usual jungle chorus of cicada and tree frogs was deafening as they moved, but it at least covered their clumsy attempts to keep quiet.

Jason found a hammock in the Bergen, a single sheet of nylon that the sergeant would normally use to sleep on, and set it up for him between a pair of large saplings. Then as gently as he could he eased his companion up and into the hammock. It was only two feet off the ground but they both agreed that it was better than lying on the jungle floor.

White stayed awake long enough to tell Jason to use his poncho slung from a couple of thick saplings and get himself off the ground, even if it was just a couple of inches. Uncomfortable though this might be, it would at least keep him free of the ants and other biting insects, unlike the night before. The Bergen was hung up on a branch and they both slept with their rifles for company. The jungle gradually quieted as they settled in. Jason slept the sleep of the exhausted.

He awoke to the now familiar high-pitched bubbling call of a Borneo gibbon in the distance and lay there listening to the jungle as it woke up. He now emulated the sergeant who listened carefully to the waking jungle before making a move of his own. Then he rolled out of his makeshift hammock and went over to Sergeant White, who was awake as usual and listening. He pronounced his leg to be feeling better; some color had come back to his gaunt features.

They wasted no time in getting themselves on the way. There was nothing they could do about the camp other than try to leave behind as little sign as possible. The stream presented a real obstacle, as it had gained some water from the rain the afternoon before. Jason took the rucksack over first and then came back for Sergeant White. Despite the care they took, they almost fell in. Jason slipped and found himself up to his waist in rushing water, while his companion hung onto a piece of wood to prevent himself from being swept down one of the waterfalls. They struggled across, Jason taking most of the weight while White held on to the rifles. They got themselves out of sight into the undergrowth on the other side and took a much-needed rest. By this time Jason was really worried about the steep hill they now had to negotiate.

His fears were justified; it took well over two hours – yesterday he'd done it in half an hour. By the time they were approaching the summit Jason was tired and Sergeant White looked even paler under his beard. Both were sweating furiously in their soaked clothes in the muggy air. The rain of the day before had done nothing to cool the air and there were more thunderheads building up overhead. Jason felt that he was living in a sauna and wondered when he would ever breathe properly again. Just as he was relaxing, his legs cramped up. The pain was excruciating and he rolled on the ground holding his thighs.

Quickly White grabbed him by the collar and thrust two white pills into his hand.

"Here, take these and a good swig of water. Can't have you throwing a wobbler now!"

Jason hurriedly threw the pills into his mouth and took a good drink of water. Within a couple of minutes he felt a lot better, but the incident had scared him.

"Christ, Dave, what was that?" he asked, blinking stupidly through the sweat pouring into his eyes.

"You've lost a lot of salt; been sweating all this time and no replacement. That can cause a Wobbler. Didn't you feel yourself drying up?"

White was a lot tougher than he looked; in spite of the wound he hadn't 'thrown a Wobbler' as far as Jason could tell. But then, he knew all about looking after himself in the *ulu*, Jason supposed. The sergeant propped himself against a tree and pronounced the location near perfect for a heli lift.

Jason, feeling somewhat better, was set to work to clear some of the more obstructive saplings and smaller trees. The new foliage was almost waist high, but he managed to find a patch that needed only a little help from his gollock. The sergeant had denied him the use of the razor sharp Gurkha Kukri that he carried, saying that he needed to keep it sharp and the gollock would do. All the while Jason worried about some huge snake lunging out and biting him.

While he was thus occupied, the sergeant got out a green metal box with a couple of dials on its front. He turned a switch and it clicked. Satisfied that it was on he pulled out a small antenna in its base and set it out in front of him. He made sure it was working and then leaned back and rested. Jason had never seen one of these devices, so when he had finished he came over to watch. Nothing seemed to be happening but the sergeant assured him that it was a search and rescue beacon and seemed to be working.

"I'm not exactly sure where we are within about two hundred yards, but they can get a cross-bearing on this signal, if they get it at all," he told Jason.

Jason squatted near by, his rifle tucked into the crook of his arm and shoulder, watched the clearing and dreamt of rescue.

They both heard the noise at the same time. It came from down the hill they had just climbed. They stared at one another. There was another sound, as though someone had slipped and fallen. Then they heard the exclamation in a language neither wanted to hear.

Without a sound Jason grabbed the Bergen and White pocketed the SARBE. There were some dense thickets off to their left about fifty yards away, but seemingly on an impulse White gestured frantically for the Bergen. Jason handed it over puzzled. The sergeant rummaged deep inside the rucksack and brought out a green plastic-looking object. It was curved slightly and had terminals at the back, attached to which were two long thin insulated green wires.

"Tie this to that tree, the outward curved surface facing this way," whispered the sergeant urgently. He handed a roll of gray duct tape to Jason. "Hurry! Make sure the terminals are at the back and we can get to the wires."

Jason complied, hands shaking, as he feverishly wrapped the strange plastic thing against the tree where they had been sitting. White hobbled over and forced it round so that it pointed back the way they had come at about waist height. He checked that the battery was in his pocket, then they crawled off hurriedly in the direction of the thicket, dragging the wires with them.

It seemed that they had only just made cover, about fifty yards away, when Jason looked back and thought he saw the heads of some men materialize in the area where they had sent off the signal.

Although it was only a brief glimpse, he knew they were Indonesians; something about the headgear they wore told him that they were not British or Gurkha. They were not in the least interested in keeping quiet. Rather they were excited and kept pointing in the direction of the saplings and small trees that Jason had recently cut down.

He was quite unprepared for what happened next. There was a deafening bang and the foliage where the soldiers were standing seemed to explode in all directions. The heads vanished in a small cloud of smoke and flame. There was total silence for a few seconds, then the screaming began.

Jason was stunned. "Oh Jesus!" he croaked. He received a kick from White and turned from his gaping to find the sergeant gesturing frantically for him to get moving. He was hurriedly pulling the wire towards him and rolling it up.

"Claymore," the sergeant whispered with a savage grin. "Our secret weapon, we've got one more. Can't leave the wires; they'll follow them."

They moved quickly to put distance between them and the enemy, and none too soon. While the horrific screaming continued, others of the soldiers who had survived began to shoot wildly in all directions. Bullets began to whip overhead and tear at the branches of the saplings and trees. A banana tree took the brunt of the shooting but it was well away from their location. It was clear the soldiers had no idea where the two Brits were hiding.

Sergeant White was cursing quietly. "The bastards must have cut our trail somewhere back by the stream. I hope they don't have any real trackers with them, if they do we're finished."

Jason looked at him tensely. "They seem to be all over the place, Sarge. Is there some kind of offensive going on?"

"Yeah, maybe, I wish I knew if our lot were aware of this or not. After Sapit I guess they have to be. That means we have to survive until our boys take the region back. We have to get out of this place as quickly as we can, come on."

They crawled deeper into the thicket. At one point Sergeant White gestured to Jason to hand over one of the HE grenades.

As Jason watched, he fashioned a trip wire with the grenade tied to a sapling.

"That's in case they find our trail." He whispered. They moved on.

Gradually the noise of the shouting Indonesians and the shooting became more distant. They continued steadily on their bellies, stopping to listen to the sounds of the jungle from time to time. Jason was actually cringing at times, waiting for the inevitable burst of gunfire that would end it all. They continued to hear voices for some time and it was evident that the Indons were looking around the place for sign of them, but no one came close enough to present a threat.

There was a rumble of thunder nearly overhead and he prayed that it would rain and cover their tracks. He was physically sick with disappointment and wondered how Sergeant White felt. The man was hard to read but Jason was sure he had to be disappointed too. Jason had no idea what they would do if they escaped from this situation, so he simply followed the slowly crawling sergeant, his mind numb.

They were a good three hundred yards from their original position when it finally began to rain. Although they were deep in cover they still got soaking wet. They lay for a while resting on their bellies, faces almost in the mud, trying to keep their rifles out of the filth of the jungle floor, listening to the roar of the rainstorm overhead.

The storm moved on and White began to move again. They continued downhill, this time on the other side of the knoll they had hoped to use as a heli pad. Slowly they clambered down the steep sides, holding onto branches and trying hard not to leave slide marks and other sign as they went. It was difficult for Jason to heft the Bergen, hold his rifle, and help Sergeant White all at the same time. The man did very well, considering how painful his leg must have been. He rarely showed his pain, seemingly totally focused upon their escape.

It was while they were negotiating the last tangle of vines and saplings near the bottom of the hill that they heard the chopper. They lifted their heads and turned towards the distant sound. The chopper seemed to be coming almost directly towards them. The beat of its blades went overhead quite fast, but then it slowed as it came towards the hilltop they had just vacated. It was being careful, still very high, a difficult shot for anyone on the ground. The chopper hovered for a short while at altitude and then moved in a large circle as though looking for any kind of sign to bring it in.

"They can't see any sign of us and are suspicious. We'd normally be out there waving hard to get them down. They won't land without some signal." White whispered.

He might have been heard by the pilot. The chopper, an RAF Wessex by the sound of it, climbed higher into the sky then moved off towards the north. Jason heard it go with a sick feeling of despair; he felt hope drain out of him. He wanted to weep and cry out, but apart from a suppressed choke he held it in.

Then they heard the muffled bang of the booby trap going off and more shooting, but as they were on the edge of the other hill by this time they could hear nothing else, and no bullets came in their direction. Jason cringed anyway, someone had tripped it and probably died. He wondered just how close the enraged Indons might be.

Sergeant White looked concerned. "Well, now the bastards know we were there for sure. They'll redouble their efforts to find us. Come on, Jason, buck up, lad. We'll just have to tab it out of here. We're not dead yet. Think of sex or something but keep your mind busy," he admonished with a tired grin. He turned away and hobbled on.

Jason watched him go. "How does he do it?" He asked himself. "*Sex! For crying out loud!*" Megan flashed briefly into his mind but he was too tired and scared to continue with that line of thought.

Slowly and carefully the two men made their way across the thickly wooded base of the hill and began to follow a compass bearing that White set, leading even further west. Jason just wanted to lie down and give up; it seemed futile to go on, but he was not about to argue with the sergeant. His growing respect for the man kept him going.

Late that evening when White considered them more secure, they bivvied down for the night. They were once again among the high primary jungle trees with their path less clogged with tangled undergrowth and new *baluka*. The going was much easier but as Jason had already learned, they were more exposed because of it.

They ate the last of their rations and shared some of the remaining chocolate that Jason had been hoarding. He was so tired he almost forgot to make his crude hammock until White reminded him sternly that he needed to get a good night's sleep, not one spent on the jungle floor. Dragging his leaden limbs about, Jason slung his own hammock and, after making sure the sergeant was comfortable, he rolled into his rubbery bed and fell instantly asleep.

* * * * *

At the RAF base in Kuching a group of lean, bearded men in jungle green clustered round an Air Force corporal who was playing with the dials of a long-range radio. The voice of the pilot of the RAF Wessex helicopter crackled in the speaker.

"We got to the L-P on the grid reference where the triangulation indicated we might find something; it's a knoll with a clearing on top, but there was no sign of Delta Whiskey.

"Seems odd though. The boys in the back are sure that the area has been cleared by someone quite recently. They checked it out carefully with binos. The signal was off too. There seemed to be lot of damage in one area to the *ulu* but no sign of anyone at all. Over."

One of the men in green took the mike off the corporal and asked, "None of the usual indicators that someone wanted to get out? Over."

"Quite frankly, old chap, it was a bit spooky. My boys in the back think there might have been a fight. It didn't look right, if you know what I mean. Over," said the pilot.

The man who had spoken earlier was Major Stanford. He turned to the others and they looked silently at one another.

"He might have been bumped before the chopper got there and had to scoot."

"Does sound fishy, Boss," one of the others offered to the major. "Dave knows all the rules. If he didn't show himself then there was something wrong. It's got to be him after the damage the Green Jackets found just north of Sapit. It makes sense now, him being all that way west and all."

"I'm beginning to think that the Indons are all over the area. We've had reports on a lot of activity up and down the border since they bumped Sapit," Major Stanford said. "Let's assume that the Indons are there. Dave was heading for Sapit when it got clobbered. He gets ambushed, but manages to escape. There's evidence of that. Then the Indons might have pushed him way over to the west, which makes some kind of sense too. But there is the added puzzle about another person with Dave. That has to be his tracker, I suppose, although Major Johnson mentioned that the boys checking out the ambush site think not. This is not making sense. We need to look at the map – isn't there a Long house somewhere over there?"

The others nodded. "We should try to insert some of ours to see if we can get to him before the Indons do, Boss," someone said.

The major agreed. "Don't forget that we have Lieutenant Norris and the other three on his trail now. I just hope they don't run into too large a group of Indons."

He turned to the single RAF officer in the stifling room.

"Thanks, John, your help is much appreciated, as always. I'd tell the pilot to come in. I think it would be dangerous to push his luck. We'll see if Sergeant White contacts us some time later; that is, if he can."

The men in green hefted their AR 15 rifles and walked silently out of the room. The corporal working the radio turned to the RAF Officer of the watch and pointed his chin at the departing men.

"If anyone spooks me it's them, sir," he said with feeling.

The officer grinned. He took up the microphone and called the chopper. "Come home, Bravo Sierra."

As he left the radio shack he said, "Rather them than me, Corporal. I don't think I could last a day in that stuff. I hope that poor bugger gets out alive. I don't know how that man can be managing out there on his own. I really don't!"

Iban

Chapter 17

Light filtered into the jungle slowly. There was not much to indicate that another day had started, just a gradual change in the illumination surrounding their base.

As usual Jason woke sharply, wide awake on the instant, but he continued lying on his platform, the habit having formed to listen before moving. He didn't want to go into the day, he was so depressed. For all his respect for the sergeant, he didn't have any confidence that they were going to get out of this predicament any time soon. In fact he was beginning to think that they were near to finished. They were out of food and the Indons were on their trail. It seemed only a matter of time now.

Slowly he got out and found Sergeant White already standing shakily on his good leg, leaning on his crutch while checking the bandages on his other. They were caked with blood. It looked as though the wound had broken open during the last difficult journey up and down the hill.

Wordlessly Jason dug into the Bergen and found some more pads; he saw that they were the last of the dressings. Sitting the sergeant down he took off the old bloody dressings carefully and gasped. Several whitish little creatures writhed off. He peered closer and swore.

They both studied the wound. To Jason it looked red and swollen; however, he didn't see any pus; the creatures were all round the opening in the wound.

"What the hell are they, Sarge?" Jason asked, but he knew already.

"Most probably maggots, so they're not such a bad thing – mind you, I'd feel better if they weren't there," White said.

Jason gulped, helped to clean off what they could, and retied the new dressings. Then he collected their things.

There was no whispered conversation. Jason made sure their bivvy was clear of obvious sign while White took a bearing, and they set off without breakfast. Jason picked up the rucksack and slung it over his shoulder on one strap.

They had only gone about four hundred yards when Jason noticed that they were following some kind of trail. Not only that, but squatting on a log watching them was a half-naked man. They instantly had their weapons up and pointed straight at him: the double snick of safeties being taken off sounded loud in the tense silence. For a couple of seconds they stared at one another. Then the man waved at them, stood up, grinned, and hurried forward, speaking to them in a quick low-toned chatter.

Sergeant White whispered back in the same language, then they sat the sergeant down, and while the man squatted facing him they began to talk.

Jason was happy enough to stop; it was hard work half-helping the sergeant and the Bergen at the same time. The damned thing weighed at least fifty pounds *and* it didn't have anything left in it of much use, he reckoned. He would have ditched it if the sergeant hadn't insisted that they keep it. He crouched next to the other two as they chattered animatedly for some minutes.

Finally, White turned to Jason. He seemed relieved.

"This man is from one of the villages not far from here. Nighan came to the village and told them about the ambush. They have been watching for the Indons. Nighan did what he was supposed to do: 'shoot and scoot.' He just scooted a bit further than he should have."

"How did he know we might be along?"

"I don't think he did. From what this fellah tells me, Nighan thinks we were topped. But they heard the noise yesterday and figured that trouble was on its way, so he was there to keep watch."

"So what do we do now, Dave?"

"This man tells me the village is not far from here, only about three thousand yards. He's going to go and get help. We should get off the trail and wait for them."

There was some more whispered conversation between the half-naked man and Sergeant White, and then he stood up and vanished up the trail to the north.

Jason helped White get off the trail and into some thick cover and there they waited for rest of the morning. They said almost nothing, the sergeant having told Jason that sound carried a really long way and they were anything but safe yet. The jungle gradually quieted as noon approached. The cicadas were muted and their regular sound plus the *chonk-chonk* of the barbets high in the trees was the only indication that the *ulu* had not completely gone to sleep.

Jason crouched at the edge of the thicket, watching the trail for any sign of Indonesians, while the sergeant rested. He watched a huge tarantula work its slow way over a dead log near by. A long line of red ants wound its way along the base of the tree they were squatting next to. At one point he started as a huge lizard scrabbled rapidly up the trunk of another tree. His leg hurt but he was damned if he would complain about a mere scratch if the sarge didn't about his leg.

His thoughts drifted to Penang and Megan. He wondered what she might be doing and wished fervently that he could be on a beach with her. Given their current run of luck it didn't seem very likely, he thought to himself. He day-dreamed of their time together while the jungle quieted around him and Sergeant White slept.

Around noon he tensed, aware that there were men on the trail. They were mostly naked, each man wearing only a loincloth. They walked carefully and watchfully as they moved. He reasoned that they might be the Ibans they were waiting for, but did nothing until they stopped on the edge of the trail and looked over towards their position. Jason stood up and silently lifted his hand to them.

Jason recognized Nighan the tracker who was with them. He grinned, flashing his gold tooth, and indicated Jason and White to his companions. He made his way swiftly over to them and all but embraced White, clucking and whispering urgently when he saw the damaged leg. Sergeant White whispered back animatedly and pointed to Jason, then to his leg. Nighan looked at Jason with respect in his dark eyes, he nodded as though in approval.

Within seconds there were ten Ibans of mixed ages clustered about, silently observing them. Nighan showed them that Sergeant White was incapacitated and after some whispering a couple went off to cut some poles. The others squatted on the jungle floor and observed the two of them. Three others headed back to the trail and vanished in the direction the two had originally come.

Before long a litter had been prepared and Sergeant White was lifted onto it, four of the men taking a corner each. Jason held onto the Bergen and placed the sergeant's rifle alongside him on the litter. White was very pale under the dark beard and looked feverish, but he grinned at Jason nonetheless and indicated that he should follow.

Silently the party moved quickly along the trail. Jason could not believe how quiet they all were. None of them had footwear and barely any clothing. All carried ancient shotguns or spears. A couple of the younger ones even carried bows, while one had what looked like a blowpipe as well as his spear.

The party arrived at a large clearing in the jungle alongside a river, three hours later. Jason was very thankful that at last there were other people helping them. Only the night before, he had almost given up all hope of ever getting out of their predicament. Now he felt a tiny ray of hope brighten his world.

There were many people about, most of them scantily clad. The boys and men who gathered about them all wore little more than a pouch in the front, held up by a string around the waist or a thicker belt of cloth. Most of the men were armed with an assortment of weapons that they carried casually.

He noted the absence of modern weapons: there were mostly spears and the usual long knives in carved wood scabbards, and several old shotguns that looked more dangerous to the owner they were in such bad condition. The one carried by Nighan was without doubt the best on display.

Jason also noted that the men and boys over a certain age were tattooed. It seemed the older they were the more tattoos they wore on their shoulders and backs. Almost all of the older men seemed to have some kind of tattoo on their throats. He wondered what that meant.

All the rumors he had heard about headhunters came back and he glanced nervously about, wondering if they were to become victims themselves. However, the inquisitive chatter and cheerful grins of welcome coupled with the obvious relief manifested by Sergeant White was reassuring.

They were taken towards a tall, very long building of attap and bamboo that appeared to be set high on many stilts. As they came closer Jason could see that the long house was parallel to a sluggishly flowing river. It was the first time he had been in any kind of large clearing and it felt good, even if the happily grinning people were close around them and making him nervous.

He tried to look happy and smiled at the men and boys clustered about. They were pointing at him and his equipment, and seemed interested in his rifle in particular. He gripped it even tighter.

The party of men and their new visitors were greeted at the base of the long house by a small delegation of elderly looking men. Again these men were almost naked, heavily tattooed, and Jason noticed that their ears had huge holes in them so that the lobes were almost down to their shoulders.

One of them, a thin wizened man with a haircut that must have been done by putting a bowl over his head and cutting round it, stepped towards them. He nevertheless looked fit as he walked forward, and he stopped in front of the litter that carried Sergeant White. He started to talk to them and the men surrounding them. Nighan chattered back and pointed to the sergeant and Jason as though explaining their presence.

The men put the litter down and Sergeant White struggled to get up. Nighan and Jason helped him to his feet. He joined in the conversation, although it was clear to Jason that he was fumbling with the words. In spite of that, there was communication. The old man turned to his colleagues and spoke rapidly to them as though explaining the situation. There was some head shaking and some nods, but Jason could not divine which way the argument was going.

Sergeant White pulled Jason over and leaned thankfully on him, allowing his leg to relax.

"They're nervous because of the Indon activity in the area and we could present them with a big problem if we're found here. The head man is discussing the situation with the others. I don't think they mean us harm, there's no love for the Indons in this area, but they have to look out for themselves as well."

"What will happen if they decide not to help us, Dave?" asked Jason nervously.

"We'll probably have to scarper with Nighan and make it on our own."

"Will they turn us over to the Indons?"

"No, I don't think so. As I said, there's no love lost between them and the Indons. Besides, our boys have been here before and helped them with medical problems. We don't mess with them and they appreciate that."

The conversation was interrupted by the head man turning and coming back to the three men. He wore a serious look on his face. He began to talk rapidly to Nighan, waving his hands at the jungle behind them, but then he seemed to say something reassuring, for Sergeant White relaxed his hold on Jason.

"He's saying that while they are very worried about the Indons being all over the place he will allow us to stay for a while and rest. He respects the help he had from the British, and would like to help us. If the Indons are spotted coming here we have to leave," White translated.

Jason was not sure how he felt about that. He was immensely relieved that they were at last among others who could provide some help and food, if even scantily. On the other hand, he did not feel that they were terribly welcome. They were viewed as bringers of potential disaster for these people.

Sergeant White was helped up one of the steep ramps towards the verandah of the huge longhouse by several men. Jason followed with the Bergen, wondering what he would find once they were inside.

He was pleasantly surprised at how spacious the interior of the attap and bamboo building was. Once on the verandah that extended all the way around the building, he could see across the river. It was about twenty yards across, a muddy, slow-moving strip of water that wound near the longhouse in a shallow loop. On the bank nearest the building were several long dug out canoes. The ground between the house and the water was stripped of trees but dense with ground cover and old stumps. On the inland side, he noticed that the jungle had also been cleared, and from his vantage point he noticed that it resembled the top of the hillside they had recently vacated. There was cultivation of some kind going on but he could not tell what.

He didn't have much time to loiter, however; they were beckoned into the entrance by not only the head man but also a group of curious women, who stood smiling at them. Jason noticed with a gulp that none of the women wore any clothing above the waist. Keeping his rebellious eyes from traveling in the wrong direction was an effort. He smiled again nervously as he followed the limping sergeant and his helpers into the gloom of the building.

They were guided along the center of the long spacious room towards a place that appeared more private. Sergeant White was lowered onto a tightly woven mat where he lay back and rested. He looked very pale to Jason.

"Are you OK, Sarge?" he enquired.

"Yeah, for the moment at least. Leg is beginning to hurt a lot though. We'll need to fix that soon."

Jason nodded. He wondered if they would be fed, he was so hungry he was getting a headache.

He need not have worried. He had laid the Bergen down within easy reach, although he still hung onto his rifle. He sat down cross-legged next to the sergeant and looked around. While he could not see down the entire length of the very long building because of the gloom at the far end, it was easy to see that there were divisions laid out that clearly marked the family spaces. He even saw mosquito nets here and there over sleeping mats. To his curious eyes there did not seem to be much privacy in the place. He wondered how they managed.

His thoughts were interrupted by Nighan, who nudged him and pointed. Some women were walking towards them bringing what looked like food. Indeed it was. Jason began to salivate at the sight and tantalizing smell of the white rice piled high on a shallow basket. Cooked vegetables arrived with the rice, and sure enough a pottery container gave off a wonderful aroma. He saw that there were some strips of what he supposed were baked fish in another. With much chatter and smiles, the women placed the food down near them and then left them to it.

Nighan wasted no time. He gestured to Jason to start eating, scooped up a handful of rice, quickly made a ball out of it, then dipped it into the bowl of vegetables and seized a morsel of the fish. Popping the whole thing into his mouth, he chewed with obvious satisfaction. Nervously Jason followed suit and found that the glutinous rice had a nutty flavor. He had no idea what the vegetables were but didn't care at that moment what he ate, as long as it was cooked. The fish had a very strange taste and was not that nice, but he still ate it. Sergeant White sat up and joined in. The three of them made short work of the food, swilled down with some water from their bottles. Jason wondered what these people drank but was afraid to ask.

With a contented burp he sat back against one of the supporting pillars and relaxed. Sergeant White ate sparingly and then lay back with obvious relief on the mat.

"Jason, we are going to have to dress this wound. We'll need some boiled water; I'll ask Nighan to get that, but you need to have a good look and make sure nothing is going septic."

Jason nodded. "OK, Sarge. When do we start?"

"Now's as good a time as any; after that, I could do with some rest."

Nighan said something rapidly to the sergeant. They talked to and fro for a couple of minutes.

"Nighan wants the shaman to come and take a look at the leg."

"You mean the witch doctor?" asked Jason incredulously.

"He's known as the *manang* here. It might be politic to do so, as long as he doesn't put any kind of shit on it." He spoke to Nighan again, who go up and went off to look for the *manang*.

Sergeant White pulled his pants down and once again Jason gingerly undid the dressings and lifted them off. The wound was still swollen and the hole black; the maggots were still there. He brushed off a curious fly and stared at it. The redness seemed to have increased in the area and his instincts told him that was not a good thing. Sergeant White turned over onto his stomach so that Jason could look at the other side of the wound. It was seeping some slightly yellow fluid. When he mentioned it, the sergeant's reaction was muted.

"I need to get to a hospital," he said briefly.

"How's the pain?"

"Bearable for the moment, but I'll have to use some more morphine tonight to help me sleep. I barely slept a wink last night."

Jason was surprised. In spite of his despair he had slept well. But then, he chided himself, he didn't have a bloody great hole in his leg.

Nighan came back with a woman who carried a bowl of steaming water. He said some thing to Sergeant White, indicating the water.

"He says it was boiled, he saw it himself," said the sergeant. "You need to wash it well, Jason, even if it does hurt me."

Jason got on with it, and for the next twenty minutes sponged and wiped the edges of the holes on both sides. Sergeant White's thigh muscles jerked as he endured the pain with clenched teeth, sweating through the ordeal.

Finally, relieved to have finished, Jason replaced the old pads, because they were down to two sets left. Sergeant White was gray with pain when he lay back and rested. Jason found another light mat near by and placed that over his legs to prevent any chill, although it was densely humid and nearing mid day.

Just as he finished, a group of Iban men came along the center of the longhouse towards them. Nighan stood up and greeted them respectfully. One of the men wore a bone ring in each ear, the lobes of which bore huge holes. He came forward and squatted next to the prone sergeant. Jason moved back against the house pole and watched. The other men clustered about, squatting or sitting on the mats in a semicircle and watching the proceedings solemnly.

The *manang* began to chant in a low tone and gradually raised his voice as he proceeded. He drew back the mat covering Dave's legs and looked at the bandaged wound. He brought forth two sharp sticks and poised them over the wound. For a horrible moment Jason thought he was going to dig them into the leg. But the man proceeded to simulate the cutting open of the wound and appeared to be pulling something out with them. He chanted in a singsong voice as he did so. To Jason it seemed as though he was having a conversation with something at the same time, ordering and commanding.

Finally, much to Jason's relief, he came to the end of his ceremony and nodded towards the prone sergeant, who spoke briefly back as though thanking him. Then the *manang* stood up and walked off.

One by one, the other men got up and left as well. Jason settled himself on a mat near to Sergeant White. He felt emotionally worn out; he needed to simply lie down and take a break. He dozed off.

A clap of thunder woke Jason late that afternoon. He jerked awake, frightened, wondering where he could be for a brief moment, then it came back to him and he glanced over at Sergeant White, who was still sleeping on the mat near by. Jason got up, went to the nearest doorway, and peered out at the sheeting rain. He noticed that the Ibans were not bothered by the downpour. Some were clustered near other openings and children were playing, screaming and splashing each other from the large puddles already forming.

The interior of the longhouse was quite dry, but he detected a slightly heavy smell, as though it was well lived in. On impulse, he began removing his sodden jungle boots, and it was with a sigh of relief that he undid the laces and pulled them off, then peeled off the soaking socks. He stared at the white wrinkled objects that were his feet. They were raw and looked as though he had kept them in hot water for hours. He took off his shirt and his shredded pants and, clad in only his tattered skivvies, he went outside onto the verandah. The rain was so intense that he felt as though he was walking into a cold pressure shower. The drops bounced on the bamboo surface of the verandah and created a kind of water surface that covered his feet. Jason wriggled his toes with deep appreciation; the sensation was intensely pleasurable. He opened his mouth and let the rain pour in. He had not brushed his teeth for days so it was a real pleasure to be able to take a mouthful of water without worrying about wasting it and then to rinse his mouth out.

The rain beat on his closed eyes to the point where it was painful. His chest and legs were sore in places where clothing and straps had rubbed him raw. It was cold but he didn't care, it was cleansing and invigorating.

Dripping, he walked back into the gloom of the longhouse to find Sergeant White sitting up watching him. Alongside was Nighan, who was smoking a thin cigarette with obvious enjoyment.

"You seemed to be having a good time out there, Jason." Sergeant White said almost enviously.

"Hey, Sarge, it was wonderful, do you want me to help you out there?"

White seemed to be thinking about it, and then abruptly he started to remove his shirt. Jason carefully helped him get his boots off and then his pants. Lifting the sergeant up onto his good leg, they staggered outside into the pouring rain. Nighan watched them go with a look that said he wanted nothing to do with them, they were mad.

While it was not coming down so hard by now, it was still a delight to simply stand in the rain and allow it to wash off the grime and refresh their bodies. They stood there, faces up to the sky, mouths wide open and drinking the clean water. White gave a bark of laughter, and Jason, with a surprised look at the man, responded with a shout of his own. The next moment they were shuffling about on the verandah in a clumsy kind of duet, shouting into the rain at the top of their lungs.

The rain lessened and there was a flash of lightning that lit up the clearing, followed by a clap of thunder that seemed directly overhead, and the two men came to their senses. Making their cautious way back into the longhouse, careful not to slip on the wet bamboo, they sat down on the mat and grinned at Nighan. He spoke to White with a grin of his own.

"He said that we are mad, the gods have put leeches in our ears to suck out what little sense we had in the first place."

Jason grinned at Nighan. "He's right about you, Sarge, you like it here. I didn't volunteer, so I'm the only one left with any sense."

He started to shiver. There were some brightly colored cloths near by, so with a look to Nighan to see if it was all right he took one and began to dry himself. He also noticed that the sergeant was looking cold, so he passed one to him.

Neither wanted to get back into their stinking uniforms, so they wrapped the cloths round their waists as sarongs. Nighan pointed to Jason's leg. With a start he realized that he had not been paying much attention to it lately. The four-inch slash was raw about the edges and half an inch deep. There were two more leeches attached to the sides, which he gingerly removed. Nighan had a look and said something to the sergeant.

"He says that you will need to have that fixed before too long – it won't heal in this wet."

"What am I supposed to do, Sarge? I don't have any medical stuff and if I did I wouldn't know what to use."

"Look in the Bergen. I might have some more of that sulphalidimide powder. You need to try and keep it dry while we're here. In any case, I need some on my leg."

Jason rummaged in one of the pockets and drew out a small tin container colored green with writing on it. It looked like a foot powder tin.

"That's it, Jason. Powder you leg with it and then put some on both sides of my leg.

They spent several minutes attending to their medical problems. Jason found that large patches of his skin, particularly around the area of his armpits and crotch, were raised and becoming red.

"It's Tinia," explained Sergeant White. "When you get back the medics will paint you green or purple to kill the fungus; then you'll look like one of your hairy Pictish ancestors!"

"Fungus!" Jason exclaimed. "I'm turning into a fucking mushroom! Not surprising, considering how manky and wet it is here. Man, but it itches and burns, that's what it does," he complained.

The storm moved on and a few rays of afternoon sunlight blazed out. Jason, who was nearer the entrance, spotted a flock of huge birds flying overhead. But then he looked harder and gasped when he realized with a prickle of superstition that they were not birds but bats. They were enormous and flew high over the longhouse and the clearing in absolute silence. The hair on the back of his neck and his forearms stood up. With a shiver, he stored it away in his memory as yet another aspect of this strange country.

The smell of cooking pervaded the air all around. The cooking huts were set apart from the longhouse, also on stilts and joined by the walkways high above the ground. There were three such huts and they were filled with women preparing the evening meal. Men were starting to come into the longhouse and children were running between the family platform areas, screaming excitedly and playing with each other.

Once again some women came to the three men and presented them with rice and boiled yams. Small portions of roasted meat, which Jason guessed might be pork, gave off a pleasant smell. Whatever it was, it tasted better than compo rations any time.

The Iban people were content to give the three men their privacy at the end of the long building for a while, but eventually the elders came towards them and sat in a semicircle around the newcomers. They were smoking the thin, rank-smelling cigarettes and began to ask questions.

While they were talking – he didn't understand a word, of course – Jason had the opportunity to observe them. The men were all very senior from what he could tell. He guessed that the wider the hole in a man's ear the older he was. You could almost put your fist through some of them. Their hair was worn in a high fringe on the front, exposing a high forehead, but was bound at the back in long braids. Some wore bangles on their legs above the calf and on their wrists. Their Asiatic eyes were large but their brows were not deep, so the effect in a couple of cases was to give the elder the look of a wise, wrinkled elf. One wore a cap that hugged his close-cropped head, enhancing the similarity. They wore only a wide loincloth with a large piece dropping down the front. In spite of the fact that they were almost naked, they still struck Jason as being very dignified.

They squatted comfortably, the soles of their feet flat on the mats covering the bamboo slats that made up the floor. They leaned their elbows on their knees and gestured with their forearms and hands. There was probably not an ounce of fat between them. Jason could see that most of the men were heavily tattooed all over their backs and upper arms and down their thighs. Most of them had a tattoo on their throats and Jason looked at it apprehensively. Some had tattoos on their fingers, which he asked Sergeant White about.

"Those are the ones who have killed more than once and taken heads – notice they are the older ones," said the sergeant out of the corner of his mouth.

Jason nodded. He hoped that these men would not take it into their minds to have a couple of extra trophies for their collection.

It was not long, however, before many more of the tribe came to have a look at these two strange creatures the jungle had thrown up. The evening meal was over and this was entertainment. The younger men clustered at the back of the crowd while the older women took what seemed to be their rightful places in among the elders. Young women with only a waist sarong wrap and girls and boys mostly naked except for a skimpy loincloth sat on the outside of the ring of people. The very young were completely naked.

As the men were tattooed so were some of the boys who were into puberty. Jason did not see any tattoos on the women. His rebellious eyes could not but appreciate some of the fine features of the younger womenfolk and their figures. He told himself to get used to it.

They all seemed to be talking at once, except when Nighan or the sergeant said anything. Then they all listened intently. But as soon as they had finished there would be a babble of conversation as they discussed the information. The elders were polite and seemed to give thoughtful responses to questions posed by the sergeant or Nighan. But several times they looked concerned after something was said by either of the two visitors. Jason learned from the sergeant that Nighan had family connections to this tribe. His uncle, one of the elders who dominated the conversation, had been a tracker for the British in Malaysia during the emergency.

Dusk settled in to the clearing outside and the jungle began its evening chorus, the cicadas and tree frogs vying with one another to make the loudest and most persistent noise. Lamps were lit and immediately huge moths began to show up, fluttering and banging against the dirty glass. A large jug was placed in front of the elders. Each one took a shallow wooden bowl and poured liquid from the jug then drank it with some relish. They indicated to Nighan and the two Brits to take some while another jug did the rounds among the men and women of the crowd.

Sergeant White took a bowl and sniffed it then took a large sip.

"It's known as *tapai*, Jason, and they expect you to drink it."

Jason took his bowl gingerly and sniffed the liquid. It was clearly something fermented and looked like muddy cider, but he was not sure.

"Its rice or tapioca wine brewed locally; think of England and swig it down," said Sergeant White.

Jason became conscious that he was being observed by the whole crowd as he tentatively brought it to his lips. It smelt sour but he wasn't going to let the side down, so he took a healthy swig and knocked it back. There was laughter as he finished and people pointed and grinned at him.

The liquid settled on his stomach and threatened to come right back up, but he swallowed again and gritted his teeth in a grimace of a smile, hoping desperately that it would stay where it was and he would not disgrace himself. Then he began to feel warmth flowing through his limbs that helped him relax, and he took another drink. It was more palatable this time, and he grinned back at the assembly. There was more laughter and pointing.

Jason estimated that he drank four of the bowls of smelly fermented wine before the roof began to move about. By this time many of the crowd had left to go to sleep, their day beginning at dawn. Some thin mattresses were presented to the three men and they were once again left to themselves. To Jason the mattress was the most comfortable thing he could remember lying on. He closed his eyes and began to snore.

Sergeant White and Nighan continued to talk to Nighan's uncle about the ongoing situation in the locality of the longhouse.

It had been made clear to both that if there was an Indonesian sighting they were to get out and head into the jungle without delay. To Sergeant White this was presenting a problem, as his leg was not getting better. He asked for plenty of warning should the event take place and was assured that the Ibans would know very early on if an Indon patrol was coming.

It was late when they eventually went to bed themselves. The longhouse settled down for the night and the jungle creatures came out of hiding to explore the clearing. Wild pigs lurched through the cultivated area looking for food, and a dog barked at the end of the longhouse as it heard them. High in the trees, about a quarter of a mile away, an orangutan male woofed to attract females, even as he slouched in his nest of light branches and leaves.

Closer to hand came the repetitive *tock-tock* of the pied hornbill.

Longhouse
Chapter 18

Jason woke with a headache. The brew he had drunk the night before was still sitting in his stomach and he wanted to retch it out. His bleary eyes took in the pillars of the longhouse and the sounds of activity further down the long floor. Instinctively he looked around for his rifle and found it near to hand. He touched it to reassure himself that it was still there and then glanced over to the sergeant and found him awake but still lying on his pallet. He looked exhausted but alert. His face was becoming more gaunt each day, Jason thought. The sergeant saw Jason looking at him and grinned at his puffy face.

"They like to party," he said unsympathetically. "You should have stopped at the second one."

Jason nodded and rubbed his eyes. Then he sat up. "Shit, Sarge! Where are our clothes?"

"The women are washing them."

"Bludy 'ell. Is this some kind of hotel?"

"They don't understand why we wear clothes in the first place. But we'll get them back this afternoon and hopefully they will be dry and still have buttons on them."

"How's the leg, Sarge?"

"Sore, but the sulpha is helping some. You need to clean the weapons."

"Right you are, Sarge."

"Dave will do."

"I know, but it's difficult...Dave."

"You've done well up to now; keep it up, Jason."

Jason glowed. "Thanks, Sarge... er, Dave."

He set about cleaning his rifle very carefully and then the AR 15. It presented some problems, as he had never encountered a rifle like this one before. Its rotating block was new to him and ingenious, but when he mentioned it to the sergeant, Dave told him, "It's light and can fire rapidly, but it doesn't pack the punch that the SLR does, that can shoot through some of the thinner trees even! But with this thing the block can jam overnight so that you can't cock it. Imagine that! You have to stamp on the bloody cocking handle to get it to move sometimes. We always keep one up the spout because of that."

"Yeah, but the SLR can fail to re-load from what the boys in A Company told me – mind you, it hasn't happened to me yet, I've got it on max gas anyway." They fell to discussing the various merits of the British weaponry against the new lighter American weapons that were beginning to show up. It seemed to help Dave take his mind off his leg.

Jason had a look at Nighan's shotgun while he was at it, then they got down to the daily routine of checking the sergeant's wound, cleaning it and re-bandaging it. The leg was beginning to swell and it didn't smell quite right to Jason but he said nothing and tried to ensure that the wound was well cleaned and well covered.

While Dave lay back and rested, Jason took some of the old dressings out of the Bergen, picked up his rifle and went down the long room looking for someone to help boil them clean. Dave told him to make sure his cut was dressed as well.

"If we run out of sulphalidimide powder you can piss on a cut like that and it will keep some of the parasites off. Try to keep the leeches off it," he added.

Jason nodded his understanding. He went out into the open along the wide verandah, dressed in his new sarong, his rifle on its sling over his shoulder, walking towards one of the cooking huts to see if there was anyone there. He came across an elderly woman who was boiling a kettle of water. Jason made his needs clear with much gesturing while the old lady squatted in front of him on the floor and cackled happily and smiling toothlessly at him.

Eventually she understood and got out a deep wooden bowl and poured water in and gave it to him.

Jason would have given his eye teeth to have a cup of tea with the boiling water, but instead took the bowl and placed the bloody bandages in it to soak.

He asked the sergeant if they were going to have breakfast and mentioned his keen desire for some tea. As they were discussing this, Nighan came back and squatted near by. The sergeant and Nighan talked for a while then Nighan grinned and went off.

"He thinks he can get some tea, but you will have to pass on the bloody biscuits, OK?"

Jason laughed. "OK, Dave. I'll take the tea."

Then a thought occurred to him. "Are you going to use that signal thing again, Dave?"

"The SARBE? It's on. Nighan left it out on the verandah – not that that should make any difference. If it's working we'll see a chopper by this afternoon."

"Great! God, I hope its working," said Jason, fervently.

Then he had to get out of the longhouse in a hurry. He only just made the edge of the jungle before he had to squat. His insides felt like they were made of water. Later, feeling weak and miserable, he made his way back to the longhouse. He was becoming more and more worried. With Dave looking worse by the day, the last thing he needed was to have an attack of dysentery. To make matters worse, his skin felt like half the parasites in the jungle had taken up residence in it. He itched from numerous bites that had ulcerated and around his leg where it had been exposed. Dave had pointed to a myriad of tiny bites and told him that they were probably chigger bites. There were remedies for both, he told Jason, except that they were not in a position to be wandering about the jungle looking for cures just now.

"Go and get a couple of blocks of cold charcoal, Jason, and eat it. Wash it down with the rainwater."

"Charcoal, Dave?"

"Yeah, it seems to soak up poisons and bugs. Don't argue, lad, go and get some. I could do with some myself. I don't know how it works but it does. First you have to help me off this platform. I'm going to make a mess otherwise."

Jason helped Dave down the steps to the edge of the jungle and waited while he did his business, and then they made their painful way back to the platform, where Dave lay back, clearly exhausted.

Jason went off and obtained some charcoal from the old woman he had talked to earlier. Puzzled, she gave him four small chunks of the black pieces from the cold fire. He brought them back and copied Dave as he crushed the blocks and ate about two spoonfuls, washing them down with water from the bottles.

Nighan brought some boiling water, and after rummaging in the Bergen they found a small plastic bag of tea. Jason felt like he was in heaven when he took his first sip of the brew.

Although Dave was not feeling well he seemed to welcome Jason's company and began to open.

"You did a stint at the Jungle School, didn't you, Jason?" he asked.

"Yeah, we did. Although the Pioneers are usually left alone, we got lumbered and had to do some training."

"Seems to me some of it paid off," said Dave dryly.

Jason grinned. "I suppose you're right. I guess it did, thinking about it."

"We had an instructor who has been in Malaya since the war. The stories he told us!"

"Give us one then, Dave. We're not going anywhere just yet."

Dave took another sip of tea. "Well, you know there are elephants in the *ulu*?" Jason nodded.

"Well, this guy has been in the *ulu* for far too long, since the war, I think. He collects butterflies! Quite famous he is, and collects them for all sorts of museums now. One day he's running about in the *ulu* chasing a particularly good specimen when he comes across a wide trail. Now wide trails are unusual in the jungle, as you might have discovered recently," said Dave in that laconic way of his. Jason grinned ruefully.

"Anyway, he charged down this jungle highway waving his net at the butterfly until he ran into a very large and wrinkled trunk. It was a granny elephant and she was looking to make him into mud between her toes. He turns and runs off as fast as he can down the very trail he has just come up, with the granny right behind him. He could feel her right behind him, so in a crazy attempt to scare her he turned and whacked her on her trunk. He told us that she just pointed it at him like to say. "That's it, Mate, you're done!" Then they were off again. The only thing that saved him was a jump off the edge of the trail down a steep bank into a river about fifty feet below him!" Dave chuckled.

"The moral of that story is, don't ever use any of the highways in the jungle; they have been put there by elephants. If a herd hears you coming, the first to run away are the bulls, who are rank cowards. Then the females go and hide with their young. However, the old grannies with a bad case of PMS hide and ambush the unwary. So ends your first lesson in jungle lore." He sat back looking tired.

"Wow! Is the jungle always so hostile, Dave?"

Dave sipped his tea.

"No, you're wrong, Jason. The one thing they teach us at Jungle School and pound it in is that the jungle is neutral. It's not out to get you, but you have to know your way around and be careful. Look at these guys, the Ibans – they live very happily here right in the middle of the *ulu*.

Jason had to ask. "Are there elephants in Borneo, and tigers?"

"There are elephants, even around these parts, but they prefer the flat lands more. No tigers here, but I ran into one in Malaysia once," responded Dave.

"Holy cow! Where?"

"We were up in the north, above the main Cameron Highlands area where there used to be lots of them; now I don't think there are that many. In any case, they are not the baddies in the *ulu*, it's the elephants."

"So how did you meet the tiger?" Jason persisted.

"We were on a long patrol, four of us, as usual. Night time, just before dawn, you know, the false dawn that you get with the *ulu*?

"It was my stag; the others were all tucked up in their hammocks while I was watching. One mistake we made was to bivvy up too near to water. Its noise drowns out a lot of other ones that you want to be able to hear. I became aware that I was being watched, kind of a sixth sense. The hair on the back of my neck started to rise. I thought it might be someone, the CCO are still around in places. It felt really bad. I was squatting, so I moved very carefully around until I was facing the direction of the stream. At first I couldn't see much but then I made out this huge shape. I realized I was staring back at a tiger. He was drinking on the other side of the small stream and watching me."

"Bloody 'ell!" exclaimed Jason. "What did you do?"

"Nothing! We sat and watched each other for about five minutes, about ten yards apart. He could tell I wasn't alone, but although I was armed to the teeth, I felt about the size of a mouse! Well, soon after that he disappeared into the darkness. The next morning I told my mates, who told me I was bullshitting. But when we went over to look, there were the pugs. Bloody huge they were!"

"Blimey!" Jason looked at the sergeant with more respect than ever. He had spent most of his army time avoiding the soldiering side, but somehow this man was living a real life. He felt humbled by it.

"I'm getting tired telling you all these *Just So* stories," said Dave. "Now let me rest." He lay back and shut his eyes.

Jason looked at him for a few seconds, observing the flush on Dave's bearded face. He was getting more and more worried but didn't know what to do. He sipped the tea he had been given, thinking about it for the hundredth time.

Later that morning he went out onto the verandah at the front of the longhouse and took a look around. The clearing was a hive of activity, mostly women and young children, although there were a couple of elders squatting near one of the canoes by the river. Jason realized that most of the men and teenage boys were gone. He wondered if they were out in the jungle checking on the Indonesians.

He negotiated the steep plank ramp down from the longhouse and walked in bare feet down to the river. His feet looked less white and sickly now, and he was enjoying being barefoot for the moment.

He acknowledged the elders who glanced at him, nodded, then went back to their discussion. Jason looked across the river and wondered how deep it was. If the Indons came they would have to escape across the river first. He guessed it might give them the edge and they could even hold them off from the other side. He looked back at the longhouse and realized that that was not an option. They could not involve the Ibans in a firefight.

He glanced up stream and saw some children playing in the water, splashing and screaming happily, while nearby some young women in their sarongs were washing clothes – green clothes, he realized: his uniform. They were beating the material on rocks and then rubbing it hard against another, rolling it and then repeating the exercise over and over. He wondered if there would be any buttons on his shirt when they had finished.

Other women were washing rice in large baskets in preparation for cooking.

He saw a couple of small boys throwing a net out onto the river near by. The whole scene was so peaceful he began to wonder how he had stumbled into this world after the hell of what he had recently been through. He seated himself on the bank and relaxed, enjoying the calm scene.

There was a small splash across the river near the other bank. He gazed intently at the point where the splash had occurred and then to his surprise he saw a kingfisher splash out of the water and fly onto a low branch with a flapping silver shape in its large beak.

He reveled in the sight of the flashing blue and white colors, and with a pang of longing he realized that he wanted to share the moment with Megan. Then he realized how absurd that feeling was. Why would he want to bring her here to this place? The more he thought about it, however, the more he wished she was here sharing the wonders of this jungle haven, and an ache began in his chest.

The wistful thoughts were interrupted when he was visited first by a couple of dogs who sniffed him all around, clearly unused to someone like him being in their universe. Then he noticed that some hairy, muddy pigs were beginning to drift his way and moved to sit on an upturned canoe to get away from them. For a while, some very small children came and stood around him, chattering and pointing to his rifle until an elderly woman came over and scolded them away, smiling apologetically at him. She chattered to him, smiling. Although she was old, he noticed her short teeth were in good condition and wondered how they did it without toothpaste. He longed to brush his teeth; they felt furry and filthy in his mouth.

His attention was drawn to a group of women and children playing with a tiny monkey near the longhouse steps. It looked like a baby. He walked up the muddy beach to watch as they laughed and teased it gently, allowing it to climb over their shoulders and hang onto their fingers. It didn't seem afraid. One of the women smiled at him and pointed to the little creature. She mimed that someone had killed its mother with a blowpipe. They had eaten the mother and they now had its baby. Jason wondered if they would eat that too. He was, however, beginning to notice that these people, while seemingly primitive, were very gentle to their children and animals.

They were also industrious. The women were constantly active, weaving baskets, washing clothes, washing rice, carrying water and performing a hundred other tasks. They rarely rested and when they did, sitting together as they talked or laughed with one another, their fingers were never still. He realized that they laughed a lot, seeming to be happy in their lives.

Hunger drove him back into the longhouse, where he found Dave awake again and Nighan tucking into the inevitable rice and vegetables. There was fruit this time and something so smelly that he almost gagged.

Dave noticed and laughed. "It's durian, Jason. Try it. This will put a few warts on your nose!"

Jason gingerly picked up one of the slimy sections of stuff from the spiky half of the durian and brought it to his mouth. He almost choked.

"Christ, Dave, what is it?'

"I told you, durian. These people love it. We are being honored, so don't let the side down. Eat it," he commanded.

Nighan was watching, his Asiatic features looking amused, as Jason tried again. This time he got it into his mouth and chewed. Surprisingly it tasted quite nice, giving off a warm feeling to his palate. Still afraid that he would gag, he swallowed and let it sit in his belly.

"I feel like I'm sitting up to my neck in a sewer, eating horse snot!" he said somewhat resentfully. "But it doesn't taste as bad as it smells. I'll say that."

Dave chuckled. "Wait till they offer you some lizard. It's disgusting. Some lizards are OK, and so is snake, but there's one that even I gag on. God help us if they give us *jarit*, I can't keep that down."

"What's that?" asked Jason apprehensively.

"It's a wad of raw pork, salt, and rice mixed, which they bury for a couple of months in some kind of bamboo container. Then they dig it up and eat it while they get pissed on *tapai*. I still don't know anyone in the regiment who can keep it down. Not even Lofty, and he's as hard as they get."

He sat up; Jason noticed that he looked more flushed, even for the time of day.

"If the chopper doesn't show, we have to find some food to take with us, Jason. That could mean dried meat or yams, but we have to start today, so work with Nighan to fill the pack. We have to last at least four days and our compo is used up. You need to bury the rubbish in the pack well outside the kampong, in the *ulu*, where it can't be found by Indons if they come through." Dave briefly talked to Nighan, who nodded.

"But the chopper will show, won't it, Dave?" Jason asked hopefully.

"I hope so, mate, I hope so," Dave said, sounding tired.

Jason continued to eat what was left of the rice and vegetables, then with Nighan he took the Bergen and descended the ramp again. They headed for the jungle nearby. Jason was still without his boots so it was hard to keep up with the leather-footed Iban, but they finally came to a spot within the jungle out of sight of the longhouse. They dug a hole about two feet deep with Jason's gollock, dumped the rubbish from the rucksack into it, and tamped it down with their feet.

Later Dave told him, "The ants will find it no matter what, but at least it will be out of sight of inquisitive Indons if they pay a visit in the near future."

While Dave rested, Jason set out to cautiously explore the longhouse again. He noticed that the construction of the building was entirely of bamboo, palm thatch, or matting made from palms or grass. Rattan cords held beams together and bound the rafters to the central house beams. The whole lengthy building was sturdy and quite waterproof, as he had discovered the day before when the storm came by. Looking up into the depths of the high roof, he could see small bundles hanging from strings, and wondered what they were.

He estimated that there were ten to fifteen different families within the longhouse itself, amounting to forty or fifty people. The sleeping platforms for the various family groups were stuffed with their personal belongings. Baskets were tightly woven and in a couple of cases he saw large earthenware jars that he guessed had been brought in from the outside. For the most part though, he was struck by how intricately made many of the worked items were. These people decorated everything, from the cloth they wove to the patterns they painted on the baskets. Most of what they had seemed to have come from the jungle.

When the Jungle is Silent

As he walked slowly along the center of the longhouse, careful not to step on items lying about, he saw something that made the hair on the back of his neck and his forearms tingle. In one corner of a family alcove high up on the wall, he saw a net, and in it were the unmistakable dusty white shapes of human skulls. Jason gave a start and could not help but stare, but quickly collected himself and looked about to see if anyone had noticed, as there were people in the house, then he walked on as though he had seen nothing untoward. Nonetheless, he was unsettled. It was not news that the Iban and Dyak tribes had once collected heads. But to actually see some was unnerving. He now believed the story of the marks on some of the older men's fingers. Didn't Nighan have some as well as his uncle? He wanted to go back immediately to talk to Dave but realized that the sergeant needed all the rest he could get, so he carried on as nonchalantly as he could.

He was soon distracted by the activities of the women sitting at openings in the walls of the longhouse, and came across a loom with an attractive young woman working it while her child sat near by sucking on something. He was impressed with her ability to weave; the patterns were angular but complex. Over by another opening were some other women weaving baskets, tight baskets that could hold water. Some were huge, which he supposed were for carrying large loads about in the jungle. They talked and laughed a lot among themselves, and as he came up they chattered to him with smiles. He smiled back and made helpless gestures with his hands to indicate that he didn't understand.

When outside, some of the women wore a very wide hat of woven palm, with a centerpiece like a frame that sat the hat on their heads and provided a huge umbrella that shielded them from both sun and rain.

They were often to be seen walking in single file from the longhouse to collect water from the river, carrying perfectly round and polished gourds that had woven handles to them. Jason began to worry about the water and resolved to capture some from the next rainstorm that came over. The water in the river was not as clear as he would have liked.

Later, as the day wore on, he noticed men and women coming in from the jungle along a well-worn trail with the huge baskets on their backs. They walked up the steep ramps to the longhouse and once inside went to another level above the sleeping platforms and poured rice grains into a large round bark container. Jason was impressed – they stored grain and then used it as they needed it;

his farmer's instincts approved and his respect for these people went up another notch or two.

Walking along the bank of the river, wondering where his clothes were, he saw something that made him pause. He had already seen how much the Ibans loved the water. The children played in it constantly while the adults washed clothes and bathed without inhibitions themselves. He now saw a group of three young girls in their puberty watching a mother bathing her baby in the water, but right alongside was a man squatting in the water washing a rooster. It was not taking kindly to the enforced bath, but he persisted, amid much laughter from the young girls.

They noticed Jason watching and by their insistent gestures and friendly smiles he realized that he was being invited to get into the water as well. He was self-conscious about it but they laughed and gestured so he took off his sarong, leaving his skivvies on, laid his rifle alongside an upturned dugout canoe and waded into the water. The mother of the baby picked it up and left, as did the man with the rooster. Jason wondered if it was a fighting cock. He would ask Dave later; there were so many questions he wanted to ask.

Now he was faced with three young women who, although they kept their sarongs on around their waists, waded into the water and surrounded him. They indicated that they would wash him if he permitted it. With a despairing look at the longhouse, he gave a feeble smile, hoping that he had interpreted the gestures correctly, and let them come closer. They proceeded to wash him in the cool water of the river, much to his enjoyment and apparently theirs. It got somewhat personal at one point, and he indicated that he could do all that for himself.

They giggled and chattered amongst themselves. It was also clear that they were flirting with him and he wondered what he should do. It was tempting to take advantage of their flirting and make some kind of move. Then he remembered the skulls and, smiling regretfully, he waded out of the water, retrieved his rifle and wrapped the sarong around his waist.

It was now early afternoon and it looked like rain again, so Jason hurried back into the longhouse and along to the area where Dave was still resting. The sergeant was sleeping when he got there, so he set about preparing to capture rain when it came. They had four water bottles between them and he wanted them full at all times.

He took the nylon hammock sheet out of the Bergen and raised one end on two sticks to a height of about two feet. Then he anchored the other end to provide a slope with a valley in the middle. He reasoned that when it rained he could fill the bottles from the run-off. Within the hour it began to rain and Jason hopped outside with the four bottles and without any trouble filled them all.

He screwed on the last of the plastic bottle-tops as he came in dripping but feeling satisfied, to find Dave awake and watching him.

"How're you doing?" he asked.

"I'll live. You've filled the bottles? Well done. We'll make a soldier of you yet, Jason." The sergeant smiled, but he looked gaunt and exhausted.

Jason grinned, but he watched Dave with concern. The flushed look denoted a temperature that had not been there yesterday and it worried him. They had to get him to a hospital – but how? Didn't this river go north? Perhaps they could take the river and get him to the coast, where they were probably safer and could get help. Jason was pleased that his dysentery seemed to have magically gone away. He felt much better for having taken the charcoal.

But it was clear they could not stay here much longer. Dave was not getting better and the Indonesians could arrive at any moment. He nervously wondered what he was going to do if the sarge got blood poisoning and began to go into a real fever. They would stay this night and then leave across the river. Perhaps he could persuade the Iban chief to provide men to carry Dave.

"No chopper though," said Jason, unhappily.

"No."

"What do we do now, Dave?"

"We get ready to leave tomorrow."

Jason turned away so that Dave could not see the bitter disappointment on his face.

The rain went away and the evening promised to be bright and clear. Jason's thoughts turned to Penang where he had enjoyed the aftermath of the rain with Megan at several places after their first wild encounter at Batu Ferengi. He sat on the mats looking out at the jungle, watching the remaining sunlight as it reflected off the wet leaves. His heart was heavy as he contemplated the thought that he would probably never see her again.

He was brought out of his reverie by Nighan, who came down the length of the longhouse and woke Dave. They talked for a few minutes and then Dave turned to Jason.

"There is going to be a party tonight and we are among the main guests. Somehow I have to be able to sit up, but there will be a lot of drinking. Don't overdo it, and be careful what you eat."

Dave settled back to rest again, and Jason took advantage of the quiet to take a nap. He dreamed of the farm in Wales. It had just stopped raining and the bracken he was wading through was wet and glistened in the weak afternoon sun. He was watching the small herd of sheep move down the steep grass-clad hill towards the gray stone farm buildings below. The two border collies were doing all the work as usual, but this time, in spite of their efforts, one of the wooly ewes broke away and headed straight for the hedge. She disappeared into the dense foliage completely, which Jason found unusual. The hedges on all the hill farms were almost impenetrable barriers to animals except the smallest, such as rabbits.

He ran over to the place where the sheep had gone and found a hole. Going down on hands and knees, he started to crawl into the hole. The problem was that in the hole was a huge tarantula and it looked as though it was going to come for him.

Jason jerked awake with a snort of fear. For a couple of seconds he was completely disoriented. He looked around for his rifle and found it where he had left it alongside him on the mattress. He sat up; he didn't need dreams like that, he thought, sweating. A sense of fear threatened to wash over him. He pushed it aside with an effort.

Looking about blearily, he noticed that someone had left their washed clothes near by in a rough bundle. He separated his shirt and trousers from those of Dave;, they were not really that dry. He checked them out. They were a shadow of their former thickness, it seemed. The left trouser leg had a huge rent in it, making them look more like some kind of green rag than a uniform. His shirt was as he had suspected, devoid of buttons now except for the sleeves. He groaned. He could not keep wearing a sarong, but the thought of getting back into these damp clothes was unappealing.

As dusk settled into the clearing, Jason sensed an air of expectation in the longhouse. There was much laughter and bustle as people began the preparations for the party. He did not see the young women who had been with him in the water and hoped that the incident had passed. However, a man who he had not seen before, middle-aged and well tattooed, came walking up to the three of them while they were sitting waiting for events to begin. Squatting near them, he lit up one of the thin, smelly cigarettes and offered one to each of them from a tin.

He began to talk to Nighan, indicating Jason with his chin a couple of times, his hands making motions as he talked. Nighan began his slow grin that wrinkled his face and made his Asiatic eyes almost disappear into the creases around them. He turned to Dave and they began to talk. Jason was sure it was about him as they were all looking at him by now. He began to feel acutely self-conscious but held his peace, waiting.

Dave contemplated him thoughtfully. "Have you been playing with the women, Jason?" he asked sternly.

Jason had the grace to look guilty. "No! Well, no, not really, Sarge! You see, these girls came up to me while..."

"While what? You made a pass at one of them?" Dave rolled his eyes as though he could not believe he was hearing this.

"No! I didn't, Sarge, really I didn't, promise."

"Well, what did you do? This old boy is here about something you did," said Dave. His bearded face betrayed nothing so Jason could only assume he was in deep trouble.

"I, er, they, three of them, gave me a washing, kind of, in the river, Dave. What could I do?"

"Three of them! What have we here, the Don Juan of the *ulu*? I can't take you anywhere! Are you ever in the shit now, Boyo! Fraternization is a complete no-no. It's in Queen's regulations somewhere, I know it is. " He had that satisfied tone that NCOs get when they have a watertight charge on their hands and the victim is wriggling on the hook.

Jason cringed. "What do you mean, Sarge?" He was sweating now.

"The old boy is asking if you want to spend the night with his daughter, you randy git!" exclaimed the sergeant with a laugh. "He feels sorry for you and wants to make you feel happy."

Jason let his breath out with weak grin, "Fuckit, Dave, you had me sweating over that one! I though he wanted my head!"

Sergeant White chuckled and turned to Nighan and the man who was watching the conversation. He spoke briefly to them and shook his head. They laughed out loud and Nighan slapped Jason on the knee while the old man, still chuckling, stood up and pointed at Jason, said something, then left.

"What did he say, Dave?"

"He said that if you changed your mind you could still live with his daughter. Nighan has told him that you are a good warrior without a woman."

Jason turned to Nighan and said, "Thanks very fucking much, Nighan. So...you told him that I didn't want to go with his daughter, Dave?"

"That's right. You could easily; they don't mind. However, she might have a boyfriend who would... who would not be pleased, and then..." he paused and sighed theatrically, "another head finds its way into the family collection!"

Jason fingered his throat. "I think I need another few cups of that whatchamacallit stuff."

"Tapai?" Dave grinned, although he still didn't look too good. "Not too much tonight, Jason. We have to get out of here tomorrow, one way or the other. I don't know if the chopper is coming. The SARBE might be used up."

They were interrupted by a gong sounding at the far end of the longhouse. They all looked down the length of the building and watched as the ceremony unfolded. Neither Dave nor Nighan had enlightened Jason as to why there was to be a celebration, so he assumed that it was for some sort of party.

He noticed that the women were wearing very pretty sarongs now and were helping other younger girls dress up. There was much laughter and giggling among the groups. The older girls were also wearing decorated nets of string and beads around their necks and many bangles around their forearms. They bound their hair up in buns and wore pretty headpieces as decoration. There were amused smiles as they watched the very young girls copying the older ones.

Decorated mats were laid out, and upon the mats were many plates of food. All kinds of ground herbs, nuts, eggs, and rice were placed in neat rows. Then about five of the well-dressed girls kneeled in a row on one side of the food, their feet tucked under them, and waited; the people behind them, Jason assumed, were their relatives. It was an assortment of older men and women with boys and very young children.

All the while a gong was still sounding down in the depths of the longhouse. The light was still good enough to see by, but lamps were being lit, and these cast long shadows against the walls.

The man whom Jason recognized as being the *manang* walked up to the long line of food and faced the girls. He sat cross-legged in front of them and also waited. After a few more minutes a man walked up to join them. He was dressed in a wide, tightly wound loincloth that left a long tail dangling in front and behind him. He was spectacularly adorned in what seemed to Jason to be a cloak of huge feathers. He realized that they were hornbill feathers, having seen a bird that morning sitting on a rail next to some children. It was a huge creature with equally large feathers and a monstrous beak. Now some of these feathers were adorning the wiry older man, who had them sprouting out of his hair and draped around his neck. A dangerous-looking knife, all of three feet long, hung in a carved wooden sheath at his side.

This forbidding-looking elder sat down next to the *manang* and the first of the ceremonies began. Dave whispered to Jason that the *manang* was blessing the house. The man took a morsel from several of the bowls and put them onto a large strip of banana leaf. Jason noticed he used rice, what seemed to be tobacco, and chicken blood. The food was wrapped carefully, a long string attached. Then another man climbed into the rafters and, balancing precariously, he attached the food on its string alongside other packages already hanging there.

"That's for the local Gods," explained Dave, after he had questioned Nighan.

Once the package had been placed, the music began. The man in the feathered dress got to his feet, drew his long knife and began to dance. The music was primitive drumming, rhythmic and insistent. Jason could make out a stringed instrument that looked like a flat lute and then noticed that it was being played by a handsome youth wearing many bead necklaces and bangles on his wrists and elbows. It had only two strings and made a plinking sound alongside the drums and gongs that sounded more like a large xylophone.

In the meantime the man was dancing, a frown of concentration on his dark face. Nighan explained to Dave that he was miming a journey where he met enemies and took their heads. He cackled with laughter at the expression on Jason's face. The

Rhino-Hornbill ritual is about headhunting, Nighan explained, and was appropriate for this party, as there was a threat of war about and the people of the longhouse needed to be reassured that their warriors understood this and would deal with it.

However, this was not just a party and a ceremony to help promote war. There was a wedding to celebrate as well. Jason noticed two young people who were sitting quietly waiting for their moment as the chief danced. The music seemed to have increased to the point where the man was dancing even harder. He seemed to be dancing himself into a trance. His long knife was flashing about in a manner that looked dangerous. The crowd appeared to like it however and watched approvingly as he went through his motions. There was clapping and calling as the dance came to a conclusion.

Then it was time for the wedding ceremony. The *manang* got up and went over to the two decoratively dressed young people. The young man, who was sitting on a cushion, was dressed in the usual wide loincloth with a decorated front-piece that fell to his knees. He too wore a headpiece of hornbill feathers, and many metal bangles on his legs and arms. He was a handsome young man, and his bride was very pretty. She was dressed in a patterned sarong and wore necklaces of large coins and glass beads. Her breasts were covered for the occasion and she too looked solemn. She was seated on a lower cushion than the groom's. No one else was solemn though, they were laughing and talking happily as the ceremony was concluded. A chicken, its neck bleeding blood, was waved over the two, and following an incantation, the two were now wed. There was clapping and much laughter again, and then the feast began.

Jason, who had watched the whole thing raptly, realized suddenly how thirsty and hungry he was. The smell of cooking pervaded the air of the longhouse as the baskets of rice and cooked fish and vegetables were brought in by older women. The crowded dwelling was awash with noise as the Iban people got going with the feast.

Food was brought to the two Brits, as they could not move very far. Dave ate only a little and seemed somewhat distracted. On closer examination, Jason saw that the sergeant was looking tired and feverish. Jason felt a gnawing fear in his stomach. If Dave went down now, their situation would suddenly become much worse.

The rest of the evening went by in a slight haze for Jason. He made Dave comfortable and gave him water to drink, then allowed himself to eat some food and drink a single bowl of *tapai*. He had become used to it and welcomed its warming feeling, but he was also worried sick about Dave; so he remained detached from the main event that was going on happily in the middle of the longhouse. The Ibans, as though sensing the Brits were tired, left them alone, except to come and present some tidbit from time to time.

Jason was feeling depressed. He was getting angrier by the minute at the situation they found themselves in. The bloody SARBE was obviously not working and Dave was getting worse. He had come to like the tough, skinny man and was sick with worry about their chances. Walking out onto the verandah, he noticed the small green box with the small antenna leaning against the outside wall. In a fit of frustration and near despair he gave it a kick that tossed it onto the other side of the doorway. Without looking at it, he walked over to the rail and peered down at the ground about fifteen feet below. The jungle was, as usual, full of the sounds of insects, cicadas and tree frogs singing. The occasional deep bellow of a bullfrog made itself heard above the usual din. High above he heard the now familiar grating sound of the hornbill sounding off. Inside the longhouse the noisy music continued, and the happy Ibans sang songs and got drunk.

Jason squatted against the attap wall outside and wondered what the next day would bring. His thoughts drifted back to Malaysia.

*   *   *   *   *

He remembered the day, soon adter their trip to batu Ferengi, the entire garrison was paraded onto the playing fields at the base of the Sergeant's mess, where the colonel addressed them. They were told that the Regiment was to prepare for Borneo. They had just under two weeks to complete arrangements and then they would ship off to Jahore Bahru for jungle warfare training.

Jason was pensive that evening when he arrived at Megan's apartment.

"What's the matter, Jason? You don't look at all happy," she said as they kissed.

He held her within the circle of his arms, they had been seeing one another for some time now and he was very comfortable around her.

"We've been told we're leaving for Jahore Bahru in less than two weeks, love."

"Jahore Bahru. Where's that?" She asked, puzzled.

"It's down in the south end of Malaya. It's where the Jungle Warfare School is; after that we go to Borneo."

He looked so miserable that she laughed.

"Come on, sit down, I'm sure it's not the end of the world."

"It is for me, Megan. We are leaving, and then you do too. I don't want that to happen," he said miserably.

Megan was quiet for a moment. "We both knew it had to happen one day, Jason. But you are right. I guess I hoped that it would go on forever. I love being with you." She said softly. She came and knelt by his chair and put her arms around his waist. "I shall miss you, my soldier boy."

"I'll miss you too, Megan," he said quietly. "Megan?"

"Yes, Jason?"

"I think I'm in love with you, you see?"

She gave him a tight squeeze. "Yes, I think I am too," she had whispered, holding back her tears.

At the RAF base in Kuching the duty corporal at the radio shack heard something. He listened and then turned up a knob on the emergency frequency used by the SAS and RAF pilots. It was routine to keep the frequency open but very unusual to hear anything. Now he could hear the repetitive signal of a SARBE emergency call sign. Corporal Stevens picked up the telephone and called the duty officer.

Ten minutes later the duty RAF officer came into the sweltering hut and asked what the problem was.

"I have a SARBE signal, sir. I think it's the same one that we had the other day."

The officer looked interested. "Is that the one we sent out a chopper for? Sergeant White, wasn't it?"

"Yessir, I'm pretty sure it is. I'm still getting a cross-ref on it. There – I think we have it."

He gave the co-ordinates of the cross-referenced signal to the officer, who took them over to the map. He marked a point on the almost bare map. There was a mark that indicated that there might be a village very close.

"Get the SAS on the phone, would you please, Corporal?" he ordered.

When a voice came on the phone, the officer told him what was going on. He gave the co-ordinates and said that he would be on standby. The phone clicked off. It was late, ten p.m., and there was nothing to be done until the morning in any case. He assumed that there would be a call soon to book a flight out at dawn. He was not disappointed; the phone rang after half an hour.

"We will need a Wessex and perhaps a scout, can you have them ready at oh-five hundred?" said the same voice he had spoken to earlier.

"I'll talk to the Senior Officer on duty, but the answer will be yes. Is it Sergeant White?"

"We think so," was the terse reply. The phone clicked off again.

Retribution
Chapter 19

Deep in the jungle of Sarawak, almost at the base of the long range of sharp hills that ran along the border, the men of the Green Jackets woke with the false dawn. There was very little noise for so many men. They were by now well used to the *ulu* and knew all the rules about keeping quiet; the Gurkhas, who were even better at this, might have been phantoms.

Major Johnson was woken with a cup of tea. It never ceased to amaze him that no matter where they might be, or what the circumstances, the British soldier could find a way to make a cup of tea. He drank it appreciatively, ate some compo biscuits, hard tack biscuits with compo cheese, and moved quietly over to the radio operator. He had a whispered conversation with Captain Scott in Padawan and was informed that Major Stanford had come in with eight men and reported that they had located their man and were going to find him. Could they borrow a few Gurkhas?

Major Johnson thought about this for a minute. He might need all the men he could get if things got bad, but he liked Major Stanford and respected the fact that he was going in after one of his own.

"I can give you one section, Phillip. Can you manage with that? Over."

"No problem, Charlie Oscar," was the laconic reply.

Major Johnson talked to Captain James Robinson about lending a section to the SAS. The captain quickly detailed off a section, which promptly made ready to head back to the RV. The men departed with a tough-looking Sabudar Major, the equivalent of a sergeant major for the Gurkhas, at their head.

Then the major concentrated on his immediate front. The Green Jackets were to go forward in three prongs, with an SAS man in each group guiding them over the tough terrain.

He went into a whispered conference with his men again to make clear the objectives. It was to be radio silence until contact. Once contact was made, the radios were to stay close to commanders and they were to listen carefully for instructions. They were to work in clear, as there was no time to code information.

The main thrust was to be Recce Platoon with the major leading in the center as a kind of blunt spear. On contact, which was assumed to be inevitable, Recce would engage while the two wings of the spear would move forward and past his position, to perform a kind of encircling maneuver. He told the men to be careful as, if he thought the resistance was strong, he was going to bring in the artillery. There were nervous grins at this. Everyone hoped fervently that he or the man calling in the Aussie artillery was going to be accurate and not drop shells onto them. They looked at Sergeant Mike Denning, who would be the man on the spot. He seemed calm enough in the gloom. The major didn't feel very calm himself. He wondered how he would do when the time came to lead his men. He took a sip of water; his mouth felt dry.

Once past the first defense they still had the hill to climb and then there would be the assault on the ravaged fort. No one knew how much effort the Indon had put into repairing the camp. They just knew he had had three days to do so; if it had been the Brits he knew it would now be a tough nut to crack.

The major looked at his watch. "Synchronize watches, gentlemen. I have twenty minutes to oh-six hundred hours." He counted the seconds in and then they set their watches on his.

"We leave in twenty minutes, on the hour. Good hunting, gentlemen."

Men grinned. "Scrappy" was looking for a fight; woe betide the Indon today!

The Recce Platoon moved out quietly with major Johnson and Sergeant Mike Denning just in front of him with a tracker. The two men were far ahead enough so that any noise from behind would not affect their judgment as they listened and moved.

The remainder of the Green Jackets started moving towards the wings at the same time, making some distance between themselves and the Recce Platoon. There were grins and thumbs-up signs from the two groups as the Brits left. The men of the Green Jackets felt a lot better with these fierce Gurkhas with them.

The movement was slow; although here the jungle was primary and there was a fair amount of space between the tall thick trees that made up the canopy overhead, the cover was not very good and the major didn't want to be surprised in poor cover. Equally he had to move steadily, for when moving tactically progress is usually slow.

Sergeant Denning was well tuned to his Iban tracker and the two of them moved very cautiously for about a thousand yards, when the ground began to rise towards the steep hillside that was another thousand yards ahead. The ground was broken here and there with gullies, and the *baluka* patches in places were quite dense. They moved past these after carefully checking them out. Soon however, the primary started to give way to denser shrubbery and deeper gullies with high banks and rises. It was at this point that the Iban stopped and squatted.

Denning knew that this meant there was something ahead and crept up to him. They had a whispered conference. Major Johnson, who was about ten good paces behind with his radio man, watched from cover, as did the rest of the platoon that had gone to ground on a hand signal. The Iban pointed to a large, dense thicket of bamboo that could just be seen further up the gently sloping hill through the saplings and bushes. In the dim light it was very hard to make out. Nonetheless, Major Johnson was sure that he could not only hear men he could smell them! He felt a tingle of excitement. Contact!

His fears for how he would be as a leader began to evaporate and were replaced by excitement as the adrenaline coursed. He was damned if he cared now! It was too late to go back, so he would trust in the Fates and deal with the front end. He was very conscious that he had to be the first to get up and face the enemy no matter what happened.

They watched the jungle for minutes and were rewarded for their patience. Major Johnson was using his binoculars to "see" into the jungle, as was the sergeant ahead of him, and he had a clear view of several men in positions at the edge of the bamboo. They seemed to be dug in behind makeshift defenses.

Sergeant Denning came crawling back to the major. He had dumped his Bergen near the Iban, who stayed forward, watching.

"We have a contact, sir. My tracker can smell them about fifty yards ahead in a stand of bamboo that stretches across our path. I have confirmed sightings of defenses. I know the area too; we have been here before. There is a way round that we could take if you want to."

The major nodded understanding but looked at him and grinned. "I don't think so, Sergeant." He gestured to his radio man who gave him the microphone. "I want the other platoons to come up level with me," he whispered. "We have contact." There was no reply other than the double click of the microphones being tapped in acknowledgement, but he knew the other two platoons were moving forward.

"I could see them too, Sergeant"

"Yes, I've seen several of theirs, sir. They are well dug in."

"Give me a grid ref then, and we will see how good the Aussies are."

While Denning worked out his grid references the major called Padawan and made sure the Australians were awake. Sergeant Denning handed the map references to him, which he whispered into the mike.

"Fire for effect," he commanded.

Everyone waited. There came a sound that all infantrymen dread. The rocketing noise a projectile makes moving through the air at a hell of a rate, and in their general direction. The shell landed about one hundred yards forward of the Brit positions with a huge explosion.

"Down fifty," called Sergeant Denning. The men in Recce Platoon ducked again as another shell came rocketing through the thick air above them. The shell landed with an enormous explosion right in the middle of the target. It tore the bamboo to shreds and even in the gloom of the jungle the men could see a huge column of earth tossed skyward.

"Fire six," yelled the major. He switched to the local frequency and through the noise he called, "All units be prepared to attack, move forward at the double on my command."

The jungle was turned into a flashing and explosive hell for five minutes as the Australians demonstrated their skill at getting shells into the air and onto their target. The British clung to the ground below and prayed that the shrapnel would not hit them. The target was so close the humming of flying metal pieces was terrifying. Some pieces even sounded like howling minies as they hurled through the air, stripping leaves and smashing into the larger trees, tearing huge scars into the trees as they struck them.

Abruptly the shelling stopped. In the brief, stark silence the men lay where they were. Then Major Johnson was up and yelling, his voice hoarse to begin with then taking on more force as he cleared his dry throat. His rifle barked and he screamed at his men to get up and at them. He ran forward, hoping desperately that he was being followed, but the madness of battle was upon him and he didn't care.

Yelling and screaming, the men of Recce jumped to their feet and raced through the jungle up the slope. As he started off Major Johnson heard Captain Robinson yell something in Gurkhali, closely followed by the banshee screams of the Gurkhas right behind. The little men had their kukris out and were looking for blood. There was no way they were going to be left out of this scrap. The two units alongside also went forward in a rush.

The resistance was minimal. The shells had done their work. The Recce platoon with Major "Scrappy" Johnson right up in the van ran out of the cover of the jungle into a moonscape of churned-up land. What had once been a dense bamboo thicket was no more; the only trees still standing were the thickest and largest, and even these were scarred and torn. Not much else remained. The few Indonesians who had been to the major's front and had survived after the hellish bombardment fired back briefly and then tried to flee.

He heard the snap and felt the wind of some bullets as he ran forward, firing his rifle from the hip. He was not sure if he hit anyone but could see men running ahead of him and continued to fire his rifle until the magazine was empty. As he frantically reloaded his own men swept past him, yelling and screaming as they went. Major Johnson paused to take stock and see what was going on, leaving his men to deal with the enemy in front of him.

There was more resistance on the wings where the shells had not been able to do so much damage, but the Brits charging towards them, shooting furiously as they ran, yelling and screaming like fiends out of hell, were more than the bravest of the Indons wanted to face just then.

The British and Gurkhas ran right through the Indon positions and stopped fifty yards beyond, reforming without being told. They fired repeatedly after the running figures that fled through the gloom of the jungle but did not pursue them. Astonishingly there were no casualties other than a sprained ankle; a Rifleman had fallen into an improvised dugout that he had not seen. Major Johnson thanked his lucky stars that the pangies they did find had mostly been torn up by the shelling. The men had run through the gaps.

His men went round checking the dead and wounded enemy, of whom there were nineteen. Sergeants called the roll and made sure the perimeter was secure. One by one they reported the situation with respect to casualties to their commanders, who were astonished and delighted at the lack of the same.

Major Johnson called in his commanders and, after taking casualty reports, addressed the next stage of the offensive. The men were elated at their first success and wanting to go but he held them in check. He made sure that the SAS were back with them and then thanked Sergeant Mike Denning for his precision. It had been very impressive, they all agreed. There was renewed respect for these men.

*   *   *   *   *

When the helicopters landed in the RV prepared for them, the group of eight SAS men picked up a section of six Gurkhas. A big RAF Wessex and a five-man scout lifted off and headed in the direction from where the SARBE signal had last come.

Major Stanford was in touch with Lieutenant Harvey Norris, who, with his three other men and two trackers, had been following the trail for two days now. They were coming towards the longhouse that coincided with the SARBE contact he was heading for.

"These are friendly Ibans, as I recall," said Major Stanford.

"Yes, I was there for a visit some months ago. Our man might have gone to ground there," said the lieutenant. "Trouble is, we are now following a large group of Indons who seem to be on his trail." He sounded tense.

"That is now going to be a problem for the Ibans in the longhouse as well as him," said the major. "How many of the baddies are there?"

"My trackers think there are about twenty of them. We are now very close to the village, which means they are probably there now."

"Move carefully, but get there. I'm going to land right in the middle of it."

The roar of the scout helicopter almost drowned out the words but there was a quick acknowledgement and Major Stanford told the pilot to get going. He didn't care to add that they might be landing in the middle of a firefight.

He leaned back and shouted in the ear of the man nearest to him. "Get everyone ready for contact as we land."

There was suddenly a lot of activity in the back as men cocked rifles and checked grenades. Bergens would have to wait until they knew what was going to happen when they landed. One man grabbed a medical pack from his Bergen and another rummaged for an extra couple of magazines and grenades. Others fingered their morphine phials and shell dressings.

Impatiently he sat forward against his straps and watched the jungle sweep under the belly of the speeding chopper.

* * * * *

Major Johnson spent a few seconds sending a compliment back to the Australians for their good work and then passed a message back to Regimental HQ reporting the first contact and his next move. After that he shut the radio down, not wanting to hear back from RHQ or GHQ, as that might mean a bollocking from the brigadier for leaving Padawan.

After a huddled conference, the commanders went back to their respective platoons. Some men were detailed to take the wounded: the Rifleman who protested that he was fine but was told to go anyway, and the Indons, as well as two unhurt prisoners. They were taken back to the RV by a small escort of Riflemen. Then the British and Gurkha men moved forward through the broken country once again, their objective this time the summit.

The climb was harder than the major had expected. The men of the Green Jackets and the Gurkhas only had to carry their

245

ammunition and other belt equipment with them. They had left their packs behind in the base. There was no well-defined trail, so they set themselves to the slopes. It was very hard going, for they not only had to keep the noise level down but watch for unpleasant interruptions from the enemy while they were at it.

The information as to what they could expect was sparse. The Hawker Hunter that had flown over the site two days ago had shown still photos of Sapit and it had looked pretty deserted; nothing appeared to have been done to repair the camp. But still photos taken from a height of several hundred feet did little to tell intelligence whether the place was still occupied today. The major did not intend to blunder into an ambush.

Sergeant Denning and his tracker moved forward cautiously, keeping ahead of the main body of men, as usual. The major saw a lot of signs that told him men had come down the slippery slopes as well as scrambling back up in a hurry. What he could not know was if there were any unpleasant surprises waiting for them when they got to the top. As it happened, they were almost within sight of the top when the tracker ahead stopped, his movements reminding the major of a pointer dog.

Suddenly there was a rumble of thunder overhead and Major Johnson looked up. Although he could not see much of the sky, he knew that this meant a lot of black cloud over the hilltop and he wondered when it would rain. It would not be long. It would be better for all concerned if they were on the ridge before the rain came. Meanwhile, ahead of him, crouching with the sergeant, the Iban was pointing, this time with his finger, to their right about forty yards ahead. Straining his eyes in the gloom the major could see some earthworks through the saplings and vines that barred the way. He froze and gave a slow hand signal to the men behind him, then crouched and watched as Sergeant Denning scanned the slopes with his binoculars, first to the right and above him, then off to the left. The major did the same and was not very happy at what he saw.

The Indons had dug in along the front of the ridge, and very well too. The only thing that seemed to have warned the Iban tracker was the fact that newly discarded earth was lying down the slope. The sergeant signaled the men behind him to stay where they were and slid carefully back down the hill to where the major crouched.

"They've built sangers just along this side of the ridge and we are about to walk into them, sir," he whispered.

"How well dug in are they, Sergeant?"

"Very well, I'd say, sir. These men know how to build crossfire sangers, and from what I've seen it's pretty thorough. We'll have a job getting past them because of the slope as well."

"Can we shell them out?"

"I think we have to, sir. Even then we might have to winkle them out one by one."

Both men's green uniforms were covered in the red mud from the slope and they were wet through from sweat. The imminent rainstorm above them was an additional problem.

"Is it going to rain?" asked the major. He looked back down the steep slope to where some of the men were just visible in the deep thickets. Rain might help him, but machine guns would be a big problem if they were used against his men as they scrambled up the steep slope toward the hidden sangers.

"I think so, sir, in less than half an hour. It might help us if we use it well. Bring the artillery in and take the line above us. Then we have to move like hell to get past and above their line. If we can break past them we will have them."

"We could go round?" It was more rhetorical than a suggestion.

"We might," agreed the sergeant, but they both knew what could happen then. If the Indons suspected a maneuver like that, they could move troops to meet them no matter where they tried to come up. It looked like the unappetizing option was what they had to go through, and that was right in front of them. The major's big card was the artillery.

"How close can we stay to their positions if we bring in artillery?" he queried the sergeant.

"I think I can walk it onto their line, sir. But we need to find good cover; where we are is close but we need to be able to get up and get in there too."

That was exactly what was bothering the major. If they went back too far and the artillery stopped, it would give the enemy survivors time to regroup and get their machine guns back up and firing. It would be a massacre.

"We stay here, dig in where we can and we watch and move as close as we dare while the artillery is going at it," he said firmly.

Sergeant Denning looked at him. There was respect in his eyes. Then he nodded and got out the map.

The major gestured to Radios, who crawled up to his position. The major called the other groups and told them to move forward very quietly so that they were nearly parallel to his location as far as they could be. He would personally skin anyone who gave their positions away.

Every man was to dump his pack, if he still had one, and keep his belt kit only: ammo, water, dressings, knives and grenades. He told them what he intended. It was not a discussion; he simply informed his commanders that they were going to have to charge up a very steep hill to take some well-entrenched positions after an artillery barrage. The acknowledgements were terse. There was flash of lightning and a clap of thunder overhead. They all braced themselves for the oncoming storm.

Sergeant Denning slid back down on his belly to the major's position and asked if he could take the radio forward with him. "I can see what I'm aiming for and call it in better that way, sir."

Major Johnson nodded his agreement but hoped that he wasn't going to lose a sergeant and a radio at the same time. Radios took off the heavy piece of equipment and slid it over to the sergeant, who lugged it back up the hill to his position.

There he and his tracker scrabbled at the soft muddy earth just behind the base of a tree and built themselves a shallow depression. The Major slid into a position behind another tree where he could see both the sergeant and still just see the bunker in the distance above him then began to scratch at the loamy soil with his jungle knife.

Near by the Brits and Gurkhas were doing the same, either digging or getting into position behind a large tree. Incredibly there were still no alarms from above. The first drops of rain began to fall.

Major Johnson watched from his position in the dense undergrowth ten yards back as Sergeant Denning laid the radio in the depression alongside him with only the antenna sticking out. He could see quite clearly as the sergeant checked his first set of co-ordinates. The major peered up the hill towards the nearest sanger with his binoculars and saw a flicker of movement inside the slit. They were clearly alert but as yet unaware of the presence of the British in their immediate vicinity. He figured that the sangers were probably staggered all along the approaches to the ridge. If there was a whole company of the enemy placed on the hillside they were going to be stretched badly if their line was longer than a quarter of a mile. In any case, what the Brits needed to do was to punch a hole through and they could roll up the sides after that.

Johnson watched as the sergeant held the microphone close to his mouth, talking to Padawan, giving the first co-ordinates. Johnson knew the words being spoken. The sergeant would ask the operator to repeat them. Then he would order "Fire for effect!"

Once again the men on the ground heard the sound of a shell rocketing through the thick air above the jungle and cringed in their makeshift holes. This time it seemed to come very close. There was a deafening explosion only twenty yards above Sergeant Denning's hole. It slammed at men's eardrums and made them wince with the pain. The ground shook and he and his tracker were tossed about in their makeshift dugouts. The major huddled deeper into his own depression as the shards of steel whined past, stripping leaves and scouring trees around and behind him. A huge column of earth was lifted into the air and chunks of red mud began to fall all around their forward position. Immediately after that there was another flash, but of lightning followed by a clap of thunder. It began to rain in earnest.

"Jesus!" The major grunted and winced as his eardrums were slammed.

He faintly heard Sergeant Denning call, "Up twenty, fire for effect."

A brief silence and then again the terrifying howl of a shell on its way. This time it was on the line. Major Johnson watched as the sanger directly in front of Denning's position was obliterated and a column of earth was tossed into the air. He heard the sergeant calling directions for the fire to move along the ridge. The shelling was devastating, and before long he was sure the guns had knocked out at least four of the bunkers within his field of view. All the time the rain came down in sheets. The men hiding in the jungle were soaked through in seconds but one thing it did was to hide their positions from desperately searching eyes.

Once and only once did a machine gun open up from the defenses ahead of the Brits and Gurkhas but it stopped abruptly after another salvo of shells struck. Johnson never knew whether it was aimed at anything.

Denning then ordered the fire to move up and had the Aussies shell the gap ahead of him with ten rounds rapid that had depth. They knew what to do. The result would be a ploughed field. After that he had them move up the slope in a wide path.

When the Jungle is Silent

The men behind Sergeant Denning crouched in their makeshift holes, put their fingers in their ears, and waited while the rain pounded down with the shells. The combined noise of shells shrieking inwards and exploding with the thunder was mind-numbing.

The Gurkhas loosened their kukris in their sheaths and grinned at one another. The barrage was awful to endure. For the British down the slope who were not being shelled it was bad enough, but for the Indonesians it must have been pure hell. At one point it was hard to tell what was lightning and thunder or a shell striking the ground.

Suddenly it was over and Denning, covered from head to foot in wet mud, waved to the major urgently. Major Johnson put a whistle to his lips and blew. There was a roar as the slopes of the ridge erupted with men, screaming and shouting, who scrambled desperately for a foothold in the muddy surface of the steep slope while shooting ahead of them. They slipped and swore in their soggy clinging clothes, as they struggled in the mud and the rain up the water-sodden hillside. But every man knew that they had to keep running no matter what; to fail to do so was to give the enemy time to recover and fire down on them with machine guns that would surely bring death.

The men of the Green Jackets followed "Scrappy" Johnson and Sergeant Denning up the seemingly impossible slope out of the jungle once again into a scene of carnage and destruction. A 105 howitzer shell can shred the jungle within a radius of fifteen yards at its center very completely, but the damage from the shards and fragments is much wider. The shells had landed in some cases directly on sangers and obliterated them. In other cases the crews were so shocked that they failed to get into position fast enough.

Howling Green Jackets soldiers ran up to them, lobbing grenades into the slits, then ran past looking for others. Those who tried to fire back found themselves fighting for their lives in the darkness of the interior with Gurkhas, who became shrieking dervishes, brandishing their wicked curved Kukris, dedicated to the War God Shiva. These rose and fell as the screaming Gurkhas butchered their victims.

The major and Sergeant Denning ran up the steep slope through the sheeting rain, followed by a tight group of men who were alongside to make sure they were kept alive. But Major Johnson was firing and screaming along with his men as they swept up the hill past the wrecked enemy sangers and drove on through the mud towards the top, their legs pounding, knees and calves aching, mouths wide open gasping for breath in the water-saturated air.

Some brave men came to meet them, shouting and yelling themselves, but the sheer firepower of the advancing Brits swept them away. There was a brief hand-to-hand fight with rifle butts, bayonets, jungle knives and kukris, but then it was over; the Brits and Gurkhas were past and charging over the crest of the hill.

Major Johnson caught a glimpse of a man's terrified face in front of him but it disappeared as he ran forward firing. His rifle stopped firing so he dropped it and hauled his pistol out, pointing it forward and firing at anyone he saw ahead of him. He nearly tripped over a body that lay in his path: he staggered forward, trying not to fall face down in the mud. It probably saved his life; while he was on one knee, a man appeared in front of him about to swing his AK rifle at him. The man was suddenly knocked over backwards as one of the Riflemen behind Johnson fired twice. The shots were so close that Johnson's ears rang. He glanced back thankfully and then staggered to his feet and ran on.

Another man reared up in front of him. He reflexively pulled the trigger twice, hitting the man in the belly. He doubled over with a gasp. The major pushed the doubled over figure out of the way then continued to run, slipping and gasping up the hill. His terror and fright were replaced by the urgency of getting to the top. He had no idea as to how many of he enemy were waiting for them up there. The knowledge that they must reach it to prevent a counter attack drove him on.

Panting and grunting with the strain, he reached the top, fell onto his knees in the mud, and turned back to see what was happening.

"God, what a slog!" he gasped, bending over to catch his breath while hurriedly changing the magazine, as his panting men staggered past him and threw themselves down in the mud to face out in a protective arc. Some were still firing furiously at retreating shadows in the forest around them. Then he saw Sergeant Denning lying against a tree about ten feet behind him. Immediately he scuttled at a crouch back down to the sergeant, who was holding his shoulder, his heaving chest covered in blood.

"You all right, Sergeant?" he shouted, kneeling by his side.

The sergeant nodded weakly. "Good man, hold on, we'll get a medic to you."

Others of his charging men came panting up towards him, and one of them immediately ran over to the sergeant and started helping him.

Johnson glanced down the slope they had just run up. It looked steeper from the top and he wondered just how they had managed it. His men were pounding up the slope in small groups, their mouths wide open as they gasped for breath, their rifles pointing up and a madness in their eyes.

Nearby were the bodies of the men who had fallen in that last desperate fight. One man was on his knees, bent at the waist, leaning forward, his head on the ground and his arms spread as though praying. A rifleman shambled over to him and cautiously pushed him with his rifle muzzle. The body fell over onto its side; the front of its head had been blown off. There were others lying like rag dolls, limp and very dead, half covered in mud, already looking as though the ground was claiming them, but others still moved feebly and some were crying for help. He was shocked to see several of them were his own men. One was clutching his stomach, groaning and crying, his head being held by his mate who was trying to reassure him.

"Don't worry, Sammy, me old mate, we'll look after yer." the rifleman said, trying to comfort him and protect his face from the rain.

The major called over. "Stay with him, Mac, but don't give him any water! Do you hear me?"

The riflemen looked over at him; one gave the thumbs up sign and the wounded one tried a weak grin. His mate called back. "He'll be OK Sir. I'll see to it."

"Well done, lads, well done!" the major said running past at a crouch.

"We have to roll 'em up, James," he called over to the wild-eyed Gurkha officer who was also covered in blood, none of which seemed to be his own. The man had lost his floppy hat, his short blond hair was streaked with filth and blood.

"Get your men together and take the right flank!" he yelled over the shooting. "Richard! Hold this center for me and watch the front, bring everyone through. I'm going for Sapit."

The officers grinned madly and nodded vigorously. Captain James Robertson began to shout in Gurkhali at his berserk men, and gradually the happy, bloody crew came together in the rain. Then they galloped off to the right flank and started to hunt for more of the luckless enemy. The screams and yells, bursts of fire and small explosions from grenades continued long after they were gone from sight.

Captain Romney-Smith yelled at his wild-eyed Riflemen to spread out, get into position to hold a perimeter and consolidate. Major Johnson called his Recce platoon together and they set off to sweep up the left flank. Men were pouring through the gap in the Indonesian defenses then forming up rapidly in crouching sections on the ridge waiting for orders. A machine gun started up, off to the right. Bullets crashed through the trees above them at head height. Men swore and dived for cover.

Major Johnson and his men ran at a crouch towards the sound. Behind him he could hear firing and the deadly burp of the platoon MGs as they cleaned up the remaining sangers. Green Jackets Riflemen helped the Gurkhas do their gristly work, yelling encouragement to one another, madness in their eyes, faces streaming water, and the blood of their victims staining their soggy uniforms. They would follow on quickly once the flanks were covered and the rear taken.

Other than the roar of the rain in the canopy, the jungle ahead had gone quiet as the riflemen worked their way forward along the ridge. Peering over the roots of a tree, down the slope to where the Indon defenses had been, the major saw several sangers still in good condition. He detailed off men to go and deal with them. The men crept down to within grenade-throwing distance and then tossed a couple into the slit trench at the back. There were loud explosions and then screams, followed by the rapid fire of SLRs, then the men dived inside with bayonets and gollocks to finish the job.

Once again the machine gun started firing, sounding oddly flat in the rain, but it was clear that the gunner had no good targets. He was simply trying to clear the ridge. He had lowered his sights so that men had to hug the ground now wherever his rounds were fired. The sound was very close; the Brits were down on the ground peering about trying to find the gunner when one pointed. He showed three fingers, meaning thirty yards, and pointed forward to the right. They would have to get a little closer to spot the man properly, but the major told a couple of men in good cover to fire in the direction of the gunner while he and three others crept along the side of the hill towards the position. The shooting began as the riflemen laid down a rapid fire to keep the

Indon gunner's head down. The fire was returned but only in short bursts as he tried to find his targets.

Major Johnson and the three riflemen with him were just about level with the sound of the firing when a man poked his head over the edge of the ridge and saw them. He gave a shout and started to run off. A burst of fire from the man behind the major who carried a Sterling submachine gun stopped him, then it was time to get going.

Quickly taking out a grenade, Major Johnson pulled the pin, counted to four and lobbed it over the edge. They ducked and waited. There was an explosion and a scream. The four of them boiled over the rim and charged wildly towards where the sound of the machine gun had come from. There were about five men sitting or lying on the ground, stunned from the effect of the grenade, but one of them still had his rifle up. He got one shot off just as he was shot to death by the riflemen charging him.

Major Johnson felt a sledgehammer blow to his left side and the next thing he knew he was lying on the soaking ground, the rain washing his face. He heard a brief burst of firing and then he saw one of his riflemen kneeling next to him.

"You all right, sir? Bloody 'ell, the major's been hit."

He yelled off to the men in the Recce platoon. "Sarge, get a medic over 'ere. Scrappy's been 'it. Sorry, sir. Didn't mean no disrespect, sir."

Major Johnson tried to sit up but the pain forced a gasp out of him and the Rifleman pushed him back down firmly. He glanced down at his waist and saw a large patch of his blood staining his shirt and pants. He felt light-headed and numb from the waist down. He soon found himself surrounded by concerned men. A few minutes later Captain Romney-Smith came and crouched next to him.

"How are you doing, Nigel?"

"Hurts a bit, Richard," he gasped. "You're in charge now. Finish it off. The boys have done a great job but you have to finish it! Off you go!"

"Right you are, sir," said Captain Romney-Smith. "We rolled up the defenses and all that is left is to get to Sapit. I think they've lost the urge to fight. Color Sergeant, stay with the major."

"Right-o, Sar," bellowed the color sergeant. He and his section started to make sure that Major Johnson was not going to die from loss of blood by tying a large shell dressing around the lower part of his torso. They pulled up his shirt and bound two dressings to him, front and back, and made him as comfortable as they could. He felt the prick of a needle as the Color gave him some morphine from the medic bag someone had dropped with them.

"You was lucky, Sar." grunted the Color as he carried out the work. "Just a few inches to yer right and you'd 'ave been a gonner."

"Thanks, Color," gasped the major. Jesus, but it hurt! He fell back against a medical pack that a rifleman had placed there to support him.

"We'll have a chopper along in no time, sir. We'll take care of you, never fear."

Major Johnson smiled weakly. "I never doubted it, Color. You men did very well."

"Good fight that was, sir, narrow squeak with the sangers and all that, but we did it!" responded the color sergeant happily.

They all stopped speaking as they heard a prolonged burst of shooting in the distance that went on for a few minutes. Then closer to hand some more, but it was only a short fusillade and then the jungle became quiet again. The rain moved off the top of the ridge with a rumble of thunder, leaving an eerie stillness in its wake. The jungle was silent, as though listening.

In the quiet the voice of the color sergeant sounded oddly loud as he made his men stay alert and watchful in their improvised perimeter. He didn't want to be surprised at this juncture. He checked on the major and gave him another phial of morphine to drink, clucking with concern and fussing about like an old maid. The major smiled to himself despite the pain.

After what seemed to be a good hour interspersed with occasional bursts of shooting followed by a prolonged silence, a runner came breathlessly into their tiny perimeter.

"Complements of the captain, sir," he said. "Objective is taken, and could the Color please bring you along?"

Major Johnson blinked the rainwater away from his eyes and grinned. "Come on, men, get me up. We have to go to Sapit and see what's there."

"Wait a minute, sir," said the Color. "Let's see what we can make for you to lie in. Come on, lads, get weaving, we've got to get the major to Sapit."

They rigged a makeshift litter out of poles and a poncho and carried him in style along the ridge for about four hundred yards, to the devastation that was Sapit. The rain had moved on, leaving a low mist in the valley, but the view of Sapit was clear.

The Indonesians had not bothered to defend it. The ravages caused by the shelling had completely destroyed the place, leaving huge craters full of stagnant water in place of the many sangers that had once been there. The remains of the pangi lines were still in place,making walking about dangerous, and coils of barbed wire were strewn all over. There was also a terrible smell, the unmistakable cloying stink of old death. There were a lot of corpses lying about, some half buried by the mud.

There were also Green Jackets and Gurkhas standing around everywhere. Major Johnson saw a small group of officers near the top of the mound who watched his arrival. Suddenly the men who were carrying him were surrounded. The soldiers were cheering him, their faces alight with victory, waving their floppy hats in the air and shouting his name, and more than once he heard "Scrappy". The noise washed over him in his light-headed state like a wave and left him dazed and slightly bewildered.

The men set him down gently on the ground and at his insistence they helped him to stand, one burly Rifleman staying with him, holding him upright. Captain Romney-Smith came over, grinning, followed by the other company officers. They were all smiling and cheering him. He waved back at the men happily but then felt like he was going to pass out and started to go limp. His men were instantly solicitous and helped him gently back down onto the litter. Someone put a small pack behind his head so that he could at least look forward and see what was going on.

Slowly the noise died down and men were put to work to deal with wounded and prisoners, of whom there were not many. The men had gone a little wild, he heard, especially the Gurkhas, who had performed feats of crazed bravery that were going to be legend before long.

Captain Romney-Smith and the other officers, all filthy, soaked and splattered with dark stains on their jungle greens, came and squatted near Major Johnson, who had a couple of protective Riflemen hovering near by.

"Bloody good piece of work, sir! Congratulations! The colonel must be pleased about this," Romney-Smith drawled, his face beaming through the mud and grime.

"I'll say, Richard! Good work yourself, and to all of you. Bloody well done, A Company, Gurkhas, all of you!" said Major Johnson. He felt enormously proud of his men at that moment.

"What are the casualties, Richard?" Now came the hard part, dealing with the dead and wounded, and later still the writing of letters to the families back home.

"Recce lost three men, Sir: Rooney, Blackman and Jones. Wounded were yourself and Sergeant Denning of the SAS, Rifleman Samuel Phelps and Rifleman Gorm Tiler. The reports for the other platoons are due in any minute."

The reports started to come in as the younger officers named their men. Major Johnson was saddened by the losses but gratified that they were not half as bad as he had anticipated. The morale of the company didn't seem to have suffered from the casualties.

"Richard, you had better get some of the wounded going as soon as possible and deal with the other issues such as defense and so on. You are in charge, as it seems I have to go back to Kuching. Wish it wasn't like this," said the major.

"Don't worry, Nigel. They can't do anything to you after this. We'll all come and defend you," said Richard confidently. There were growls of agreement from the men within hearing.

"Another thing, Richard."

"Yes, sir?"

"I want all of Harper's platoon recovered any way we can. I want them buried with full military honors back in Minden Barracks. I don't want them left here."

"Very good, sir. I shall take care of it; you can rely on me. We all want them to come home with us."

"Thanks, Richard, the sentiment is much appreciated," he told his captain.

He made a point of thanking Captain James Robinson for his support. The Captain was embarrassed at the praise, but Major Johnson was determined that this young officer, who now looked like a scarecrow in his filthy and bloody uniform, be mentioned in dispatches. His men had performed exceptionally well.

Then he asked for the SAS men, who sauntered up. Sergeant Denning was somewhere being taken care of by the Green Jackets medic, who passed the message that he was stable and would be fine. His shoulder blade was broken but it would mend. Major Johnson was determined that the man would get the Military

Medal for the work he had done that day. The others came and squatted like natives next to his litter and waited to hear from him.

"Couldn't have done it without you fellows," he said, sitting up with a wince of pain.

"That's all right, sir. Glad to have come along," said one of the men.

"I'll be talking to Major Stanford and the Brig – you can be sure of that, gentlemen. Thanks again for a job well done."

They looked uncomfortable. He laid back and closed his eyes for a moment but when he opened them they had gone.

Several hours later, the helicopter pad had been reconstructed and the distant sound of helicopters could be heard. It was now late afternoon and it was necessary to get the wounded out of the jungle to a hospital before it was too dark to evacuate them. The dead would leave at a later time.

The roar of chopper engines drowned out all other sounds as the RAF Wessex helicopters swooped in like huge dragonflies, picked up the wounded and left.

It was time for Major Johnson to go. The Riflemen who had become his unofficial bodyguard picked him up and carried him the short distance to the open doorway of the Wessex. The burly men placed him gently on the floor of the noisy craft as though he were a child, then they stood back and saluted him smartly, to which he waved his hand in answer.

As the chopper lifted off, by sitting up and leaning on his elbows he could see the men working on the defenses, then as the aircraft turned to head for home he could just see from his litter the savaged jungle where they had come up the ridge.

Major Johnson lay back with a grimace of pain but he then smiled to himself. Now he could face the music; he really didn't care.

Providence
Chapter 20

Jason came awake to find he was being shaken urgently. It was Nighan, and in the gloom of the dawn he looked very worried., For a frightening instant Jason thought that Dave had died or something. But Nighan indicated, by signs and urgent words, that they were to get dressed very quickly and leave. A lot of activity was going on all around, a muted bustle everywhere in the darkness of the longhouse. A child began to cry, obviously sensing that there was something badly wrong. It was quickly hushed and the preparations to leave went on feverishly.

Dave was fumbling as he tried to pull on his pants. Jason dealt with his own damp clothes and then hurriedly helped him. Then it was shirts on and the task of pulling on canvas boots, praying that a scorpion hadn't taken up residence during the night, and frantically lacing them up.

"What's going on, Dave?" asked Jason as he helped, although he thought he knew.

"Nighan says the Indons are a quarter of a mile away and coming here."

"Oh shit."

Dave had sounded slurred but as Jason couldn't see his face in the gloom he left it at that for the moment. They were ready within five minutes and then there was a panicked hunt for bits and pieces, belt kits, rifles and ammo. Jason ran out onto the verandah to look for the SARBE. Dave didn't want to compromise the Ibans any more than he had to with careless signs of their being there. He felt exposed while on the verandah and prayed the Indons weren't already in the clearing and looking for them. He found the box on the verandah and threw it into the Bergen. He didn't know how to switch it off, and in any case it wasn't working as far as he knew. More weight to carry, he thought resentfully. But he also knew Dave was right: they could not compromise these people.

Jason and Nighan lifted Dave to his feet, and while Jason hefted the Bergen and the rifles, Nighan helped Dave to hobble along to the far end of the building. It was almost completely empty of people by now. The Iban women and children were hurrying off into the jungle. No one wanted to meet the Indons; they had a bad reputation with villages. Jason wondered where the men might be but didn't have time to think about it. They had to negotiate the steep ramp with Dave, who was not doing at all well. He was breathing heavily, and when Jason touched his forehead it was very hot.

"Oh God!" he thought. "I don't even know where to go!"

Nighan was talking rapidly to him, pointing towards the trail that led out of the village to the west. Jason had seen women coming that way from somewhere with large baskets of rice the other day. He nodded and cocked his rifle as he did so, what the hell? They couldn't swim the river now. He and Nighan got Dave between them, an arm draped over a shoulder each, and then they hurried along the path from the longhouse towards the opening in the jungle ahead.

They were just into the narrow pathway when Jason heard a shout from back up at the other end of the longhouse clearing. The Indons had arrived. He wondered how quickly they would realize that no one was there and start looking for the avenues of escape. A thought began to take shape in his mind; he remembered what Dave had done the other day and wondered if he could repeat the exercise. In the meantime they were trying to put as much distance as they could between themselves and the longhouse. It occurred to him to wonder why they were using the trail instead of going into the jungle, but then he realized that if the Indons had arrived in force, they could easily find and surround the trio. They were better off trusting Nighan, he thought.

They hobbled painfully along the narrow winding trail for about a hundred yards. It was dark, as the sun had not yet risen, but there was enough light to see ahead to what looked like an opening. Sure enough, they came out into a wide open space. This was where the rice was grown. They stood on a small rise looking west over a cleared space of jungle comprising about six acres of very uneven ground full of waist high stubble and the shells of burnt stumps of trees.

It had been fired some months ago. In the dim light Jason could see that the land gradually rose towards the other end of the clearing where the dark shape of a hut nestled among a couple of large mounds that had stumps and new growth starting around it. There was a small gap in the rise of the land in front of the hut, which was on stilts and well protected from wind and rain. Behind the hut was another larger hillock that was partially cleared, and which would give them a good field of view if they could only get there without being detected.

Jason pointed to the hut and indicated that they should go there. Nighan didn't much like the idea but he didn't argue either, so they set off as fast as they could across the burnt-out land. It was hard going and their path was slowed by large burnt stumps and blackened tree trunks lying across the line they wanted to take. They came to a well-worn path very shortly however, and made better progress.

Jason was looking around desperately for some place they could hide but there was nothing, only what lay ahead. He had a huge lump in his stomach as he began to realize that they were not going to make it and that they would now have to find an alternative. Dave had made it very clear that being taken prisoner was not an option. Jason remembered the story Dave had told him about how the Indons had captured a wounded SAS man once and butchered him without mercy. He had informed Jason that if cornered they would have to fight and that would be that.

Now Jason was trying to estimate where best they could make the stand. Fear gripped him and threatened to paralyze his mind, but he shook it off and concentrated on getting Dave across the open ground. They were all but running now; the Bergen felt terribly heavy and he wondered if he should ditch it. Then he remembered the claymore.

Abruptly he stopped and let Nighan support Dave.

"I'm going to hold them up. Go!" he said urgently, pointing towards the hut and the cleft in the mounds before it. "Go! Dave, can you hear me? Stay with Nighan, get to the cover of the hills near the hut, I'll be along."

Dave didn't argue. "OK, Jason, be careful; remember how we did it before." He was sweating profusely and looked very sick.

Nighan hobbled off with Dave dragging along beside him. Incredibly Dave still had his AR 15 slung over his shoulder. Desperately rummaging in the Bergen, Jason pulled out the claymore and then hunted feverishly for the battery. He couldn't find it for a couple of seconds and started crying with frustration. Then he found it. Seizing his rifle he began to sprint back the thirty yards towards the opening in the trees that denoted the pathway to the longhouse.

He expected any moment for the gap to be filled with gun-firing Indons, but amazingly it was quiet. Nervously he set the claymore upright in the middle of the path, its convex side facing down the path, near a small bend that would not make it easily visible for anyone coming towards it. Then he ran the cables out for fifteen yards to a point where he could watch the trail and be protected from the blast by a tree. He had a hundred-yard dash once he had fired the claymore and didn't relish the thought at all. He peered down the trail, panting. His heart was pounding with adrenalin and fear.

"Fuck it, I'm not cut out for this kind of shit!" he muttered to himself. His mouth was dry and he desperately wanted to take a pee. But he stayed where he was, watching the light begin to illuminate the path ahead. He was in deep cover but if they started firing at him he would be in trouble.

A small sound caught his attention, then a flicker of movement, and all of a sudden there were men on the trail ahead of him. They advanced cautiously, but the ones in front were bunched. Even Jason knew that was a bad thing to do. He had already tied one of the wires from the claymore onto the battery; he waited, trying to keep his breathing from telling the world where he was.

The men came down the path walking quickly, and it dawned on Jason that they were more interested in simply finding out where it was going than worrying if there was danger. They did not appear to be tactical. He began to wish they had just gone to ground in the jungle but then realized that these men had tracked them here. They could do so again and this time Dave was near to finished.

He fired the claymore just as the first man was within five yards of the device. There was a mind-numbing "bang!" and the men seemed to disappear in a large puff of smoke and flame.

Jason didn't wait. He jumped up and began to run for his life back the way he had come. He heard the screams dimly but his heart was pounding in his chest and his labored breathing was so loud that he didn't pay much attention. His leg hurt like hell and his back felt like a huge target as he pounded down the open area towards the Bergen. Why he did so he never knew, but he scooped it up, slung it over his back, and continued running flat out for the gap in the low mounds ahead. But now his leg was not working very well and each pace became a red-hot agony. He knew that if he stopped he was finished so he screwed up his face and continued to run, the pain burning a line down his calf.

The first bullets began to smack by just as he was within ten yards of the opening. He glimpsed Nighan off to the side watching and waving to him. He could not see Dave. Terrified, Jason began to weave as more bullets slammed past him, getting closer. Then he saw Dave, lying in the long grass with his rifle up and pointing down the field. He began to shoot back in the direction of the Indonesians.

The snappy bark of his rifle joined in the loud crack from theirs. Jason had just scooted through the gap and was in the act of throwing himself down when he felt a huge blow in his back. The blow had the effect of accelerating his forward motion so that he virtually dived about ten feet to land face forward in the prickly stubble, just behind where Dave was lying.

He lay there for a long couple of seconds, sobbing for breath, his face scratched and bleeding from the impact, wondering if he was going to die. There was a lot of pain in his back and it was difficult to breathe. He rolled over and tried to take the Bergen off; it was difficult but eventually he managed, and then lay there gasping while Dave fired off a lot of rounds in the direction of the attackers.

"Jason, are you all right?" Dave croaked.

"I think so, Dave; something hit me in the back. I... I can hardly breathe!"

"Are you bleeding?" Dave asked, firing off another couple of shots.

"No, I don't think so."

"Then stop skiving and get up off your effin'arse! Help me with this lot, they look really pissed."

"Fuckin' NCOs," Jason grumbled to himself. "Never give a man a moment's peace!" He had a crazy impulse to laugh. His back hurt like hell just under his right shoulder blade.

"I heard that, you insubordinate bastard. If we get out of here I'm going to put you on a charge!" croaked Dave, but he was grinning through his pain. "Come on lad; let's give them shit while we can. Bloody good job back there, by the way!"

"Bloody right, Sarge!" gasped Jason. Did nothing bother this man?

Jason rolled over and retrieved his rifle. Then he rolled to the other side of the gap and found some good cover. After that he took a look down the clearing towards the tunnel where he had set off the claymore.

While it gave him a clear view of the entire field, it was not reassuring. There seemed to be many more than ten men coming towards them in short runs then going to cover. They were doing a classic section assault on this position; it was bringing them closer by the minute. He counted another five off to the right who seemed to be intent upon going around their position to encircle them.

He heard a loud "*ponk*" sound from back near the tunnel and something went into the sky. To his horror, he realized what it was.

Dave heard it too and exclaimed, "Shit! The baddies have a two-inch bloody mortar! Now we're for it!"

The first bomb landed well in front of their position and went off with a loud crack. A piece of shrapnel whined over head, but it was enough to make Jason duck.

Then he popped his head up and took aim at one of the men scampering along on the wings. He was trembling so much he couldn't take aim properly. He quietly cursed himself and took a deep breath. He tried again and found that the rifle was much steadier. He aimed just in front of his intended victim and had the satisfaction of seeing the man jerked into the shrubs from the impact.

The others went to ground too quickly for him to fire at them again. Jason pulled his last HE grenade off his belt and wrenched out the pin. He knelt and then threw the grenade as high and as far as he could in the direction of the men to the right. He heard it go off but didn't see or hear any reaction. He fired several rounds in their direction to keep them there and then turned his attention back to the front, diving down under cover as several rounds snapped past him.

The recoil of the rifle on its present gas setting was heavy on his shoulder, which already hurt like hell, but at least the bloody weapon was reloading. He was calmer now, the knot in his stomach had eased and he felt ready to deal with whatever was coming. He glanced over at Dave.

Dave was firing methodically at the men in front and had clearly done a lot of damage; they were less inclined to get up and move now, although they could hear someone shouting furiously at the reluctant attackers. Jason looked behind him at the hut. They could retreat there but it would not give much cover, bullets would go straight through the attap walls. It would be a trap. His eyes went to the hillock behind it. If they could only get up that low hill they might be better off than down here in the gully, he thought.

His thinking was interrupted by another popping sound and another of the bombs soared into the air above. Fascinated, he watched the small dark object go high into the sky, slow, then turn over and accelerate down towards him. It disappeared for a few seconds and then there was a huge explosion just in front of them. Small rocks and shards of shrapnel whined past the two men, who clung to the ground.

Jason looked around for Nighan; he had disappeared. He cursed softly, so this was what they were now up for. Nighan had deserted and they were on their own.

"Dave, Nighan has scarpered."

"Most probably gone to get help from his pals the Ibans," croaked Dave. He fired off another few rounds and was rewarded by a scream.

Jason decided to concentrate. In spite of his leg Dave was still every bit the soldier, so he felt he should be too. He sucked in a breath and sighted on a man who was hiding behind an old stump. He carefully squeezed the trigger and saw the stump shake while the man behind it threw up his arms and fell back.

"Dave, this thing can really knock 'em over," he shouted gleefully, his fear put aside for a couple of seconds. He felt a crazy impulse to get up and run down shooting at the enemy in one wild charge. But the bullets snapping by only just overhead reminded him that prudence was also part of his survival, so he huddled down and concentrated on available targets, letting the bullets fly past, also keeping an eye on the men off to the right.

There was a lull in the firing, which Jason took advantage of to take a drink. His back and shoulder were so stiff he could hardly move his right arm now. He felt something wet dribbling down his back and when he tried to touch it his hand came back red. He swore quietly. He felt that their world was beginning to close in on them and he began to feel very frightened. He glanced over at Dave and noticed that he was cradling his face in his forearms.

"Dave! You alright?" he called although they were only five feet apart. Dave lifted his head, looking disoriented; he shook his head and peered down at the area ahead of them.

"Yeah, I think so," he muttered, thickly. He took aim and his rifle barked, the shell case flying over to land next to Jason.

* * * * *

The SAS patrol led by Lieutenant Norris moved carefully to just inside the edge of the jungle and surveyed the longhouse in front of them. It was eerily quiet. Only the sound of a couple of pigs rooting in the mud under the building disturbed the hush. No Ibans and certainly no Indonesians. The men were very tense, listening and watching intently for anything that might mean an ambush.

It was then that they heard the boom of something going off and distant screams, and soon after that they heard a lot of gunfire. It was well off to the west but it was unmistakable: there was a firefight going on. Their man was in trouble!

They looked urgently at one another. The temptation to rush out and then charge down to the other side of the longhouse was enormous. But SOPs demanded that they did not do stupid things like this and run into an ambush themselves. Giving the order to drop Bergens, Lieutenant Norris nonetheless led the way out of the surrounding jungle as rapidly as he could without making any noise. They moved tactically towards the longhouse and checked it for occupants; no one at all. Very cautiously he went up the steep stairs with another man and carefully checked to see that there was no one waiting to attack them from behind. All the time there was a lot of shooting going on to distract them.

Lieutenant Norris hurried down the steps and silently pointed towards the opening in the trees that indicated there might be a pathway. They now ran in a crouch towards the entrance of the opening and there went to ground to watch and listen. They too heard the popping sound and the explosion that followed.

One of the men silently mouthed to him, "Two-inch! Where did they get that?"

He nodded. It must have been captured at Sapit or was a World War II relic. He didn't think the Chinese made them and that was where the Indons got a lot of their arms from. Things were sounding bad for their man. He got up and slipped quickly into the jungle followed by his men and their Iban trackers. They kept abreast of the pathway although it was difficult, as the new growth was dense in places. However, they made good progress until they came to the point where the claymore had gone off. The carnage was clear for them to see. There were at least four bodies in pieces lying about and the jungle nearby was shredded. There was even one wounded man crawling about groping with his hands for something, his face a mass of blood.

Lieutenant Norris looked at the gristly work approvingly. Sergeant White was giving the Indon a very bad time of it. He certainly wasn't going to go out easily. The man in front suddenly stopped and used a hand signal for them to get down. Then he moved forward very slowly and looked out of the cover. There was a loud "PONK!" sound close by, followed after some seconds by a distant explosion.

They were right on top of the mortar crew! Norris didn't hesitate. He signaled that they were to rush the three men with the mortar and then get out onto the open space and deal with the Indons in the field. He and his men got into position, and just as another mortar was fired they charged out of the jungle. They were firing as they went, and the crew of the mortar went down without a sound. Then the men and Lieutenant Norris were running and weaving out onto the field, looking for cover as they spotted the Indonesians in front of them.

A very desperate and noisy firefight developed as the Indons realized that they were caught in the middle. The leader tried to rally the men and get them off to the far side so that they could regroup. His men were disciplined and made good progress in spite of the withering fire from the newcomers.

Both Dave and Jason continued to fire at whatever targets they could find, but the Indons were canny, prepared to take this one cautiously. They had probably judged that there were only two of them by now, but they had experienced how nasty a sting the two men could hand out, so they were careful.

The dreaded popping sound came again. Jason knew where it was going so he didn't waste time looking at it and instead tried to make himself as small as he could. The explosion was so close his ears popped. The whistle and hum of steel shards was also so close he was sure he would be hit, but amazingly neither of them were. They compared notes and then went back to watching for targets and shooting down the field at anything that moved. Jason thought he could hear the sound of a helicopter but discarded the idea as being ridiculous and concentrated on the men off to the side.

But then Dave said drunkenly, "Is that a chopper?"

They listened, and now Jason was sure Dave was right, but it was far away.

"Could be –" but he never finished. The popping sound came again and the two men curled into balls and waited. The bomb landed on the hillock just above Jason and threw him about two feet towards Dave. He felt a burning sensation in his right shoulder, just above the armpit, but other than being winded from the blow he thought he was all right.

He scrambled back into position and fired a couple of rounds off to the right to keep the heads down over there. He received a long burst of fire back that made him duck. They were getting pissed and far too close for comfort he thought.

At the same time he heard a furious burst of firing down at the far end of the clearing where the mortar was located. It died out and then four green-clad figures appeared, running and weaving out of the cover of the tunnel to disappear into the long grass behind logs and other cover. They started firing at the men in front of Jason and Dave.

Jason stared in total surprise. "Dave!" he screamed. "I think we have help!" the pain in his ribs doubled him over and shut him up, but he continued to point wordlessly.

Dave lifted his head and peered myopically down the slope towards the open field. "Where?" he croaked.

"There! Right in front of us! Some men took out the mortar and now they're shooting at the Indons from behind. Wonder if they're SAS?" He stopped again; his ribs hurt like hell and the pain lanced through his side.

Dave didn't reply, his fever was now raging and he was slipping into unconsciousness. Despite his own pain Jason crawled over to him and pulled him back from his firing position.

"Dave!" he shouted over the noise of the battle taking place at their front. "Not now, Dave. Hang on, mate. Christ, Dave, you have to hang on!"

The desperation of their situation up to this point... and the light he could now just see at the end of this awful tunnel... then to see Dave slipping away... It made him sick to the point of weeping.

* * * * *

The pilot nudged Major Stanford. "RAF is telling me that the signal has moved," he shouted over the noise of the scout engines.

"Do you know where?" shouted Stanford.

"About three hundred yards off to the west, they say."

Major Stanford wondered if he could get in touch with Lieutenant Norris but decided that there wasn't time

"Head for the new bearing," he shouted back. He peered forward and thought he could see the clearing where the longhouse was located. There was a river running near by, and then he saw in the distance another larger clearing. As he peered at it in the haze he was sure he saw an explosion and some smoke.

"Head for that area over there, and tell the other chopper to follow you," he commanded.

The pilot looked uneasy but he complied. They flew directly at the larger space, and as they drew near the smoke seemed to increase and there was another explosion. The pilot brought the chopper over the clearing and then at the major's insistence moved the scout down to the south. There was a man waving frantically up at them. It was one of the men with Lieutenant Norris.

"Put us down right where he is," shouted the major.

"They're bloody shooting at us!" the pilot yelled.

"Well blimey, so they are! Get us down then you can piss off. Hurry!"

"You're fucking mad! But OK." As the pilot threw the chopper down, the men in the back were already shooting at targets from inside the doorway. The loud crack and bark of weapons being fired briefly competed with the sound of the motors.

The chopper dropped like a stone and Major Stanford shouted, "Out, men, get out!" They jumped the last few feet and went to ground.

A few bullets whipped past them as they landed and one hit the wall of the helicopter with a loud "Wang!" The pilot pulled out of there as fast as he could go, but he did remember to tell the other pilot that the crazy major expected him to unload his men as well, and to hurry up. He climbed to a safe height and waited the outcome of the battle below, hoping that the bullet he had heard hadn't done any real damage.

* * * * *

Jason had noticed that the sound of the helicopter was much louder and he realized that it was not just one but two. One swept over the large clearing and hovered at the site nearest to the tunnel. One of the newcomers was standing up recklessly waving at it. The chopper came down fast. There were men inside who were shooting down at the Indonesians even as the chopper came to a height of four feet above the ground. The men jumped down and ran forward, still shooting furiously. It all happened within a minute and the chopper was lifting off again. The Indonesians had few chances to take any potshots at Jason and Sergeant White, as they were now preoccupied with dealing with this new threat from behind.

Jason watched from his cover and then concentrated on shooting anyone who he saw that exposed himself from among the enemy. But he soon stopped; he could not be sure of who was out there and didn't want to hit any of the newcomers.

He continually looked over at Dave, who he had laid out on his back in a small patch of shade provided by a bush.

Then to his amazement and delight another chopper, a huge Wessex, came thundering down into the clearing, again guided by that crazy man who seemed to be oblivious of danger. It too hovered, and again men piled out of it, firing weapons as they did so, and they too went to ground. The chopper lifted off with a roar that drowned out the sound of firing from all around the area.

The newcomers were aggressively moving forward, much as the Indonesians had, but this time they used a lot of firepower.

The survivors of the first attack were driven towards the left of Jason's position. He fired at them if it looked like any were thinking of coming his way.

He heard a boom, then a scream off to his right, and swiveled his head just in time to see one of the four men who had been in that area blown sideways by the blast of a shotgun. Then there was a fusillade of firing punctuated by the boom of a large Browning shotgun going off repeatedly, more screams, and then some yelling and chanting as a group of Ibans came running out of the jungle to pounce on the dead Indons. What followed next chilled him. In his exhausted state he watched numbly as Nighan and other Ibans took the heads.

The shooting was beginning to die down. He looked over to where the main battle had taken place and saw only men he recognized as British soldiers and some darker men who looked like Gurkhas who were rounding up a few of the Indonesians and tying their arms behind them. Men were moving towards him.

He shuffled over on hands and knees to where Dave was lying and checked to see if there was a pulse. He was breathing in shallow gasps, so Jason quickly soaked his neck cloth and wiped his face, then poured some water onto his neck.

"It's over, Dave! The cavalry got here; looks like it's your boys. They've taken care of everything. Hang on, mate. Just hang on for a bit longer, Dave!" he pleaded, gasping for breath, almost sobbing.

He didn't notice the arrival of the men who stood over him until one put a hand on his shoulder.

"It's all right now, chum. We've got him. Let us in there and we'll get him out, OK?"

Jason looked up at the man standing over him and then glanced round at the other men who were beginning to cluster about.

"You've got to get him to a hospital! He was shot in the leg and it's going bad. I got the bullet out but I think he's got blood poisoning; don't let him go!" He was babbling as the relief of the moment set in, but also from his fear that after all they had been through Dave might not make it. He was heedless of the tears running down his face as he looked up at them.

Another man quickly crouched next to Dave and began to examine him professionally. He rapidly took the pulse, glanced at the leg and said, "He's right, boss. Dave is in a bad way. We need the chopper now!"

"OK, get Dave off in the scout and take the other two who got hit. Patrick and Mike, wasn't it? Stevens, you go with them back to Kuching. Radios, call in another chopper, Wessex type – we'll need it."

There was a flurry of activity as the men made a makeshift stretcher for Sergeant White and very quickly they were carrying him down to the flat part of the open area.

While they were doing this a man was on the radio calling in both of the helicopters. The sound of their engines became a roar as they swept back in, guided by the soldiers on the ground.

Jason was desperately tired now and he could not use his right arm; for some reason it was beginning to seize up, and he was gasping for air because his ribs hurt so much. He barely felt the needle go in that deadened the pain. The men then got to work, took his bloody shirt off, looked at the three black puncture holes in his right shoulder and remarked on the huge livid bruise under his shoulder blade and across his back.

He sat numbly still as the man poured some water over the wounds, washed off the blood, injected him with something, then bound a dressing pad over the punctured area. Then the same efficient man had a look at the calf. He clucked over that, sprinkled some powder over it, then put on a clean shell dressing and bound it tight.

"Needs looking at," he said to the others. "He's got shrapnel in his back, don't think it's in a lung but he may also have a broken rib or two."

The tall man who had come up to him first came back and knelt on one knee in front of him. He stared at Jason who sat with his head down. The major noted the rags that Jason wore and the tattered boots, the bandaged shoulder, the scratched and bloody face with many days' growth of beard, and he noted the hollow-eyed exhaustion of the scarecrow figure sitting on the ground in front of him.

"Where did you come from? What's your name, soldier?" he asked gently.

"Rifleman Griffith, Green Jackets, sir. I got out of Sapit when it went down. Seems a long time ago now," Jason muttered. His tongue felt thick, it was so dry. He tried to get up.

"Stay right where you are, young man. My name is Major Stanford. We didn't expect to find Dave in such good company." He smiled at the bewildered Jason. "We have to get Dave out of here first, Rifleman Griffith, but we will put you on the very next chopper out after that, is that OK?"

Jason nodded. "Yesir, that's just fine. Sir, will he be all right then?"

Major Stanford nodded. "I think so; it looks as though you took good care of him. We're grateful. He is too good a man to lose now." He put a hand on Jason's good shoulder, gripped it, then got up and left. Another man came and squatted next to Jason. He looked up, the sun was in his eyes but he realized it was Nighan.

"Nighan! You old bandit! I thought you'd scarpered. Good to see you, boyo!" Jason gasped. He grinned tiredly at the man.

Nighan touched him on the shoulder, grinned back at him, his gold teeth gleaming, and then said something seriously to him. Jason blinked, understanding nothing of what was being said.

Another man squatting near by spoke rapidly to Nighan, who answered him and then they spoke together for a few minutes. Nighan was pointing at Jason and gesticulating.

The man crouched next to Jason. "I'm Sergeant Jack Fielding, Rifleman Griffith. What's your first name?"

"Jason, Sarge."

"Well, Jason, this man Nighan is one of our trackers, and he has been saying some pretty good things about you. Looks like you have impressed the hell out of him actually. He wants to know if you would like a tattoo for the kills you have made."

Jason grinned weakly at Nighan. "Tell him thanks, I'll give it some thought but right now I've had enough punctures for one day."

Sergeant Fielding laughed quietly. "You'll do, lad, you'll do! Time to get you onto the chopper."

Jason was helped to his feet by the men around him; instinctively he looked for his rifle.

"Me rifle! I've got to get me rifle...and Dave's Bergen, anyone know where it is?"

There were surprised chuckles from the men nearby. Sergeant Fielding said, "You *have* learned, Rifleman, haven't you? Don't worry, Jason; we'll bring them down to the chopper with you."

They guided him down the slope to the large Wessex that was sitting on the stubble, its rotors turning slowly. He was helped on board and then six of the SAS got on board with him. They made him comfortable on the floor and then the chopper revved its engines to a howl and the rotors began to spin; it lifted off after a few minutes and he could look down on the place where he had been so very sure he would not be leaving.

The men showed him the huge rent in the back of the Bergen, the dented and disfigured mess tins and the smashed SARBE. They told him they now understood the huge bruise on his back and the probable broken ribs. He had been very lucky.

He sleepily asked them how they had known to find Dave and him. They replied it had been the SARBE. He shook his head in disbelief; it had worked after all! Jason had been given some morphine to ease the pain of his shoulder so he was asleep before they got to Kuching.

The Wessex helicopter landed in the middle of the afternoon at the RAF base, whereupon the sleeping Jason was transferred to an ambulance and taken to the hospital near by.

Reunion
Chapter 21

The Colonel of the Green Jackets stepped out of his Landrover and walked up the steps to the entrance Brigade HQ. The Gurkhas went through their routine of snapping to attention and presenting arms, to which he gave a quick, distracted salute. His lean face was tense. He expected a serious telling off from the Brig and wasn't looking forward to it. Once inside he was greeted by the same starched captain who had met him the last time.

They strode into the cool interior of the building where the usual bustle of a busy headquarters prevailed, then up to the now familiar door of the brigadier's office. He was announced by the captain, and as he walked in, the door was closed softly behind him.

The colonel saluted smartly.

Brigadier Whiley-Carrick strode round his desk and walked up to the colonel with his hand outstretched.

"Richard! Good to see you!" he said as they shook hands. "Come on over, let's have some tea and you can tell me all you know."

Colonel Barker-Hollingsworth took off his hat and smiled his relief at his commanding officer.

"That would be nice, sir," he agreed.

The brigadier barked at a hovering servant for some tea and they sat down on the large rattan chairs.

"Now tell me how it went. I do hear that it went well, at least?"

"Oh yes, sir. They took Sapit back and everyone did very well. The Indon had fortified the ridge but the lads and the Gurkhas managed to storm it after softening it up with the help of the Australians."

"Damn good job, Richard. There'll be a few gongs for this, I have no doubt. It looks like we did the right thing, sending Nigel back."

"Er, yes indeed, sir. Actually he led the charge, it would seem."

The brigadier frowned. "What d'you mean, Richard?"

"Well, sir, I gave him permission to join his men at the sharp end. I rather think that had I not he would have disobeyed orders and gone anyway, so I agreed rather than let him add to his list of misdemeanors. If you know what I mean?"

"Cheeky bugger!" said the brigadier slowly staring at him.

The colonel was sure his lips twitched with a tiny smile.

"Yes rather, sir. Er...actually he led the charge and was quite badly wounded during the attack."

"Wounded you say?" The Brig looked alarmed. "Damn, Richard. Is he going to be all right? What are we going to do now?"

"Beg pardon, sir? What do you mean?" The colonel was watching the brigadier keenly.

"Well damn, it's a little difficult to court martial a hero, isn't it, old boy?"

The colonel shifted in his seat and nodded agreement, waiting.

"Tell you what. Make out a full report on the whole incident and let me have it within a few days. I'll have to send it into GOC Singapore, with my own recommendations, of course." His voice had a tone of finality. This time colonel was sure he had the trace of a smile on his lips.

"Yes Sir. I shall do this immediately."

"I expect to hear good things about my Gurkhas in that report, as well as the Green Jackets, Richard."

"Oh, absolutely! No question about that, sir!" said the colonel.

* * * * *

Megan was restless, she didn't know quite why. Since Jason and the Green Jackets had disappeared into the strange jungle world the British soldiers now appeared to live in, she had been fretful and moody.

She missed him badly. It had puzzled her during their first meetings as to what it was exactly that attracted her to him. She found his shyness attractive for one thing, but he didn't really lack in confidence. During their time together she had warmed to his interest in the world about him, although he was not in the league of her student acquaintances when it came to education. Nonetheless, his wry humor had captured something within her that now delayed her departure.

For the first days of his absence she had moped, although the work helped take her mind off things for a while. She had not expected to feel this strongly about Jason. He was a nice boy from Wales, but their lives were so totally different there had not seemed to be much of a future. However, now she was missing him very badly.

She began to dread the weekends. She thought that taking a trip to Batu Feringgi might help, but it had been miserable, in spite of the sunny beach and the calming effect it had on her.

It was now several months and many letters since he had gone off to the wilds of Borneo. He had described life in Jahore, where they had seemingly spent weeks in the jungle with brutal instructors who chased them all over the place. Then that strange boat trip. Why didn't the Brits just fly the troops over to Kuching? She didn't know much about armies and how they moved around, but from what she could tell, the British Army seemed to move its men in the same manner the Americans had during the Second World War. From what Jason had written, they didn't seem to have much in the way of modern equipment.

She wondered what the conditions at the "front" were like for him.

His last letter had mentioned that he was going "up country", whatever that meant. The English language was full of strange expressions and it seemed that the boys in the British Army had a language entirely of their own.

Some of her acquaintances from the Peace Corps were due to visit in a couple of days, so she was busy making things ready for them in the spare room of her apartment. The unwelcome visitors

Dale and Jan had left a long time ago, but somehow there was still a kind of presence left that bothered her.

She thought of visiting Matt and Krista but remembered that they were visiting Singapore and would not be home for a couple more days.

She decided that she wanted to go for a walk and clear her head. She quite enjoyed walking the streets of the old town. It was composed of a curious mixture of Chinese and colonial buildings that dated back to the beginning of the previous century, and some long before that. Nothing quite like it in the US, she reflected. No one had ever accosted her while she walked along the crowded old streets other than to stare at her as she went by, and of course to talk about her. Unlike San Diego, she thought, where a young woman simply didn't walk alone in certain areas.

Her walk took her past the E&O Hotel. Its old façade was a throwback to the times when the British had ruled this country. Megan didn't think it looked as though it had made many concessions to the changing times since they had left, some paint was flaking on the entrance pillars and the shutters looked cracked and old. On principle she disapproved of the colonial aspect left behind by the Brits, but on impulse she decided to go in and see what was happening, even if it was to simply have a quiet drink in the long, old-fashioned bar.

There were a few couples in the main lounge, mainly European women and their husbands. They looked hot despite the fans that were working hard to move the humid air about the large room. Most looked like Brits to her; a couple were bright red with sunburn. The men stared while their florid wives scowled at their ogling husbands and envied the slim attractive girl walking past, but she ignored them.

Megan was dressed in her white linen skirt and sandals with a colorful orange blouse with the long sleeves turned up. She felt cool and relaxed now; the tropical heat didn't bother her any more. All the same, she was not entirely comfortable within herself.

She made her way into the long, cool, dark room where the bar was situated and ordered rum and Coke, which she took to the table off to the side nearest the window. Seated in the huge rattan chair she could see out into the gardens from there. She was aware that two youngish men sitting at the bar were watching her, and after a quick glance decided that they were British officers and thus, according to Jason at least, to be avoided.

Megan had just settled back into the large rattan chair and taken a sip of her drink when she became aware that someone was standing nearby. She glanced up with a look of enquiry on her face. The young man, one of those who had been at the bar, shifted uneasily, then Lieutenant Graham asked politely, "Hello, Miss, would you mind if we joined you?"

Megan thought about it for a minute. If these men were from the same unit as Jason then perhaps they might know something about him.

She nodded noncommittal agreement and Graham smiled. The other man came and joined them.

"Are you with anyone, Miss?"

Megan looked around theatrically. "Do I look as though I am?"

He blushed, but then asked, "Are you American, Miss?"

"Yes, is there a problem with that?" she said a little sharply, not in the mood for some pickup.

"Er, no... In fact, I'm, uh, Roger Graham... Lieutenant Graham, Green Jackets actually. How do you do?" He held out his hand.

"Megan. Fine, what can I do for you, Lieutenant?" she asked politely but coolly, touching his hand with hers briefly.

"This is David; er, David, this is Megan from America." Graham introduced his companion in a friendly manner.

The two men sat down awkwardly as though they had rehearsed their lines but had now forgotten them and were stuck for words. David was looking embarrassed.

She looked directly at them and decided that they were not threatening. In fact Roger's freckled face was open and his blue eyes guileless. The other officer, David, was as lean as his companion and both seemed to be very young to be in the army. They were dressed in loose white flannel trousers and white sleeveless shirts, rather like a uniform she thought.

"We don't meet very many European girls as young or as pretty as you on this side of the straits," David said disarmingly. "We thought you might be Australian, or with a party." Despite herself Megan had to smile, it broke the ice and both men grinned back at her with relief.

Roger was the one leading the charge, as it were. "Megan, we were thinking of going to have a meal at one of the Chinese restaurants on the coast and wondered if you would like to come with us?"

"I'm sorry, I would love to but I am probably not the best company right now. You see I..." she hesitated. "You are from the British camp on the island, aren't you?"

"Yes that's right, Minden Barracks, Green Jackets. Why do you ask?" enquired David.

"Do you know a Rifleman called Jason Griffith?"

Both men looked stunned, then Roger leaned forward, placed his glass carefully on the glass table top and looked at her.

"Do you know a Rifleman Griffith?" he asked her casually, with a glance at his companion.

"Yes, I do. I have not heard from him in a while and I just wondered...if you might, well...know if he is OK." She stared at him.

"Well, this is a bit awkward really. I, er, I'm so sorry." David said. He looked very embarrassed now, and Roger looked distinctly uncomfortable.

Megan sat up. "Why are you sorry? Is something wrong? Is Jason alright?"

"Jason? Oh, Rifleman Griffith. Oh no – well, actually, yes, in fact."

Megan was now becoming alarmed.

"Can I please buy you another drink?" Roger asked.

'Yes, yes, OK. Do you know something?"

"Actually, I wonder if I've seen you once before at the polo club; you came and watched the game with, er, Jason?"

Megan nodded; she remembered how interested in the game Jason had been.

"So here you are and I, I mean we, really didn't mean to intrude. Jason... Rifleman Griffith is going to be all right."

Megan looked at him hard. "It's OK, but what do you mean, Lieutenant, he is 'all right'? Why shouldn't he be?"

Lieutenant Stevens interjected. "You don't know?"

"Guys, what am I supposed to know?" asked Megan, "I haven't heard from him in weeks!" She was beginning to feel exasperated. What were these people getting at?

"I'm sorry, I should probably start from the beginning," said Graham.

"Yeah, that would be a good idea!" said Megan, an impatient edge to her voice. Then they had to wait in silence as the 'boy' came over and placed fresh drinks in front of them.

Finally Roger said, "Well, there was a bit of a scrap up country, you see." There was that expression again.

"Do you mean at the 'front'?" she asked.

"Actually, um, yes. Well, Rifleman... Jason was caught up in the middle of it."

Megan felt a chill move down her back. She stared at the man with wide eyes. Her stomach felt cold.

Graham hurried on. "It was a hill fort, place called Sapit, probably shouldn't tell you its name. Never mind; in any case, Jason managed to get out before it all got run over."

"Mister Graham! Is he all right?" Megan's voice was almost shrill in the still room.

"Yes...well, he did get wounded, but we don't know quite how badly. Apparently he was found with another man, also wounded, in the jungle. They say he is going to be fine and that he did rather well, in fact. Isn't that so, David?"

"Oh yes, they say he was found fighting off a bunch of Indons. Bloody good show, by all accounts," agreed Lieutenant Stevens, nodding vigorously.

Megan felt the floor move a little and her stomach suddenly had a huge lump in it. "Is there...is there any way I can see him?" she asked in a small voice.

"Well, actually, it's one heck of a coincidence, but we simply didn't know, you see. Not often one sees a pretty girl in this place." Roger looked embarrassed again. "Sorry, didn't mean to be rude, but now that we know who you are, of course we can help," he added kindly. David nodded enthusiastically.

"Rifleman Griffith... Jason should be arriving in Butterworth airport tonight from Singapore, and now we would be delighted to offer you a lift over there to see him. It will have to be tomorrow though, because they will probably have to do some processing and so forth. He's a bit of a hero, actually, so we wanted to see him too; he is in my company, you see."

Megan didn't answer. There were a lot of emotions swirling about inside her that threatened to overwhelm her. Jason was wounded? They were telling her he was OK, but what did that mean? To her horror she found that tears were welling in her eyes.

Damn! She searched for a handkerchief in her small bag and couldn't find one but one of the officers gave her his. She thanked him and dried her eyes and blew her nose in it.

"I'm sorry, I didn't mean to be a crybaby," she said, and then looked at the hanky, abashed. "I'll wash it and return it tomorrow. Yes, I'd like that very much. You are very kind."

The two young officers were plainly embarrassed, but Lieutenant Stevens said, "Please don't apologize, Megan, we quite understand.   Please forgive us for the misunderstanding. Good. Then where shall we pick you up?"

"Why not here? I live nearby, and it is only a short walk for me."

"Why don't we pick you up at around two in the afternoon, tomorrow?" asked Lieutenant Graham gently.

She nodded silently, looking down. They bade her a polite goodnight and left.

Megan finished her drink slowly and then went home. Her mind was whirling with questions, but there were few answers. What on earth had happened to Jason? She barely slept that night.

*   *   *   *   *

Jason didn't really remember much about his first night at the hospital that was situated in the grounds of the HQ in Kuching. They carried out a preliminary operation the night he arrived and he woke up in a clean military bed with bandages wrapped firmly around his right shoulder. It hurt like hell and so did his back. He found that breathing was sometimes difficult, especially when he coughed. Then he discovered that his right calf was bandaged. Not only that, but his face stung, and when he looked down at himself he noticed that under his army pajamas he was colored bright purple in places and green in others and red in even others. Most of the places were under his arms and chest or his crotch and legs. What the hell had happened to him? he wondered.

He looked around groggily and then groaned as the pain washed over him from all quarters. There were brisk steps on the brightly polished linoleum covered floor ,and a nurse in her crisp light blue uniform with red shoulder tabs stood over him.

"Well. Hello there! How are we today?" she asked kindly, her voice carrying the trace of a Yorkshire accent. She popped a

282

thermometer into his mouth, told him to keep it under his tongue and not to speak, then efficiently took his pulse, holding his wrist firmly in her cool hand while she looked at her watch.

Jason had the opportunity to observe some of the others in the ward with him, but he felt tired so when the nurse let him go that he settled down into the bed and fell asleep again.

The doctor and matron came to see him later in the morning. Despite the humid heat that the fans did little to alleviate the latter wore her cloak of office and looked very official. Her gray hair was pinned back under her cap and she wore a pair of small bi-focal glasses on her nose, making her look very severe and definitely not some one trifle with. Her dress uniform made no concessions whatever to the humidity and the heat.

They stood over Jason and discussed him as though he were some inanimate object. It appeared that they would have to send him on to Singapore to finish the operations, as there were still pieces of shrapnel in his back.

For the rest of the day he slept and tried to forget what had happened for the last few days, but the one thing that bothered him was Dave White. Jason wondered what had happened to him.

He had the opportunity to ask the question when he was visited by the colonel of the regiment late that morning. There was a lot of noise outside as people came and went and then matron came bustling in with two nurses. Under her direction, they helped the men lying in bed to sit up and then came to Jason and helped him up, plumping pillows behind him. Matron admonished him to be "correct" to the colonel, who was coming to visit the men. The others in the ward received the same treatment, about eleven of them, most from the Green Jackets; some of the Riflemen knew him and had called out earlier when they noticed he was awake. Then there were some dark men among them who looked like Gurkhas; some seemed to be badly hurt. They were told not to talk by the Yorkshire nurse as Matron ran a sharp ship and they didn't want to run afoul of "the Dragon" as she quickly became known.

The colonel was preceded by the Regimental Sergeant Major. Instinctively the men in their beds braced as the RSM marched in. His pace stick held firmly under his left arm, he marched the length of the ward and then turned about and stood rigidly to attention, his stern face impassive. No one said anything. Then in strolled the colonel with the adjutant, and another tall thin man in crumpled jungle greens without insignia. Jason recognized the man as the officer who had come with the rescue unit at the longhouse.

The colonel stopped at every bed and talked briefly with the man there, asking him how he was and congratulating him on the good fight at Sapit.

When he came to Jason he looked down at him and said, "Well, Rifleman Griffith, how are you feeling?"

Jason croaked a reply. Then the colonel said, "The Green Jackets and the Gurkhas took Sapit back, Griffith, did you know that?"

"No, sir."

"You were the only survivor. I have been hearing a lot of interesting things from the Special Air Service about you. I would like to hear the whole story from you one of these days."

"How is Sergeant White, sir?" Jason directed his question at Major Stanford.

The major grinned and looked at the colonel as though for permission to speak. The colonel smiled and nodded.

"He is doing well, Rifleman Griffith. He will recover and they say we will save his leg. If you had not been there to help, however, he might not have survived. Thank you for the good work. He has not said much, as he is full of penicillin, other antibiotics and such like. But he asked after you."

Jason flushed with embarrassment. "I'm fine, sir. Tell him not to worry about me."

They moved on, but not before the colonel had said to Jason, "We are all very proud of you, Griffith. Get well soon."

The RSM, in an awful attempt at humor, leaned over Jason and said, "You are improperly dressed, Rifleman. Do your top button up this minute!"

Jason gulped and reached to do so but the RSM winked and whispered, "Well done, lad!" He marched off stiff as a ramrod behind the officers as they continued around the ward.

*　*　*　*　*

They came to take the more seriously wounded and those who needed further operations off to the airport after lunch. Along with the others Jason was dosed with something that made him sleepy.

They were taken aboard a large plane, and with some nurses in attendance they were flown back to Singapore.

Another operation at Princess Alexandra's Hospital and he woke up in the familiar surroundings of a military hospital ward.

He endured the impersonal but not unkind treatment of the nurses who came and stared at him and the others from the Green Jackets and Gurkhas as they lay there nursing their wounds. They were something of celebrities, for they were survivors of the first real casualties in any numbers of the Confrontation.

Jason was beginning to feel bored and lonely. They continually came and checked his pulse and temperature as they did with the others, but there was little to do and there were few books to read. By this time he was able to hobble about on a crutch and visit the others at their bedsides.

He learned from his roommates that they had all been in the battle for Sapit. They told him how A Company and the little 'Gurks' had stormed the hill and taken it back, but that the major, "Scrappy" Johnson, had been badly wounded. He was probably being spoilt rotten in a private ward by the nurses, they said, but they didn't begrudge the major his good fortune. They loved their commander.

Jason realized that by comparison to the others he had gotten off fairly lightly, so he didn't make much of his hurts. They pounded him with questions, which he answered somewhat hesitantly, always surprised at their praise for his having made it.

Two days later, he and a couple of other walking wounded were put on board another plane and flown north to Butterworth. The plane landed in the early evening and he was taken in a stretcher to the small but efficiently run hospital in the Australian camp. It was very late, and once again he was dosed with some kind of drug that made him sleepy. In an absurd kind of way he had the feeling that he was coming home. The doctor told him that he would be released to go back to Minden Barracks within a few days.

His thoughts went to Megan. He wondered how she was and if she was even on the island of Penang. She had told him that she was not going to stay for much longer. He felt depressed at the thought that she had gone.

* * * * *

Megan was picked up at exactly 2 p.m. by the two young lieutenants in a small Morgan car with the cover down. It was a sunny day and very pleasant. They were elaborately polite and Lieutenant Graham helped her into the passenger seat. Lieutenant Stevens sat in the cramped rear seat, his knees almost at his chin. They were in a cheerful mood, and despite Megan's qualms about Jason she relaxed.

They sped down to the ferry point and drove onto the crowded ferry. The Chinese and the Indians watched them curiously as they got out and strolled onto the top deck. Megan had a sense of déjà vu as they walked to the front of the ferry to watch the water traffic go by as the ferry chugged across the straits.

The two officers, despite their youth, were good company and filled in some of the questions that she asked about the incident in Borneo. They were very excited at the success of the battle and it was clear they both wished that they could have been there. Megan shook her head. Men! When they were not drinking or chasing women, they were off fighting and getting killed. In spite of herself she liked them though; they carried with them the eternal optimism of young men anywhere.

They drove off the ferry at the Butterworth side and then along the shoreline north to the main Australian airbase. The officers showed their passes and explained Megan's presence to the guard, who saluted and let them in.

They drove up to the large building that was the hospital and parked. Megan was tense. Lieutenant Graham went off to find out where the ward was that held the Green Jackets, while Megan and Lieutenant Stevens waited at the entrance in the cool of the air-conditioned hallway. He came back within a few minutes with a nurse in tow.

She smiled at Megan and said she would show them up. It was a quiet trio that followed the nurse in her crisp uniform up the wide stone stairs to the second floor. They passed the usual stainless steel trolleys being wheeled about by nurses, and the cleaners still working the corridors. The place smelt of antiseptic. The sound of their shoes on the tiled floor was loud in the otherwise quiet of the hospital.

The nurse came to an open doorway that led off the verandah and said to someone inside, "You've got a visitor, young man." Then she indicated to Megan to go in and gave her a smile. Megan looked at the men with her. They grinned and waved her in.

"We'll be outside. Take your time," said Lieutenant Graham.

Megan walked in cautiously. Jason was sitting on the edge of the bed, a book lying next to him, half read. He was staring at her, a look of total surprise on his battered face.

"Megan?" he whispered, and stood up. He stood there wobbling, and if Megan had not taken two long strides, he might have fallen. Jason looked terrible, his chest was swathed in bandages and it seemed as though someone had painted him different colors after having beaten him about the face. He fell forward into her arms.

They stood there just holding each other for a long time. She realized she was crying and heard him snuffle into her shoulder.

"It's all right, Megan, it's all right, love. I'm back now."

The End

Author's note.

This story is about British soldiers in the little known war in Borneo euphemistically known as the Confrontation. While it was not a 'secret' war it was not well publicized. The British Services up till quite recently have been very coy about letting the press see how they fight their 'Bush Fires" as they became known. This one was particularly successful.

The regiments of the Light Infantry all have a distinguished history, as is that of the Green Jackets 60th Rifles which is one of the very best.

While the Confrontation did occur. In fact the British, and Commonwealth forces and in particular the SAS and the Gurkhas so dominated the jungle and the border that the Indonesians, much as they would have liked to, never could make any serious of inroads into Sarawak and Sabah.

The story of the assault on Sapit never happened. However this was a war fought deep in the jungles of Sarawak and Sabah by dedicated and first rate soldiers to whom I have tried to give personality and human faces. Their allies were the indigenous people of the jungle the Iban and Dyak people whom the Brits got to know and respect, and so it is fitting that they be included in this story.

James Boschert

About the Author – James Boschert

James Boschert grew up in the then colony of Malaya in the early fifties. He learned first hand about terrorism while there as the Communist insurgency was in full swing. His school was burnt down and the family while traveling, narrowly survived an ambush, saved by a Gurkha patrol, which drove off the insurgents.

He went on to join the British army serving in remote places like Borneo and Oman. Later he spent five years in Iran before the revolution, where he played polo with the Iranian Army, developed a passion for the remote Assassin castles found in the high mountains to the north, and learned to understand and speak the Farsi language.

Escaping Iran during the revolution, he went on to become an engineer and now lives in Arizona on a small ranch with his family and animals.

ASSASSINS OF ALAMUT
BY
JAMES BOSCHERT

An Epic Novel of Persia and Palestine in the Time of the Crusades

    The Assassins of Alamut is a riveting tale, painted on the vast canvas of life in Palestine and Persia during the 12th century.

On one hand, it's a tale of the crusades—as told from the Islamic side—where Shi'a and Sunni are as intent on killing Ismaili Muslims as crusaders. In self-defense, the Ismailis develop an elite band of highly trained killers called Hashshashin whose missions are launched from their mountain fortress of Alamut.

But it's also the story of a French boy, Talon, captured and forced into the alien world of the assassins. Forbidden love for a princess is intertwined with sinister plots and self-sacrifice, as the hero and his two companions discover treachery and then attempt to evade the ruthless assassins of Alamut who are sent to hunt them down.

It's a sweeping saga that takes you over vast snow-covered mountains, through the frozen wastes of the winter plateau, and into the fabulous cites of Hamadan, Isfahan, and the Kingdom of Jerusalem.

"A brilliant first novel, worthy of Bernard Cornwell at his best."—Tom Grundner

GREEK FIRE
BY
JAMES BOSCHERT

In the fourth book of Talon, James Boschert delivers fast-paced adventures, packed with violent confrontations and intrepid heroes up against hard odds.

Imprisoned for brawling in Acre, a coastal city in the Kingdom of Jerusalem, Talon and his longtime friend Max are freed by an old mentor from the Order of the Templars and offered a new mission in the fabled city of Constantinople. There Talon makes new friendships, but winning the Emperor's favor obligates him to follow Manuel to war in a willful expedition to free Byzantine lands from the Seljuk Turks. And beneath the pageantry of the great city, seditious plans are being fomented by disaffected aristocrats who have made a reckless deal to sell the one weapon the Byzantine Empire has to defend itself, *Greek fire*, to an implacable enemy bent upon the Empire's destruction.

Talon and Max find themselves sailing into perilous battles, and in the labyrinthine back streets of Constantinople Talon must outwit his own kind - assassins - in the pay of a treacherous alliance.

PENMORE PRESS
www.penmorepress.com

Historical fiction and nonfiction
Paperback available for order on line
and as Ebook with all major distributers

A Falcon Flies

by

James Boschert

Talon has returned to Acre, the Crusader port, a rich man after more than a year in Byzantium. But riches bring enemies, and Talon's past is about to catch up with him: accusations of witchcraft have followed him from Languedoc. Everything is changed, however, when Talon travels to a small fort with Sir Guy de Veres, his Templar mentor, and learns stunning news about Rav'an.

Before he can act, the kingdom of Baldwin IV is threatened by none other than the Sultan of Egypt, Salah Ed Din, who is bringing a vast army through Sinai to retake Jerusalem from the Christians. Talon must take part in the ferocious battle at Montgisard before he can set out to rejoin Rav'an and honor his promise made six years ago.

The 'Assassins of Rashid Ed Din, the 'Old Man of the Mountain', have targeted Talon for death for obstructed their plans once too often. He is forced to take a circuitous route through the loneliest reaches of the southern deserts on his way to Persia to avoid them, but even so he faces betrayal, imprisonment, and the threat of execution.

His sole objective is to find Rav'an, but she is not where he had expected her to be.

PENMORE PRESS
www.penmorepress.com

Historical fiction and nonfiction
Paperback available for order on line
and as Ebook with all major distributers

Force 12 in German Bight

by

James Boschert

Considering that oil and gas have been flowing from under the North Sea for the best part of half a century, it is perhaps surprising that more writers have not taken the uncompromising conditions that are experienced in this area – which extends from the north of Scotland to the coasts of Norway and Germany – for the setting of a novel. James Boschert's latest redresses the balance.

The book takes its title from the name of an area regularly referred to in the legendary BBC Shipping Forecast and one which experiences some of the worst weather conditions around the British Isles. It is a fast-paced story which smacks of authenticity in every line. A world of hard men, hard liquor, hard drugs and cold-blooded murder. The reality of the setting and the characters, ex-military men from both sides of the Atlantic, crooked wheeler-dealers, and Danish detectives, male and female, are all in on the action.

This is not story telling akin to a latter day Bulldog Drummond, or even a James Bond, but simply a snortingly good yarn which will jangle the nerve ends, fill your nose with the smell of salt and diesel oil, your ears with the deafening sound of machinery aboard a monster pipe-dredging ship and, above all, make you remember never to underestimate the power of the sea.

'Roger Paine, former Commander, Royal Navy'.

PENMORE PRESS
www.penmorepress.com

Historical fiction and nonfiction
Paperback available for order on line
and as Ebook with all major distributers

www.ingramcontent.com/pod-product-compliance
Lightning Source LLC
Chambersburg PA
CBHW070438170726
48291CB00002B/568